T0356998

VOLUME 1 • FOOTHOLD

RIGSBY WI

S.E. CASE

IRON CIRCUS COMICS

ARTIST · AUTHOR
S. E. CASE

MANAGING EDITOR
KEL McDONALD

PROOFREADER
ABBY LEHRKE

PREPRESS TECHNICIAN · BOOK DESIGN
HYE MARDIKIAN

PUBLISHER · EDITOR-IN-CHIEF
C. SPIKE TROTMAN

ISBN   978-1-63899-140-3 (ebook)
       978-1-63899-141-0 (print)

FIRST EDITION,   · March 2025
FIRST PRINTING

Printed in China

RIGSBYWI.COM

IRON CIRCUS COMICS
STRANGE AND AMAZING

329 West 18th Street, Suite 604 • Chicago, Il 60616 • ironcircus.com • inquiry@ironcircus.com

Contents © 2025— S. E. Case. All rights reserved. No part of this book may be reprinted or reproduced in any manner (except for journalistic, educational, or review purposes) without written consent of the publisher and creators. The stories, institutions, and characters in this book are fictional. Any resemblance to persons living or dead, except for satirical purposes, is purely coincidental. All characters herein and distinctive likenesses thereof are properties of their respective creators.

Publisher's Cataloging-in-Publication
(Provided by Cassidy Cataloguing Services, Inc.).

Names: Case, S. E., author, artist. | McDonald, Kel, editor. | Mardikian, Hye, designer | Spike, 1978-
         publisher, editor.

Title: Rigsby WI. Volume 1, Foothold / artist, author, S.E. Case ; managing editor, Kel McDonald ;
         proofreader, Abbe Lehrke ; prepress technician, book design, Hye Mardikian ; publisher, editor-
         in-chief, C. Spike Trotman.

Other titles: Rigsby Wisconsin. Volume 1, Foothold | Foothold

Description: First edition. | Chicago, IL : Iron Circus Comics, 2025.

Identifiers: ISBN: 978-1-63899-141-0 (print) | 978-1-63899-140-3 (ebook)

Subjects: LCSH: Rural teenagers--Wisconsin--Comic books, strips, etc. | High school students--
            Wisconsin--Comic books, strips, etc. | Friendship--Comic books, strips, etc. | Dysfunctional
            families--Comic books, strips, etc. | Mothers and daughters--Comic books, strips, etc. | LCGFT:
            Graphic novels. | Coming-of-age comics. | BISAC: COMICS & GRAPHIC NOVELS / Coming of Age.
            | COMICS & GRAPHIC NOVELS / School Life. | COMICS & GRAPHIC NOVELS / Slice of Life.

Classification: LCC: PN6727.C3878 R54 2025 | DDC: 741.5973--dc23

For
A & M

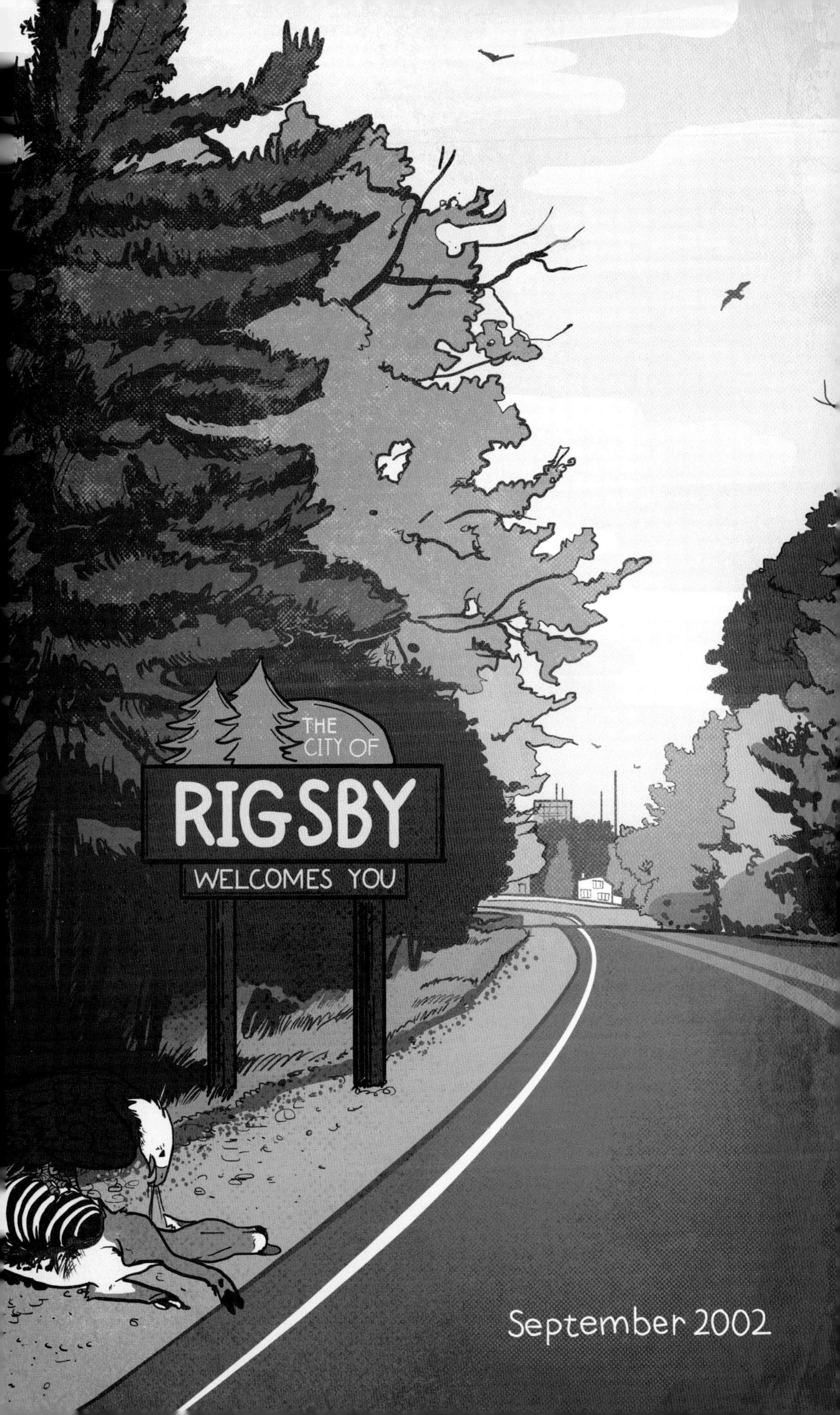
THE
CITY OF
RIGSBY
WELCOMES YOU
September 2002

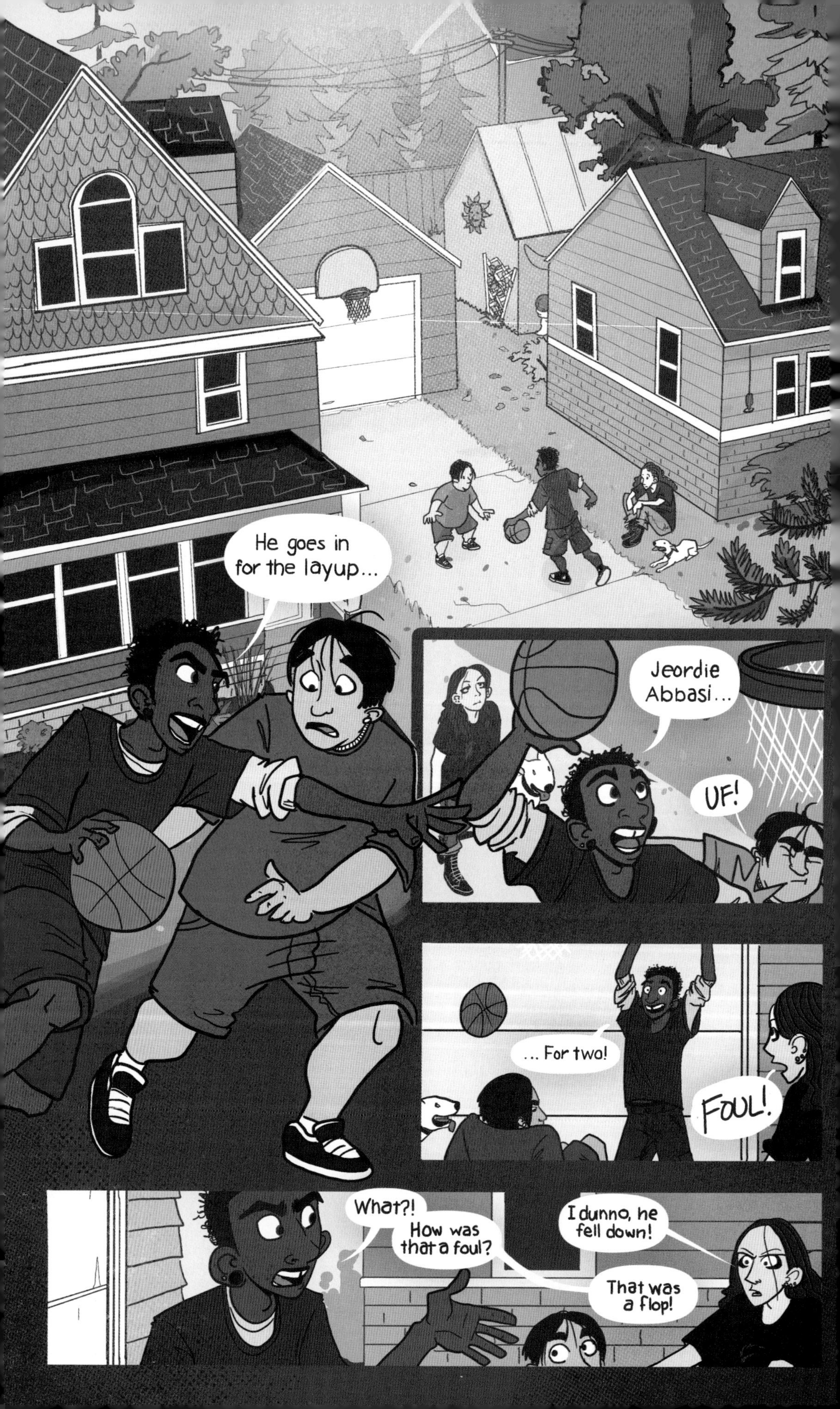

He goes in for the layup...
Jeordie Abbasi...
UF!
... For two!
FOUL!
What?!
How was that a foul?
I dunno, he fell down!
That was a flop!

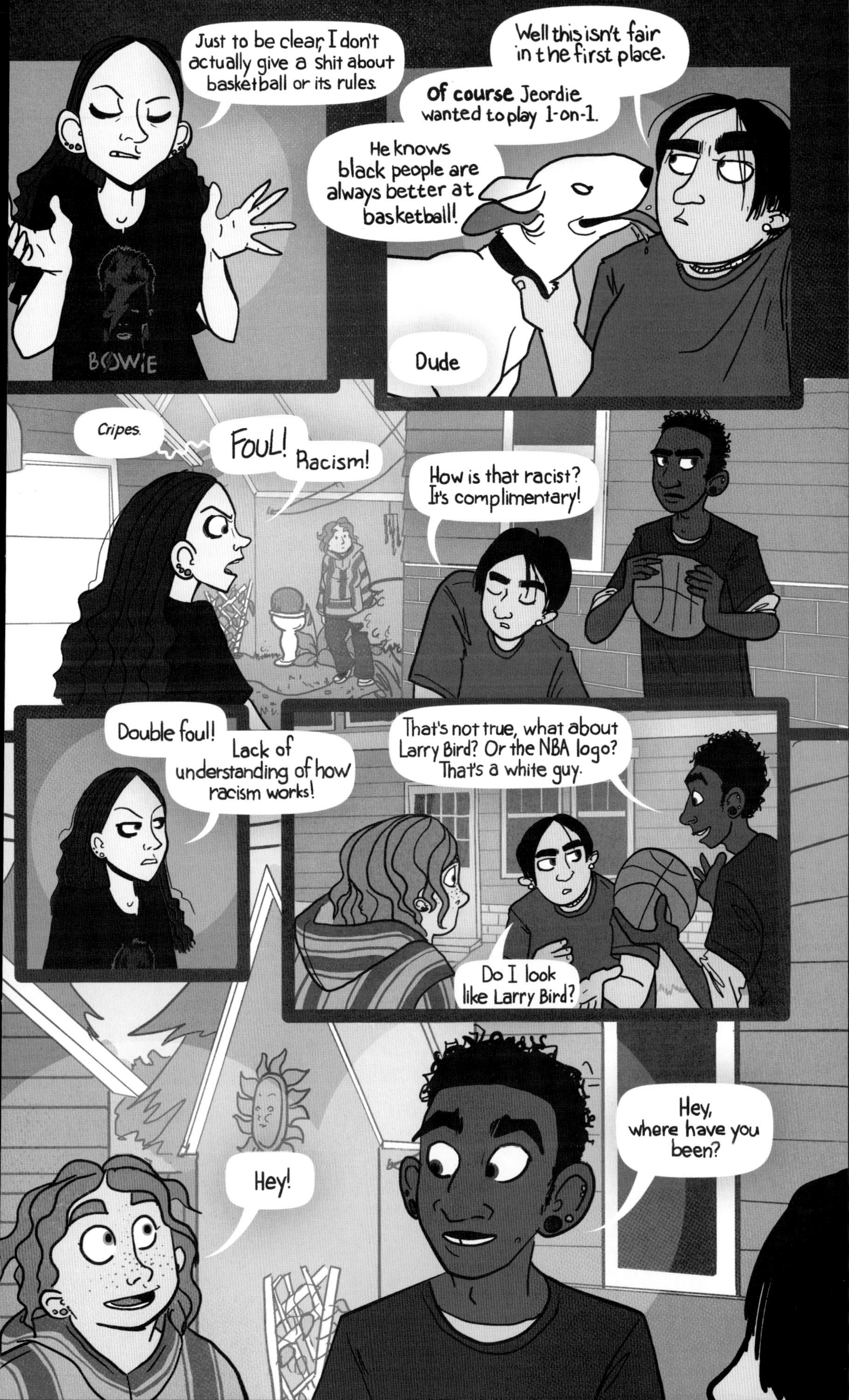
Just to be clear, I don't actually give a shit about basketball or its rules.
BOWIE
Well this isn't fair in the first place.
Of course Jeordie wanted to play 1-on-1.
He knows black people are always better at basketball!
Dude
Cripes.
FOUL!
Racism!
How is that racist? It's complimentary!
Double foul!
Lack of understanding of how racism works!
That's not true, what about Larry Bird? Or the NBA logo? That's a white guy.
Do I look like Larry Bird?
Hey!
Hey, where have you been?

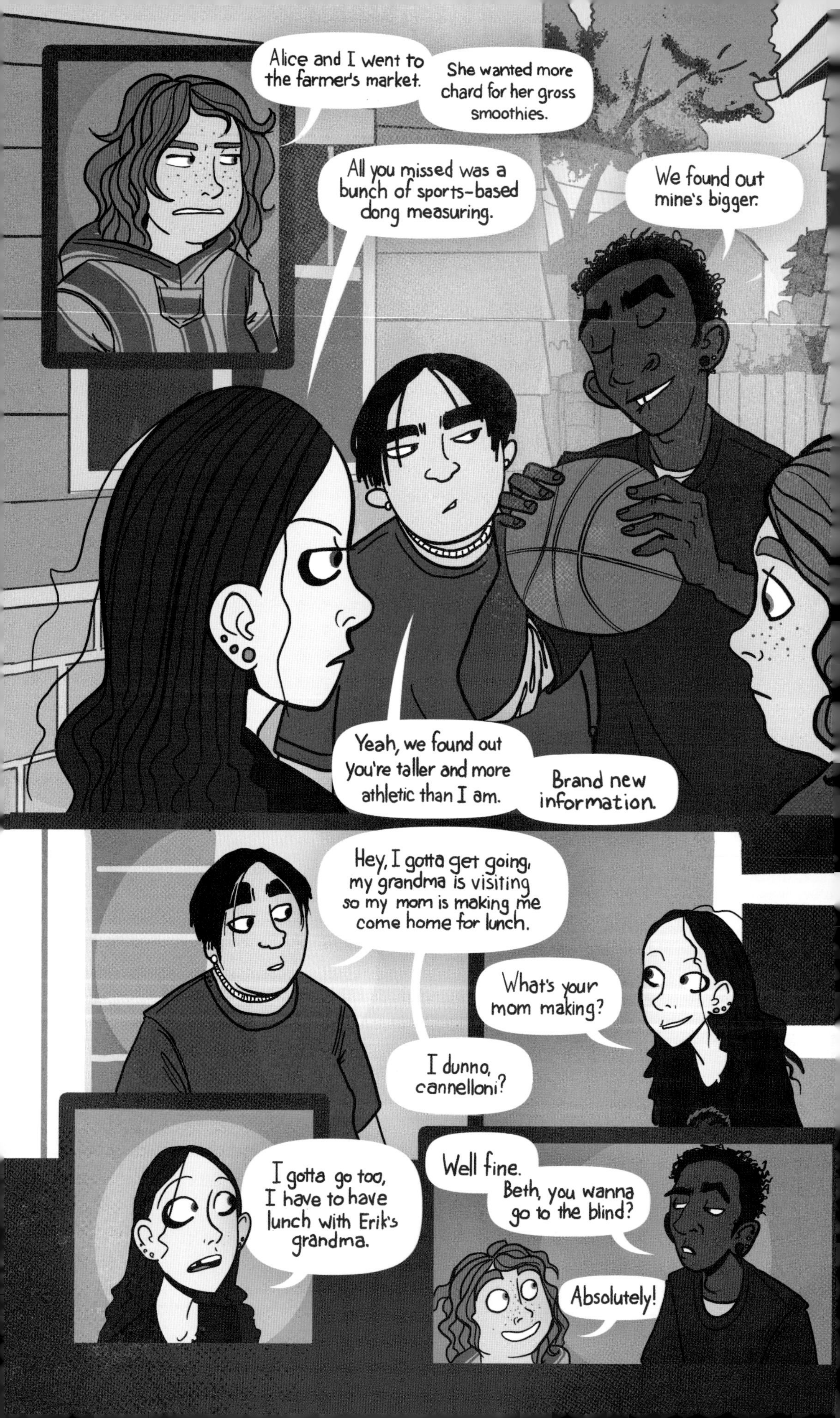
Alice and I went to the farmer's market.
She wanted more chard for her gross smoothies.
All you missed was a bunch of sports-based dong measuring.
We found out mine's bigger.
Yeah, we found out you're taller and more athletic than I am.
Brand new information.
Hey, I gotta get going, my grandma is visiting so my mom is making me come home for lunch.
What's your mom making?
I dunno, cannelloni?
I gotta go too, I have to have lunch with Erik's grandma.
Well fine.
Beth, you wanna go to the blind?
Absolutely!

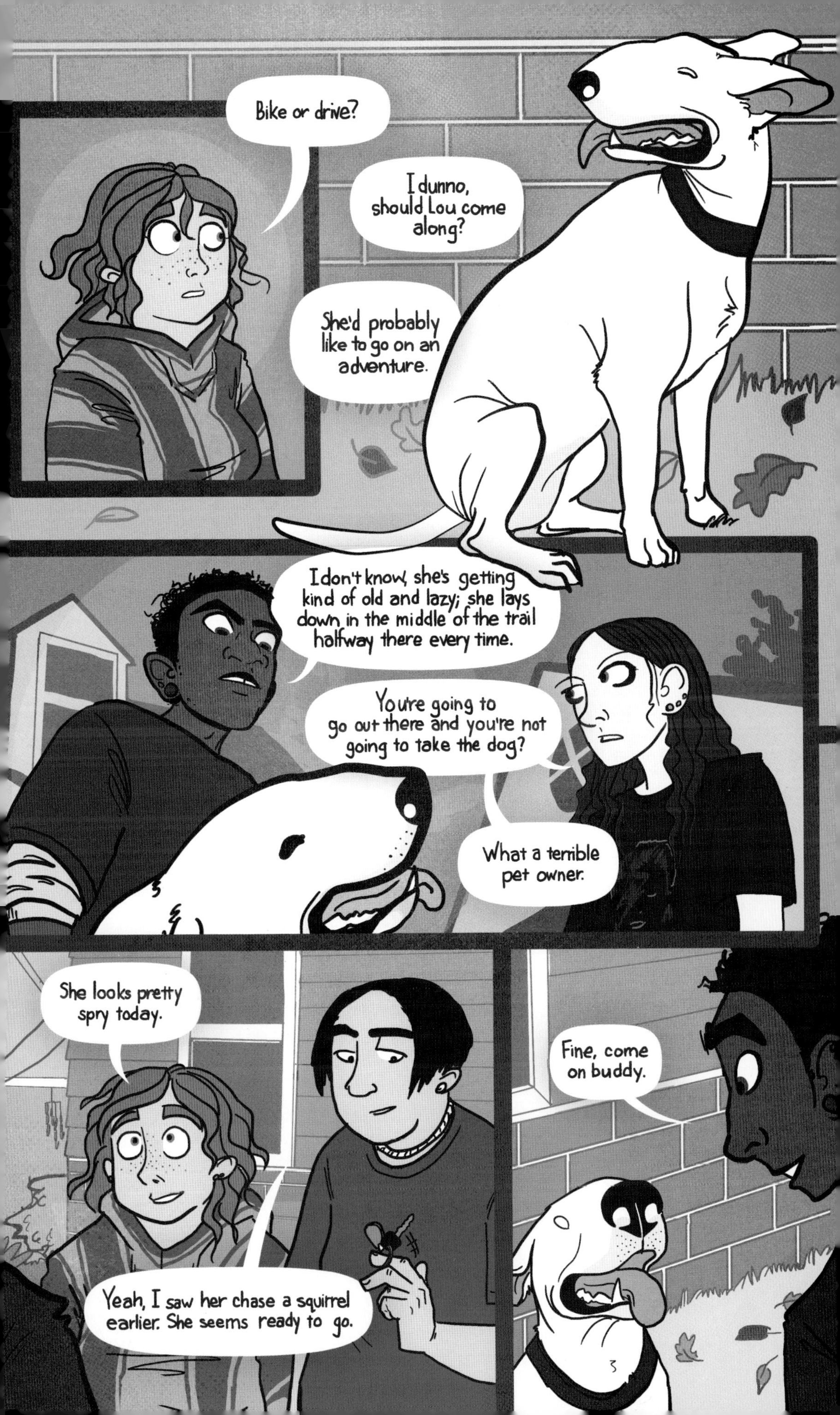

Bike or drive?
I dunno, should Lou come along?
She'd probably like to go on an adventure.
I don't know, she's getting kind of old and lazy; she lays down in the middle of the trail halfway there every time.
You're going to go out there and you're not going to take the dog?
What a terrible pet owner.
She looks pretty spry today.
Yeah, I saw her chase a squirrel earlier. She seems ready to go.
Fine, come on buddy.

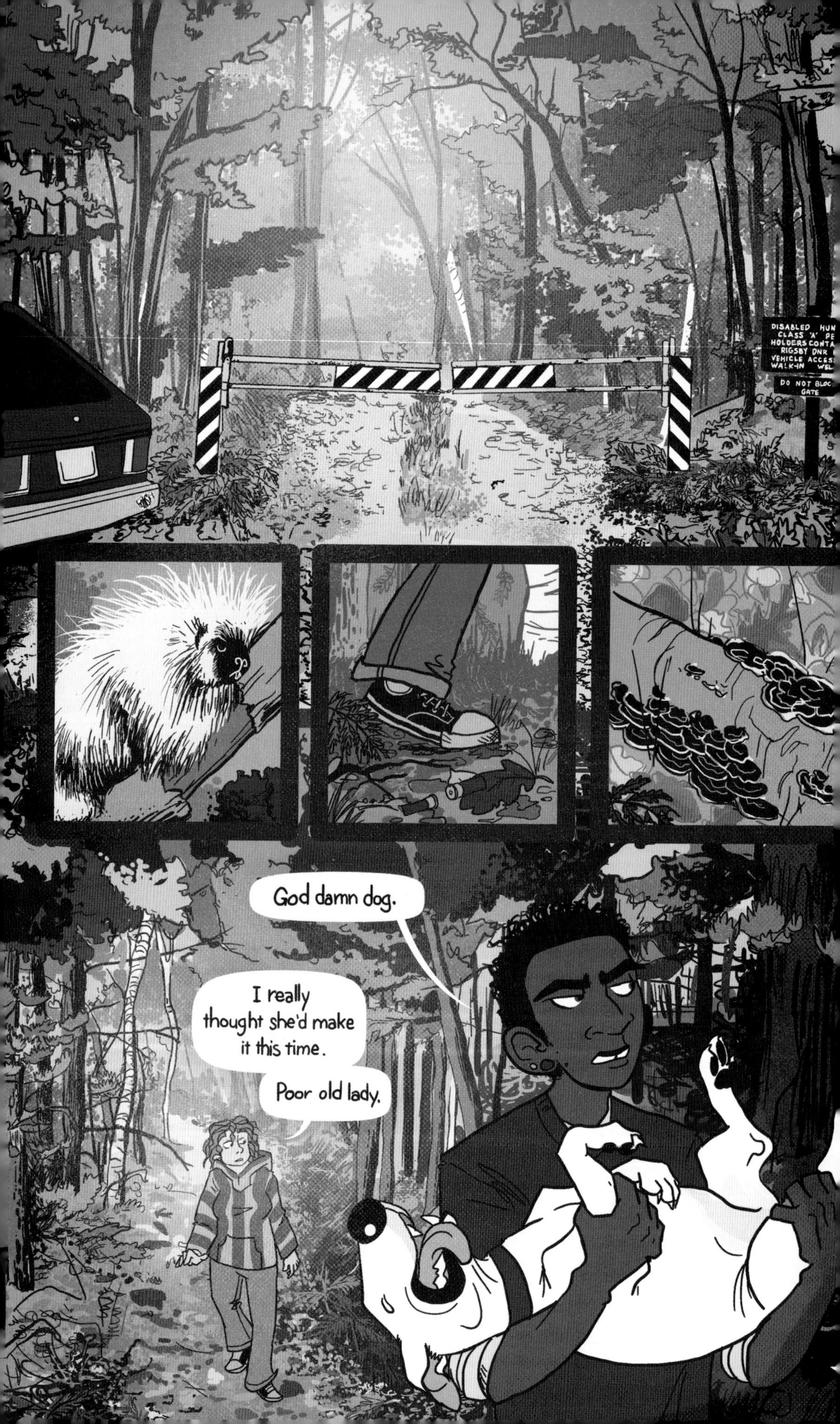

DISABLED HUN
CLASS 'A' PE
HOLDERS CONTA
RIGSBY DNR
VEHICLE ACCESS
WALK-IN WEL
DO NOT BLOC
GATE
God damn dog.
I really thought she'd make it this time.
Poor old lady.

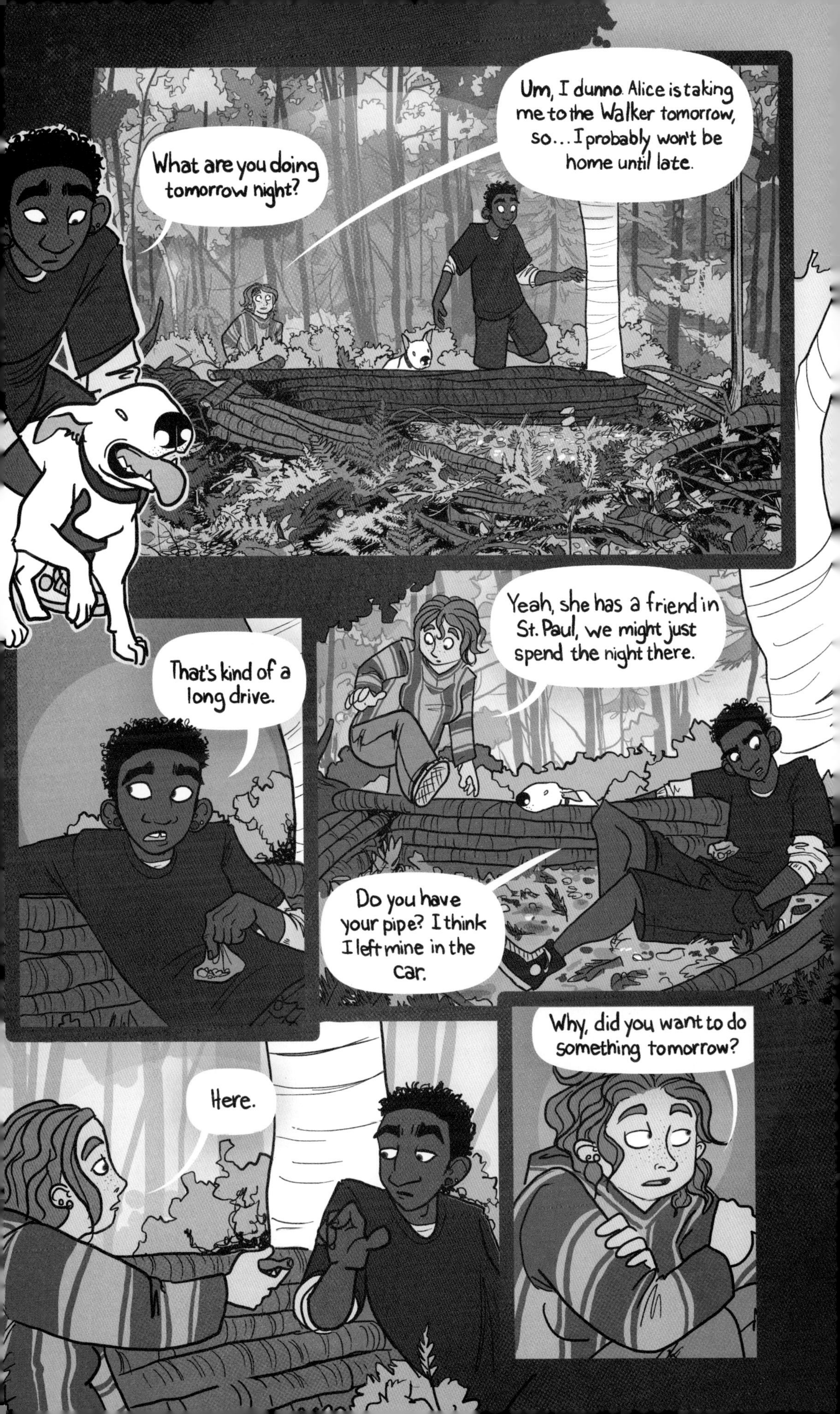
What are you doing tomorrow night?
Um, I dunno. Alice is taking me to the Walker tomorrow, so... I probably won't be home until late.
That's kind of a long drive.
Yeah, she has a friend in St. Paul, we might just spend the night there.
Do you have your pipe? I think I left mine in the car.
Here.
Why, did you want to do something tomorrow?

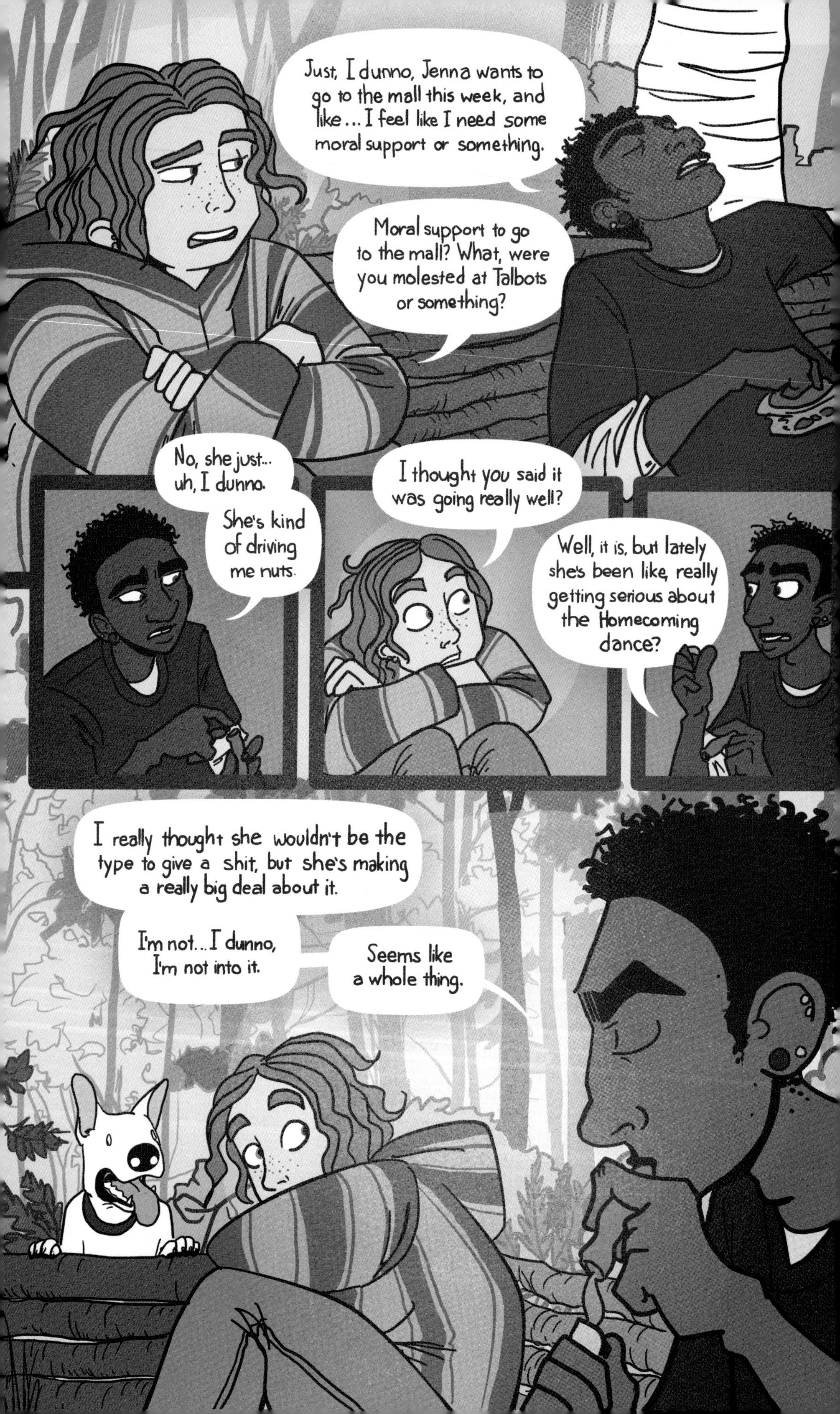
Just, I dunno, Jenna wants to go to the mall this week, and like... I feel like I need some moral support or something.
Moral support to go to the mall? What, were you molested at Talbots or something?
No, she just... uh, I dunno.
She's kind of driving me nuts.
I thought you said it was going really well?
Well, it is, but lately she's been like, really getting serious about the Homecoming dance?
I really thought she wouldn't be the type to give a shit, but she's making a really big deal about it.
I'm not... I dunno, I'm not into it.
Seems like a whole thing.

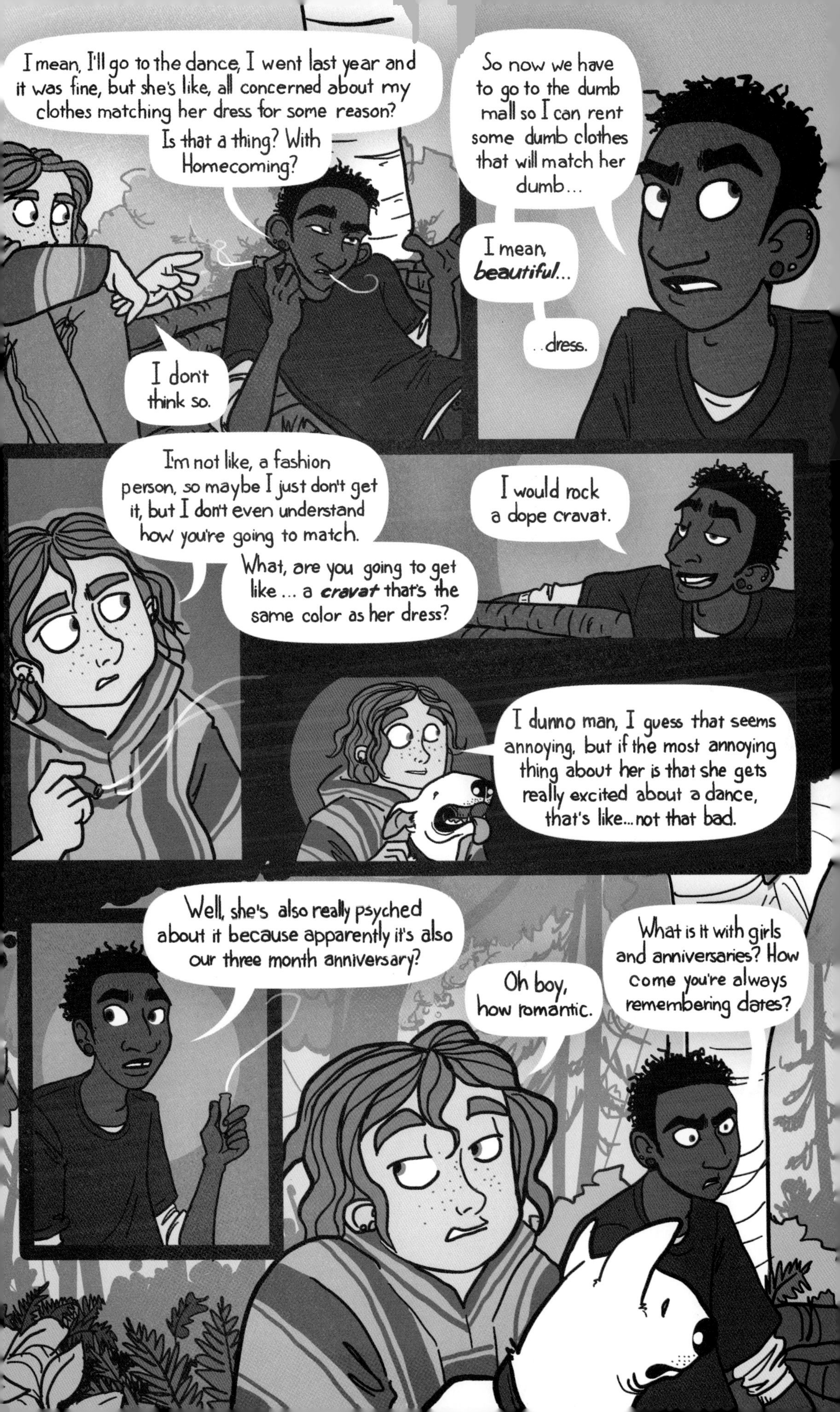
I mean, I'll go to the dance, I went last year and it was fine, but she's like, all concerned about my clothes matching her dress for some reason?
Is that a thing? With Homecoming?
I don't think so.
So now we have to go to the dumb mall so I can rent some dumb clothes that will match her dumb...
I mean, ***beautiful***...
...dress.
I'm not like, a fashion person, so maybe I just don't get it, but I don't even understand how you're going to match.
What, are you going to get like ... a ***cravat*** that's the same color as her dress?
I would rock a dope cravat.
I dunno man, I guess that seems annoying, but if the most annoying thing about her is that she gets really excited about a dance, that's like...not that bad.
Well, she's also really psyched about it because apparently it's also our three month anniversary?
Oh boy, how romantic.
What is it with girls and anniversaries? How come you're always remembering dates?

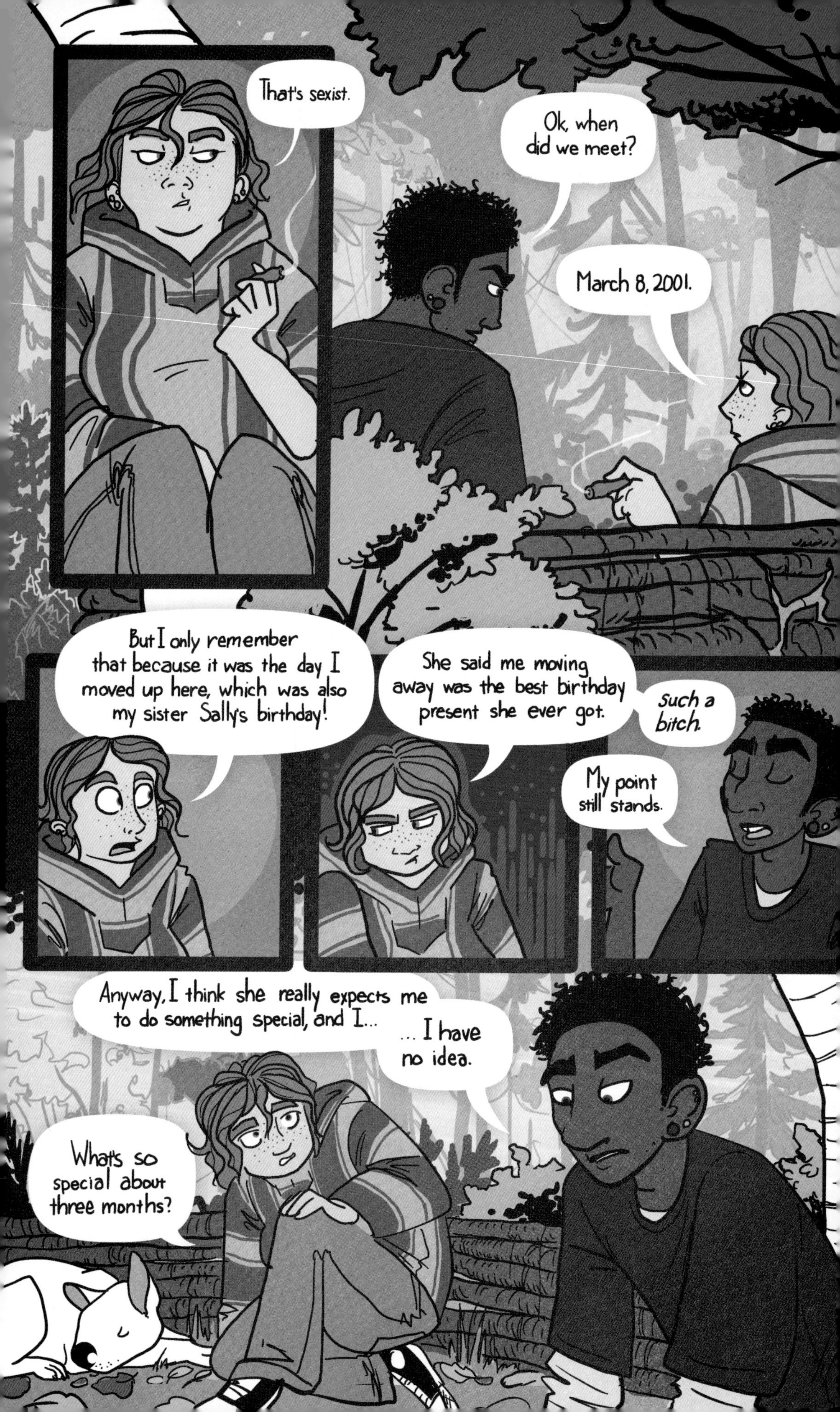
That's sexist.
Ok, when did we meet?
March 8, 2001.
But I only remember that because it was the day I moved up here, which was also my sister Sally's birthday!
She said me moving away was the best birthday present she ever got.
such a bitch.
My point still stands.
Anyway, I think she really expects me to do something special, and I...
... I have no idea.
What's so special about three months?

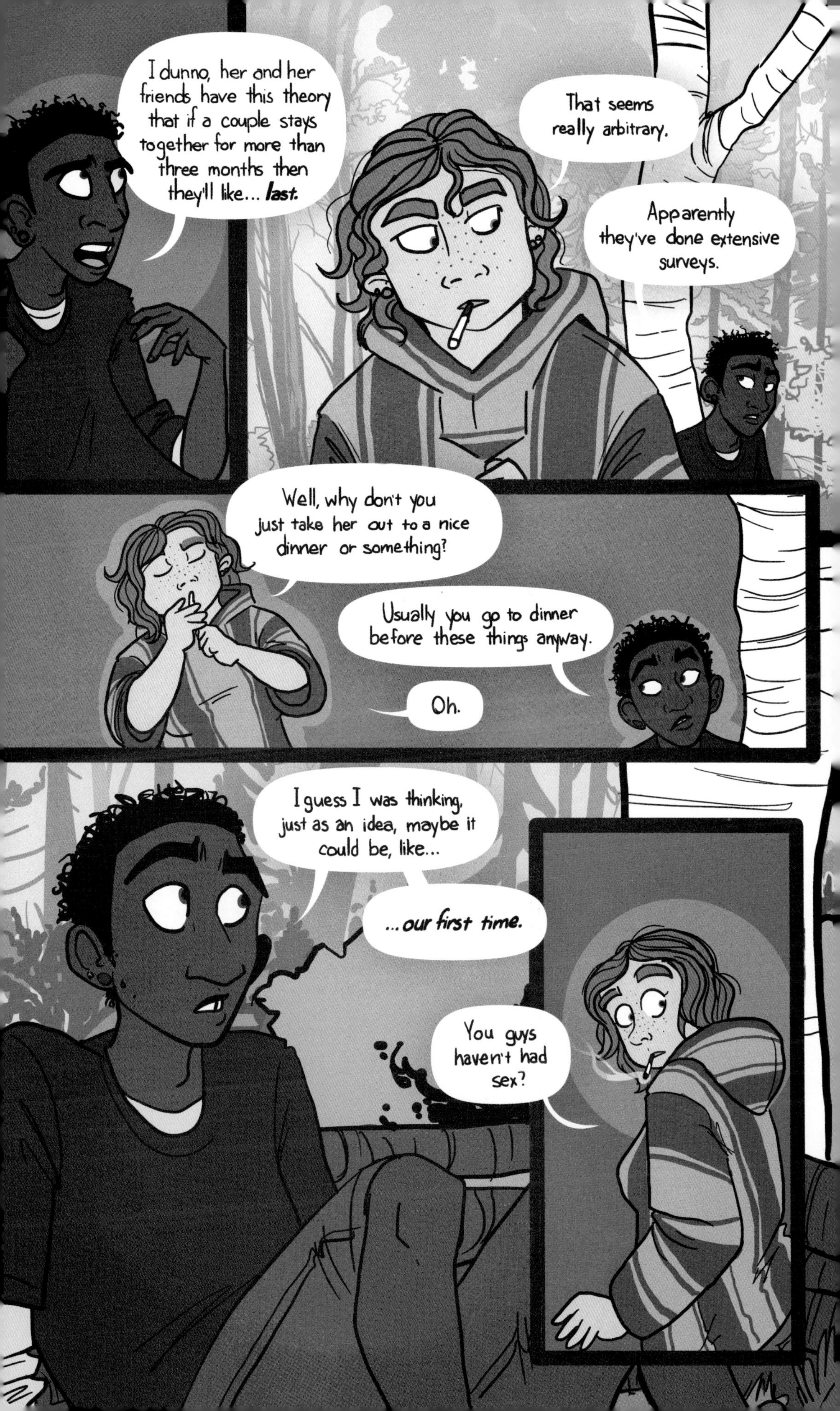
I dunno, her and her friends have this theory that if a couple stays together for more than three months then they'll like... **last.**
That seems really arbitrary.
Apparently they've done extensive surveys.
Well, why don't you just take her out to a nice dinner or something?
Usually you go to dinner before these things anyway.
Oh.
I guess I was thinking, just as an idea, maybe it could be, like...
...our first time.
You guys haven't had sex?

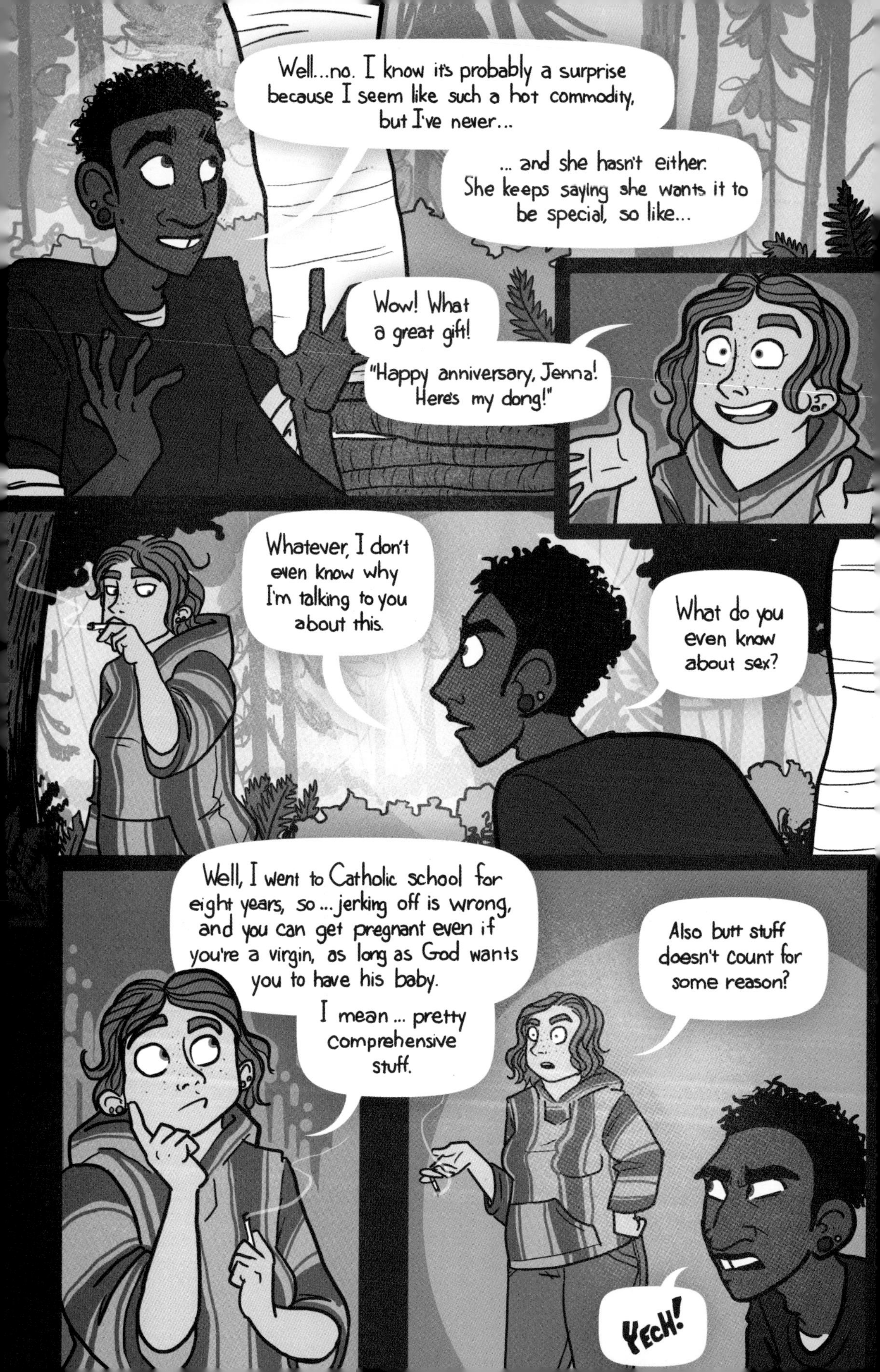
Well...no. I know it's probably a surprise because I seem like such a hot commodity, but I've never...
... and she hasn't either. She keeps saying she wants it to be special, so like...
Wow! What a great gift!
"Happy anniversary, Jenna! Here's my dong!"
Whatever, I don't even know why I'm talking to you about this.
What do you even know about sex?
Well, I went to Catholic school for eight years, so ... jerking off is wrong, and you can get pregnant even if you're a virgin, as long as God wants you to have his baby.
I mean ... pretty comprehensive stuff.
Also butt stuff doesn't count for some reason?
YECH!

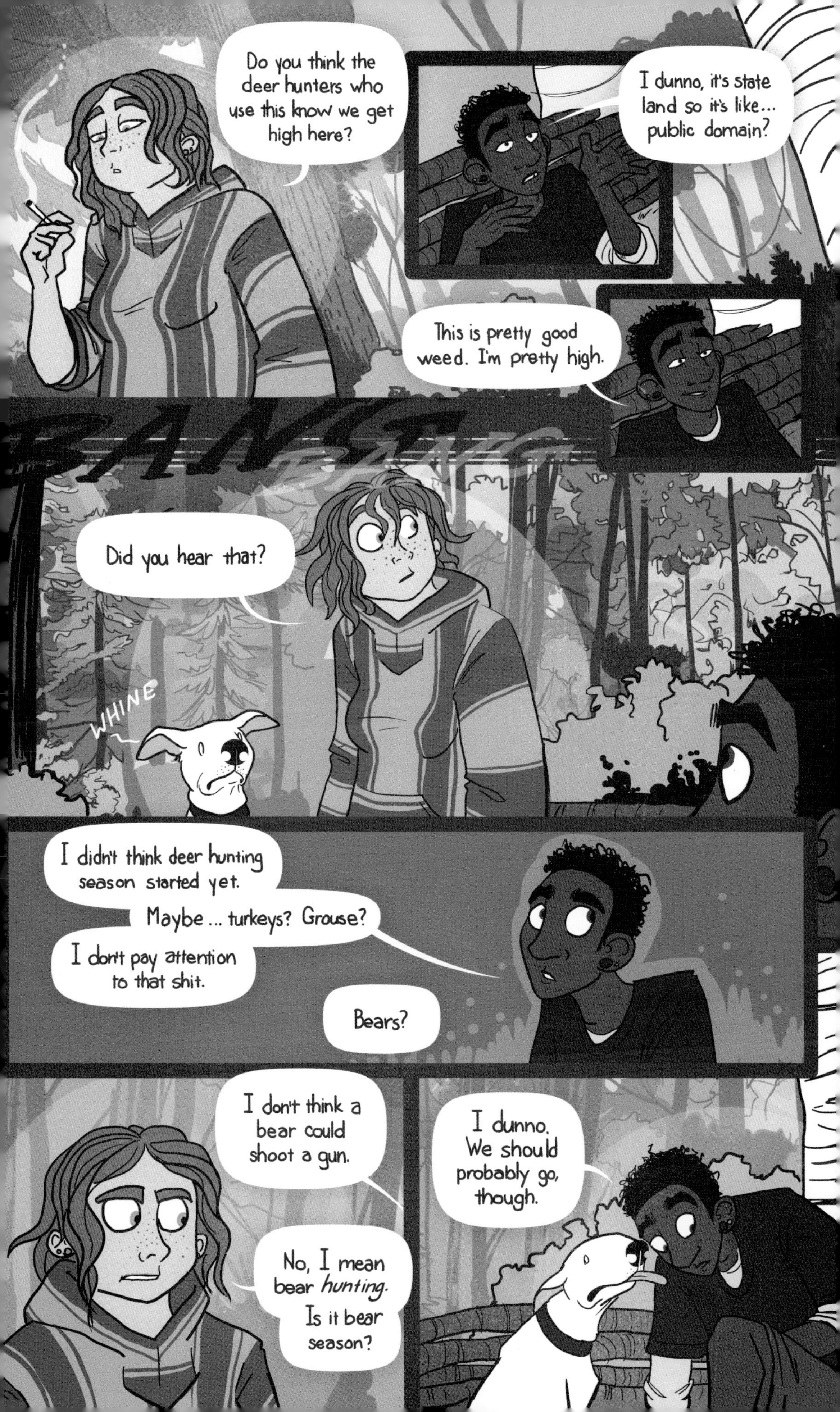

Do you think the deer hunters who use this know we get high here?
I dunno, it's state land so it's like... public domain?
This is pretty good weed. I'm pretty high.
BANG
Did you hear that?
WHINE
I didn't think deer hunting season started yet.
Maybe ... turkeys? Grouse?
I don't pay attention to that shit.
Bears?
I don't think a bear could shoot a gun.
No, I mean bear *hunting*. Is it bear season?
I dunno. We should probably go, though.

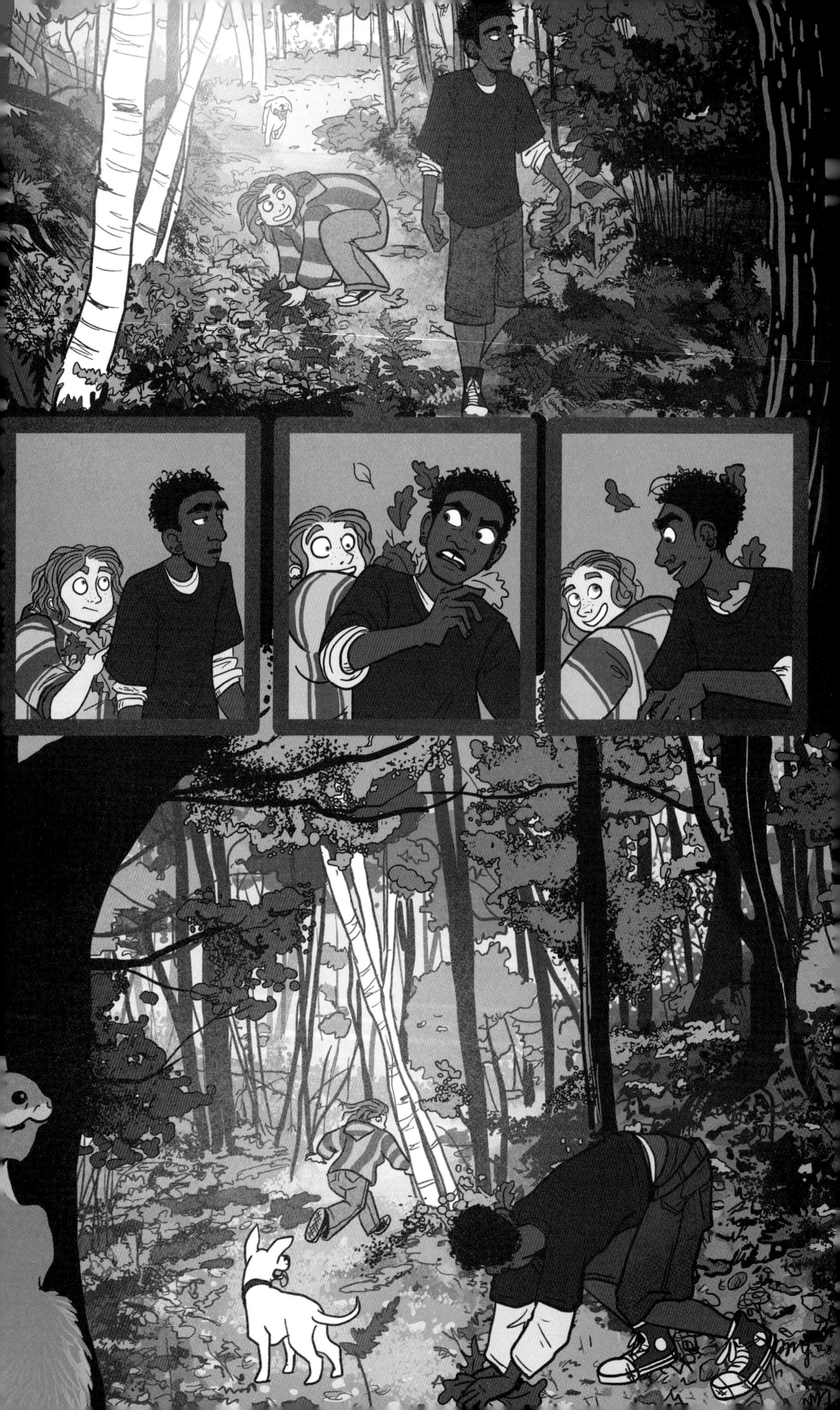

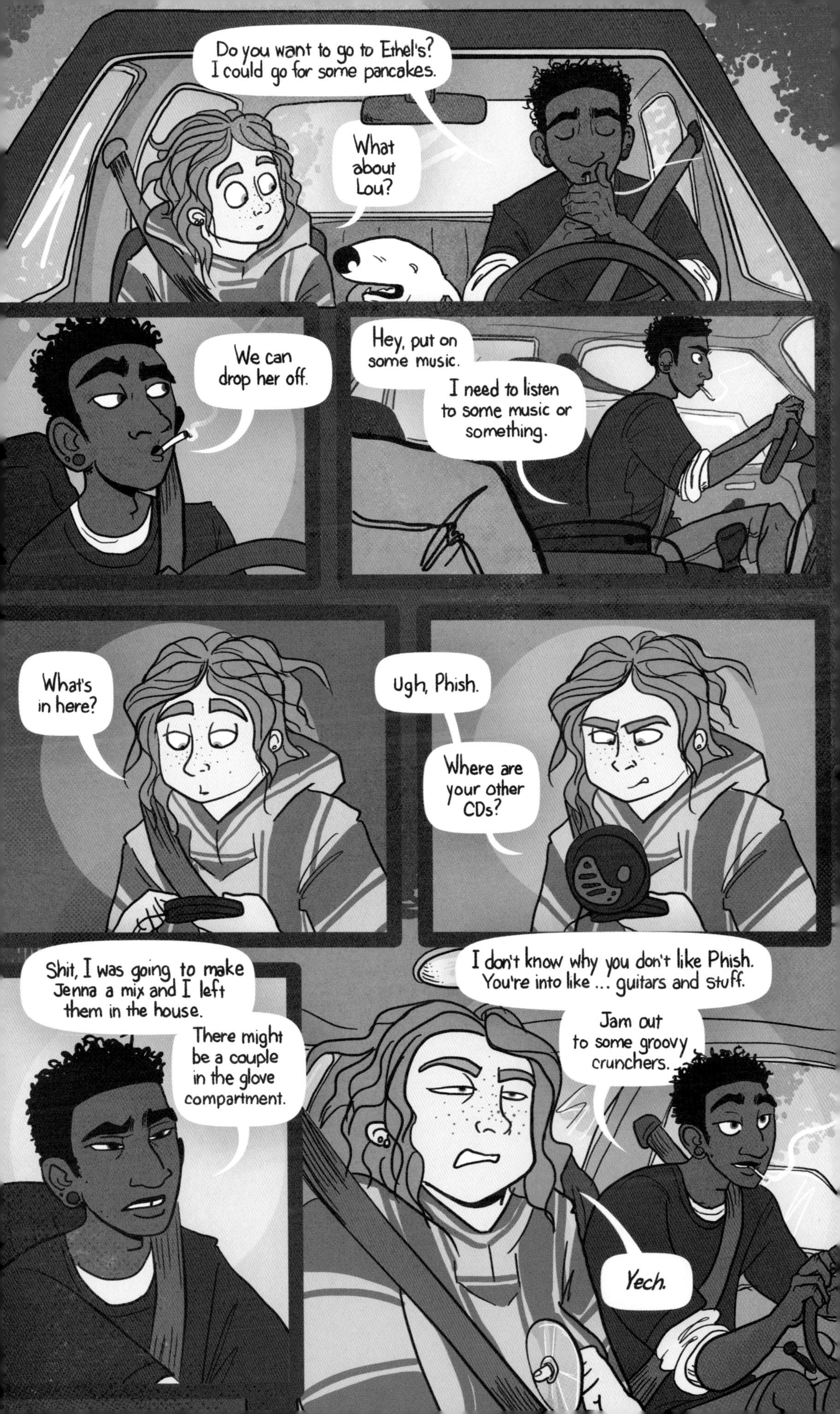
Do you want to go to Ethel's? I could go for some pancakes.
What about Lou?
We can drop her off.
Hey, put on some music.
I need to listen to some music or something.
What's in here?
Ugh, Phish.
Where are your other CDs?
Shit, I was going to make Jenna a mix and I left them in the house.
There might be a couple in the glove compartment.
I don't know why you don't like Phish. You're into like ... guitars and stuff.
Jam out to some groovy crunchers.
Yech.

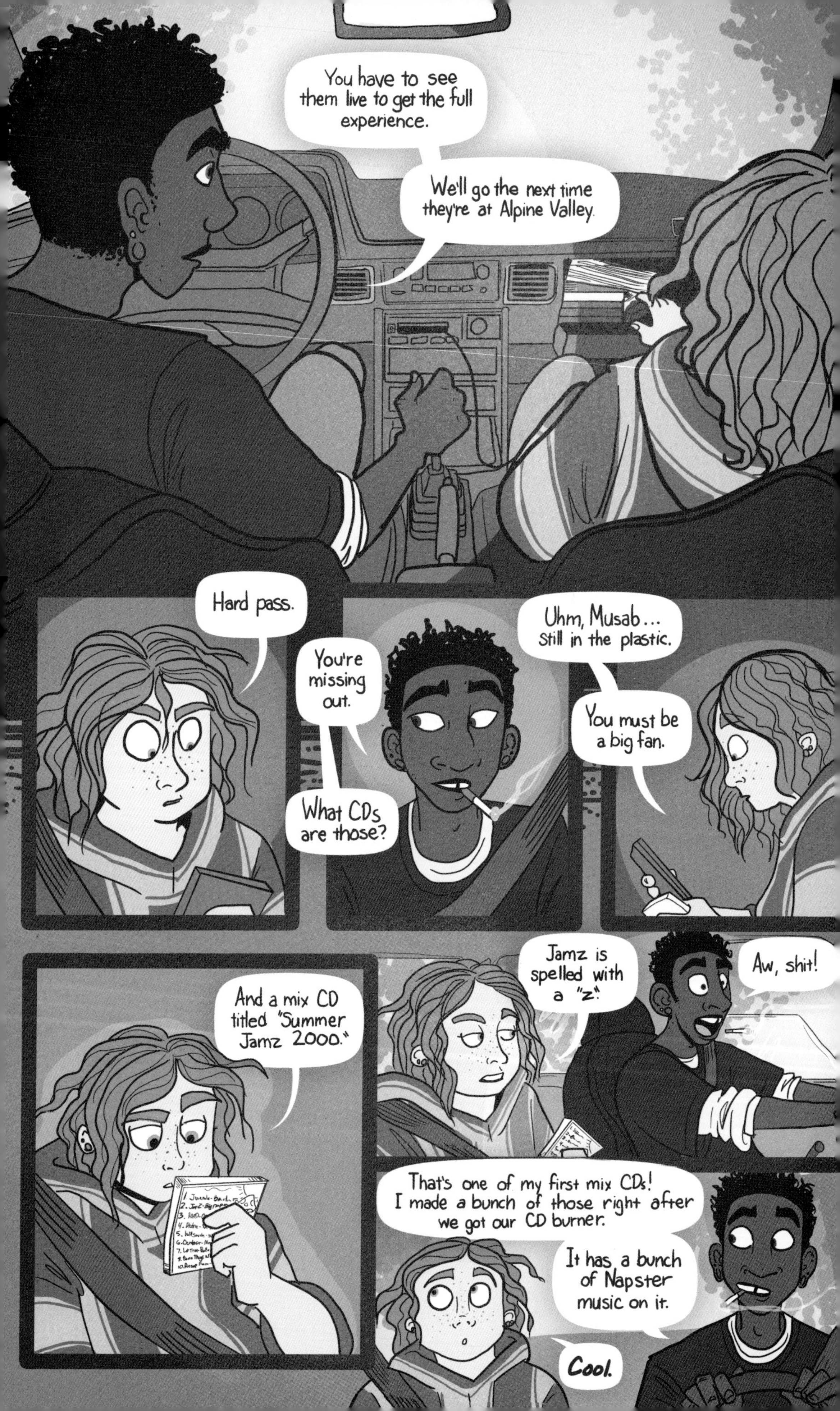
You have to see them live to get the full experience.
We'll go the next time they're at Alpine Valley.
Hard pass.
You're missing out.
What CDs are those?
Uhm, Musab... still in the plastic.
You must be a big fan.
And a mix CD titled "Summer Jamz 2000."
Jamz is spelled with a "z."
Aw, shit!
That's one of my first mix CDs! I made a bunch of those right after we got our CD burner.
It has a bunch of Napster music on it.
Cool.

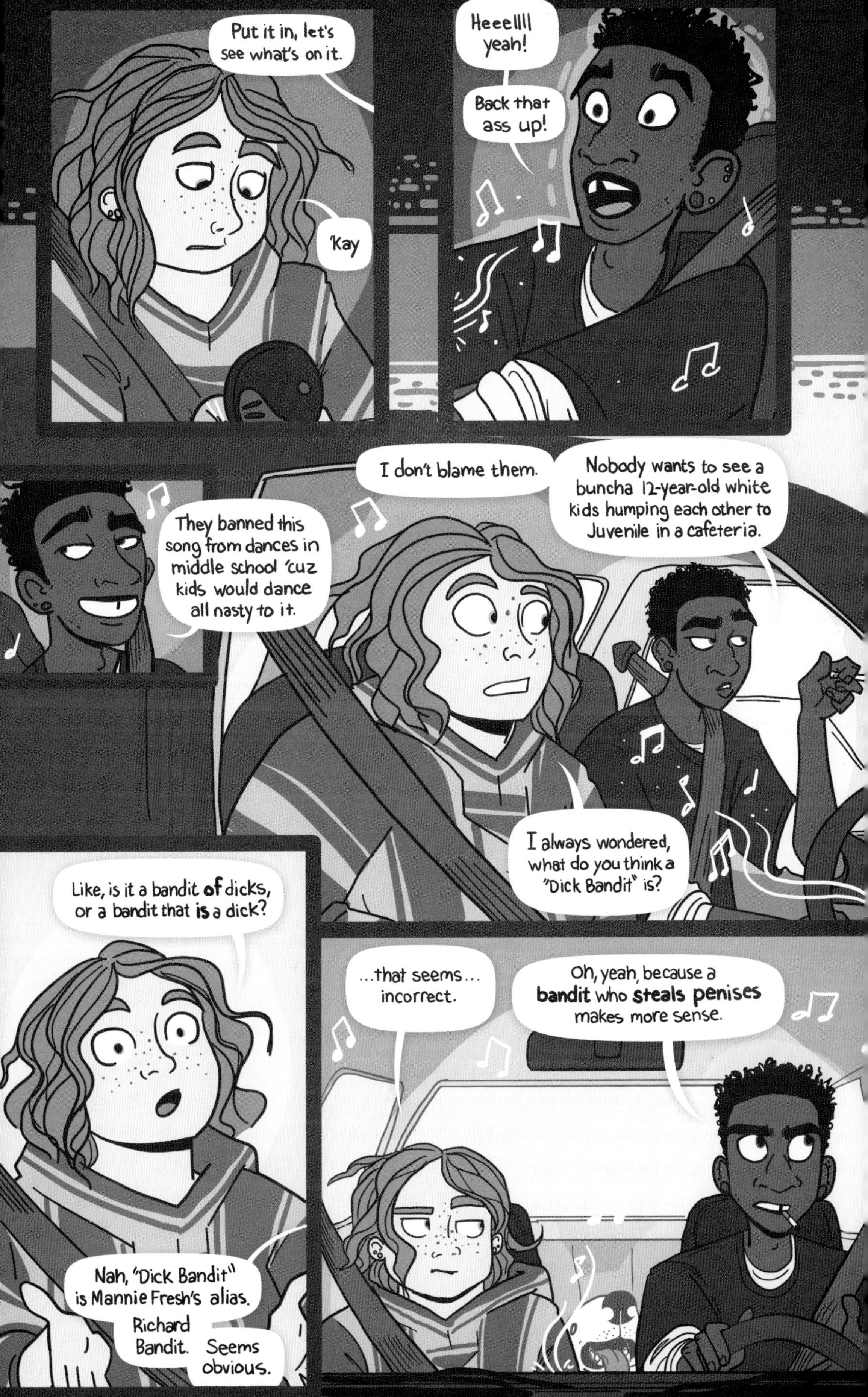
Put it in, let's see what's on it.
'Kay
Heeelll yeah!
Back that ass up!
They banned this song from dances in middle school 'cuz kids would dance all nasty to it.
I don't blame them.
Nobody wants to see a buncha 12-year-old white kids humping each other to Juvenile in a cafeteria.
I always wondered, what do you think a "Dick Bandit" is?
Like, is it a bandit **of** dicks, or a bandit that **is** a dick?
Nah, "Dick Bandit" is Mannie Fresh's alias.
Richard Bandit.
Seems obvious.
...that seems... incorrect.
Oh, yeah, because a **bandit** who **steals penises** makes more sense.

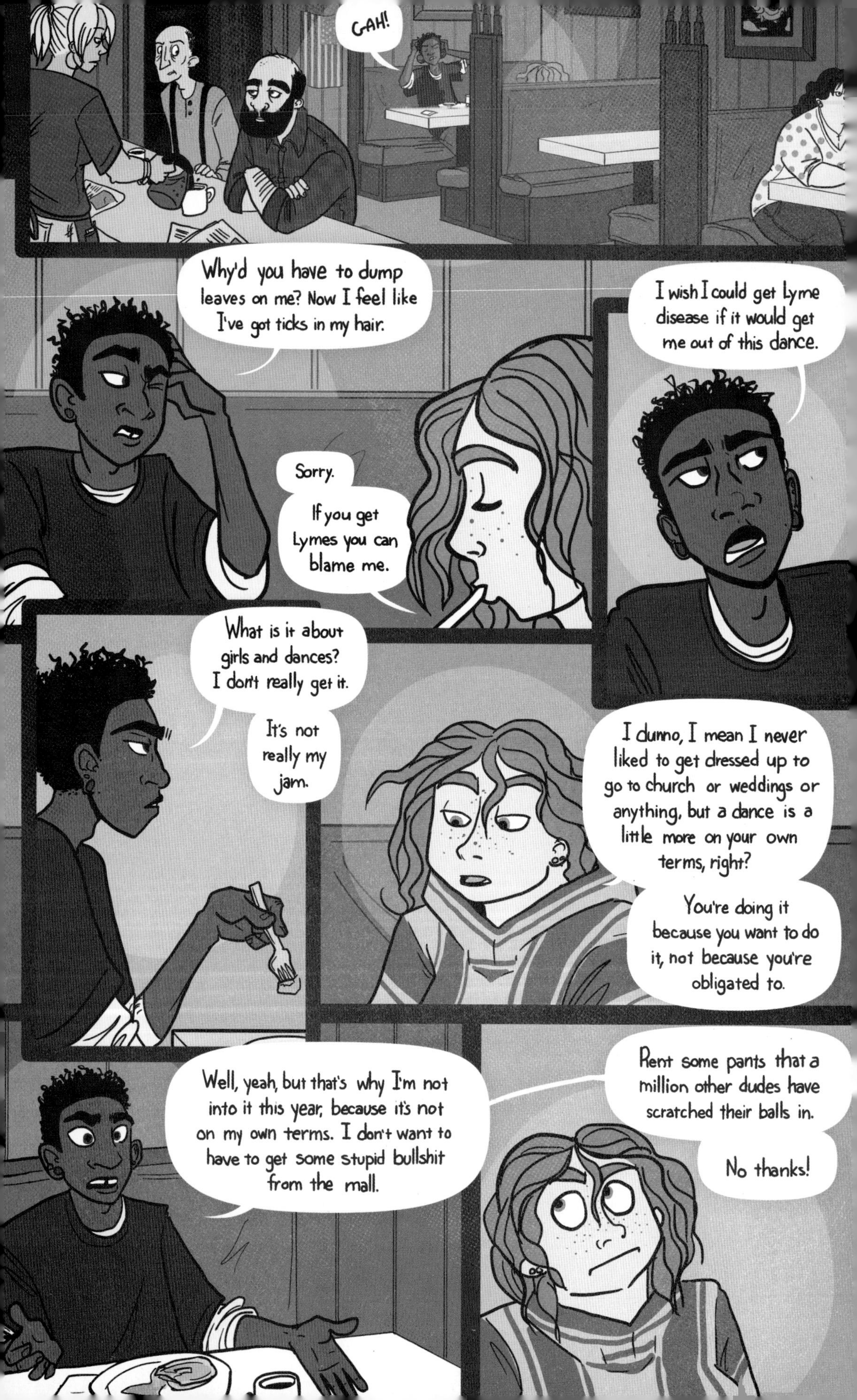
GAH!
Why'd you have to dump leaves on me? Now I feel like I've got ticks in my hair.
Sorry.
If you get Lymes you can blame me.
I wish I could get Lyme disease if it would get me out of this dance.
What is it about girls and dances? I don't really get it.
It's not really my jam.
I dunno, I mean I never liked to get dressed up to go to church or weddings or anything, but a dance is a little more on your own terms, right?
You're doing it because you want to do it, not because you're obligated to.
Well, yeah, but that's why I'm not into it this year, because it's not on my own terms. I don't want to have to get some stupid bullshit from the mall.
Rent some pants that a million other dudes have scratched their balls in.
No thanks!

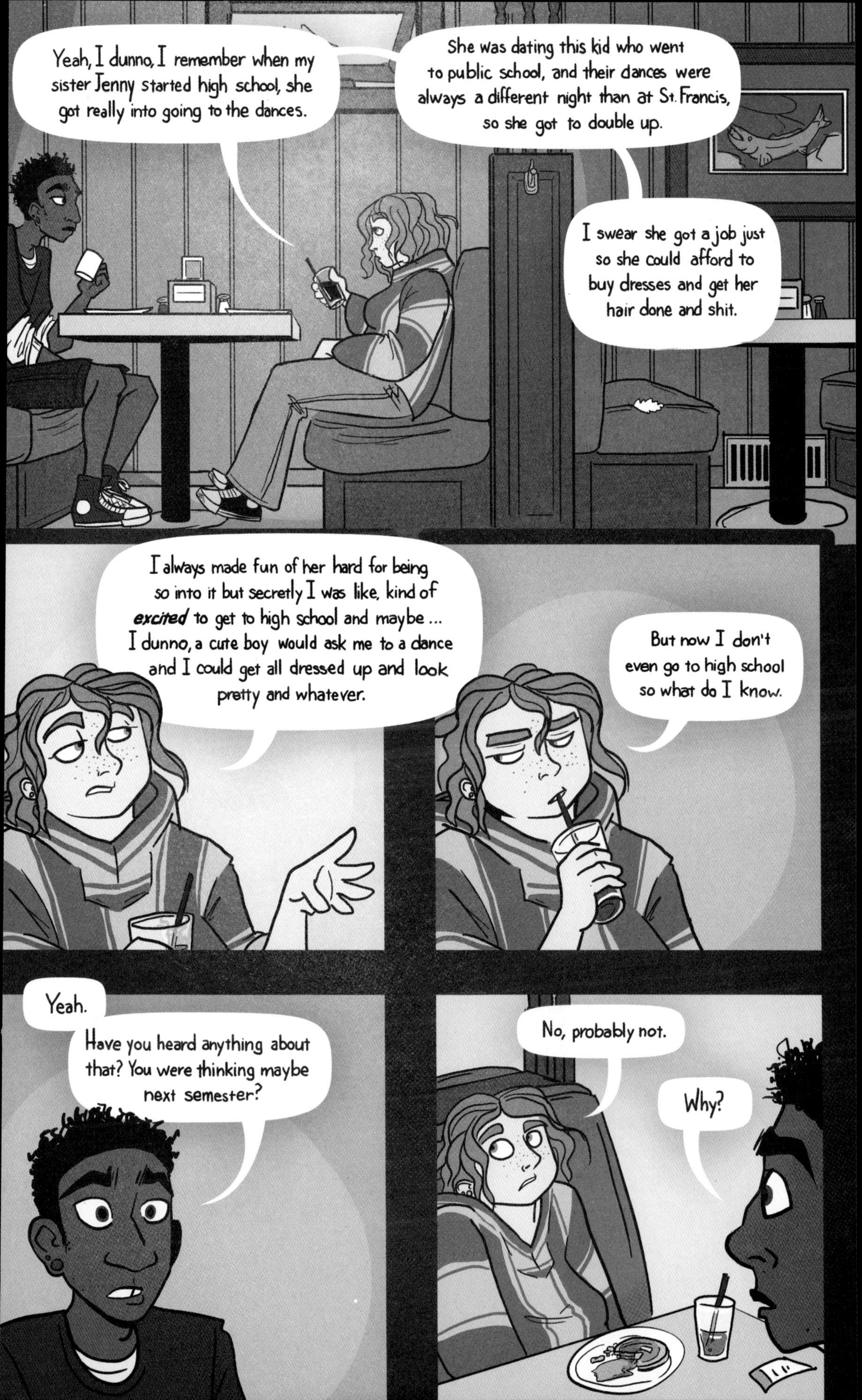
Yeah, I dunno, I remember when my sister Jenny started high school, she got really into going to the dances.
She was dating this kid who went to public school, and their dances were always a different night than at St. Francis, so she got to double up.
I swear she got a job just so she could afford to buy dresses and get her hair done and shit.
I always made fun of her hard for being so into it but secretly I was like, kind of *excited* to get to high school and maybe ... I dunno, a cute boy would ask me to a dance and I could get all dressed up and look pretty and whatever.
But now I don't even go to high school so what do I know.
Yeah.
Have you heard anything about that? You were thinking maybe next semester?
No, probably not.
Why?

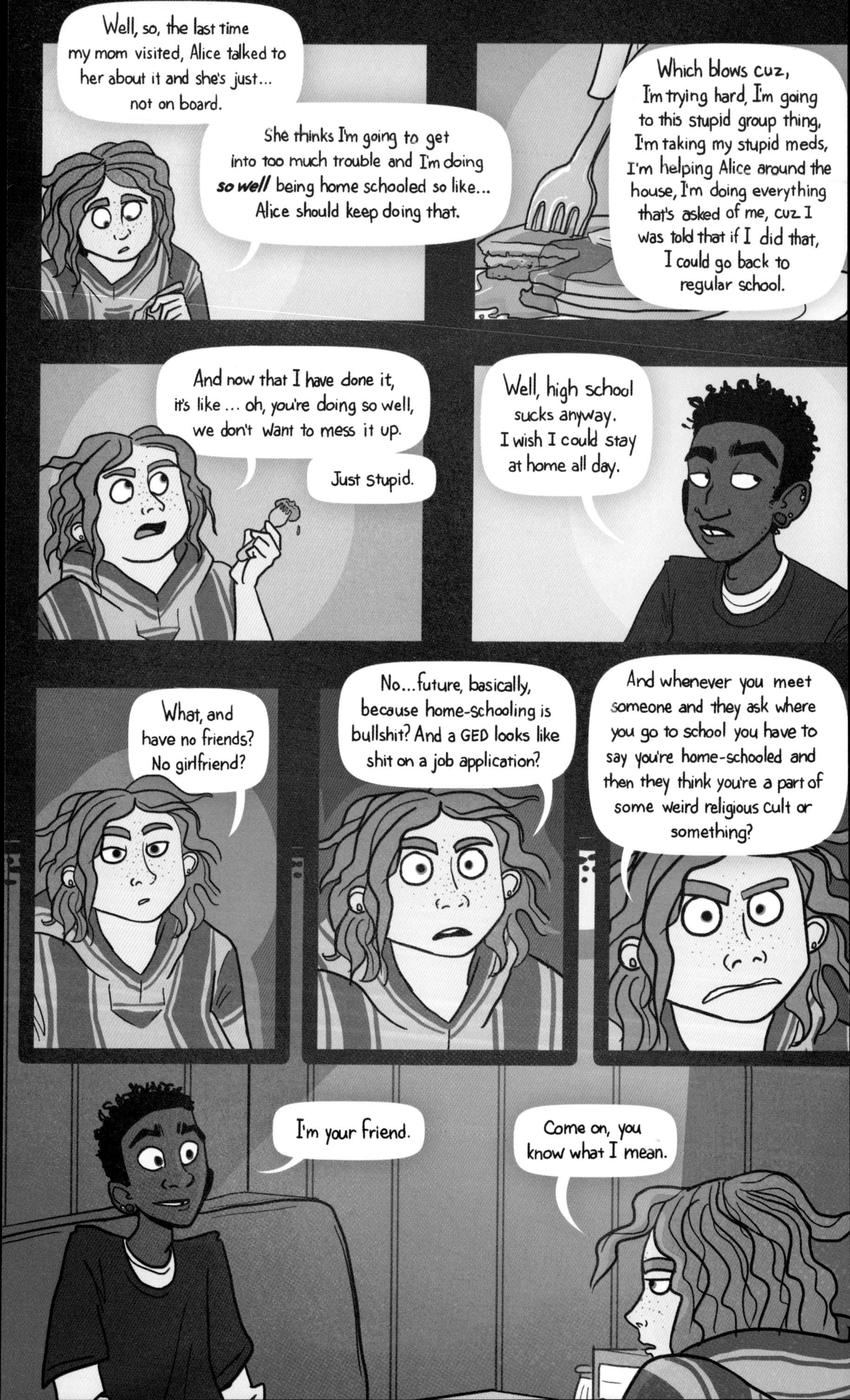
Well, so, the last time my mom visited, Alice talked to her about it and she's just... not on board.
She thinks I'm going to get into too much trouble and I'm doing ***so well*** being home schooled so like... Alice should keep doing that.
Which blows cuz, I'm trying hard, I'm going to this stupid group thing, I'm taking my stupid meds, I'm helping Alice around the house, I'm doing everything that's asked of me, cuz I was told that if I did that, I could go back to regular school.
And now that I have done it, it's like ... oh, *you're* doing so well, we don't want to mess it up.
Just stupid.
Well, high school sucks anyway. I wish I could stay at home all day.
What, and have no friends? No girlfriend?
No... future, basically, because home-schooling is bullshit? And a GED looks like shit on a job application?
And whenever you meet someone and they ask where you go to school you have to say you're home-schooled and then they think you're a part of some weird religious cult or something?
I'm your friend.
Come on, you know what I mean.

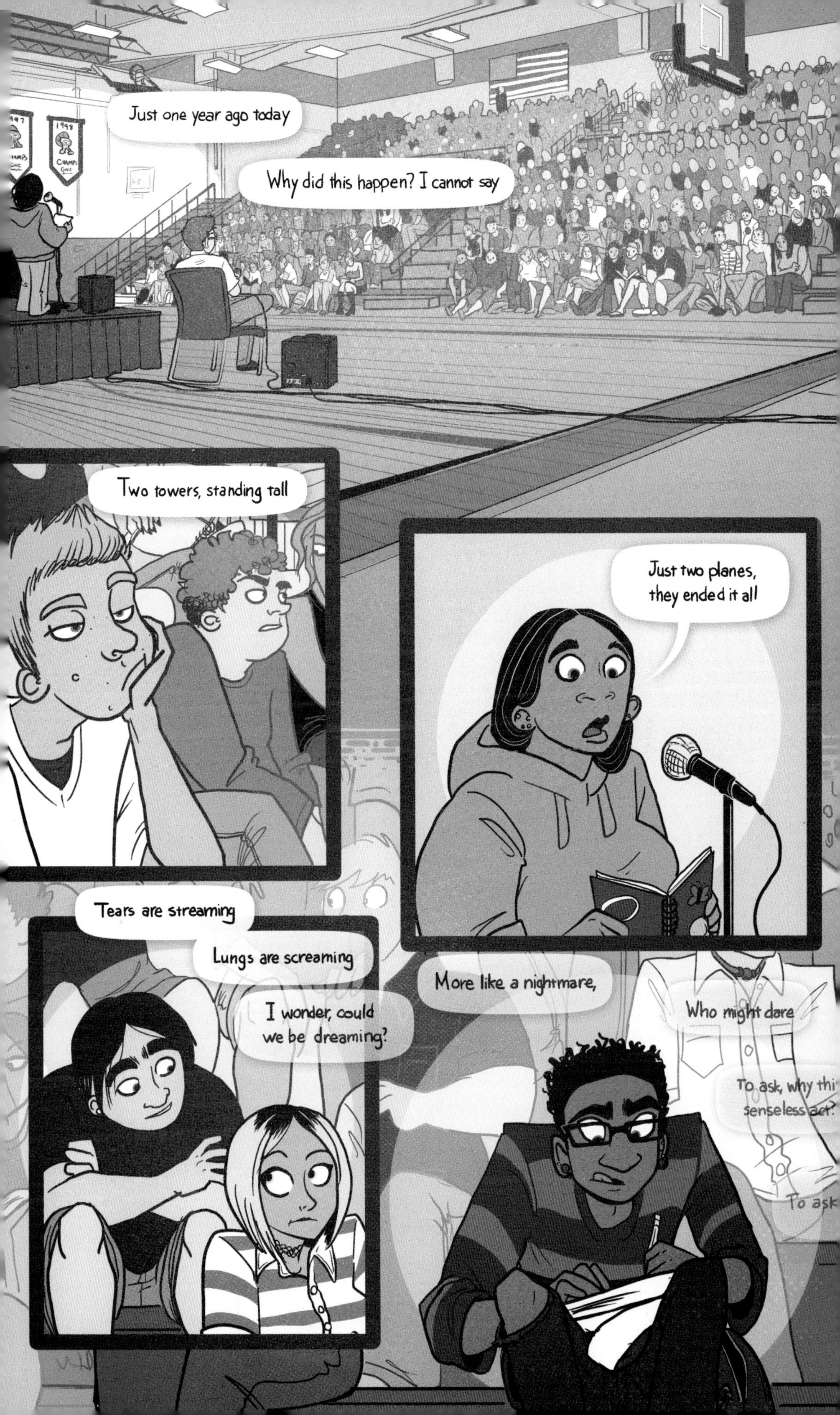

Just one year ago today
Why did this happen? I cannot say
Two towers, standing tall
Just two planes, they ended it all
Tears are streaming
Lungs are screaming
I wonder, could we be dreaming?
More like a nightmare,
Who might dare
To ask, why thi
senseless act?
To ask

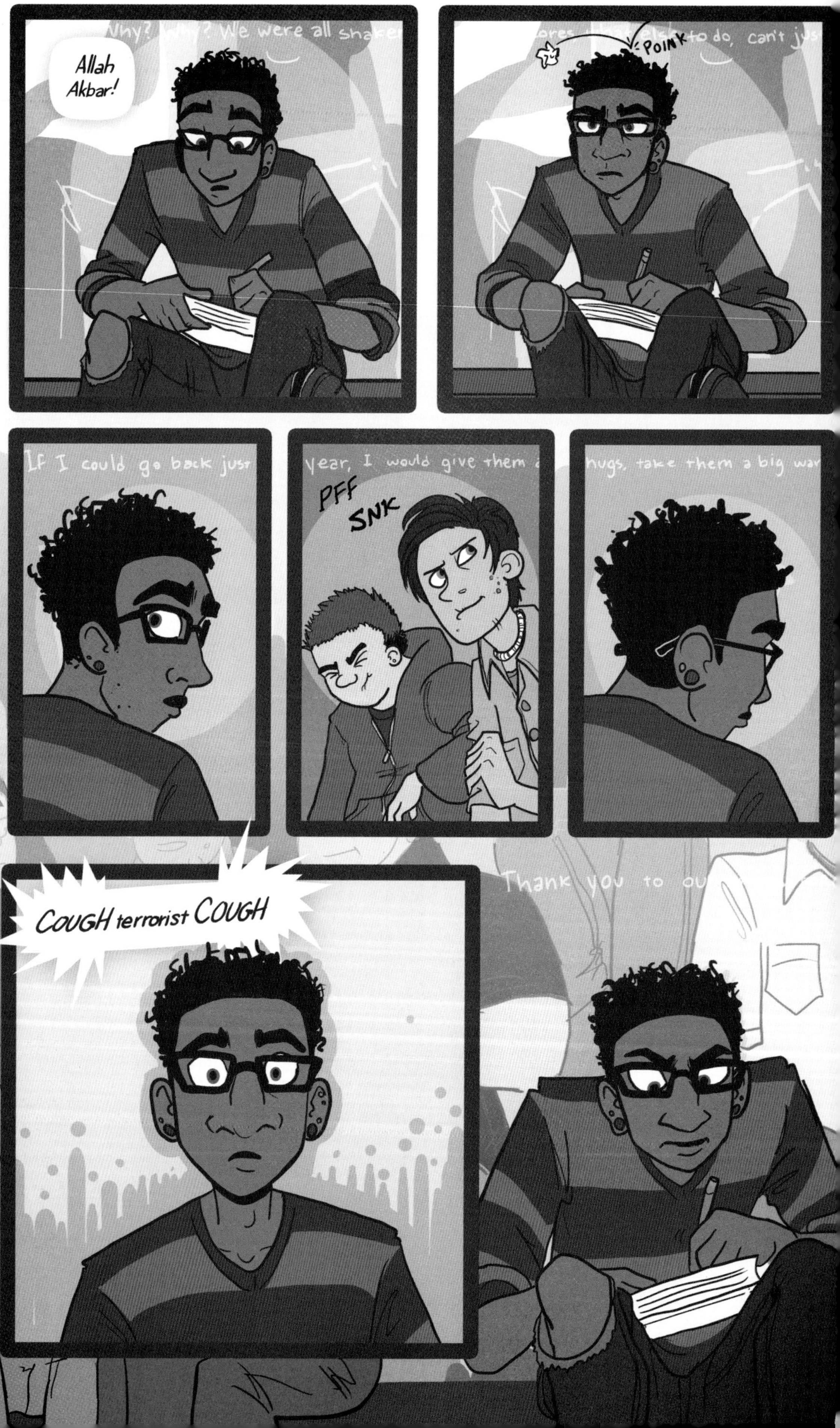
Allah Akbar!
POINK
If I could go back just
year, I would give them a
hugs, take them a big wa
PFF
SNK
COUGH terrorist COUGH
Thank you to ou

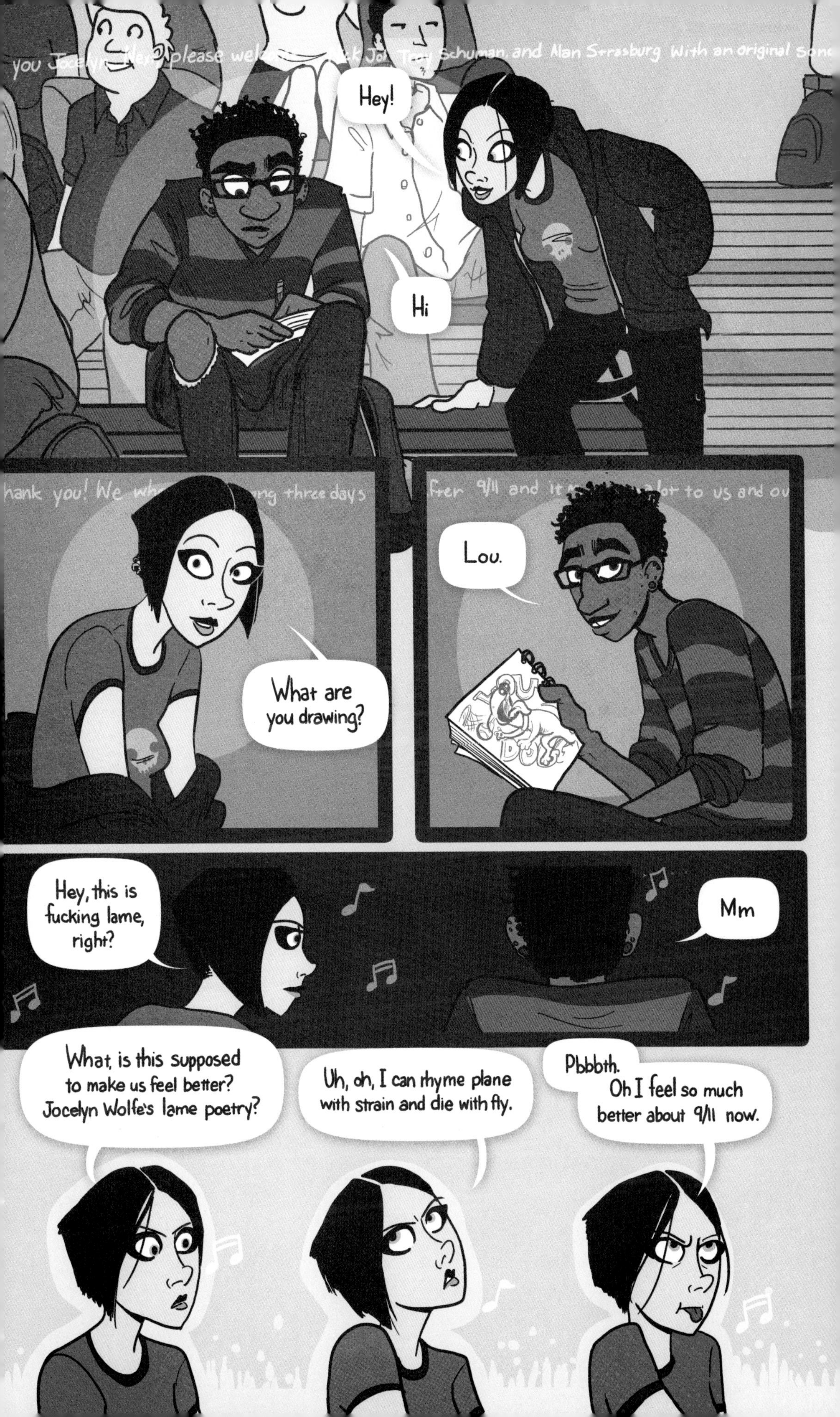

Schuman, and Alan Strasburg with an original
Hey!
Hi
three days
9/11 and it
lot to us and
What are you drawing?
Lou.
Hey, this is fucking lame, right?
Mm
What, is this supposed to make us feel better? Jocelyn Wolfe's lame poetry?
Uh, oh, I can rhyme plane with strain and die with fly.
Pbbbth.
Oh I feel so much better about 9/11 now.

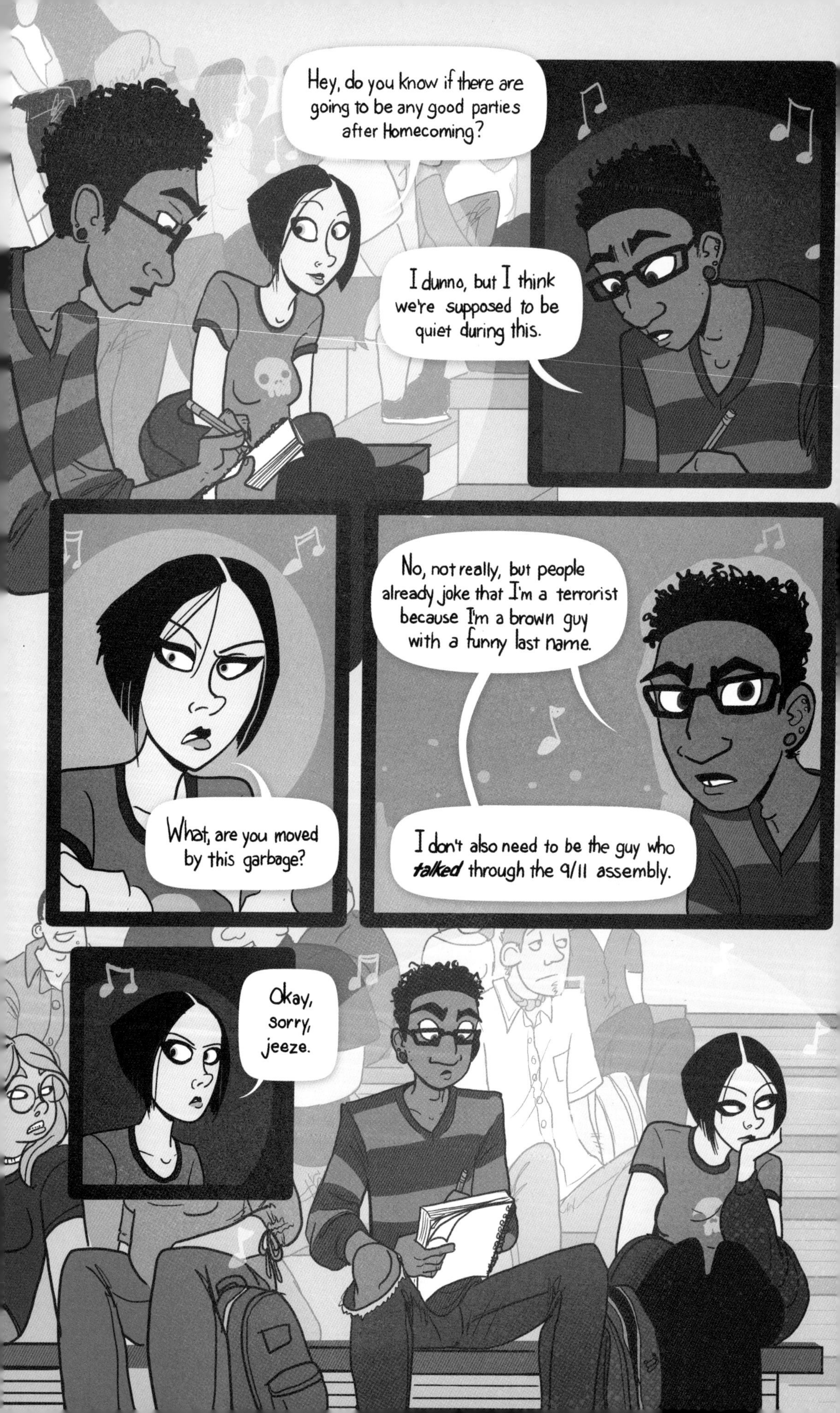
Hey, do you know if there are going to be any good parties after Homecoming?
I dunno, but I think we're supposed to be quiet during this.
What, are you moved by this garbage?
No, not really, but people already joke that I'm a terrorist because I'm a brown guy with a funny last name.
I don't also need to be the guy who *talked* through the 9/11 assembly.
Okay, sorry, jeeze.

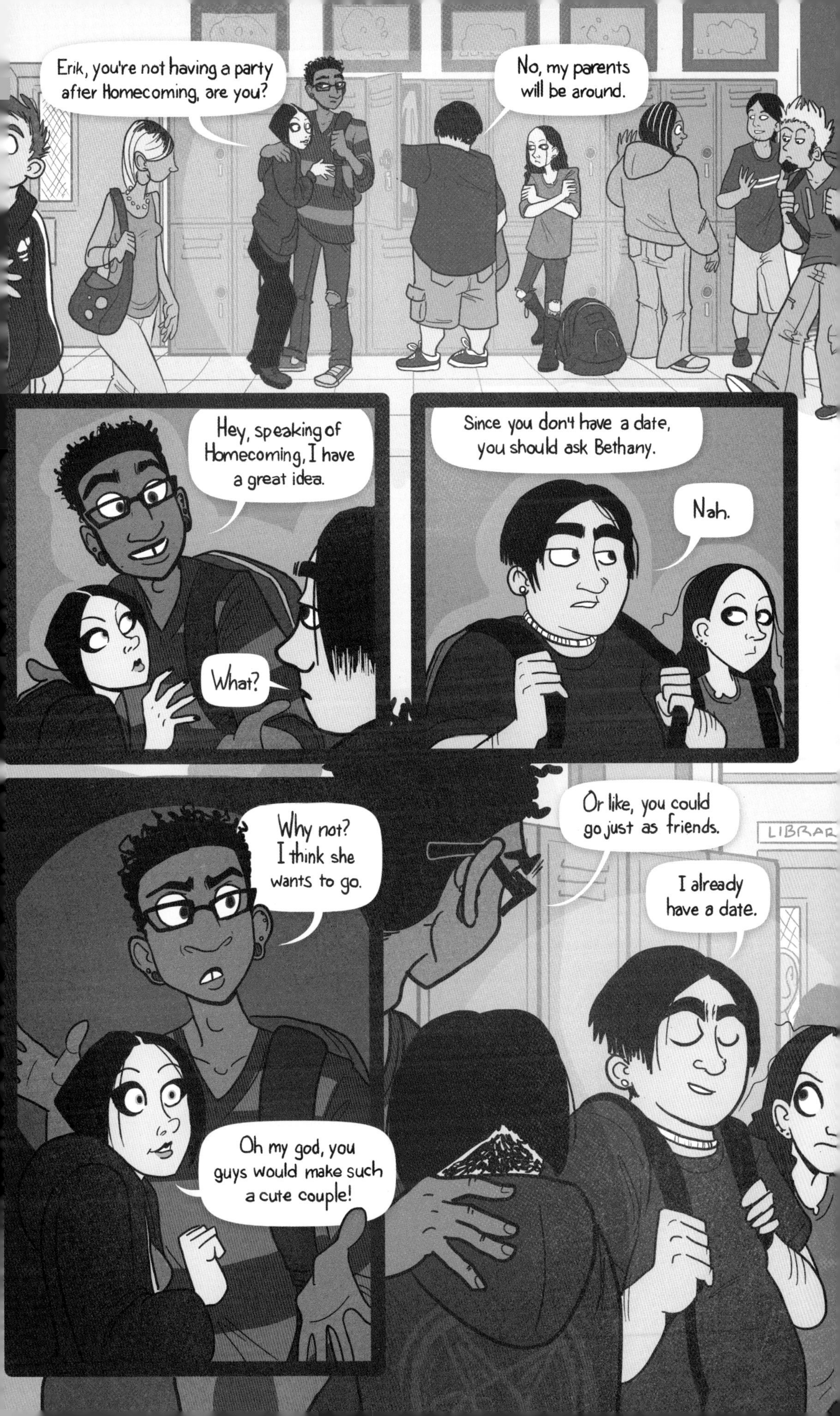
Erik, you're not having a party after Homecoming, are you?
No, my parents will be around.
Hey, speaking of Homecoming, I have a great idea.
What?
Since you don't have a date, you should ask Bethany.
Nah.
Why not? I think she wants to go.
Oh my god, you guys would make such a cute couple!
Or like, you could go just as friends.
I already have a date.
LIBRAR

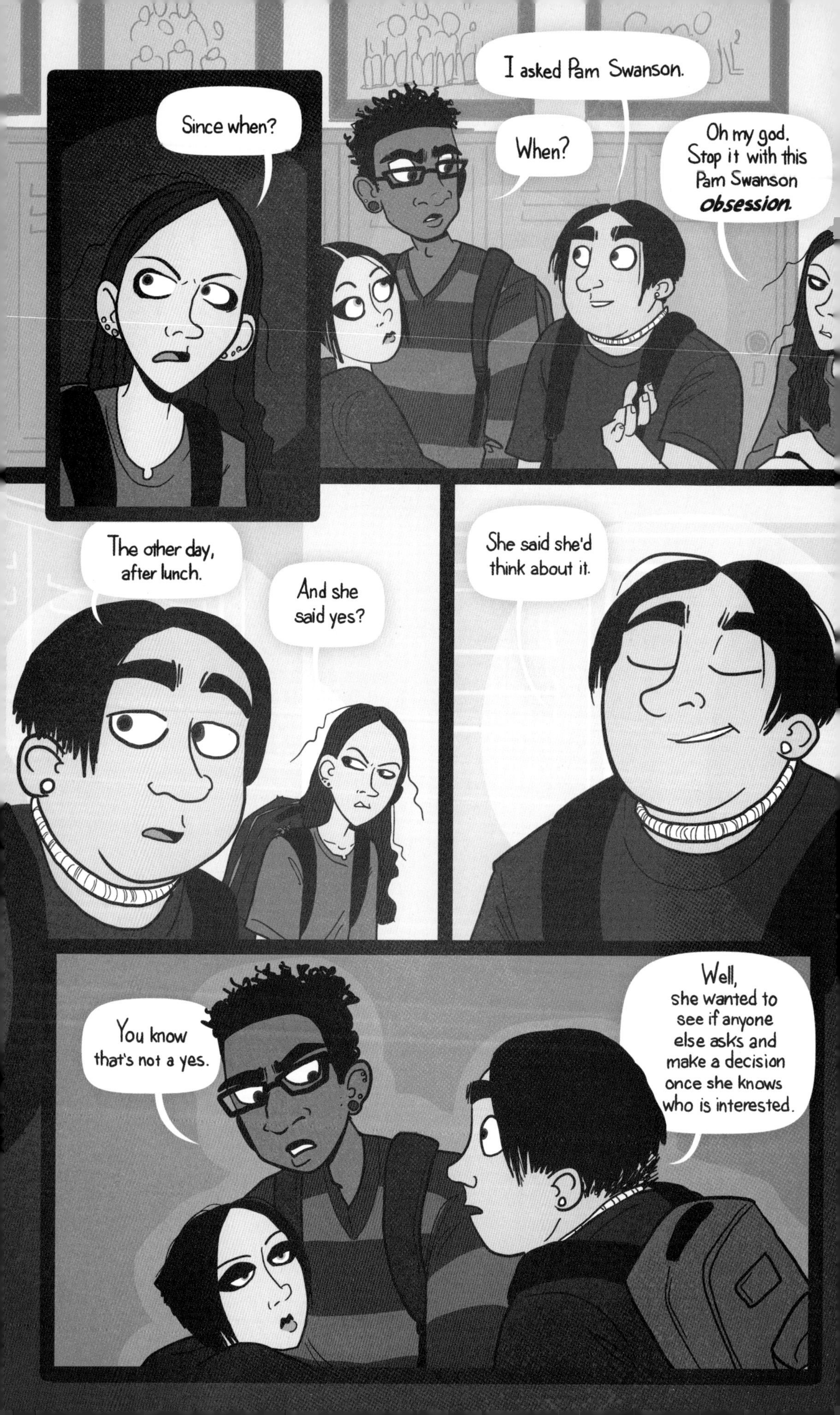
Since when?
When?
I asked Pam Swanson.
Oh my god. Stop it with this Pam Swanson **obsession**.
The other day, after lunch.
And she said yes?
She said she'd think about it.
You know that's not a yes.
Well, she wanted to see if anyone else asks and make a decision once she knows who is interested.

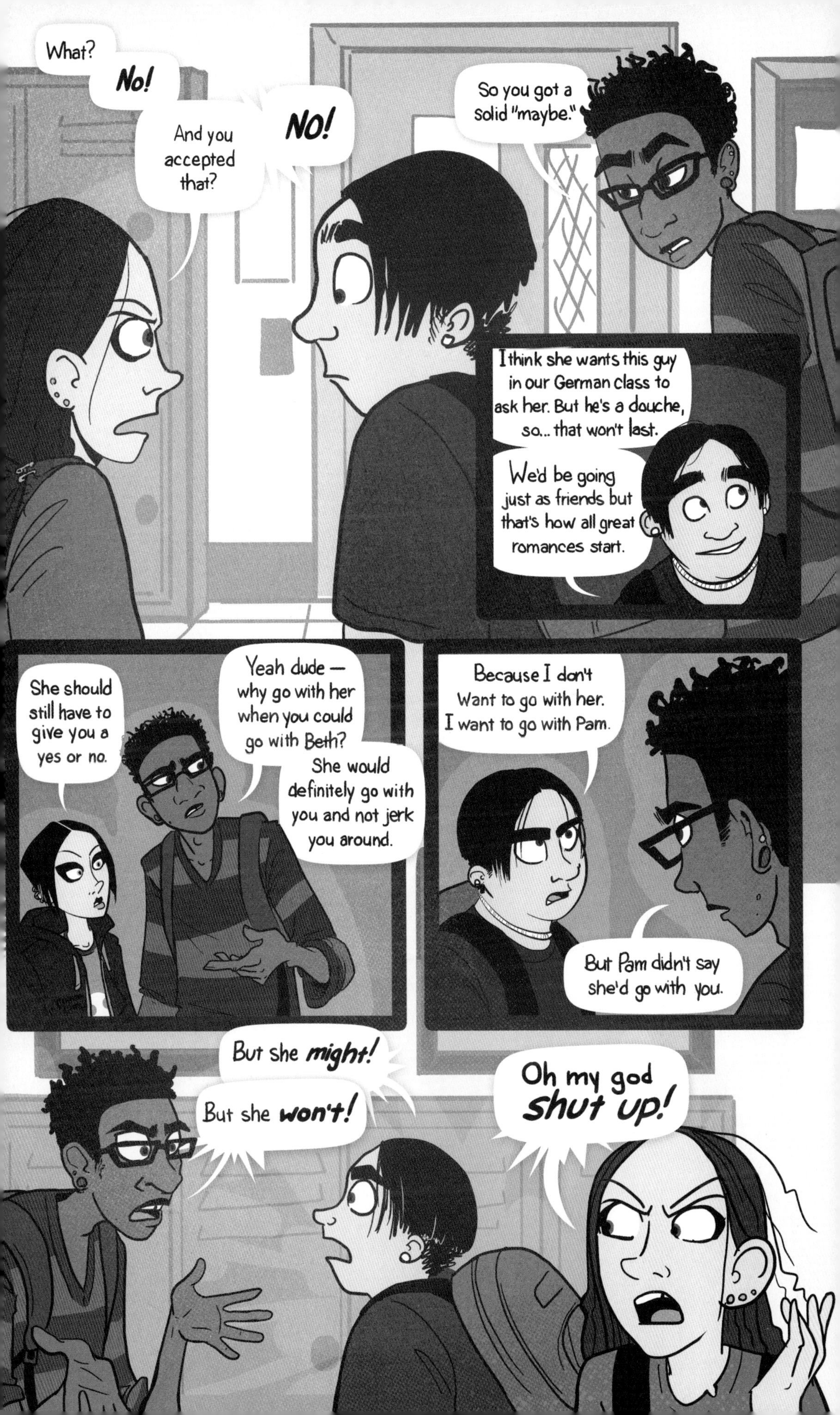
What?
No!
And you accepted that?
NO!
So you got a solid "maybe."
I think she wants this guy in our German class to ask her. But he's a douche, so... that won't last.
We'd be going just as friends but that's how all great romances start.
She should still have to give you a yes or no.
Yeah dude — why go with her when you could go with Beth?
She would definitely go with you and not jerk you around.
Because I don't Want to go with her. I want to go with Pam.
But Pam didn't say she'd go with you.
But she might!
But she won't!
Oh my god shut up!

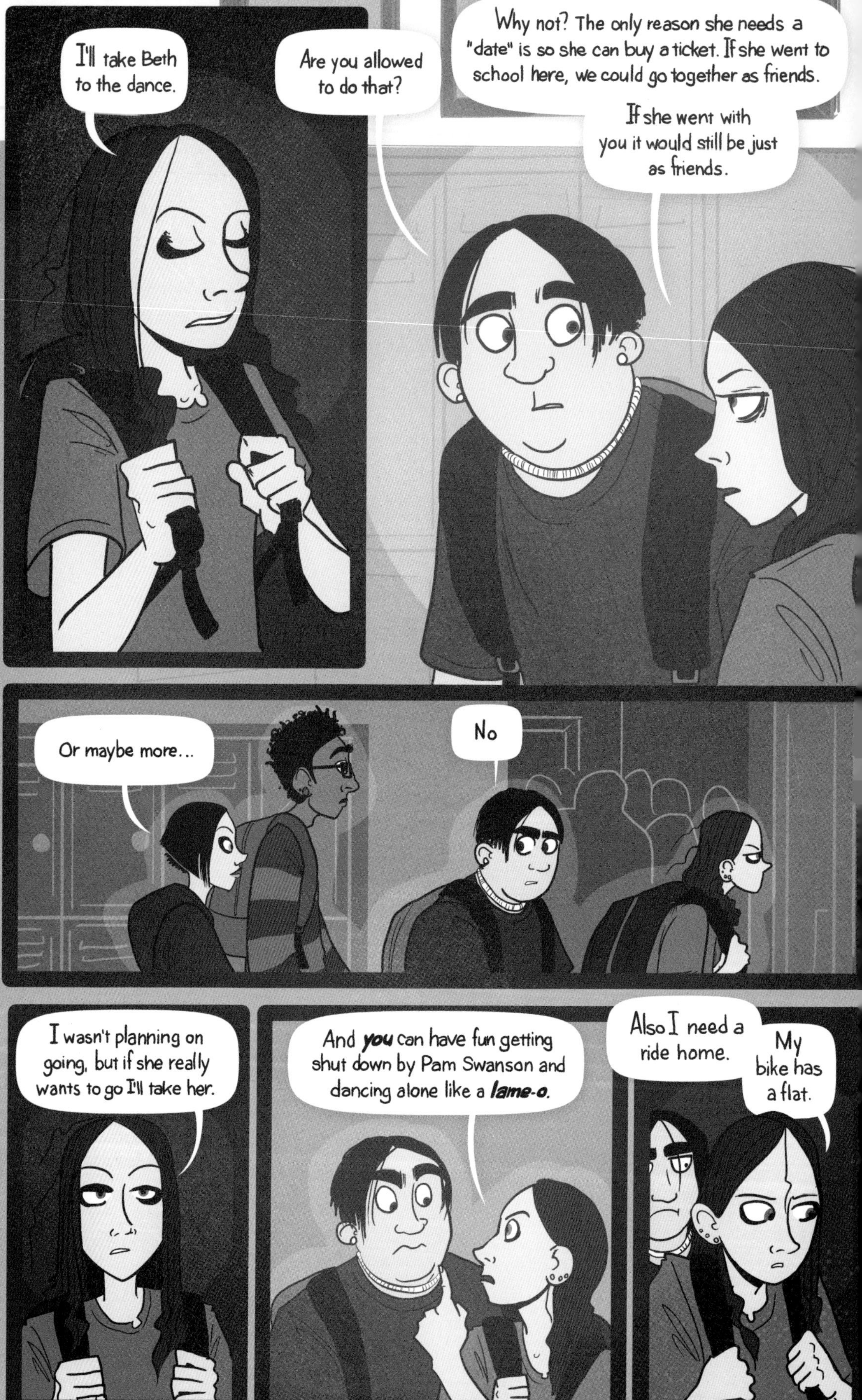
I'll take Beth to the dance.
Are you allowed to do that?
Why not? The only reason she needs a "date" is so she can buy a ticket. If she went to school here, we could go together as friends.
If she went with you it would still be just as friends.
Or maybe more...
No
I wasn't planning on going, but if she really wants to go I'll take her.
And *you* can have fun getting shut down by Pam Swanson and dancing alone like a *lame-o*.
Also I need a ride home.
My bike has a flat.

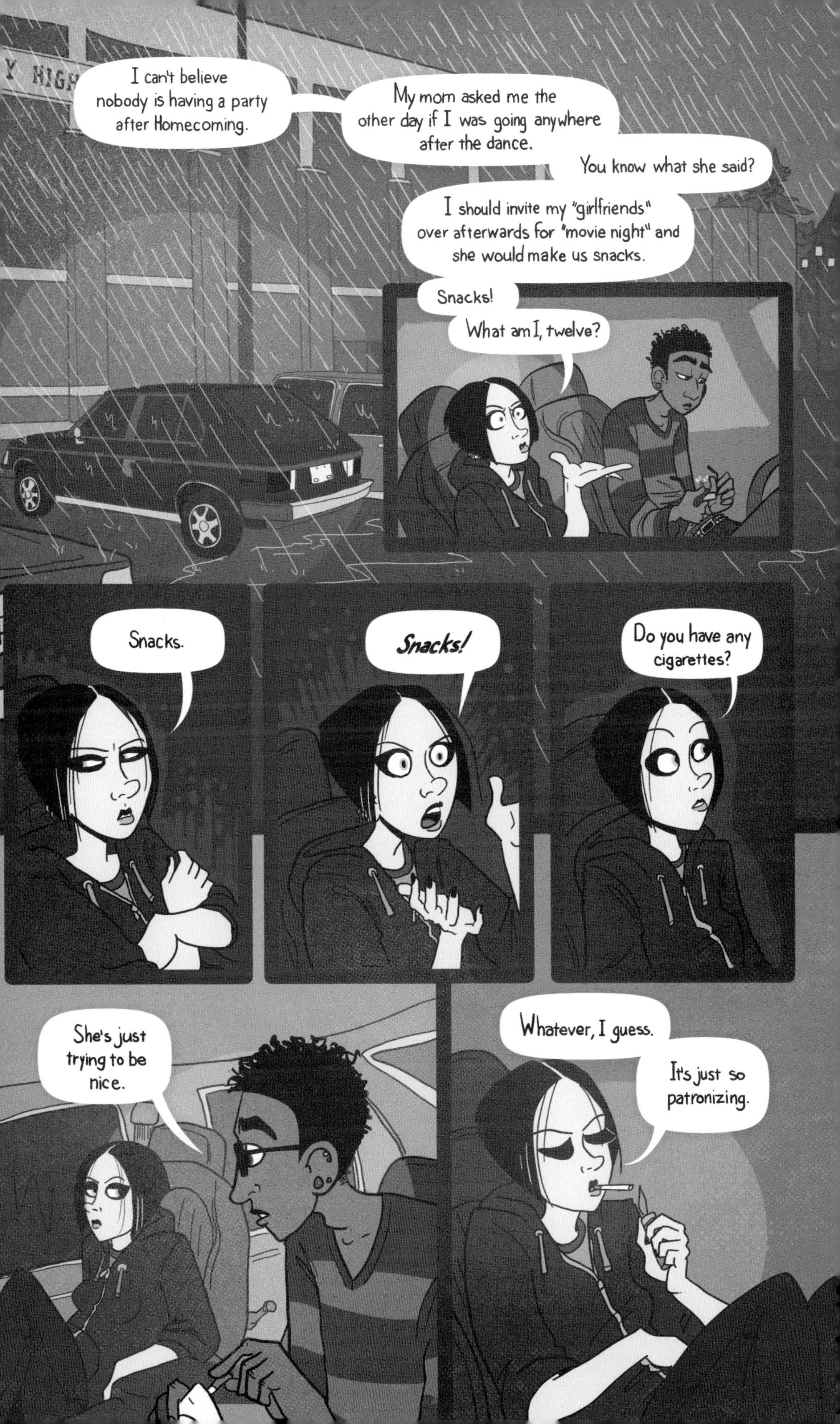
I can't believe nobody is having a party after Homecoming.
My mom asked me the other day if I was going anywhere after the dance.
You know what she said?
I should invite my "girlfriends" over afterwards for "movie night" and she would make us snacks.
Snacks!
What am I, twelve?
Snacks.
Snacks!
Do you have any cigarettes?
She's just trying to be nice.
Whatever, I guess.
It's just so patronizing.

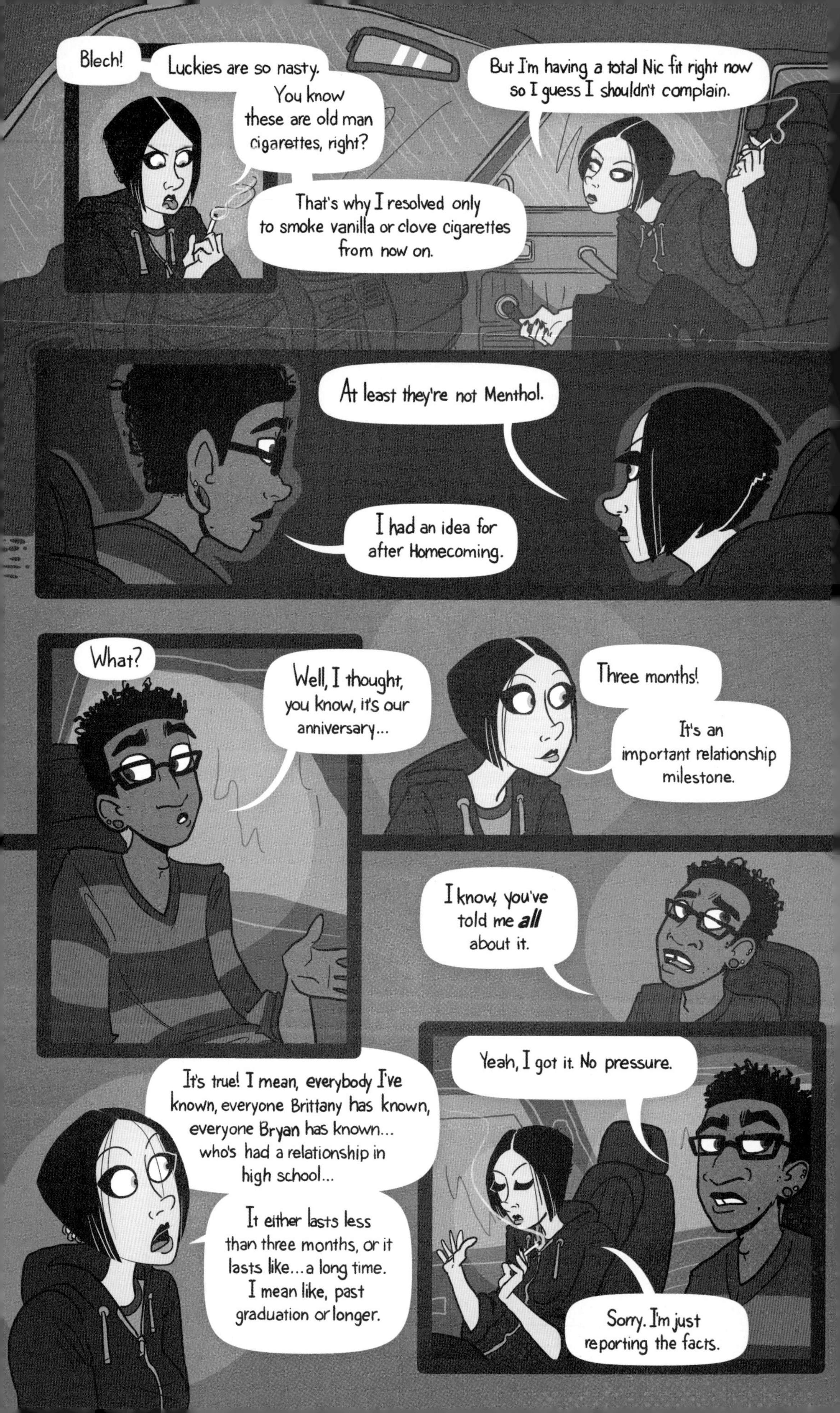

Blech!
Luckies are so nasty.
You know these are old man cigarettes, right?
That's why I resolved only to smoke vanilla or clove cigarettes from now on.
But I'm having a total Nic fit right now so I guess I shouldn't complain.
At least they're not Menthol.
I had an idea for after Homecoming.
What?
Well, I thought, you know, it's our anniversary...
Three months!
It's an important relationship milestone.
I know, you've told me *all* about it.
It's true! I mean, everybody I've known, everyone Brittany has known, everyone Bryan has known... who's had a relationship in high school...
It either lasts less than three months, or it lasts like... a long time. I mean like, past graduation or longer.
Yeah, I got it. No pressure.
Sorry. I'm just reporting the facts.

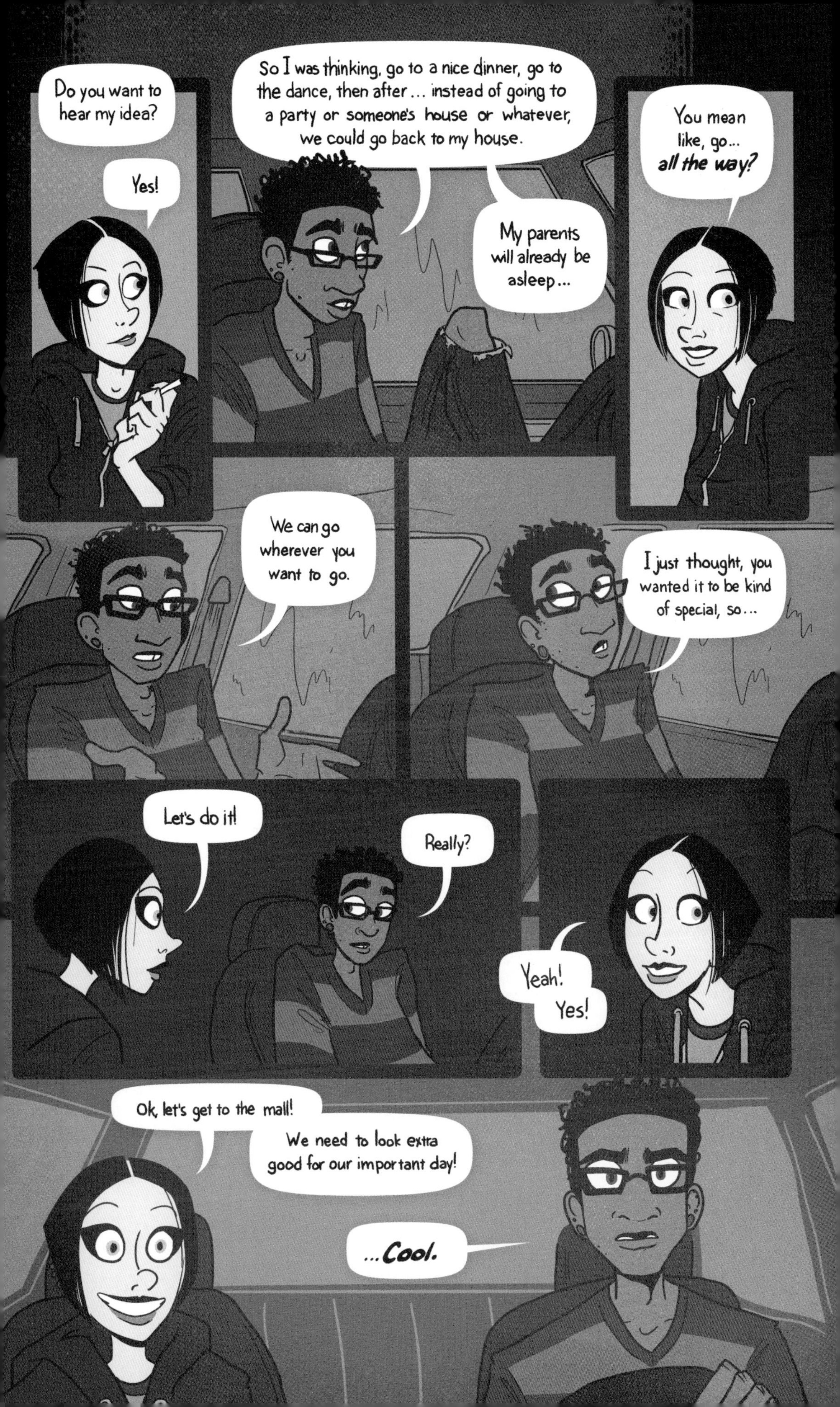
Do you want to hear my idea?
Yes!
So I was thinking, go to a nice dinner, go to the dance, then after ... instead of going to a party or someone's house or whatever, we could go back to my house.
My parents will already be asleep...
You mean like, go... *all the way?*
We can go wherever you want to go.
I just thought, you wanted it to be kind of special, so...
Let's do it!
Really?
Yeah! Yes!
Ok, let's get to the mall!
We need to look extra good for our important day!
...*Cool.*

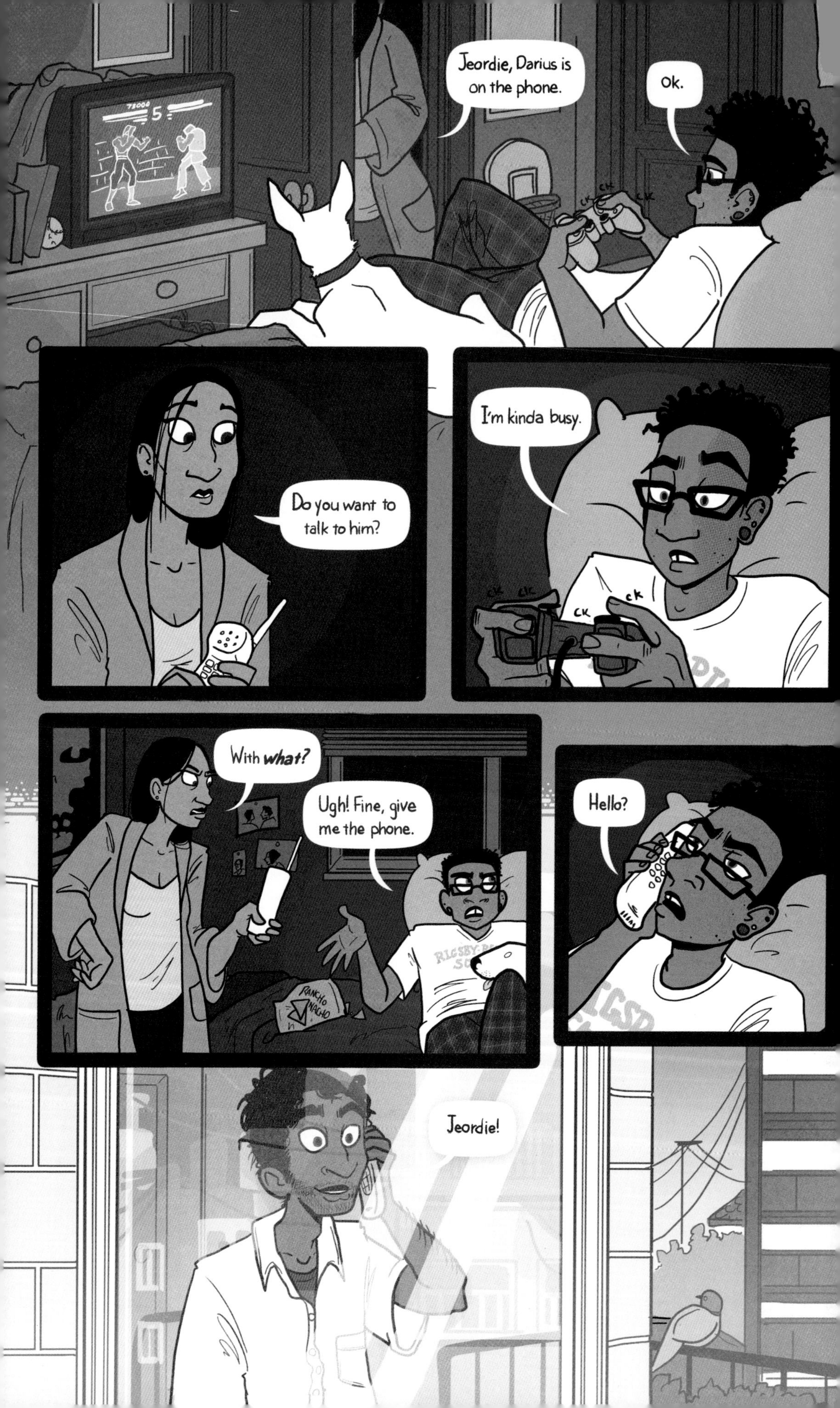
Jeordie, Darius is on the phone.
Ok.
CK CK CK
Do you want to talk to him?
I'm kinda busy.
CK CK CK CK
With ***what?***
Ugh! Fine, give me the phone.
RANCHO NACHO
Hello?
Jeordie!

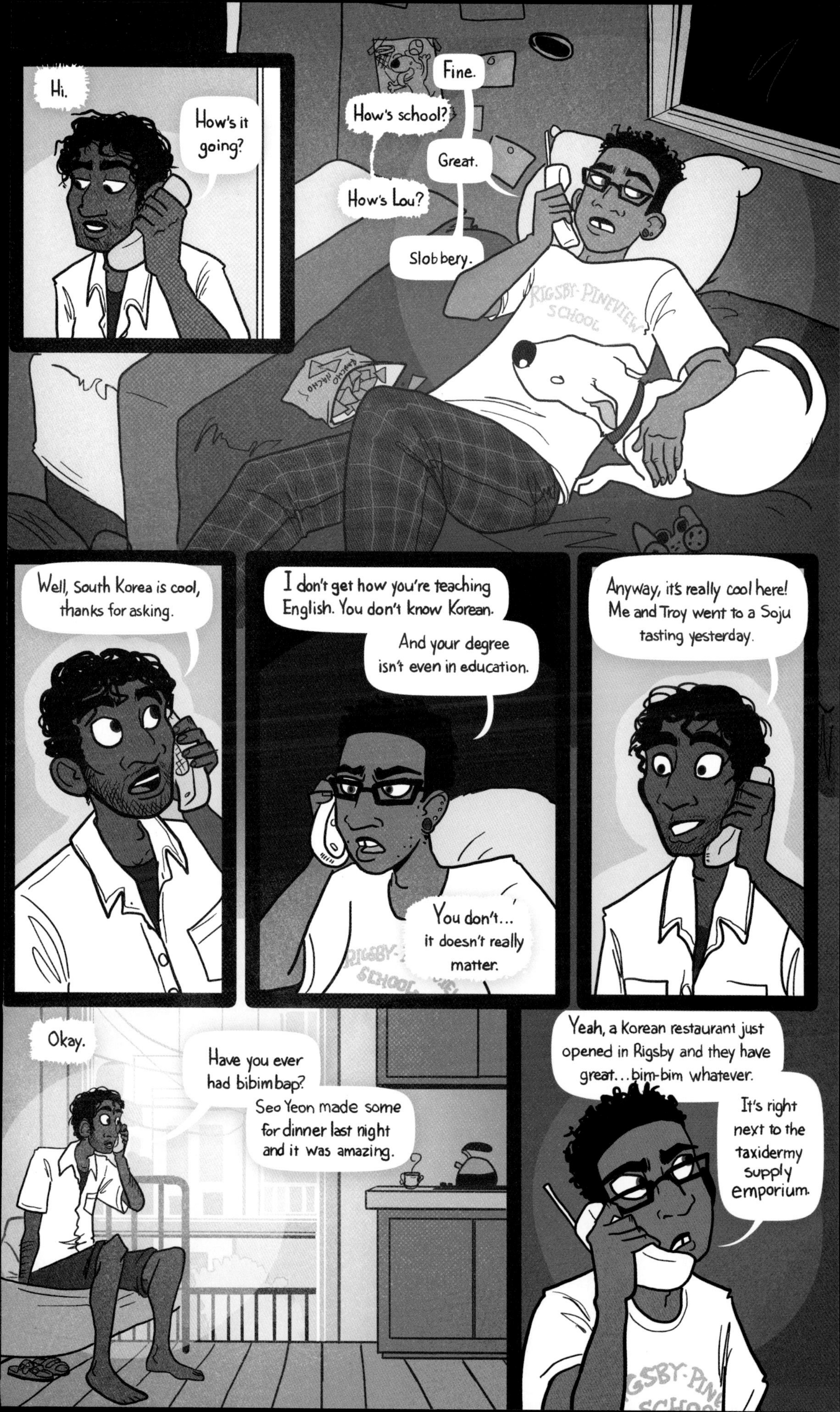
Hi.
How's it going?
Fine.
How's school?
Great.
How's Lou?
Slobbery.
RIGSBY-PINEVIEW SCHOOL
Well, South Korea is cool, thanks for asking.
I don't get how you're teaching English. You don't know Korean.
And your degree isn't even in education.
You don't... it doesn't really matter.
Anyway, it's really cool here! Me and Troy went to a Soju tasting yesterday.
Okay.
Have you ever had bibimbap?
Seo Yeon made some for dinner last night and it was amazing.
Yeah, a Korean restaurant just opened in Rigsby and they have great... bim-bim whatever.
It's right next to the taxidermy supply emporium.

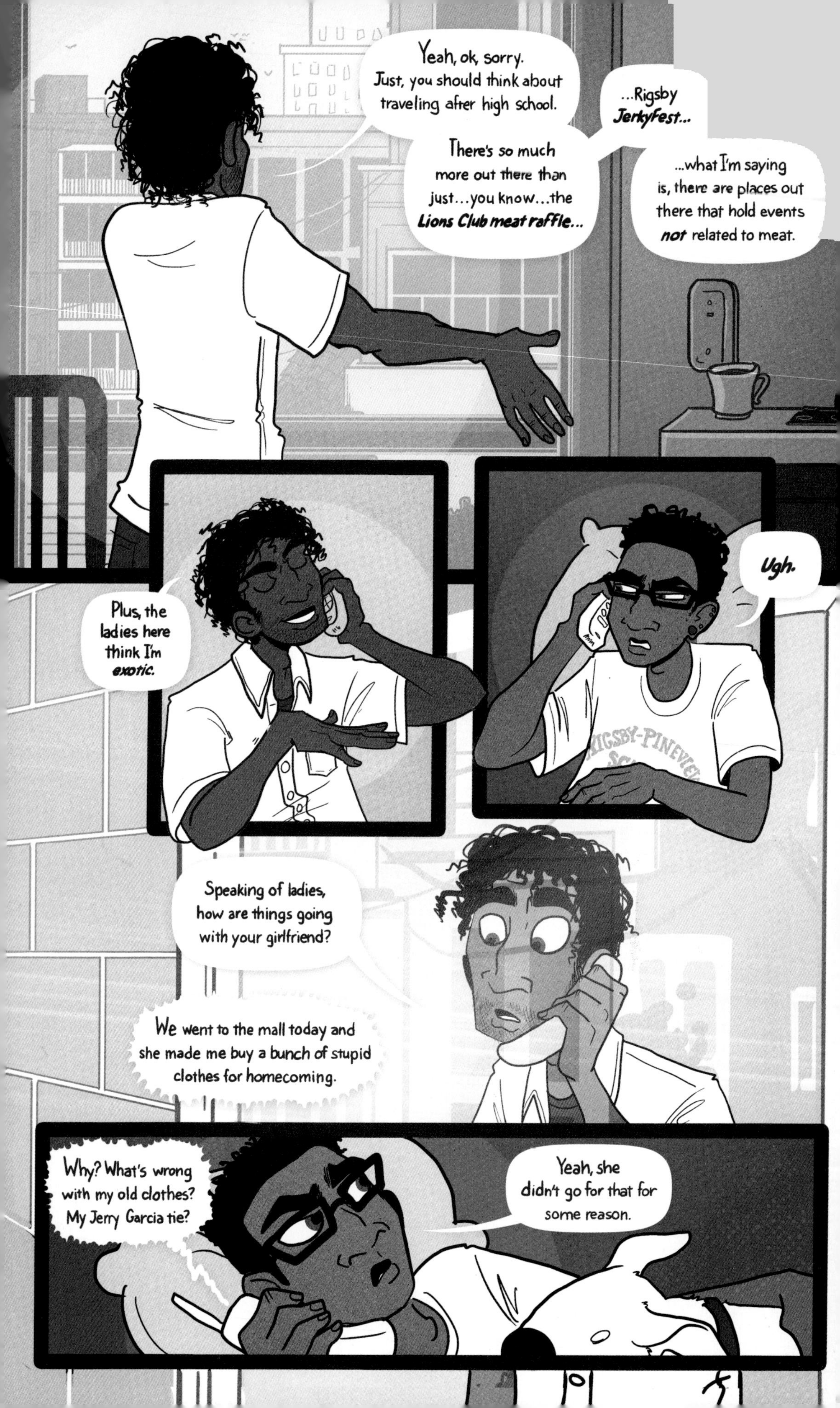
Yeah, ok, sorry. Just, you should think about traveling after high school.
There's so much more out there than just...you know...the **Lions Club meat raffle...**
...Rigsby **JerkyFest...**
...what I'm saying is, there are places out there that hold events ***not*** related to meat.
Plus, the ladies here think I'm ***exotic.***
Ugh.
RIGSBY-PINEVIEW SC
Speaking of ladies, how are things going with your girlfriend?
We went to the mall today and she made me buy a bunch of stupid clothes for homecoming.
Why? What's wrong with my old clothes? My Jerry Garcia tie?
Yeah, she didn't go for that for some reason.

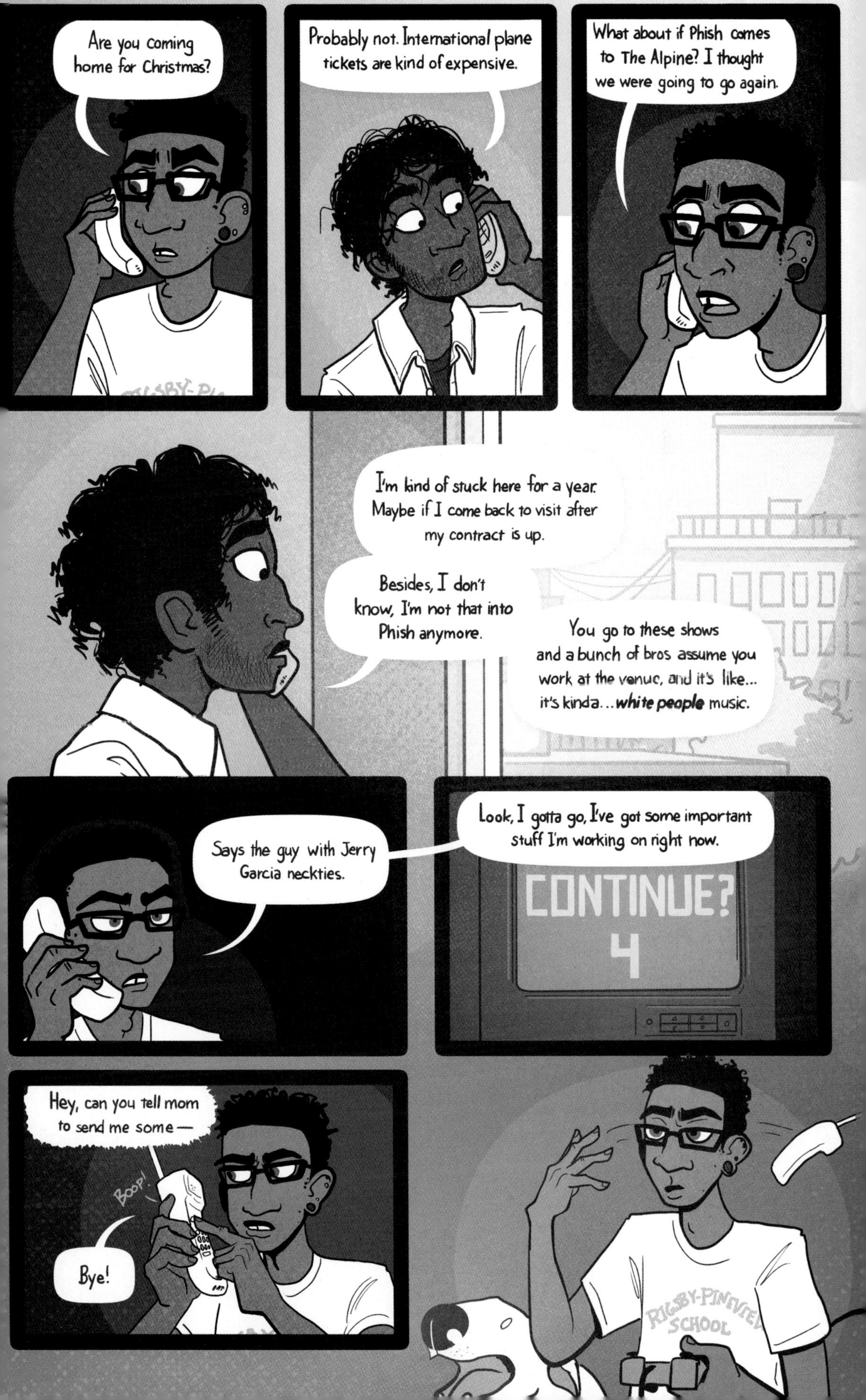

Are you coming home for Christmas?
Probably not. International plane tickets are kind of expensive.
What about if Phish comes to The Alpine? I thought we were going to go again.
I'm kind of stuck here for a year. Maybe if I come back to visit after my contract is up.
Besides, I don't know, I'm not that into Phish anymore.
You go to these shows and a bunch of bros assume you work at the venue, and it's like... it's kinda...*white people* music.
Says the guy with Jerry Garcia neckties.
Look, I gotta go, I've got some important stuff I'm working on right now.
CONTINUE?
4
Hey, can you tell mom to send me some—
BOOP!
Bye!
RIGSBY-PINEVIEW SCHOOL

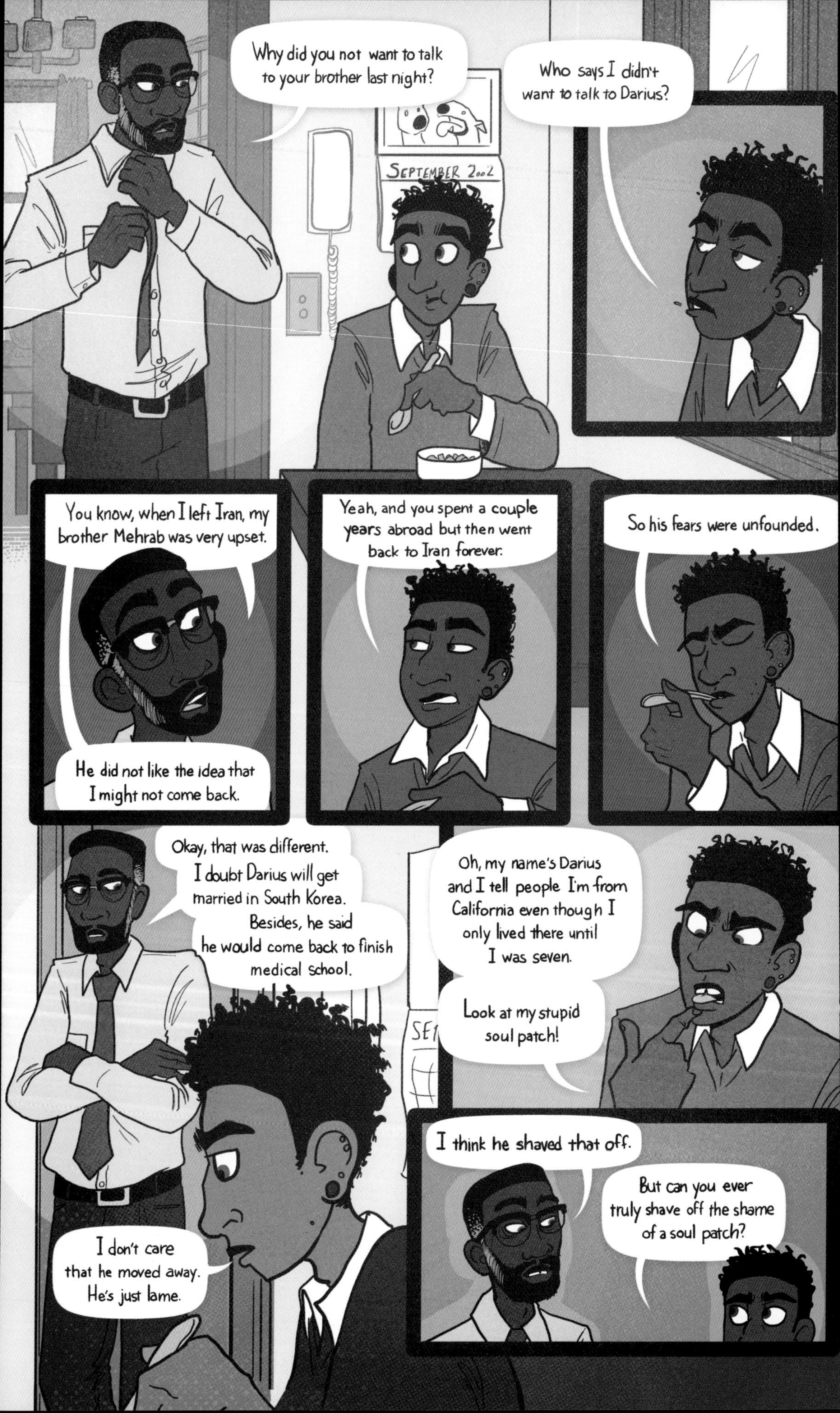
Why did you not want to talk to your brother last night?
SEPTEMBER 2002
Who says I didn't want to talk to Darius?
You know, when I left Iran, my brother Mehrab was very upset.
He did not like the idea that I might not come back.
Yeah, and you spent a couple years abroad but then went back to Iran forever.
So his fears were unfounded.
Okay, that was different. I doubt Darius will get married in South Korea. Besides, he said he would come back to finish medical school.
I don't care that he moved away. He's just lame.
Oh, my name's Darius and I tell people I'm from California even though I only lived there until I was seven.
Look at my stupid soul patch!
I think he shaved that off.
But can you ever truly shave off the shame of a soul patch?

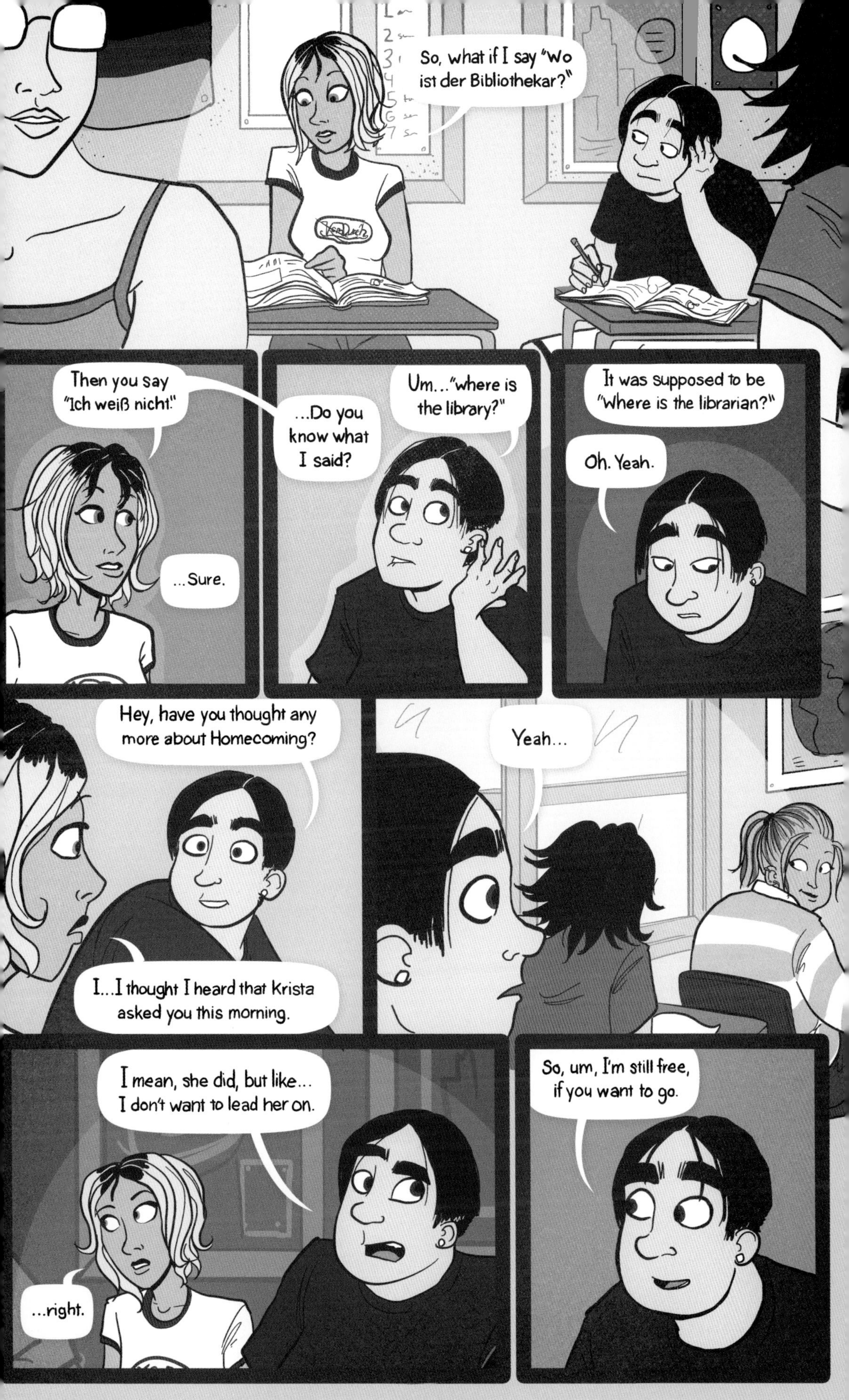
So, what if I say "Wo ist der Bibliothekar?"
Then you say "Ich weiß nicht."
...Do you know what I said?
...Sure.
Um..."where is the library?"
It was supposed to be "Where is the librarian?"
Oh. Yeah.
Hey, have you thought any more about Homecoming?
I...I thought I heard that Krista asked you this morning.
Yeah...
I mean, she did, but like... I don't want to lead her on.
...right.
So, um, I'm still free, if you want to go.

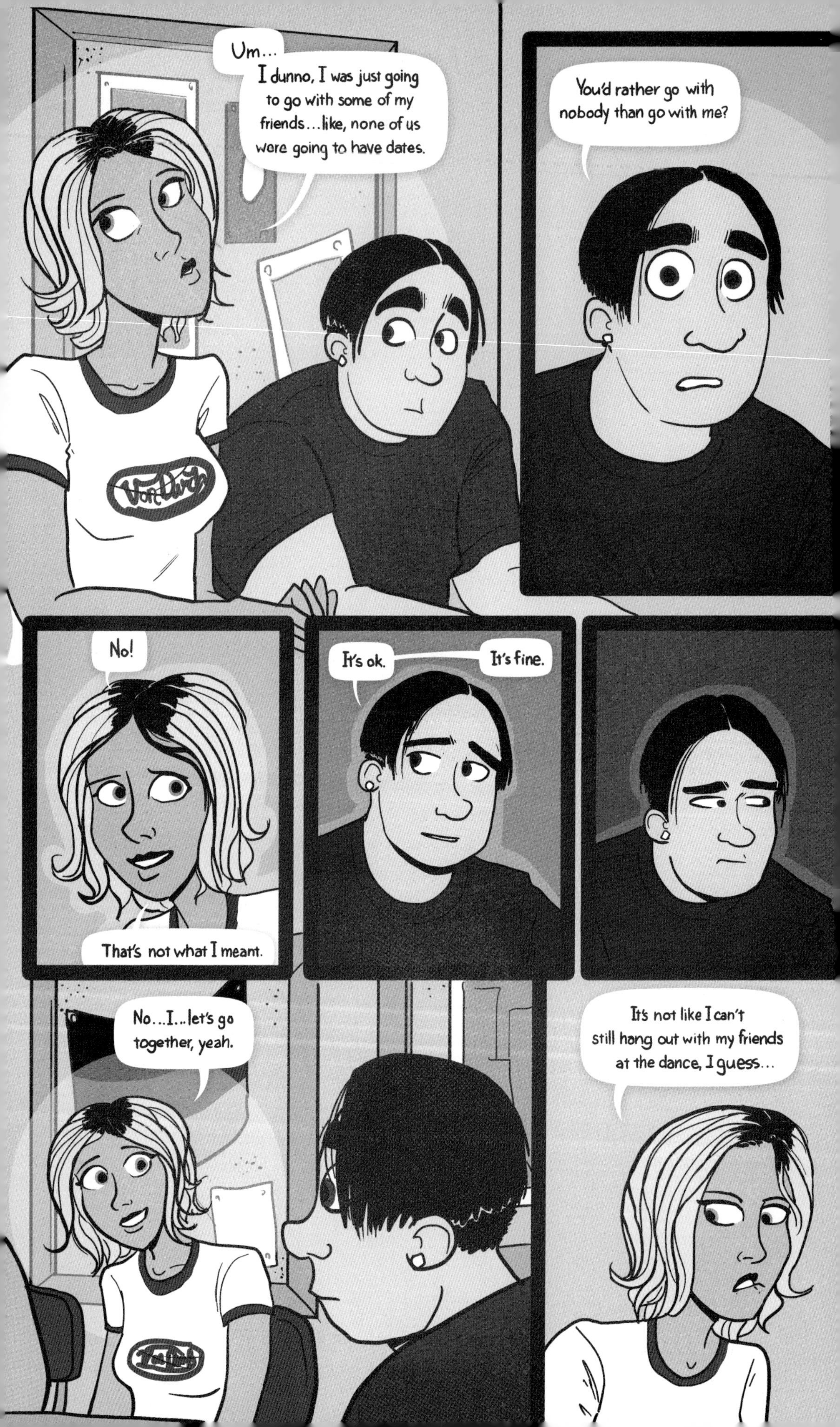
Um...
I dunno, I was just going to go with some of my friends...like, none of us were going to have dates.
You'd rather go with nobody than go with me?
No!
That's not what I meant.
It's ok.
It's fine.
No...I...let's go together, yeah.
It's not like I can't still hang out with my friends at the dance, I guess...

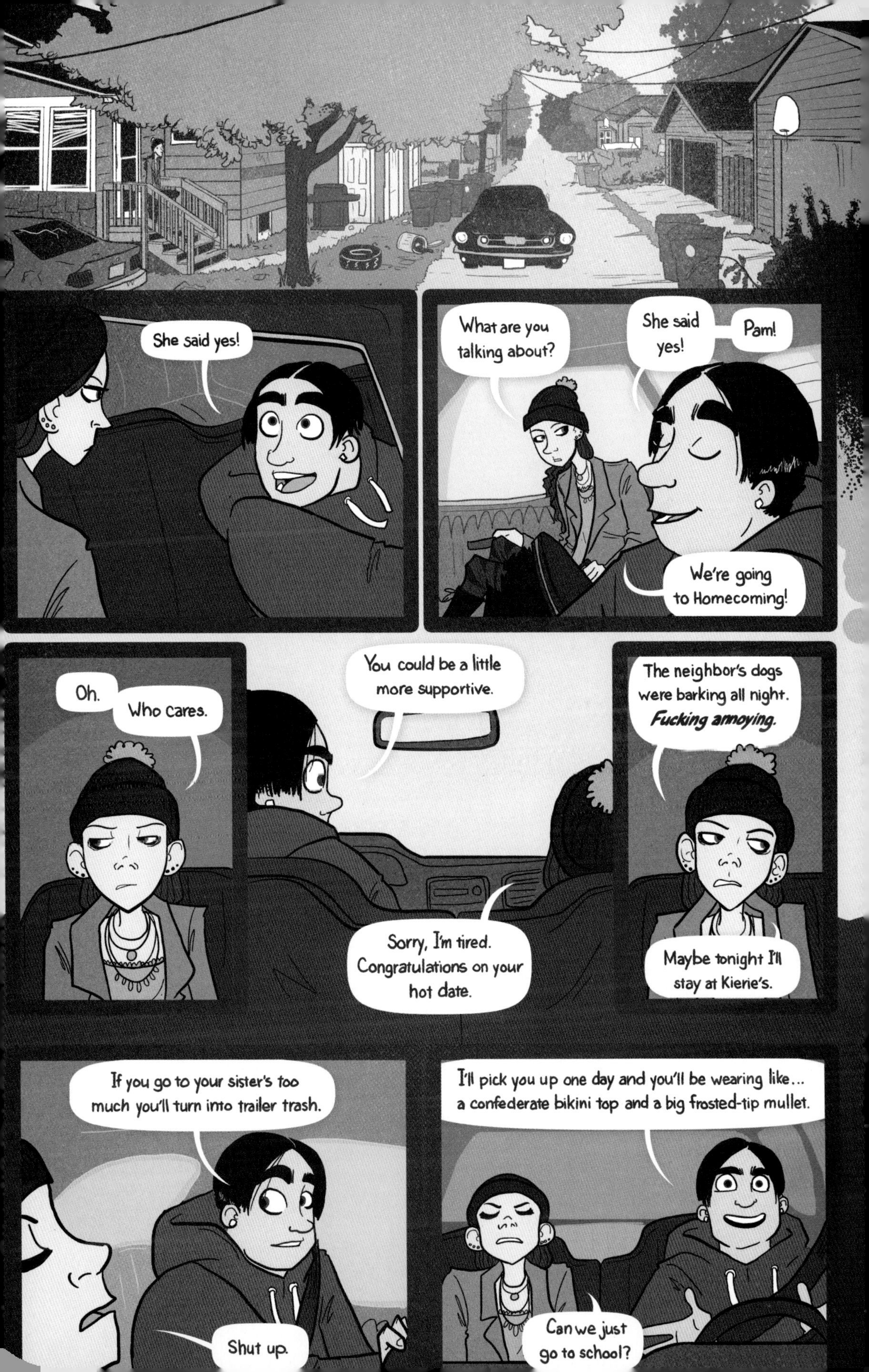
She said yes!
What are you talking about?
She said yes!
Pam!
We're going to Homecoming!
Oh.
Who cares.
You could be a little more supportive.
Sorry, I'm tired. Congratulations on your hot date.
The neighbor's dogs were barking all night. *Fucking annoying.*
Maybe tonight I'll stay at Kierie's.
If you go to your sister's too much you'll turn into trailer trash.
Shut up.
I'll pick you up one day and you'll be wearing like… a confederate bikini top and a big frosted-tip mullet.
Can we just go to school?

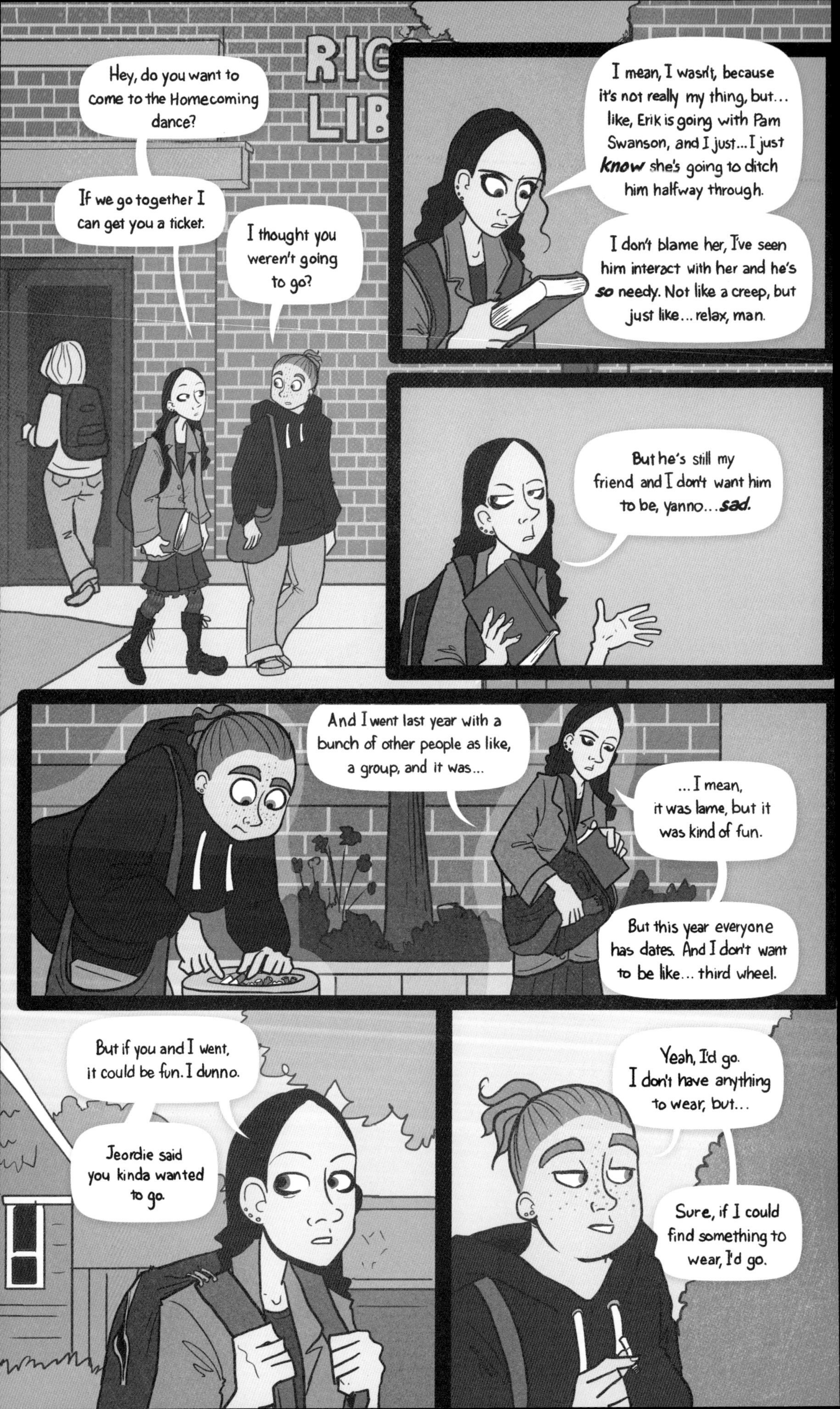

Hey, do you want to come to the Homecoming dance?
If we go together I can get you a ticket.
I thought you weren't going to go?
I mean, I wasn't, because it's not really my thing, but... like, Erik is going with Pam Swanson, and I just... I just **know** she's going to ditch him halfway through.
I don't blame her, I've seen him interact with her and he's **so** needy. Not like a creep, but just like... relax, man.
But he's still my friend and I don't want him to be, yanno... ***sad.***
And I went last year with a bunch of other people as like, a group, and it was...
...I mean, it was lame, but it was kind of fun.
But this year everyone has dates. And I don't want to be like... third wheel.
But if you and I went, it could be fun. I dunno.
Jeordie said you kinda wanted to go.
Yeah, I'd go. I don't have anything to wear, but...
Sure, if I could find something to wear, I'd go.

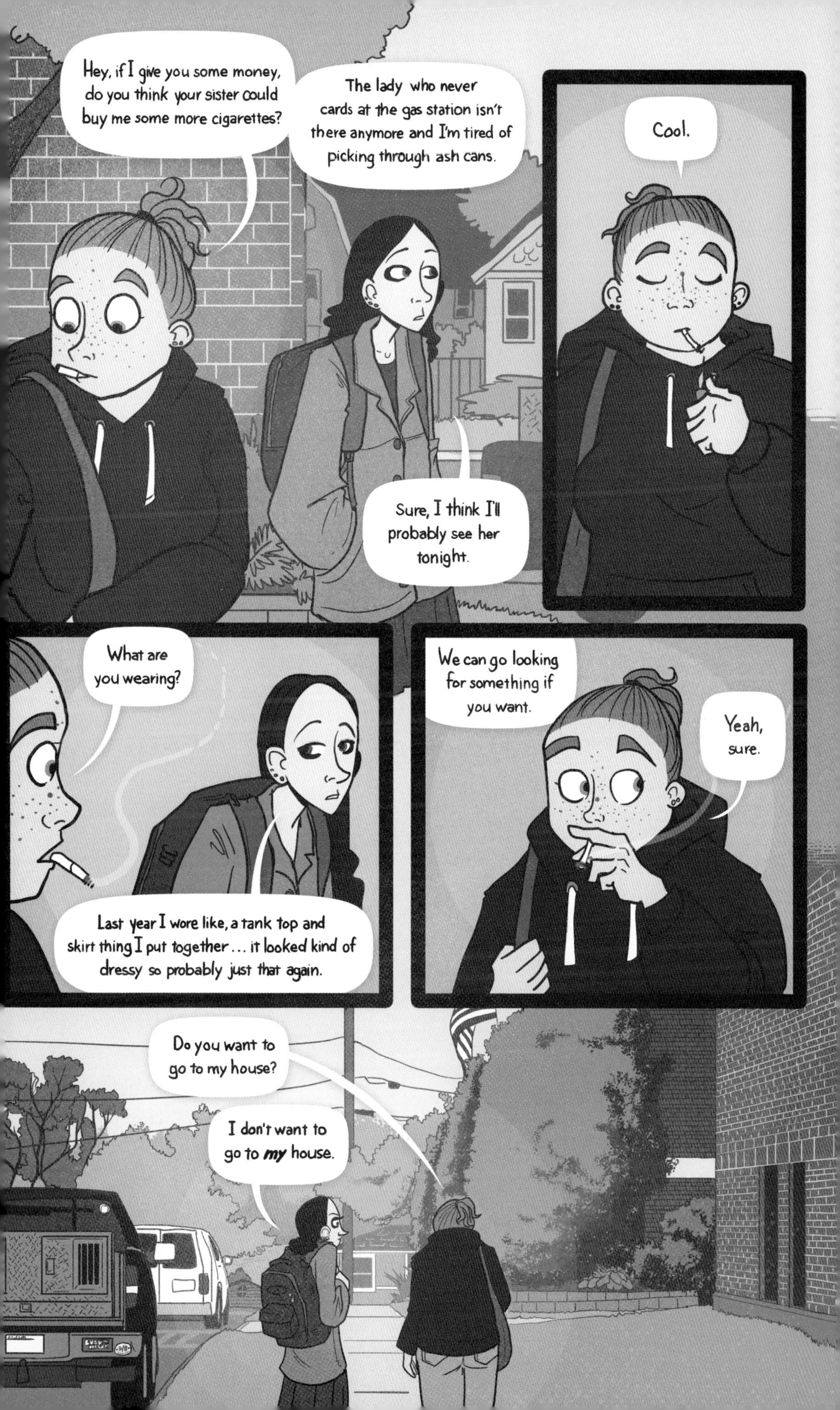
Hey, if I give you some money, do you think your sister could buy me some more cigarettes?
The lady who never cards at the gas station isn't there anymore and I'm tired of picking through ash cans.
Sure, I think I'll probably see her tonight.
Cool.
What are you wearing?
Last year I wore like, a tank top and skirt thing I put together... it looked kind of dressy so probably just that again.
We can go looking for something if you want.
Yeah, sure.
Do you want to go to my house?
I don't want to go to ***my*** house.

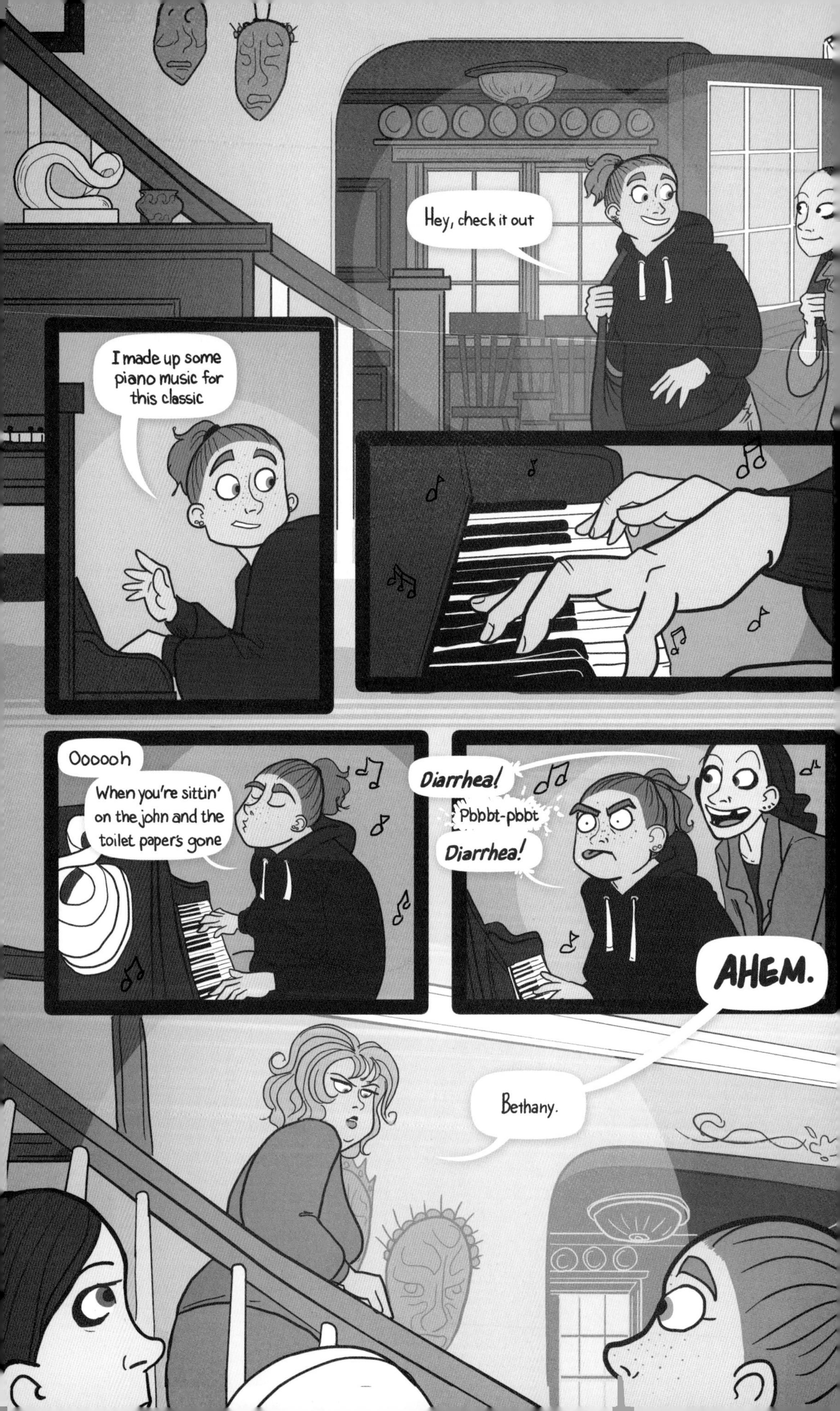
Hey, check it out
I made up some piano music for this classic
Oooooh
When you're sittin' on the john and the toilet paper's gone
Diarrhea!
Pbbbt-pbbt
Diarrhea!
AHEM.
Bethany.

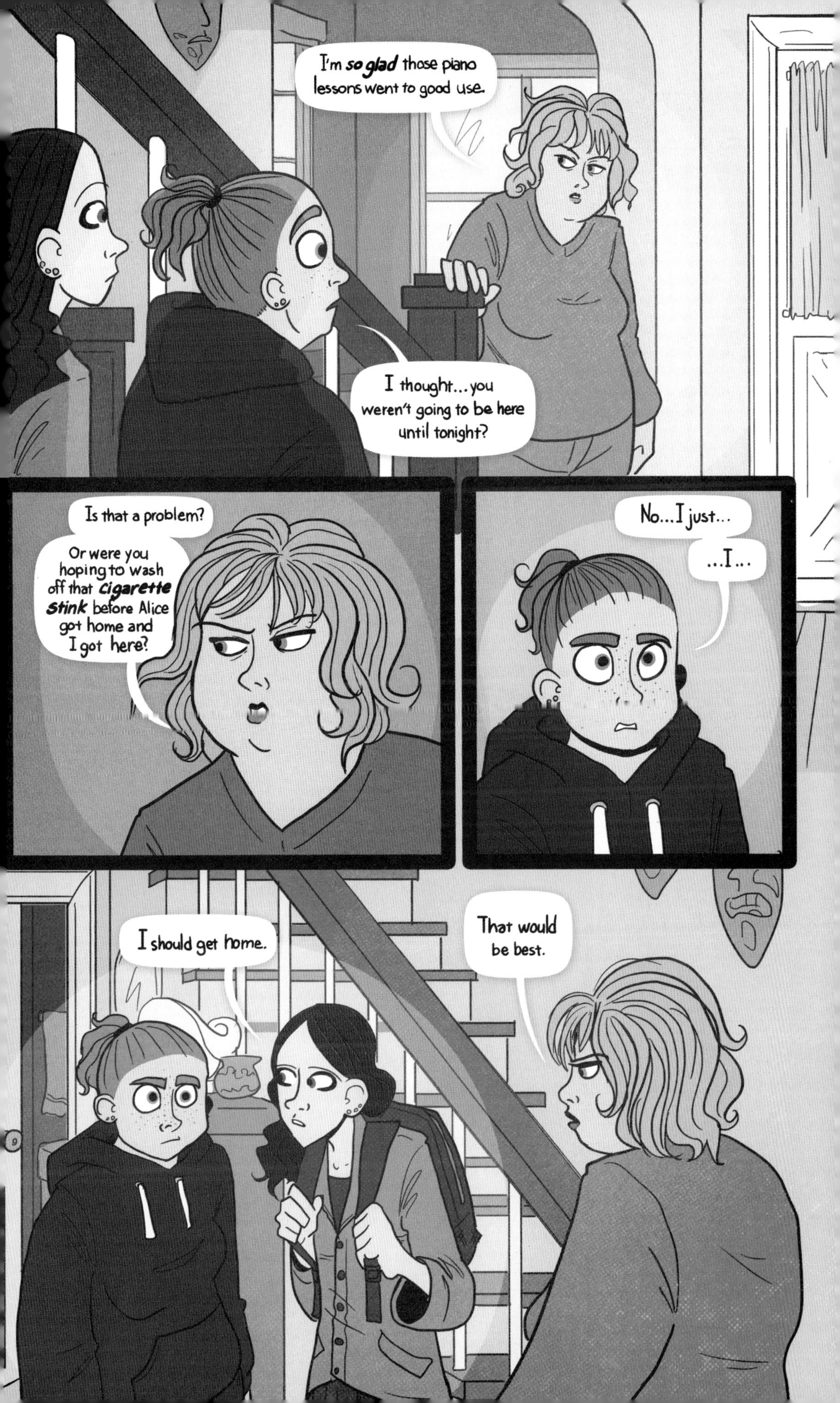

I'm so glad those piano lessons went to good use.
I thought... you weren't going to be here until tonight?
Is that a problem?
Or were you hoping to wash off that cigarette stink before Alice got home and I got here?
No... I just...
...I...
I should get home.
That would be best.

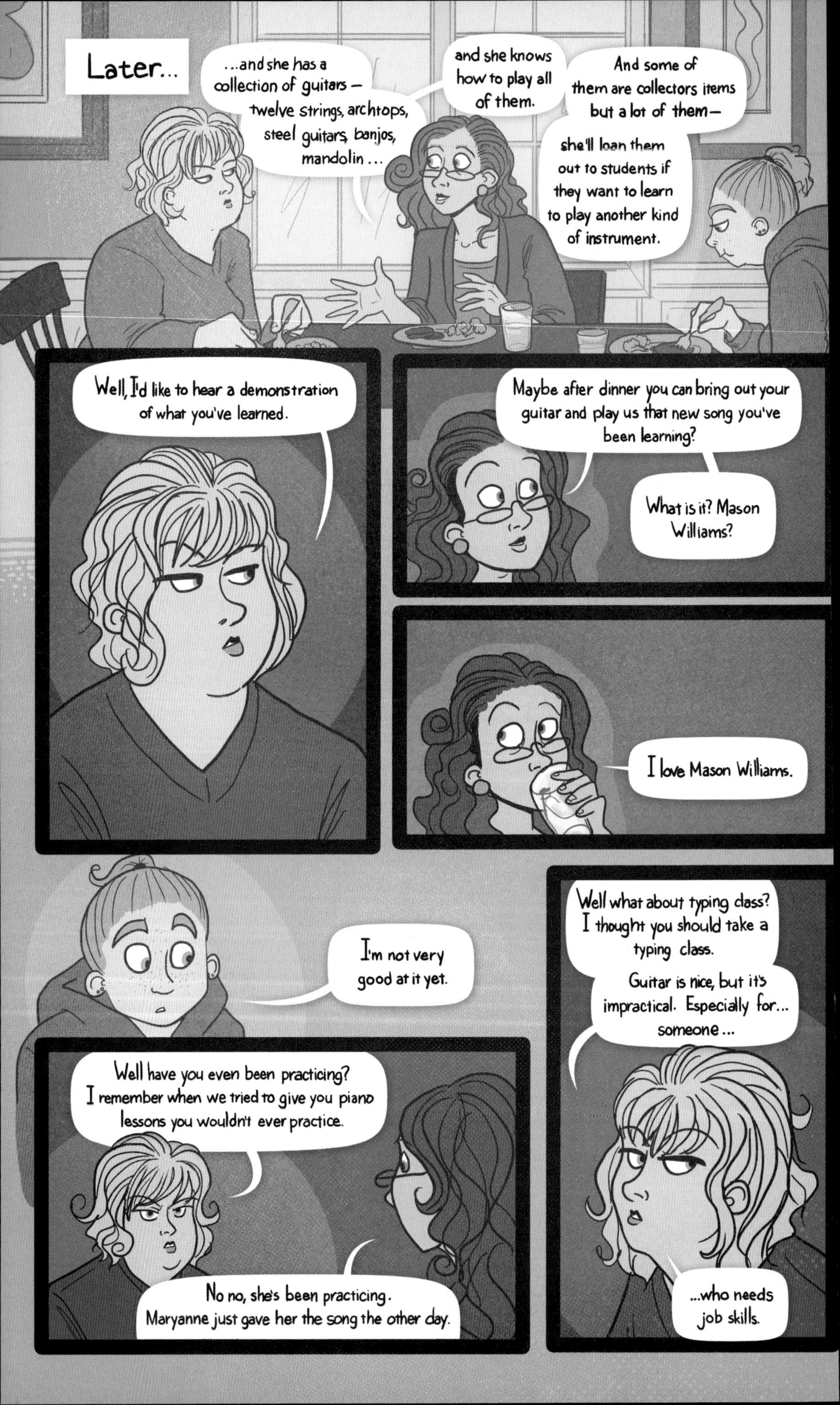
Later...
...and she has a collection of guitars — twelve strings, archtops, steel guitars, banjos, mandolin...
and she knows how to play all of them.
And some of them are collectors items but a lot of them—
she'll loan them out to students if they want to learn to play another kind of instrument.
Well, I'd like to hear a demonstration of what you've learned.
Maybe after dinner you can bring out your guitar and play us that new song you've been learning?
What is it? Mason Williams?
I love Mason Williams.
I'm not very good at it yet.
Well have you even been practicing? I remember when we tried to give you piano lessons you wouldn't ever practice.
No no, she's been practicing. Maryanne just gave her the song the other day.
Well what about typing class? I thought you should take a typing class.
Guitar is nice, but it's impractical. Especially for... someone...
...who needs job skills.

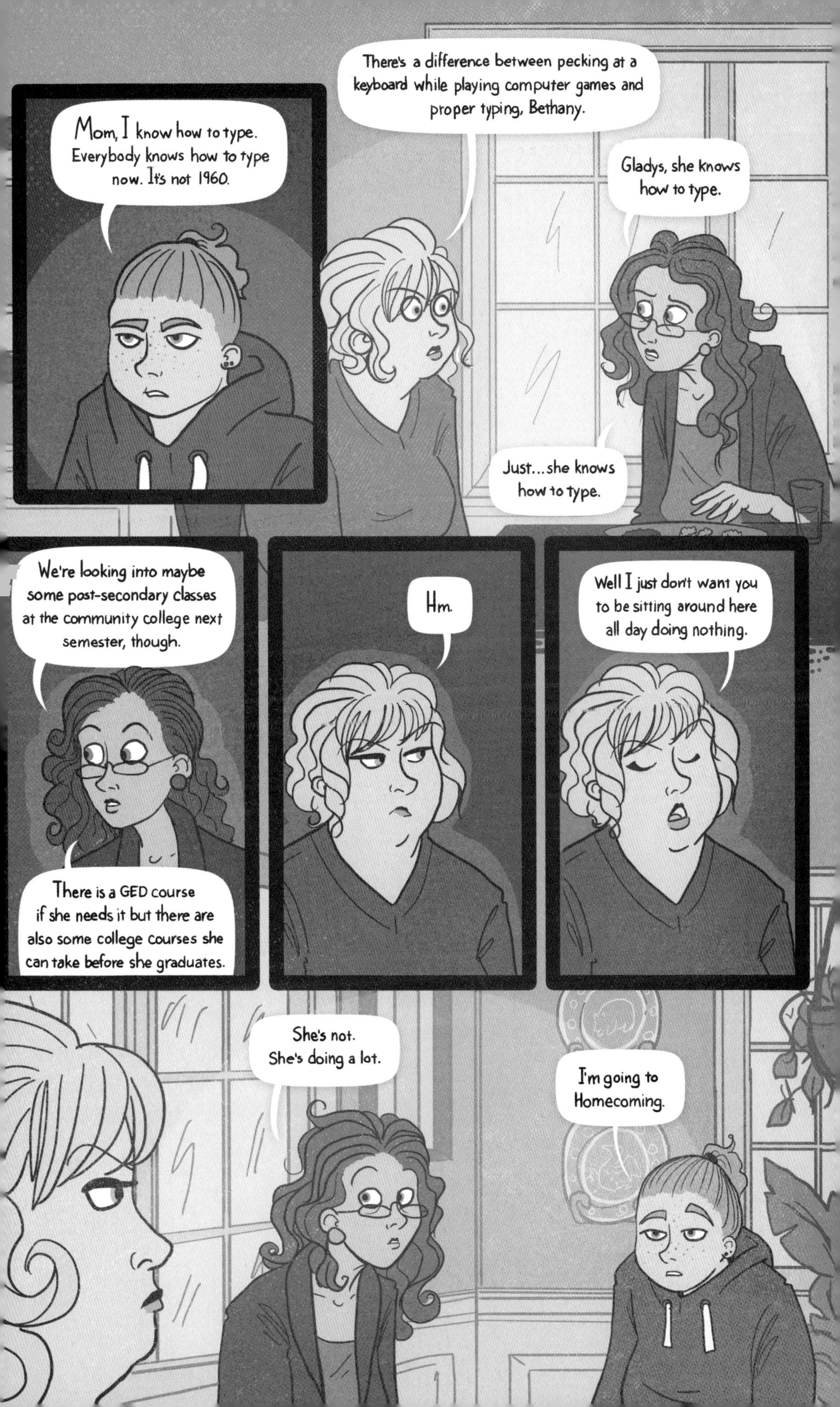
Mom, I know how to type. Everybody knows how to type now. It's not 1960.
There's a difference between pecking at a keyboard while playing computer games and proper typing, Bethany.
Gladys, she knows how to type.
Just...she knows how to type.
We're looking into maybe some post-secondary classes at the community college next semester, though.
There is a GED course if she needs it but there are also some college courses she can take before she graduates.
Hm.
Well I just don't want you to be sitting around here all day doing nothing.
She's not. She's doing a lot.
I'm going to Homecoming.

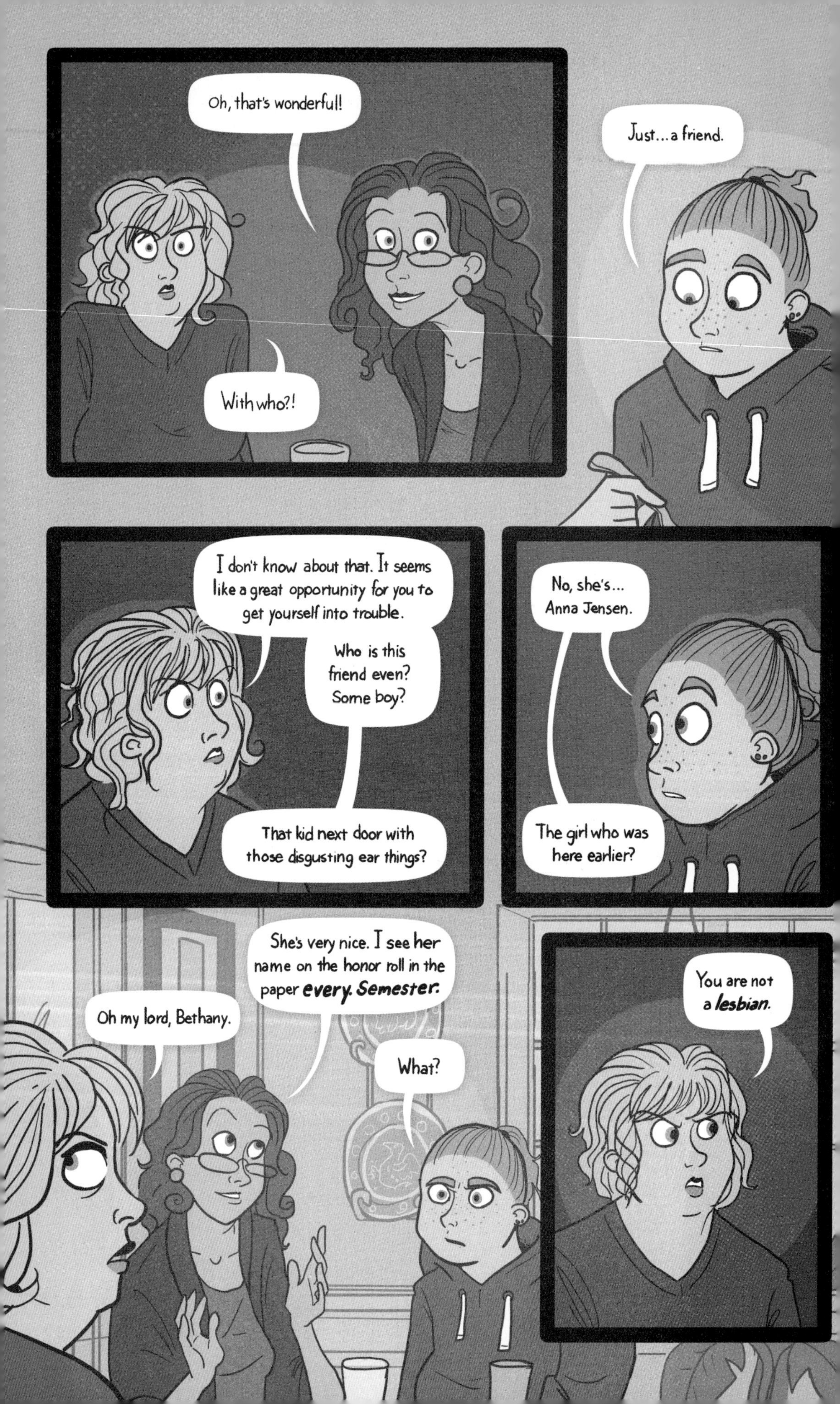
Oh, that's wonderful!
With who?!
Just... a friend.
I don't know about that. It seems like a great opportunity for you to get yourself into trouble.
Who is this friend even? Some boy?
That kid next door with those disgusting ear things?
No, she's... Anna Jensen.
The girl who was here earlier?
Oh my lord, Bethany.
She's very nice. I see her name on the honor roll in the paper **every. Semester.**
What?
You are not a ***lesbian***.

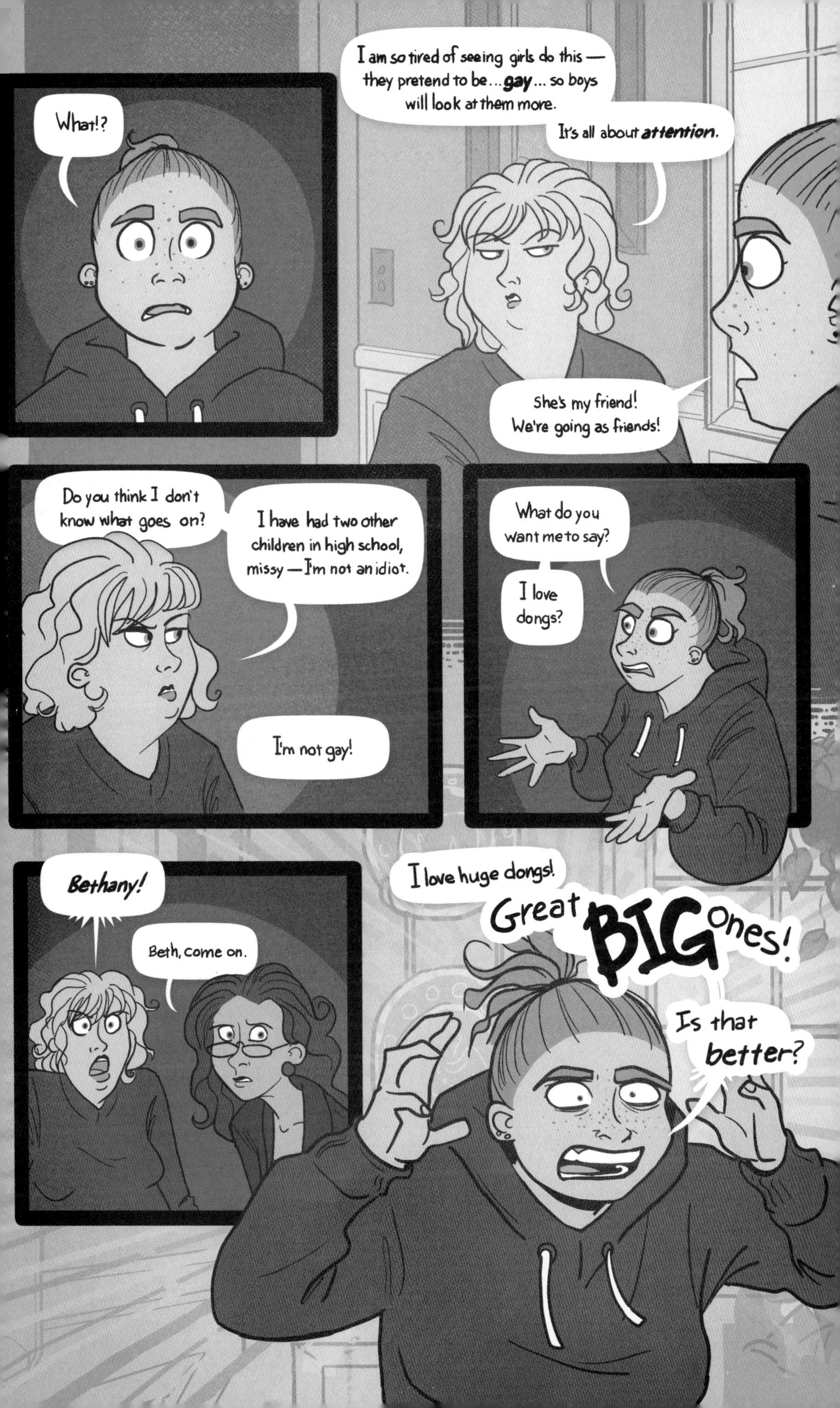
What!?
I am so tired of seeing girls do this — they pretend to be... **gay**... so boys will look at them more.
It's all about ***attention.***
She's my friend! We're going as friends!
Do you think I don't know what goes on?
I have had two other children in high school, missy — I'm not an idiot.
I'm not gay!
What do you want me to say?
I love dongs?
Bethany!
Beth, come on.
I love huge dongs!
Great BIG ones!
Is that *better?*

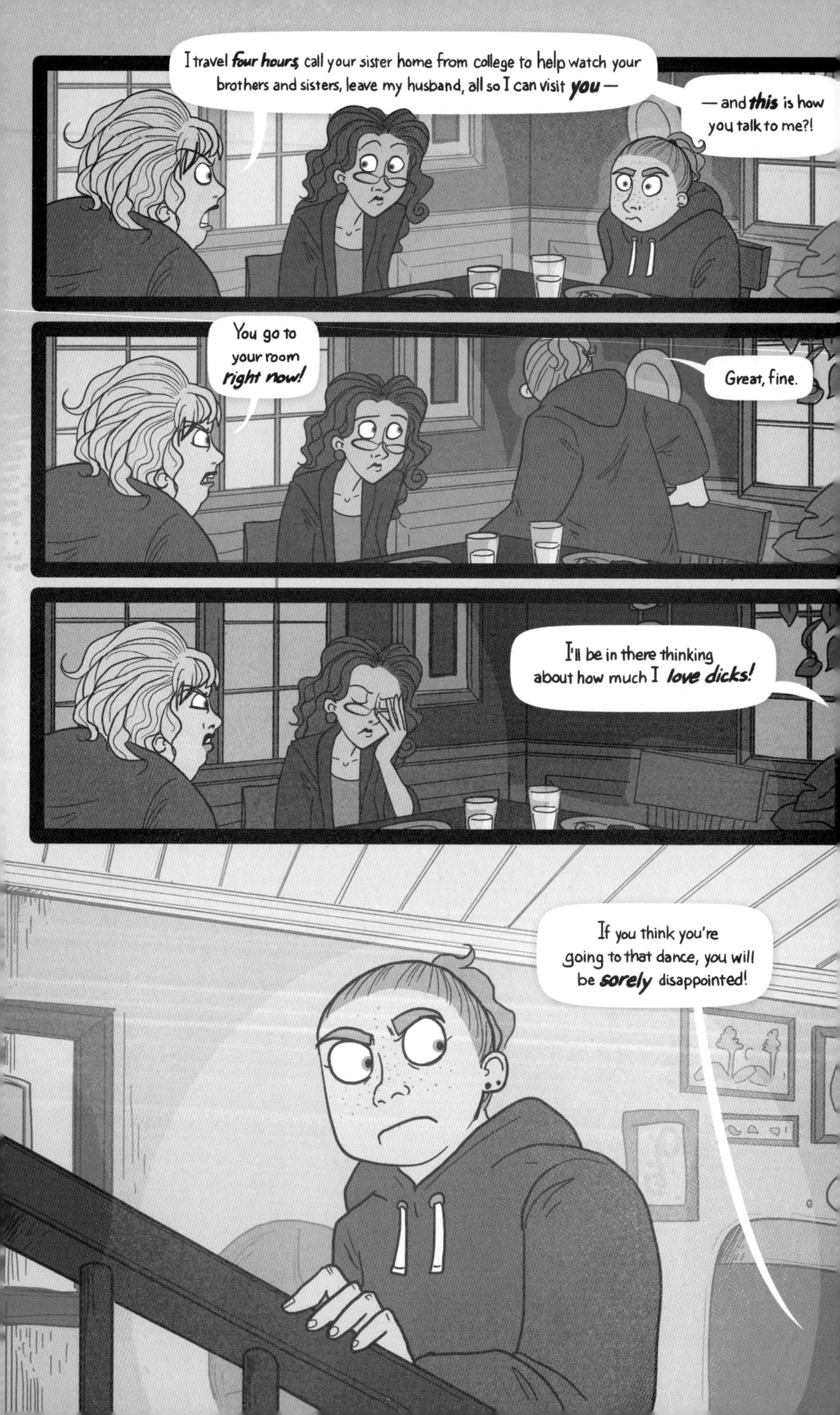
I travel **four hours,** call your sister home from college to help watch your brothers and sisters, leave my husband, all so I can visit **you**—
—and **this** is how you talk to me?!
You go to your room **right now!**
Great, fine.
I'll be in there thinking about how much I **love dicks!**
If you think you're going to that dance, you will be **sorely** disappointed!

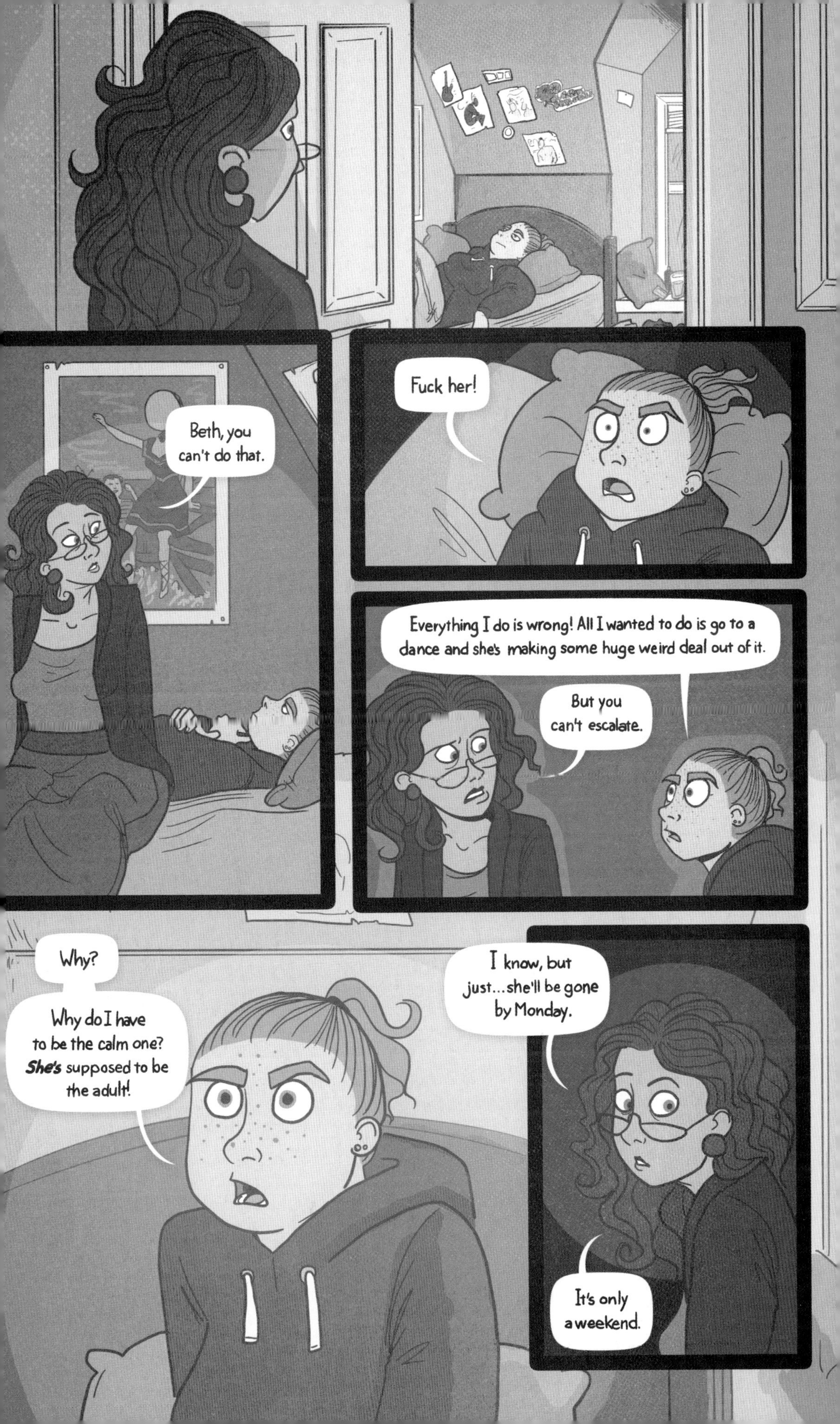
Beth, you can't do that.
Fuck her!
Everything I do is wrong! All I wanted to do is go to a dance and she's making some huge weird deal out of it.
But you can't escalate.
Why?
Why do I have to be the calm one? ***She's*** supposed to be the adult!
I know, but just...she'll be gone by Monday.
It's only a weekend.

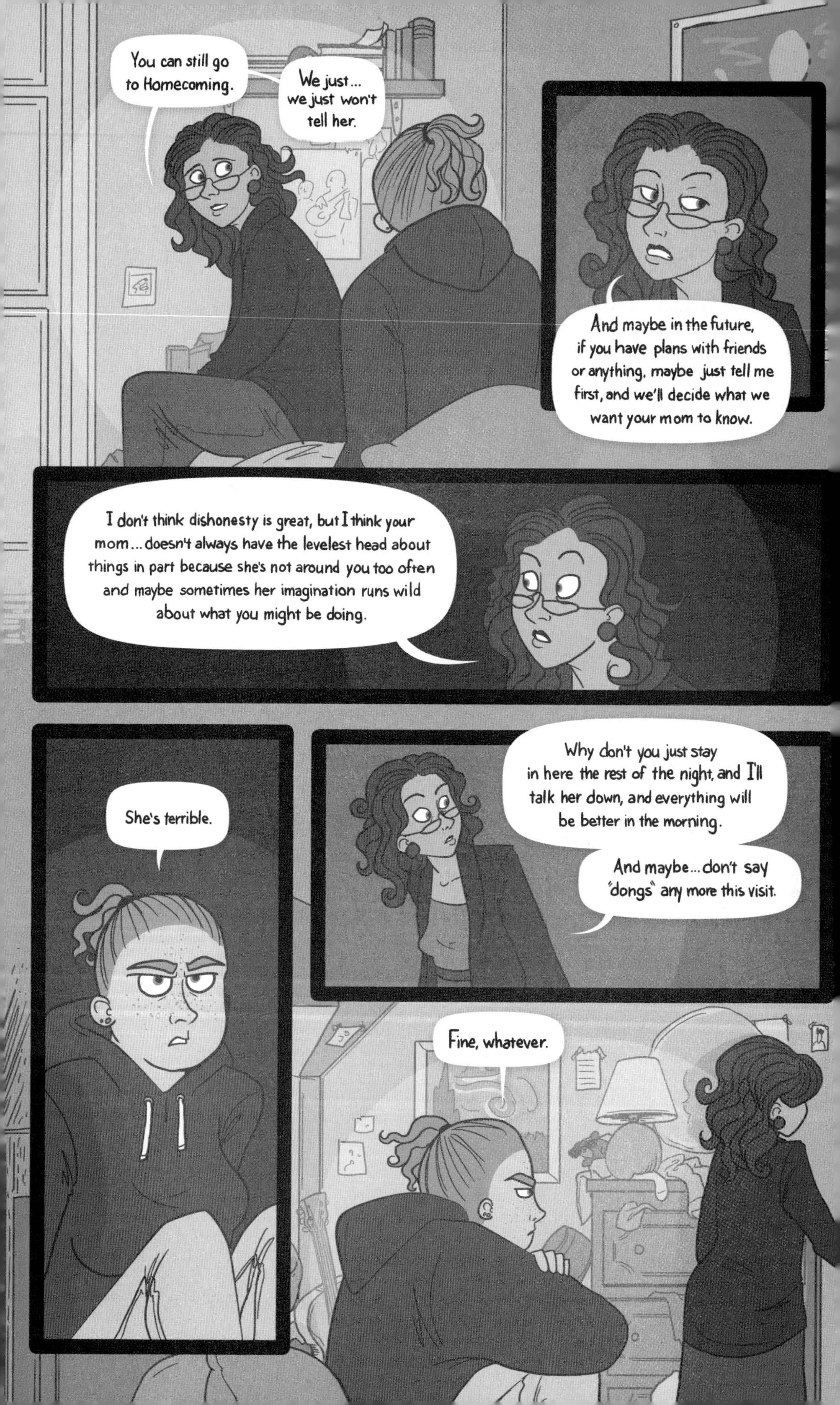
You can still go to Homecoming.
We just... we just won't tell her.
And maybe in the future, if you have plans with friends or anything, maybe just tell me first, and we'll decide what we want your mom to know.
I don't think dishonesty is great, but I think your mom... doesn't always have the levelest head about things in part because she's not around you too often and maybe sometimes her imagination runs wild about what you might be doing.
She's terrible.
Why don't you just stay in here the rest of the night, and I'll talk her down, and everything will be better in the morning.
And maybe... don't say "dongs" any more this visit.
Fine, whatever.

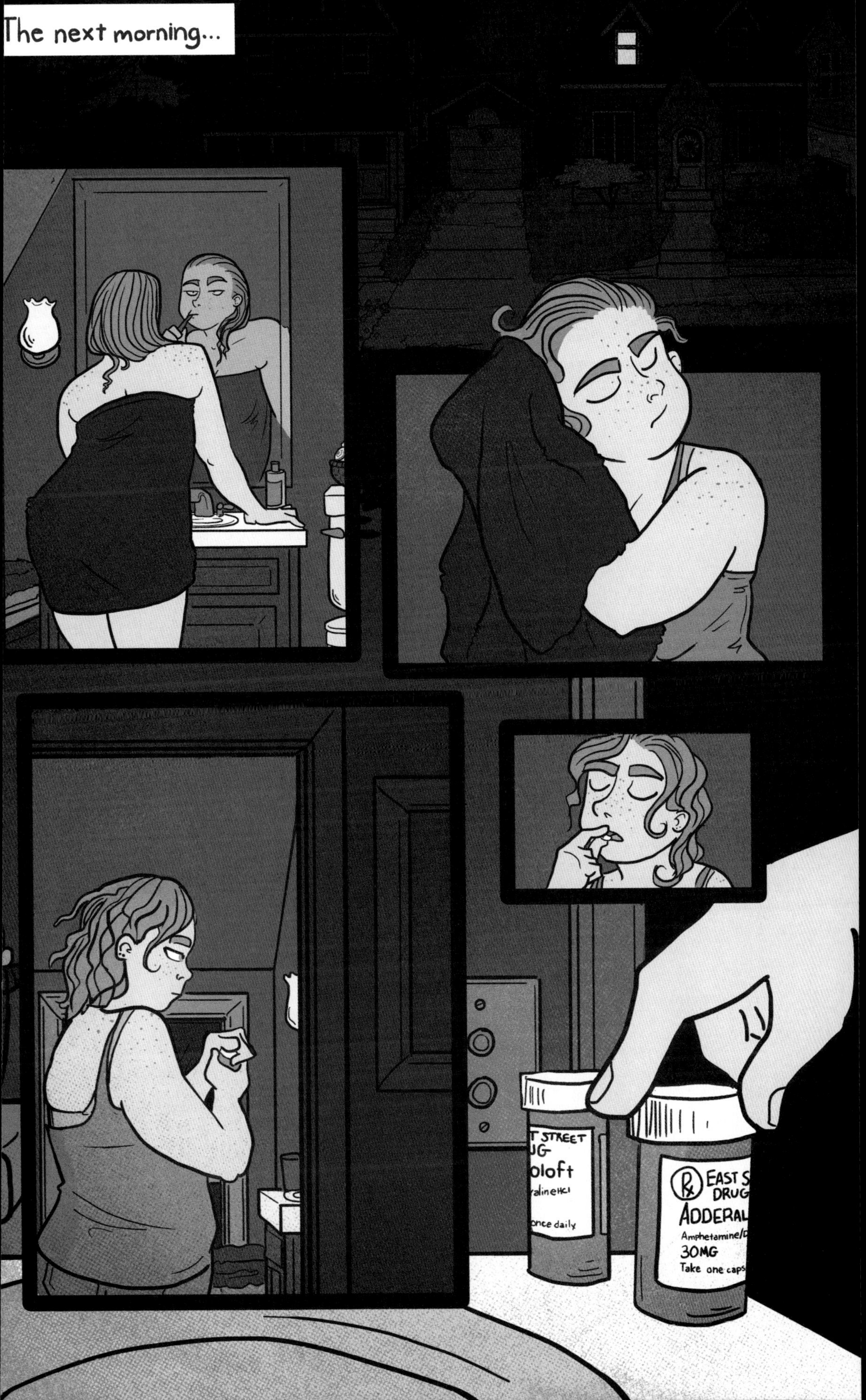
The next morning...
T STREET
UG
oloft
ralineHCl
once daily
Rx EAST S
DRUG
ADDERAL
Amphetamine/D
30MG
Take one caps

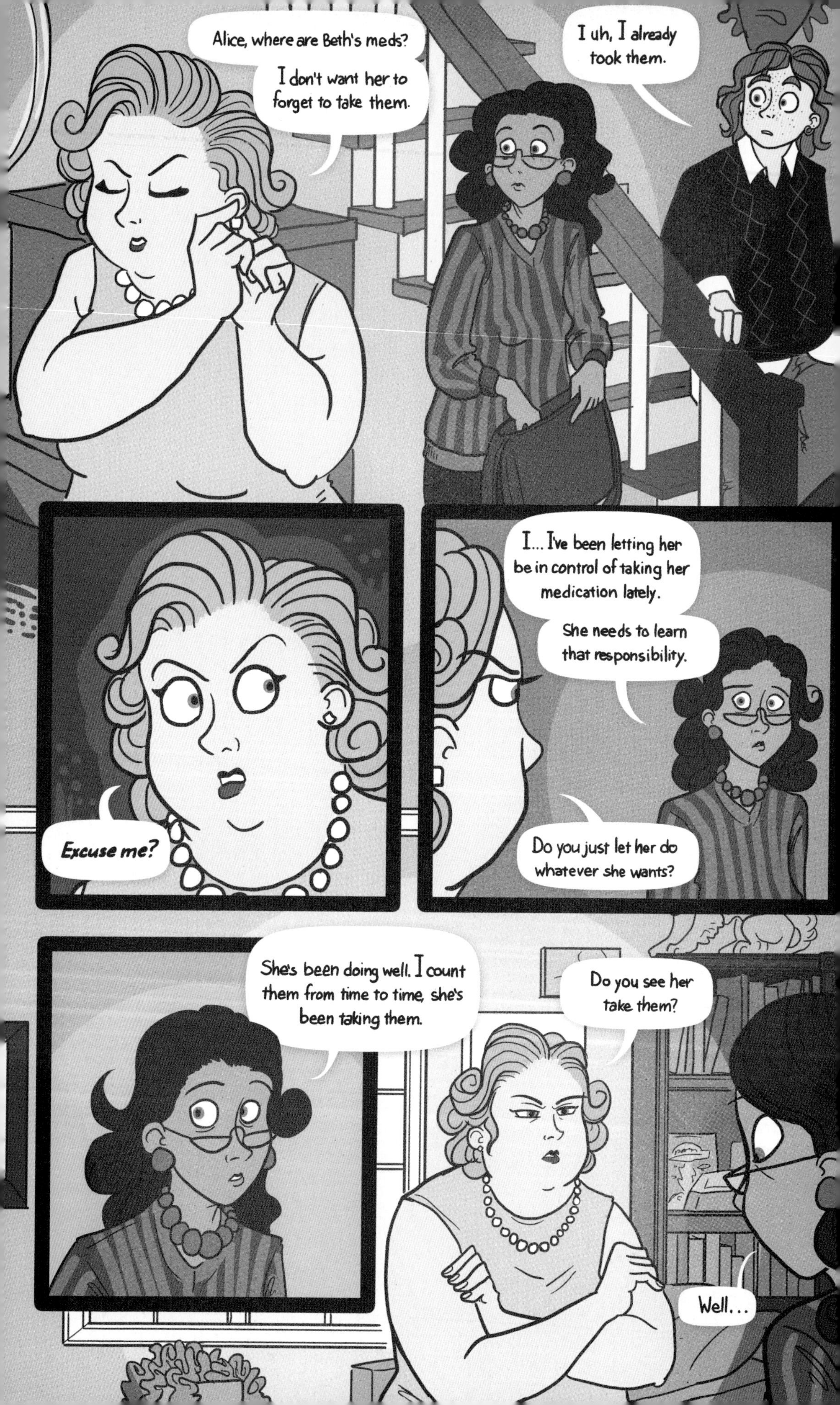

Alice, where are Beth's meds?
I don't want her to forget to take them.
I uh, I already took them.
Excuse me?
I... I've been letting her be in control of taking her medication lately.
She needs to learn that responsibility.
Do you just let her do whatever she wants?
She's been doing well. I count them from time to time, she's been taking them.
Do you see her take them?
Well...

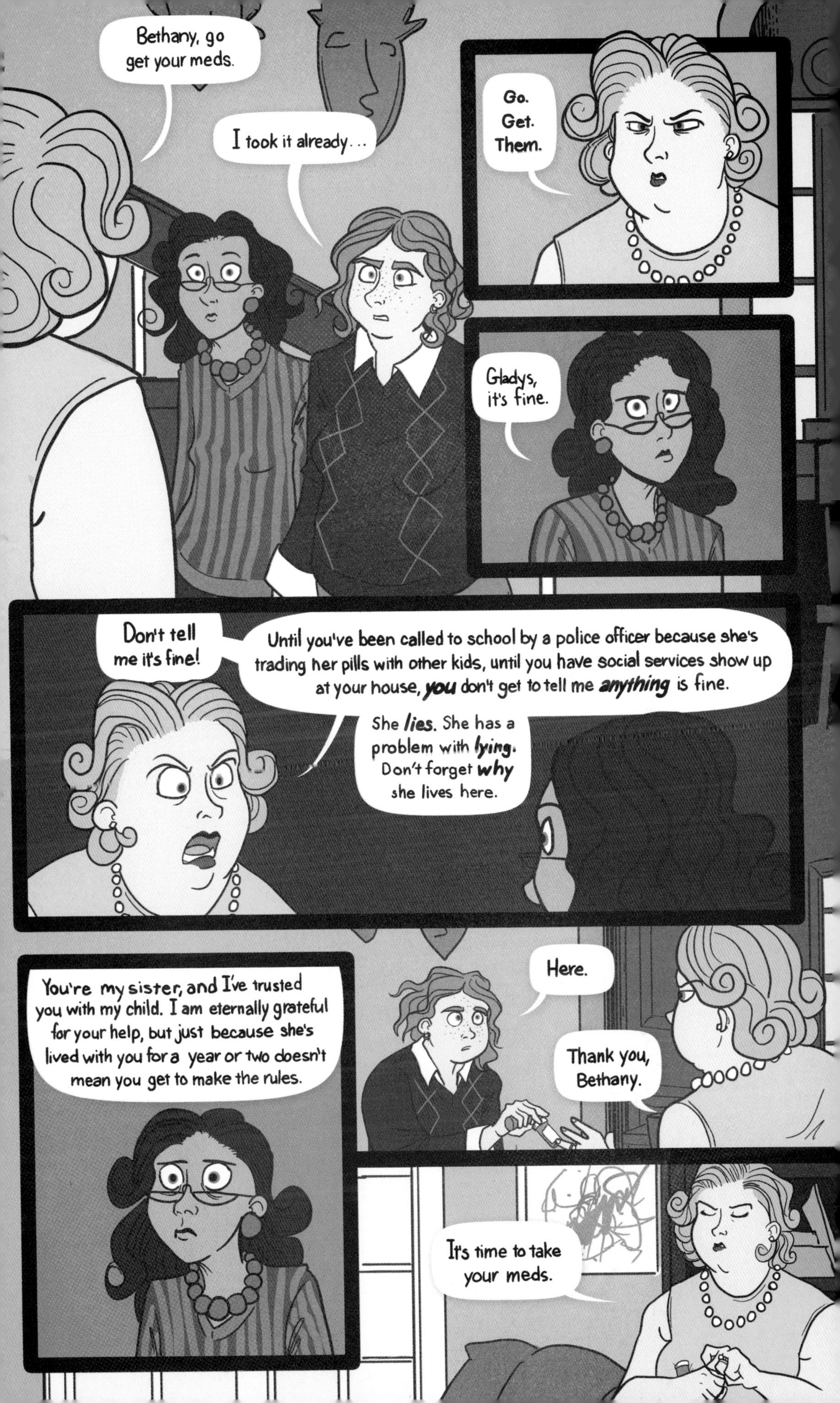
Bethany, go get your meds.
I took it already...
Go. Get. Them.
Gladys, it's fine.
Don't tell me it's fine!
Until you've been called to school by a police officer because she's trading her pills with other kids, until you have social services show up at your house, *you* don't get to tell me *anything* is fine.
She *lies*. She has a problem with *lying*. Don't forget *why* she lives here.
You're my sister, and I've trusted you with my child. I am eternally grateful for your help, but just because she's lived with you for a year or two doesn't mean you get to make the rules.
Here.
Thank you, Bethany.
It's time to take your meds.

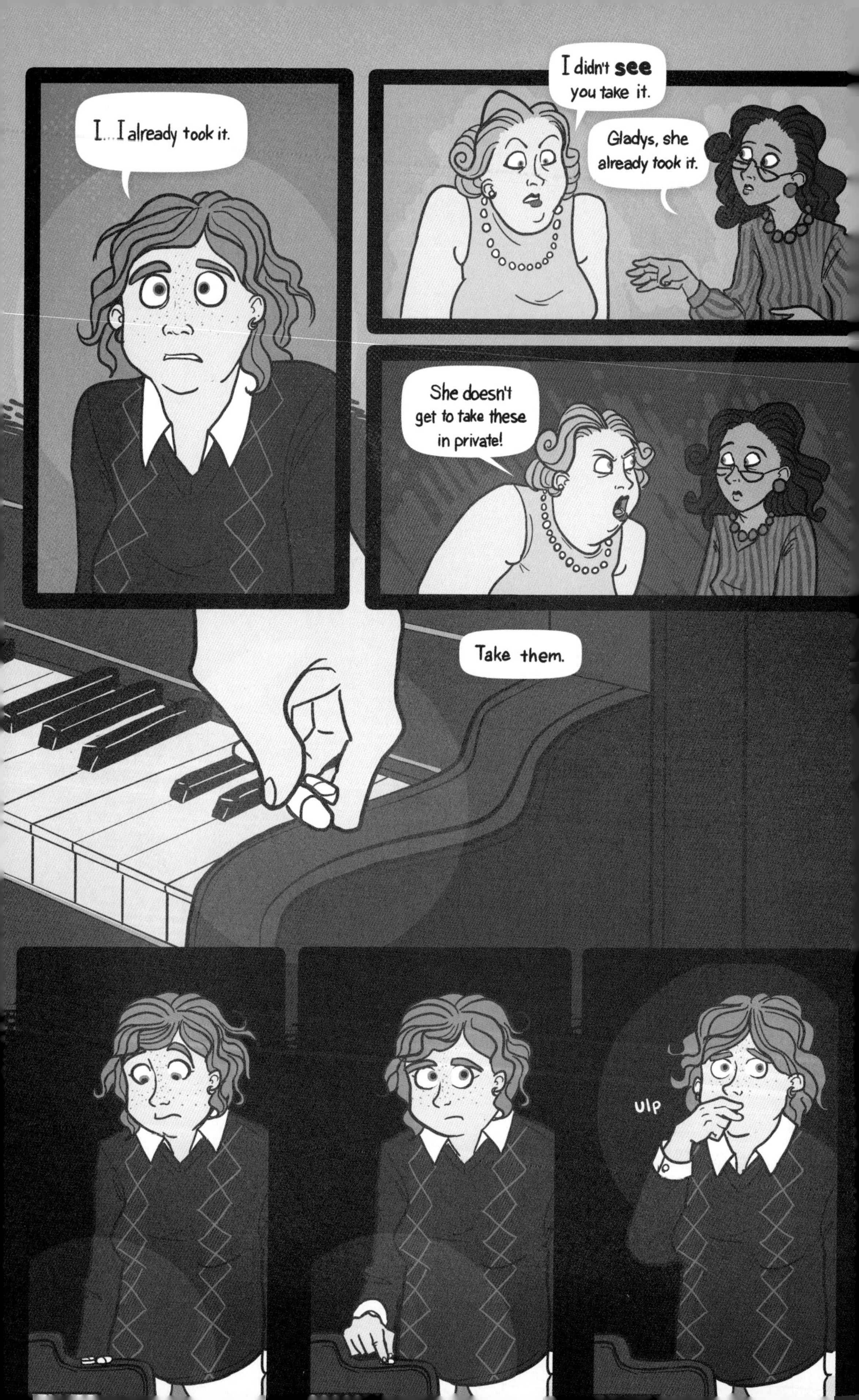
I...I already took it.
I didn't **see** you take it.
Gladys, she already took it.
She doesn't get to take these in private!
Take them.
ULP

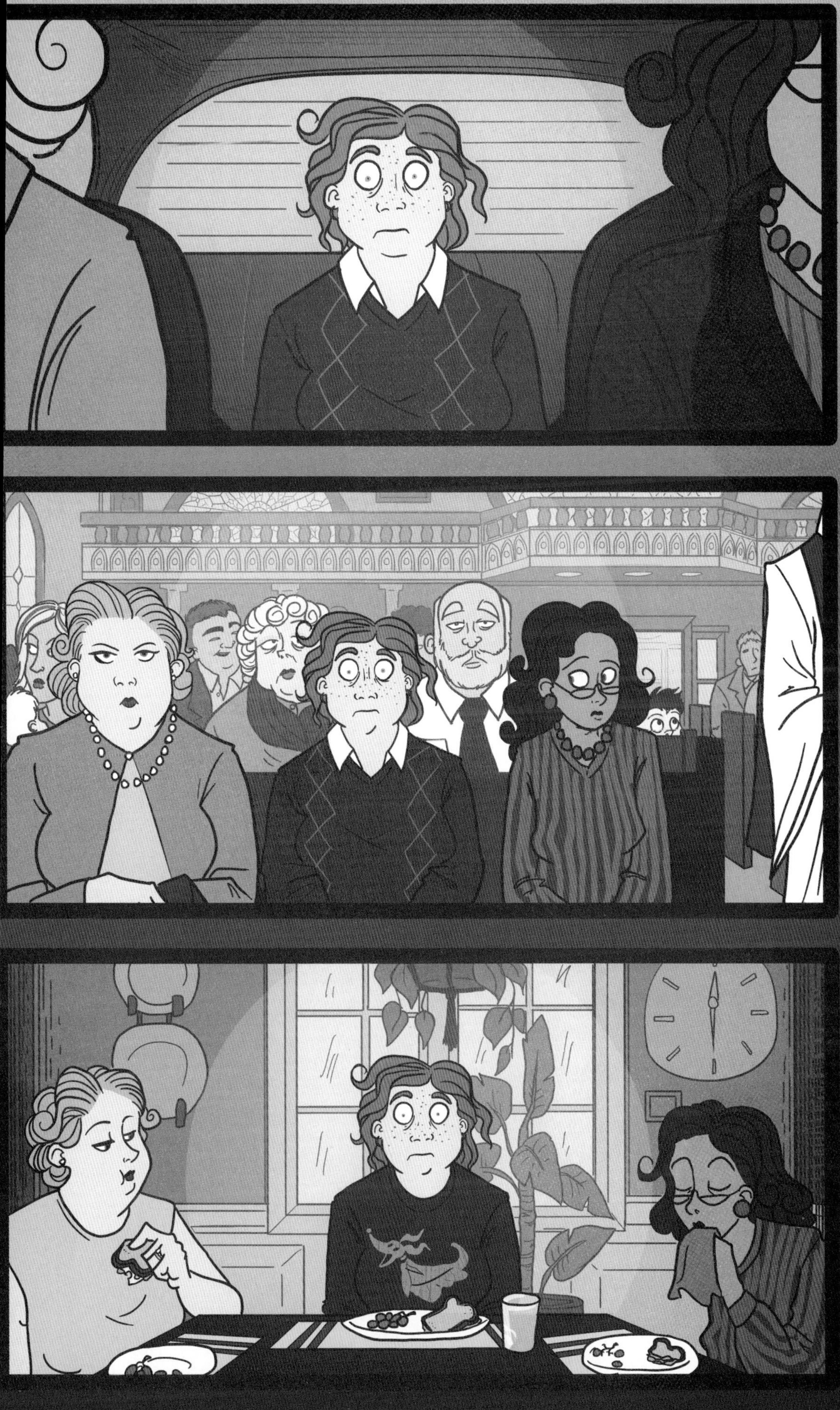

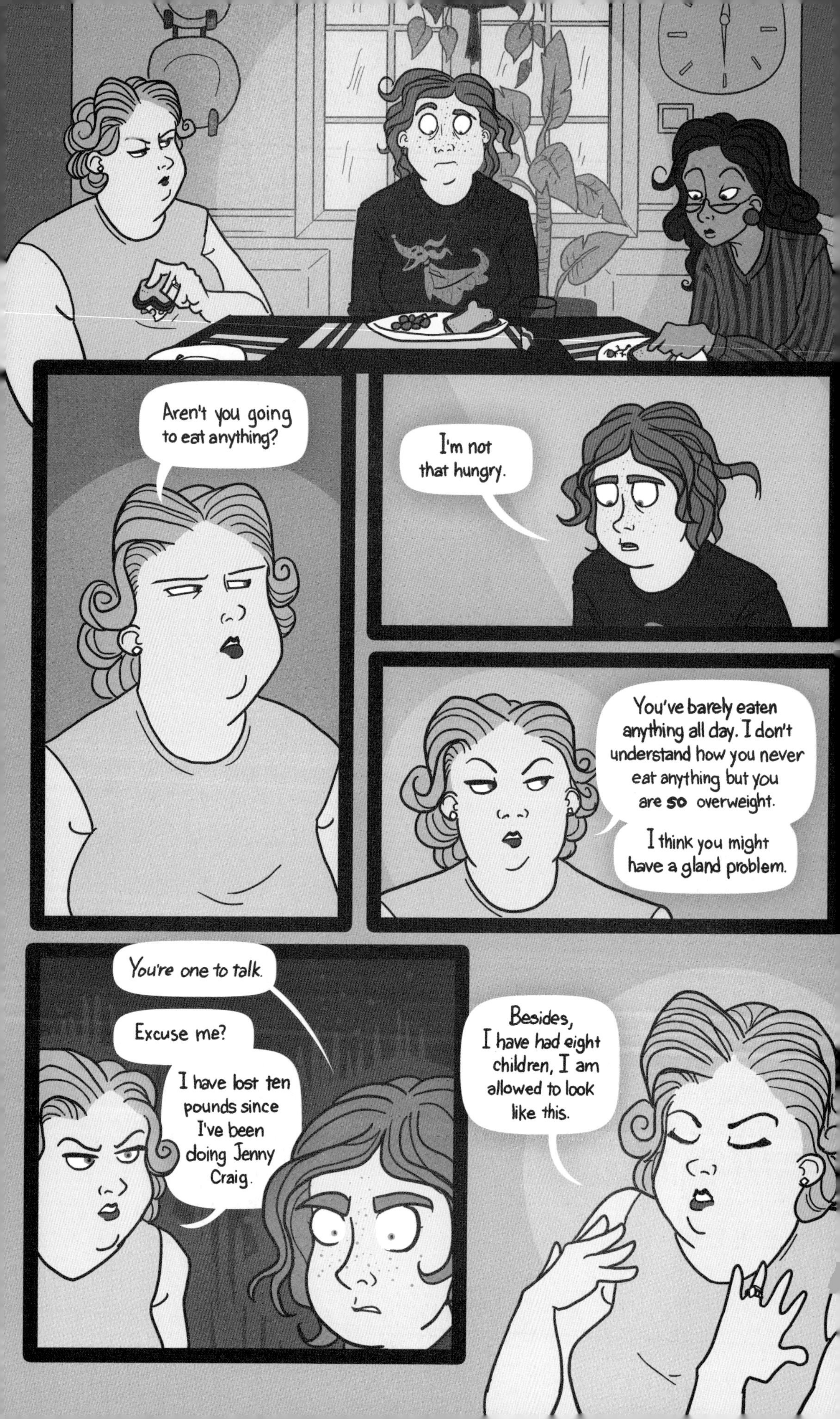
Aren't you going to eat anything?
I'm not that hungry.
You've barely eaten anything all day. I don't understand how you never eat anything but you are **so** overweight.
I think you might have a gland problem.
You're one to talk.
Excuse me?
I have lost ten pounds since I've been doing Jenny Craig.
Besides, I have had eight children, I am allowed to look like this.

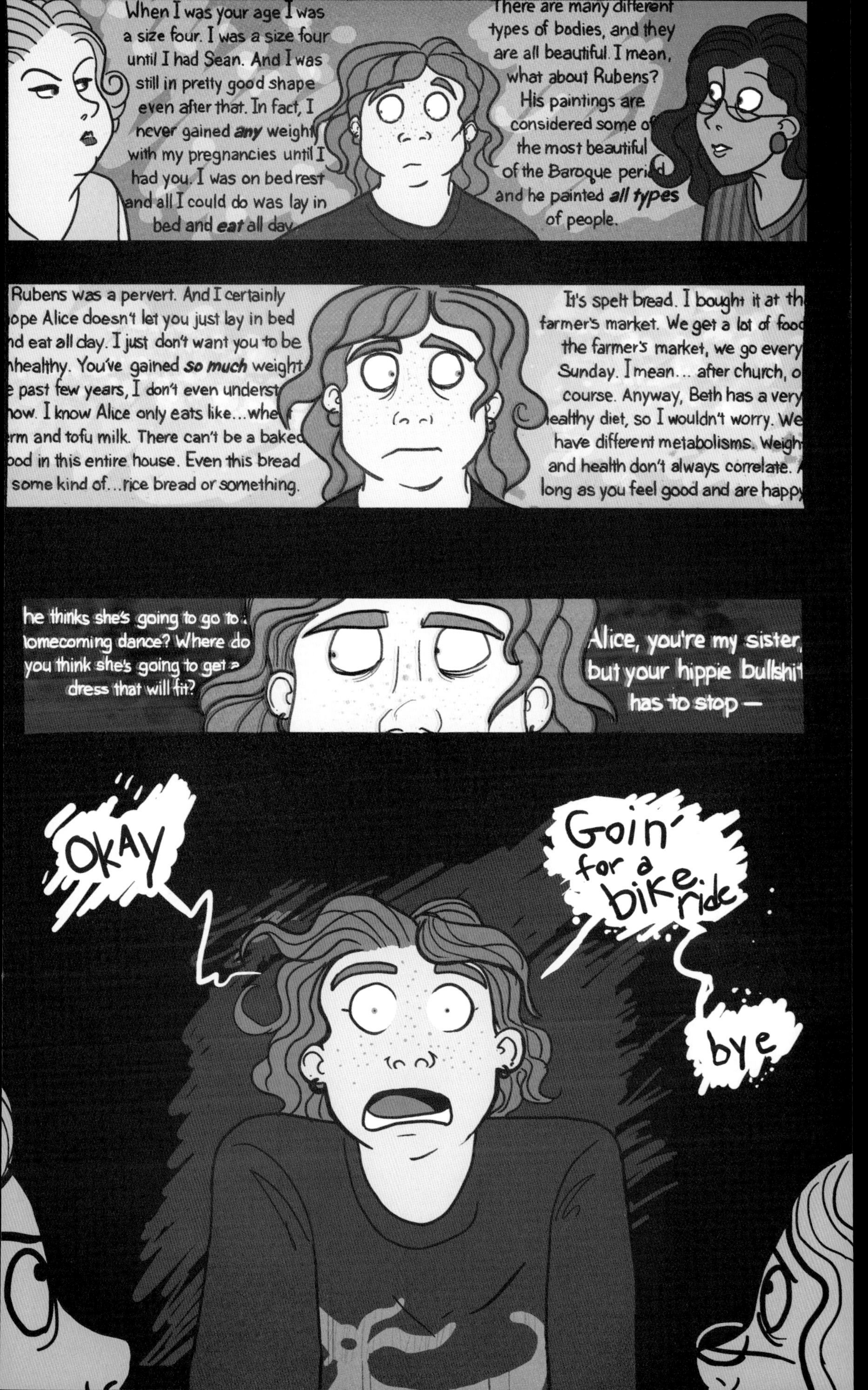
When I was your age I was a size four. I was a size four until I had Sean. And I was still in pretty good shape even after that. In fact, I never gained **any** weight with my pregnancies until I had you. I was on bedrest and all I could do was lay in bed and **eat** all day...
There are many different types of bodies, and they are all beautiful. I mean, what about Rubens? His paintings are considered some of the most beautiful of the Baroque period and he painted **all types** of people.
Rubens was a pervert. And I certainly hope Alice doesn't let you just lay in bed and eat all day. I just don't want you to be unhealthy. You've gained **so much** weight the past few years, I don't even underst... how. I know Alice only eats like... whe... germ and tofu milk. There can't be a baked good in this entire house. Even this bread some kind of... rice bread or something.
It's spelt bread. I bought it at th... farmer's market. We get a lot of food the farmer's market, we go every Sunday. I mean... after church, of course. Anyway, Beth has a very healthy diet, so I wouldn't worry. We have different metabolisms. Weight and health don't always correlate. As long as you feel good and are happy
...he thinks she's going to go to a homecoming dance? Where do you think she's going to get a dress that will fit?
Alice, you're my sister, but your hippie bullshit has to stop —
OKAY
Goin' for a bike ride
bye

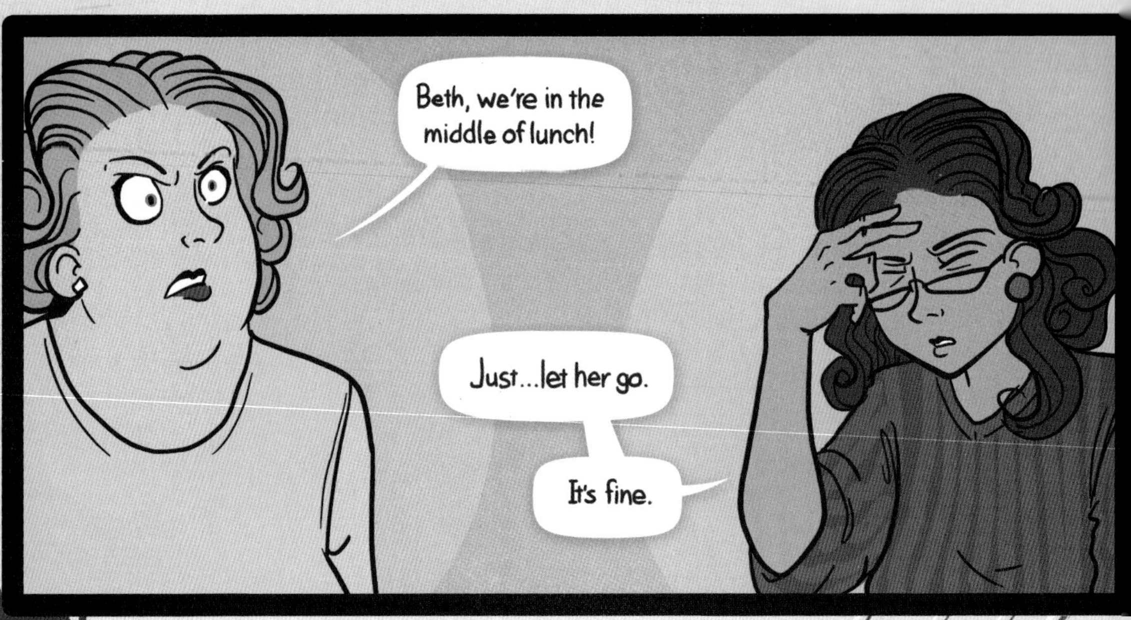
Beth, we're in the middle of lunch!
Just...let her go.
It's fine.
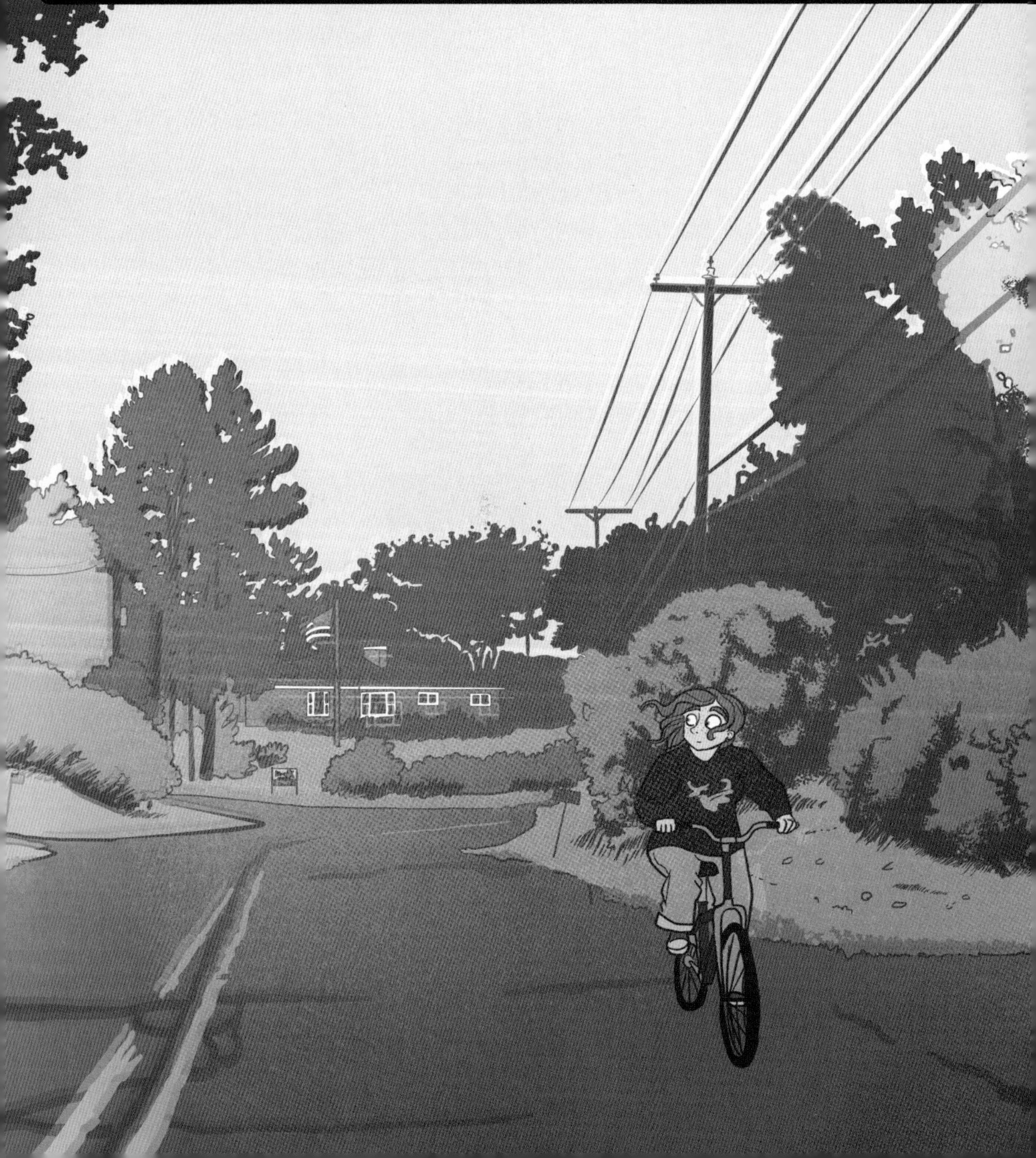

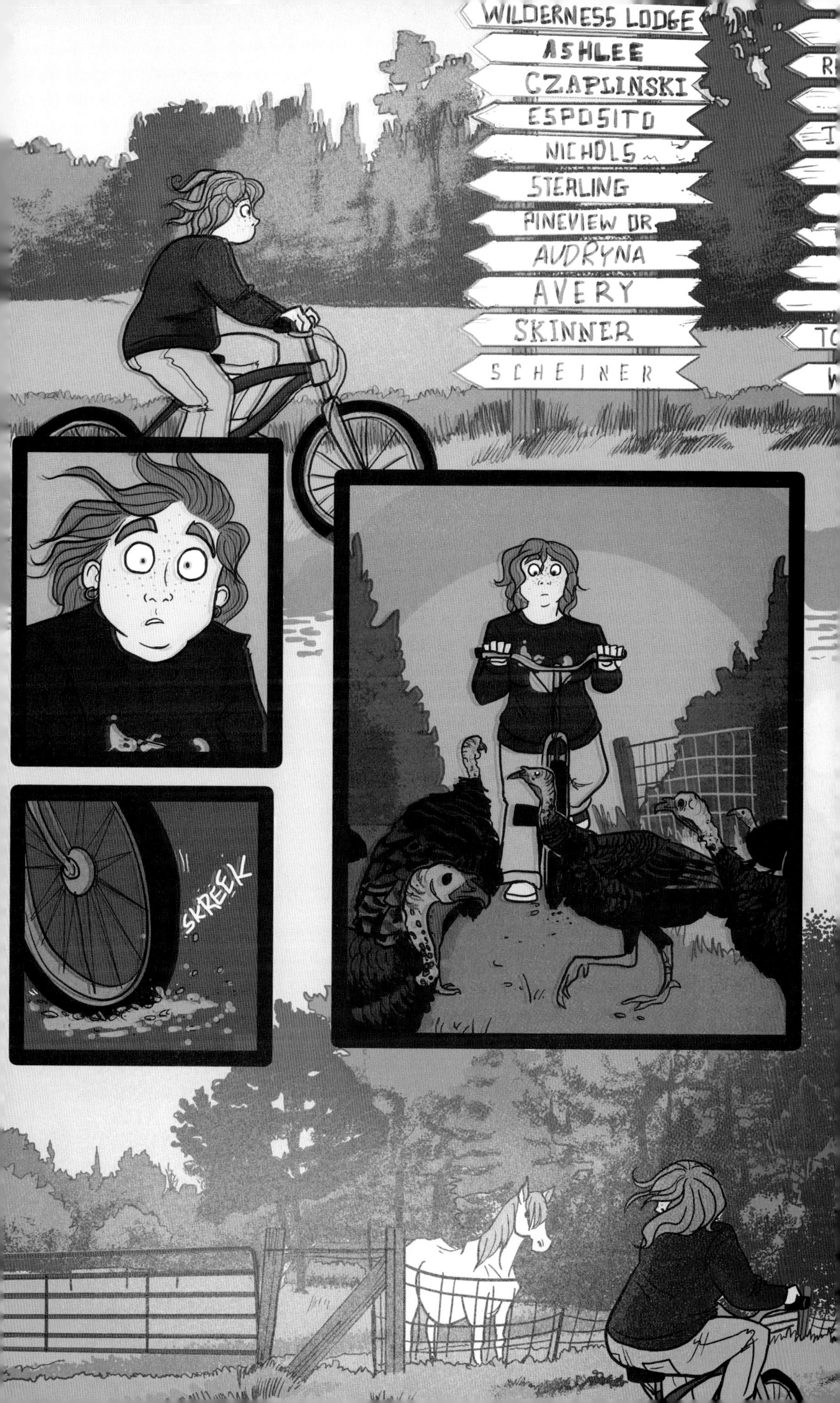
WILDERNESS LODGE
ASHLEE
CZAPLINSKI
ESPOSITO
NICHOLS
STERLING
PINEVIEW DR.
AUDRYNA
AVERY
SKINNER
SCHEINER
SKREEK

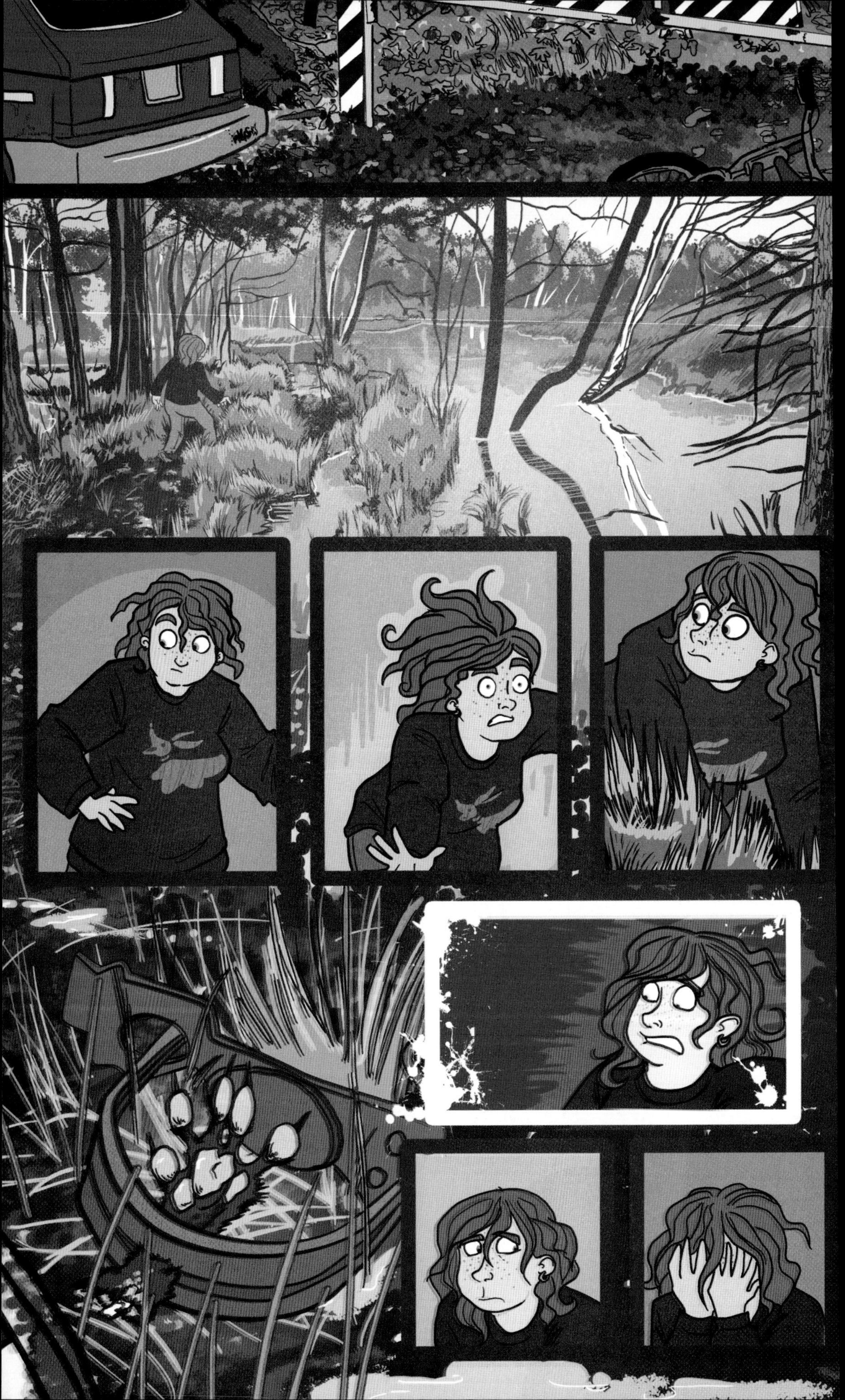

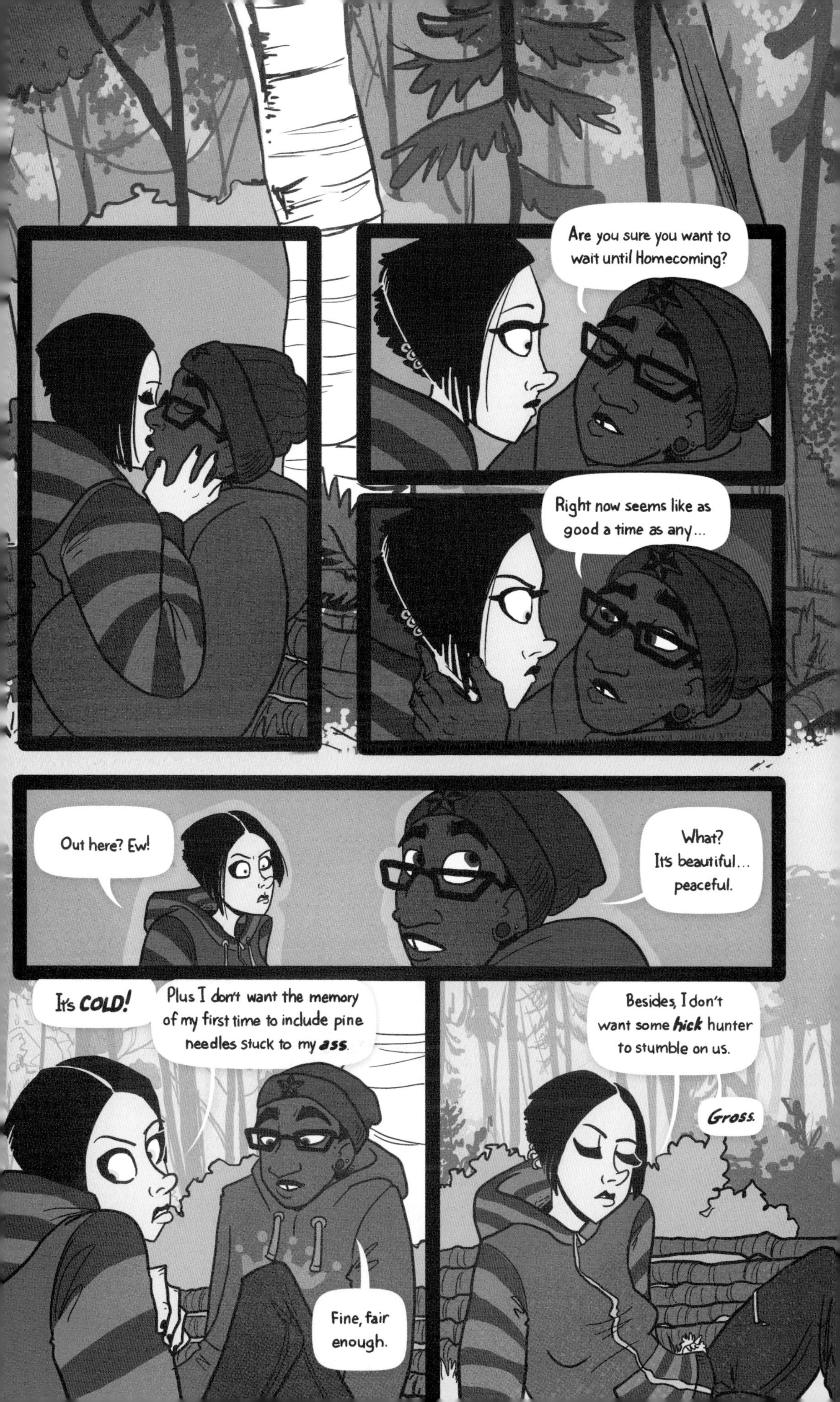

Are you sure you want to wait until Homecoming?
Right now seems like as good a time as any...
Out here? Ew!
What? It's beautiful... peaceful.
It's COLD!
Plus I don't want the memory of my first time to include pine needles stuck to my ass.
Fine, fair enough.
Besides, I don't want some hick hunter to stumble on us.
Gross.

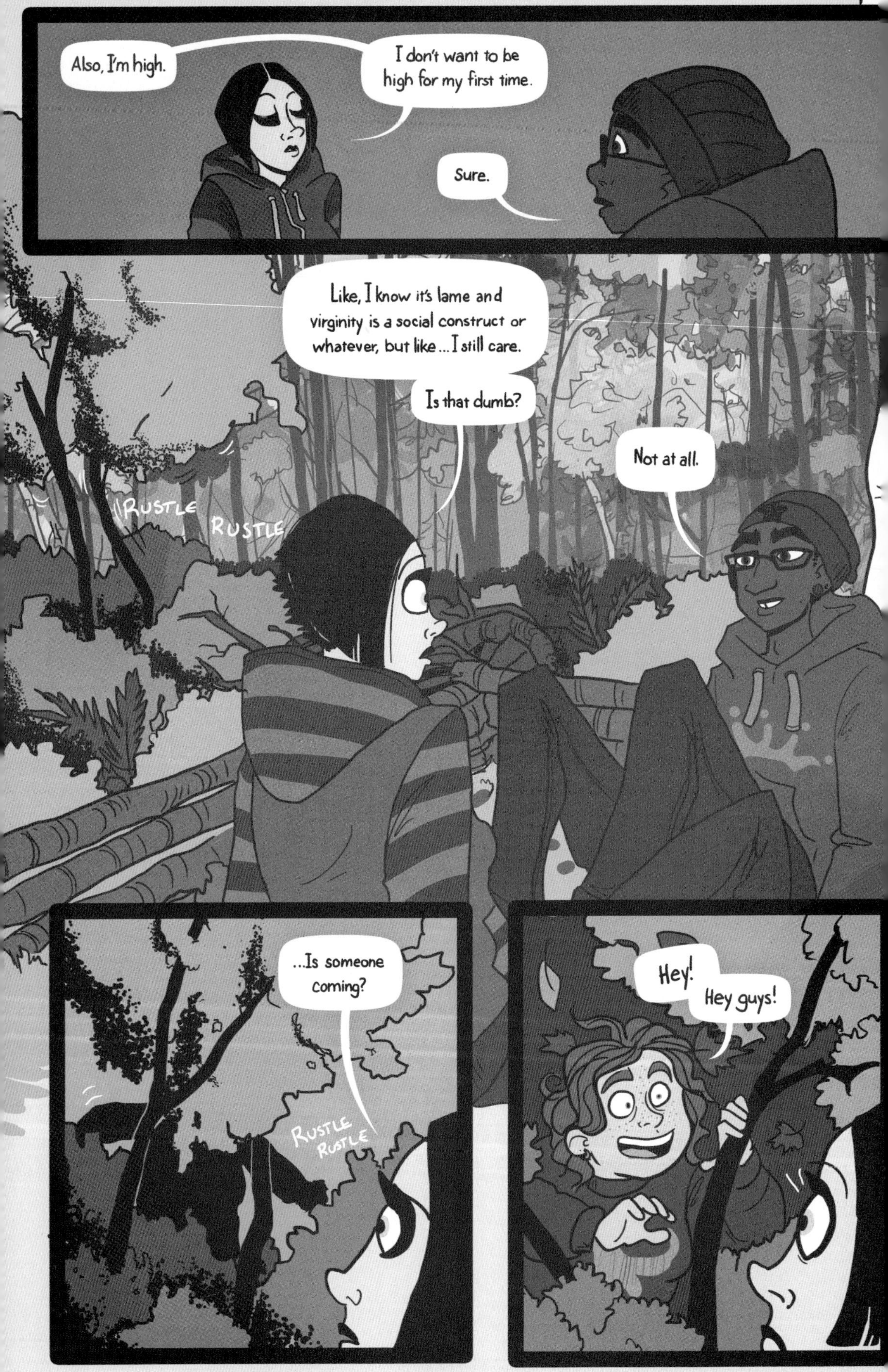
Also, I'm high.
I don't want to be high for my first time.
Sure.
Like, I know it's lame and virginity is a social construct or whatever, but like... I still care.
Is that dumb?
RUSTLE
RUSTLE
Not at all.
...Is someone coming?
RUSTLE RUSTLE
Hey!
Hey guys!

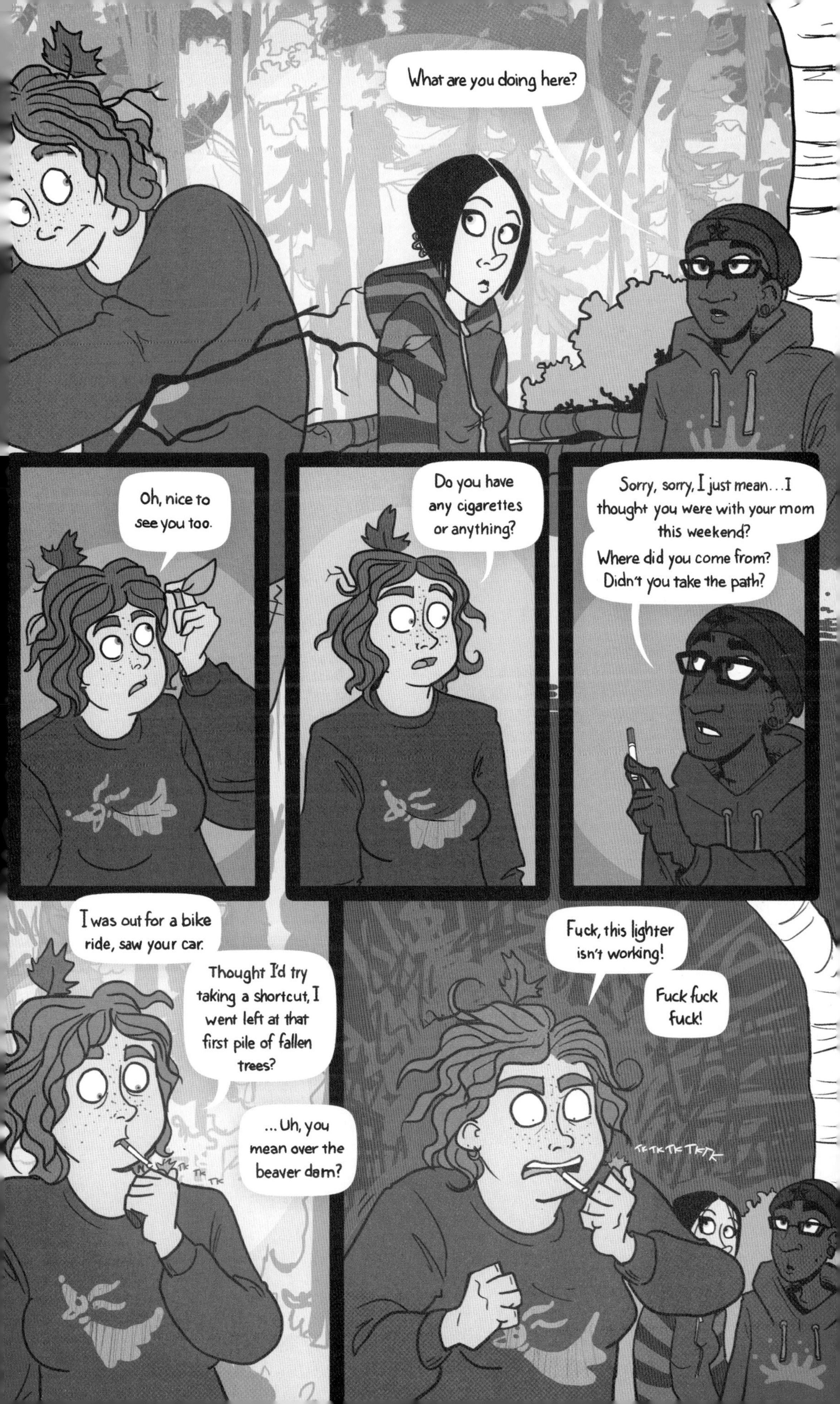

What are you doing here?
Oh, nice to see you too.
Do you have any cigarettes or anything?
Sorry, sorry, I just mean...I thought you were with your mom this weekend?
Where did you come from? Didn't you take the path?
I was out for a bike ride, saw your car.
Thought I'd try taking a shortcut, I went left at that first pile of fallen trees?
TK TK TK
...Uh, you mean over the beaver dam?
Fuck, this lighter isn't working!
Fuck fuck fuck!
TKTKTKTKTK

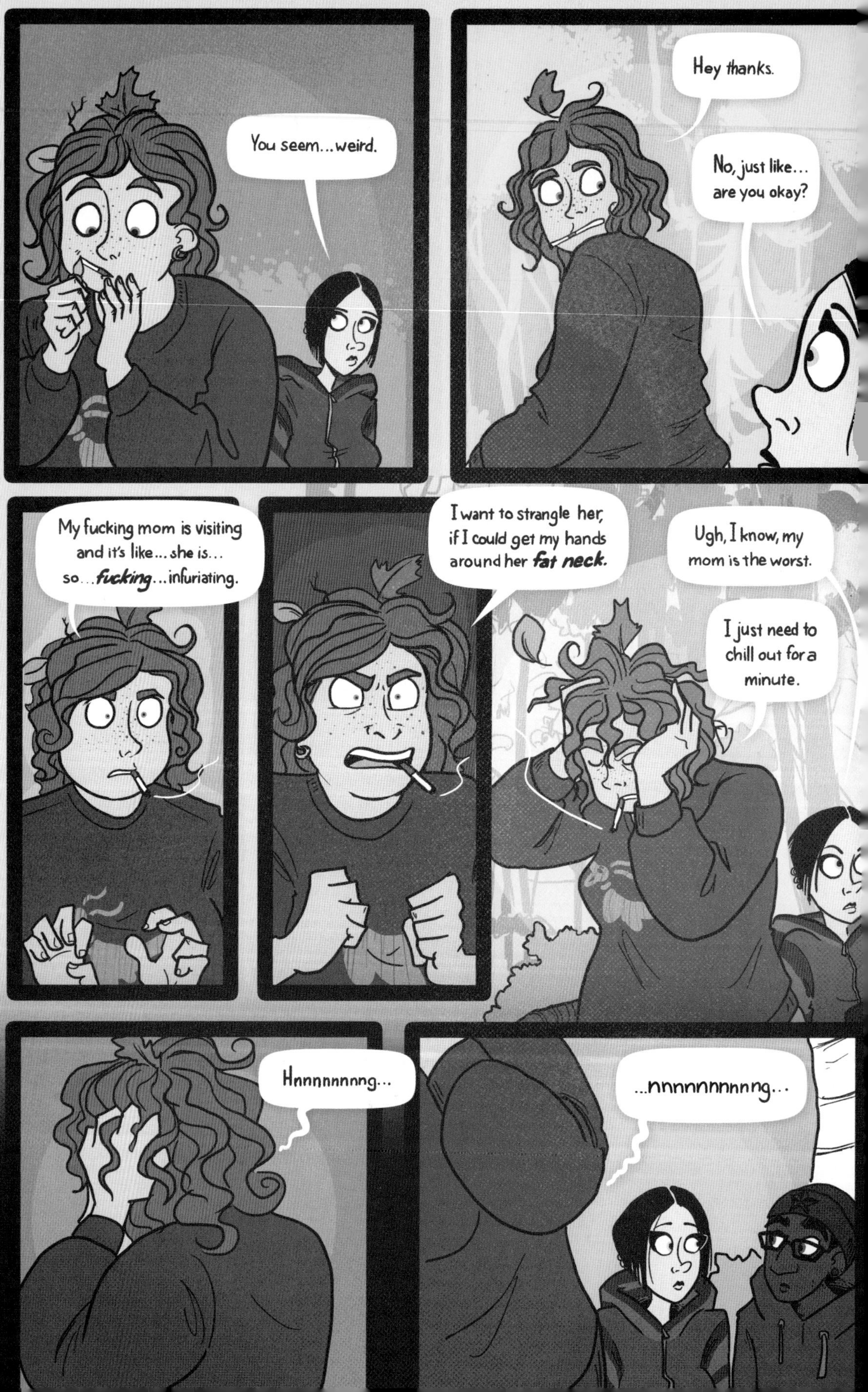
You seem...weird.
Hey thanks.
No, just like... are you okay?
My fucking mom is visiting and it's like... she is... so... **fucking**... infuriating.
I want to strangle her, if I could get my hands around her **fat neck.**
Ugh, I know, my mom is the worst.
I just need to chill out for a minute.
Hnnnnnnnng...
...nnnnnnnnng...

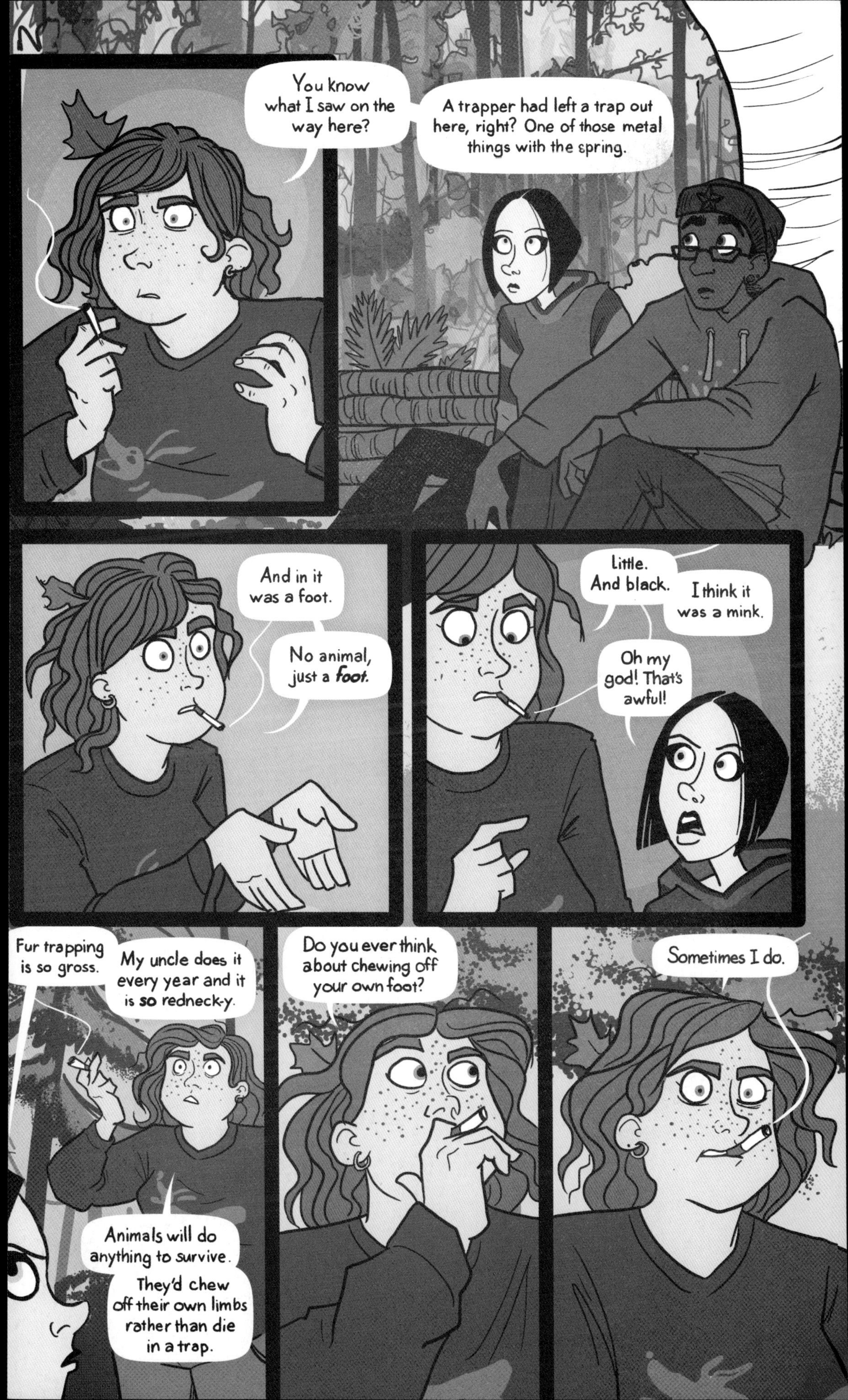

You know what I saw on the way here?
A trapper had left a trap out here, right? One of those metal things with the spring.
And in it was a foot.
No animal, just a **foot**.
Little. And black.
I think it was a mink.
Oh my god! That's awful!
Fur trapping is so gross.
My uncle does it every year and it is **so** redneck-y.
Animals will do anything to survive.
They'd chew off their own limbs rather than die in a trap.
Do you ever think about chewing off your own foot?
Sometimes I do.

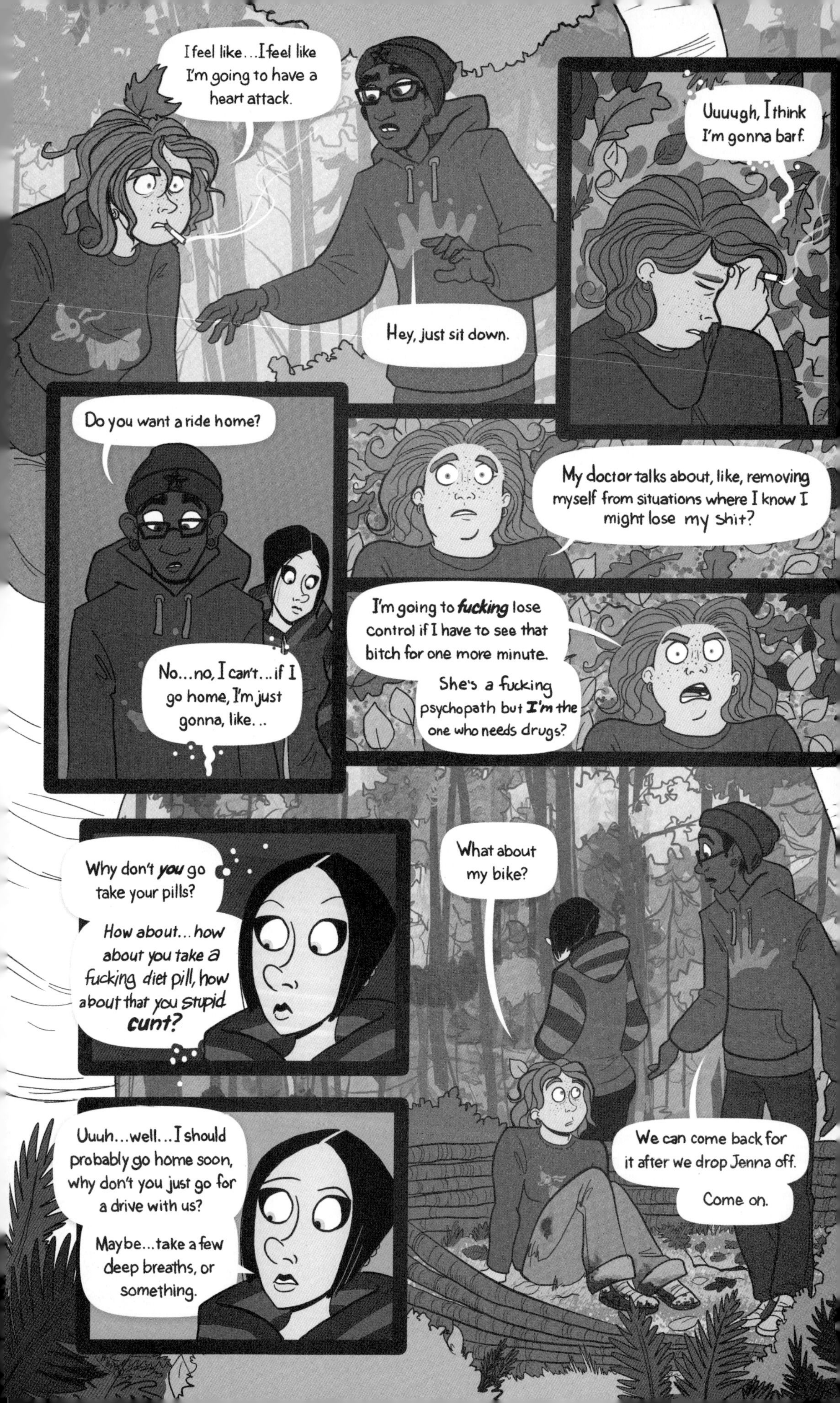
I feel like... I feel like I'm going to have a heart attack.
Hey, just sit down.
Uuuugh, I think I'm gonna barf.
Do you want a ride home?
No... no, I can't... if I go home, I'm just gonna, like...
My doctor talks about, like, removing myself from situations where I know I might lose my shit?
I'm going to ***fucking*** lose control if I have to see that bitch for one more minute.
She's a fucking psychopath but ***I'm*** the one who needs drugs?
Why don't ***you*** go take your pills?
How about... how about you take a fucking diet pill, how about that you stupid **cunt?**
Uuuh... well... I should probably go home soon, why don't you just go for a drive with us?
Maybe... take a few deep breaths, or something.
What about my bike?
We can come back for it after we drop Jenna off.
Come on.

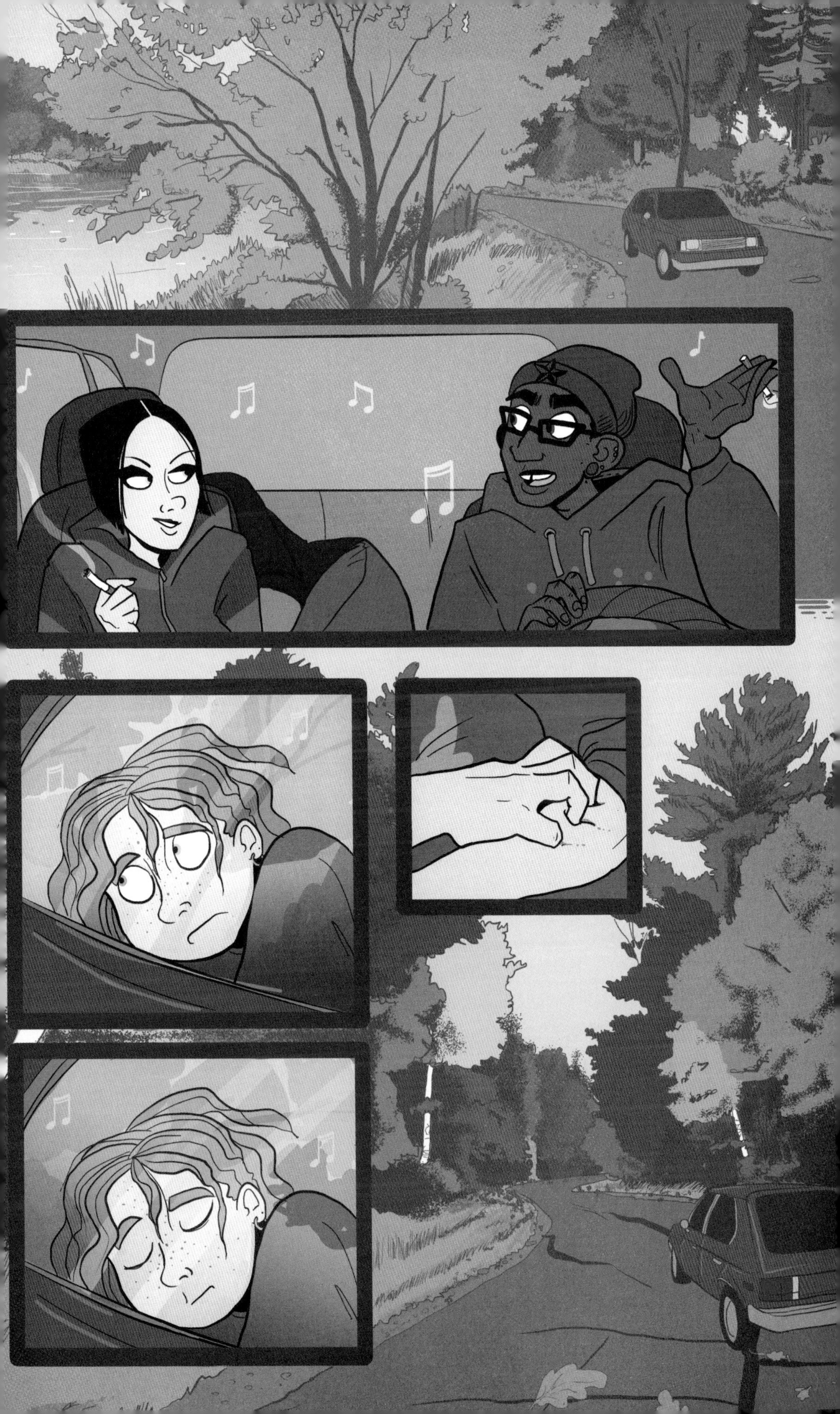

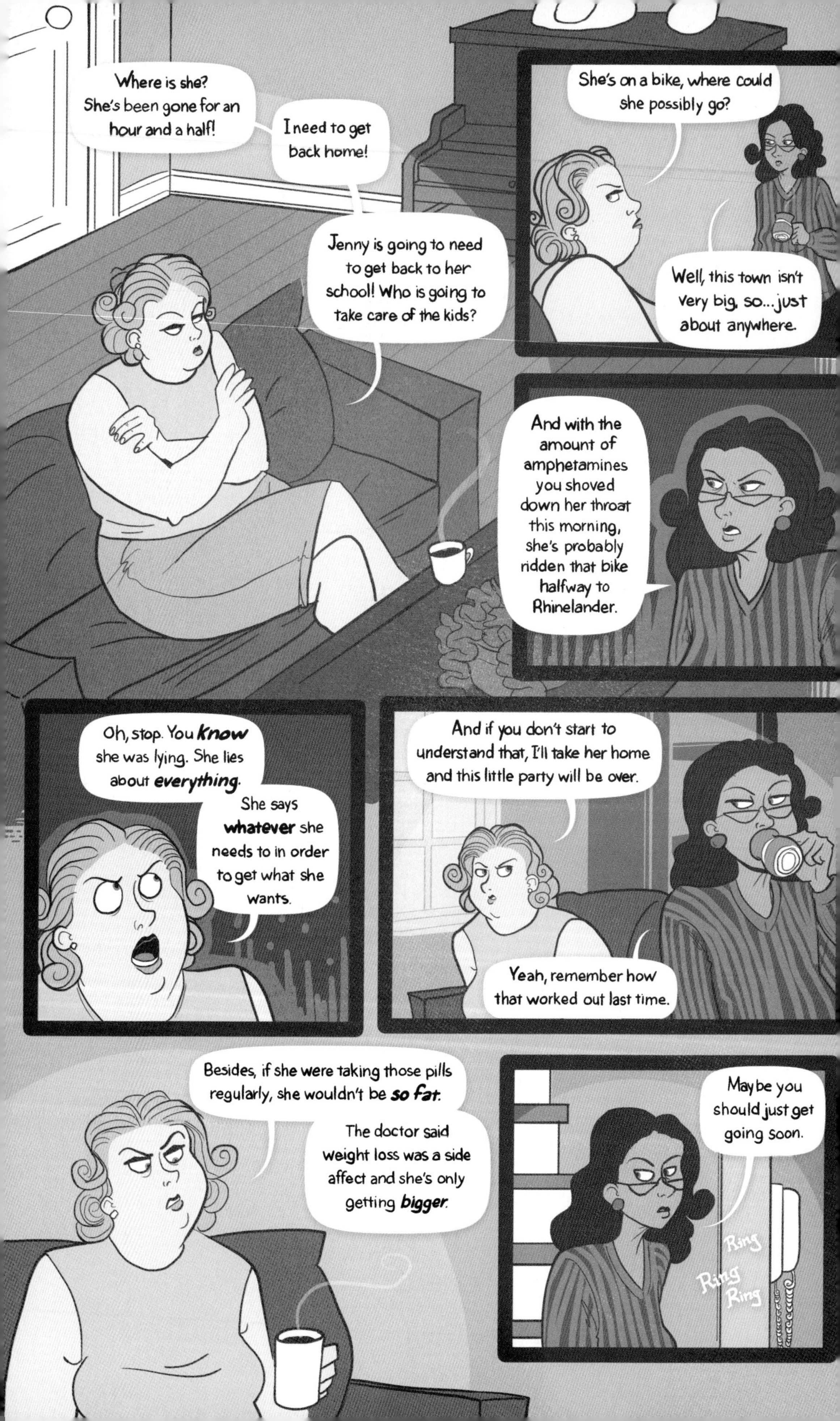
Where is she? She's been gone for an hour and a half!
I need to get back home!
Jenny is going to need to get back to her school! Who is going to take care of the kids?
She's on a bike, where could she possibly go?
Well, this town isn't very big, so...just about anywhere.
And with the amount of amphetamines you shoved down her throat this morning, she's probably ridden that bike halfway to Rhinelander.
Oh, stop. You **know** she was lying. She lies about **everything**.
She says **whatever** she needs to in order to get what she wants.
And if you don't start to understand that, I'll take her home and this little party will be over.
Yeah, remember how that worked out last time.
Besides, if she were taking those pills regularly, she wouldn't be ***so fat***.
The doctor said weight loss was a side affect and she's only getting ***bigger***.
Maybe you should just get going soon.
Ring
Ring
Ring

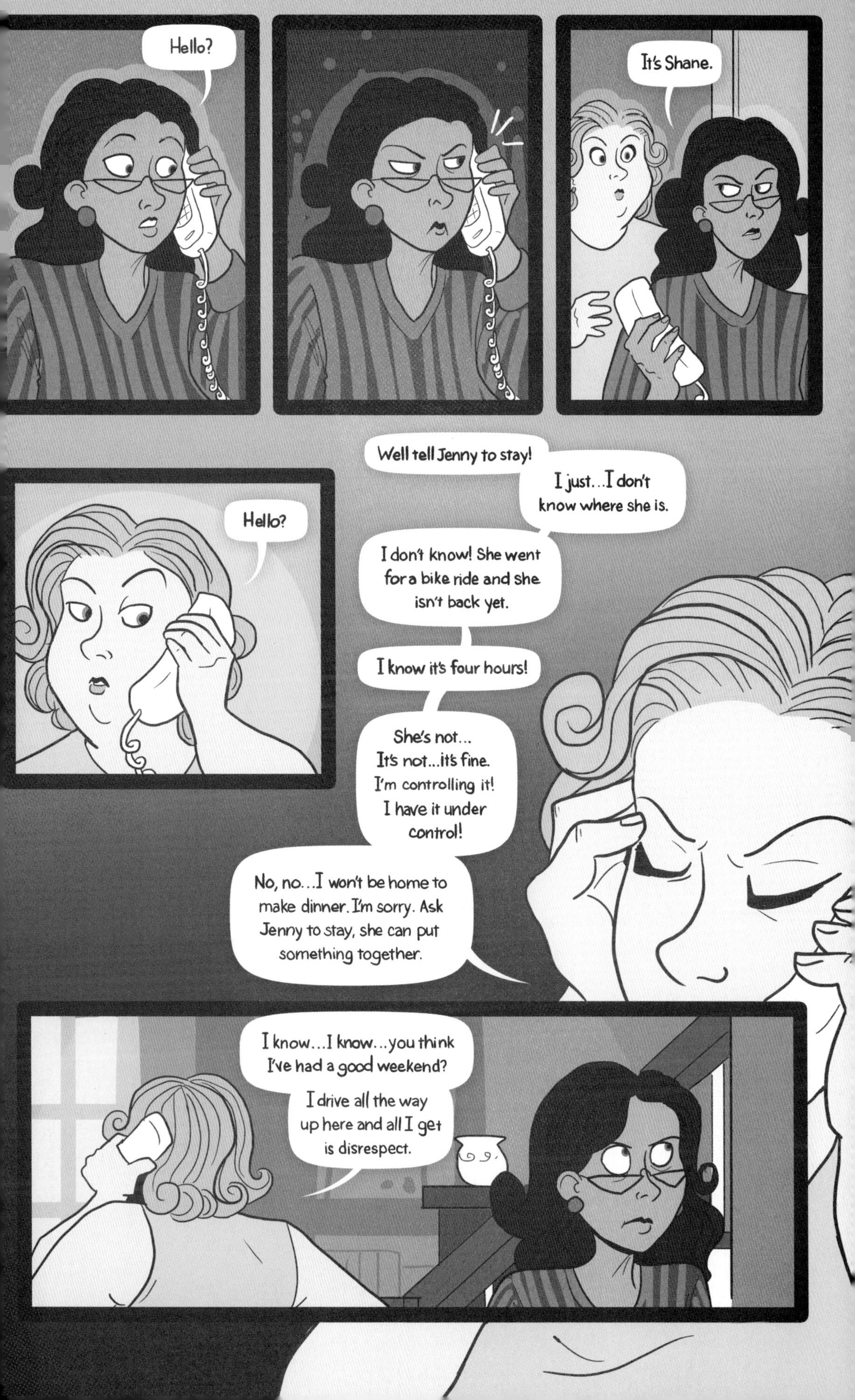
Hello?
It's Shane.
Hello?
Well tell Jenny to stay!
I just...I don't know where she is.
I don't know! She went for a bike ride and she isn't back yet.
I know it's four hours!
She's not... It's not...it's fine. I'm controlling it! I have it under control!
No, no...I won't be home to make dinner. I'm sorry. Ask Jenny to stay, she can put something together.
I know...I know...you think I've had a good weekend?
I drive all the way up here and all I get is disrespect.

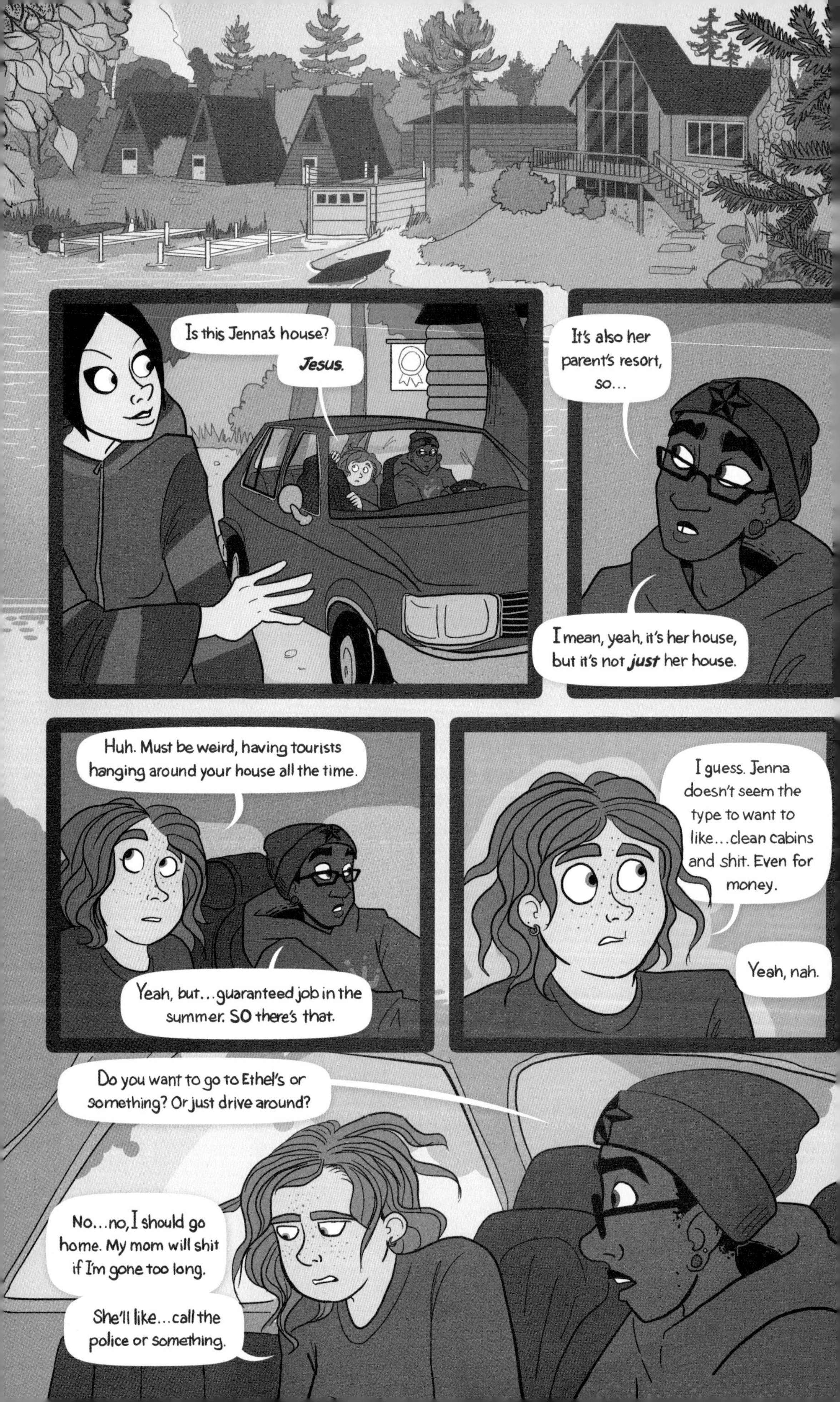
Is this Jenna's house?
Jesus.
It's also her parent's resort, so...
I mean, yeah, it's her house, but it's not *just* her house.
Huh. Must be weird, having tourists hanging around your house all the time.
Yeah, but...guaranteed job in the summer. SO there's that.
I guess. Jenna doesn't seem the type to want to like...clean cabins and shit. Even for money.
Yeah, nah.
Do you want to go to Ethel's or something? Or just drive around?
No...no, I should go home. My mom will shit if I'm gone too long.
She'll like...call the police or something.

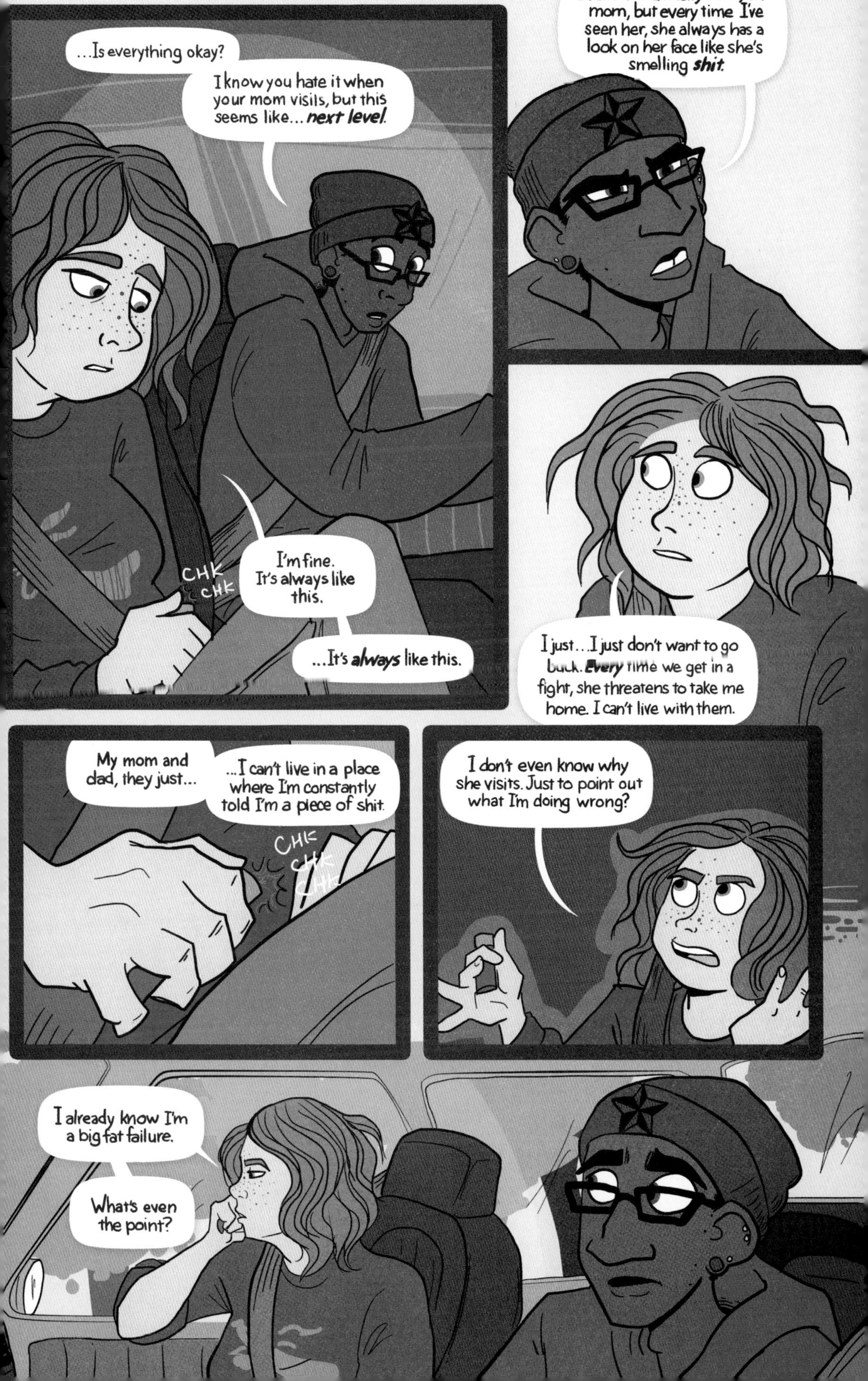
...Is everything okay?
I know you hate it when your mom visits, but this seems like... *next level*.
CHK CHK
I'm fine. It's always like this.
...It's *always* like this.
I've never actually met your mom, but every time I've seen her, she always has a look on her face like she's smelling *shit*.
I just... I just don't want to go back. *Every* time we get in a fight, she threatens to take me home. I can't live with them.
My mom and dad, they just...
...I can't live in a place where I'm constantly told I'm a piece of shit.
CHK CHK CHK
I don't even know why she visits. Just to point out what I'm doing wrong?
I already know I'm a big fat failure.
What's even the point?

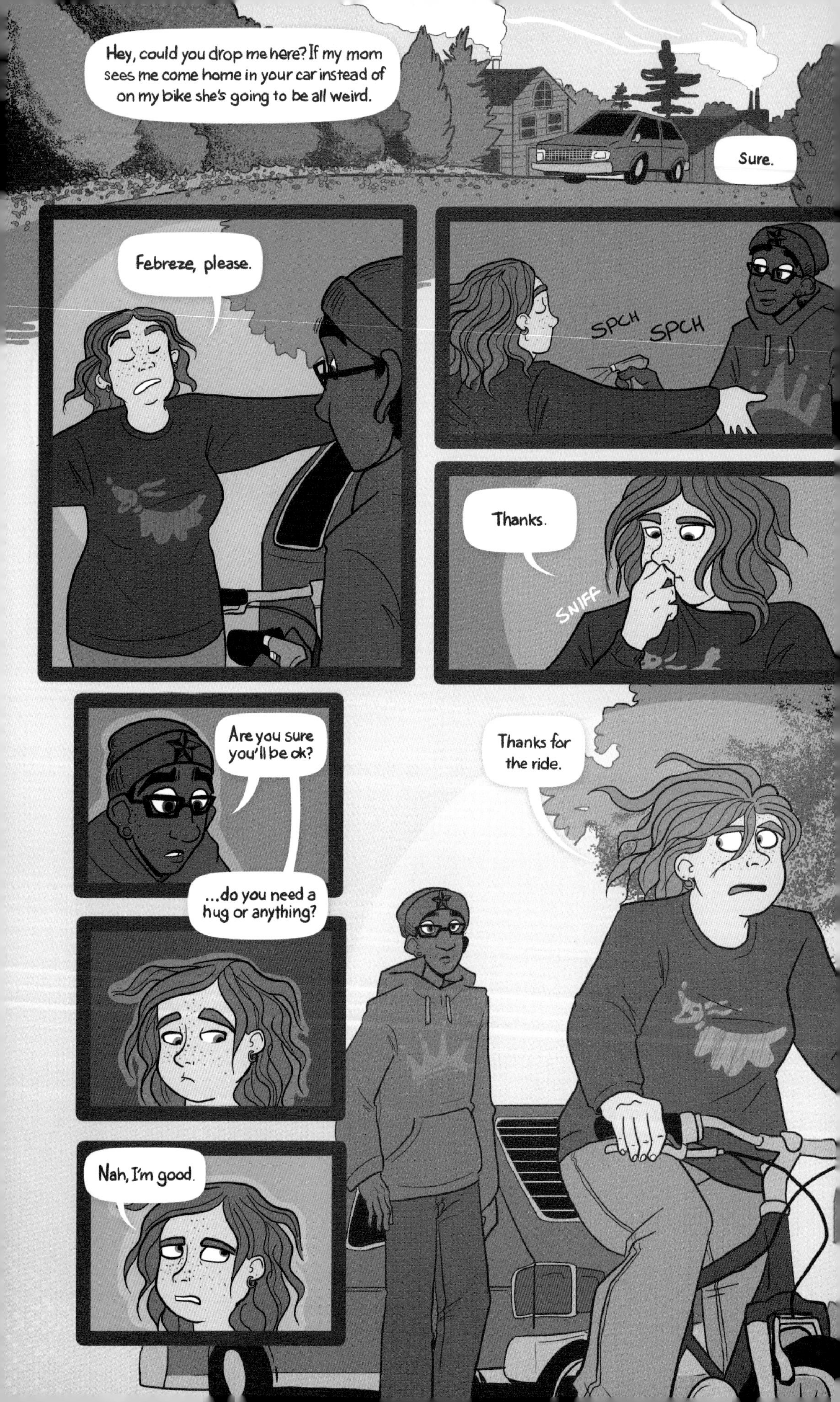
Hey, could you drop me here? If my mom sees me come home in your car instead of on my bike she's going to be all weird.
Sure.
Febreze, please.
SPCH SPCH
Thanks.
SNIFF
Are you sure you'll be ok?
...do you need a hug or anything?
Nah, I'm good.
Thanks for the ride.

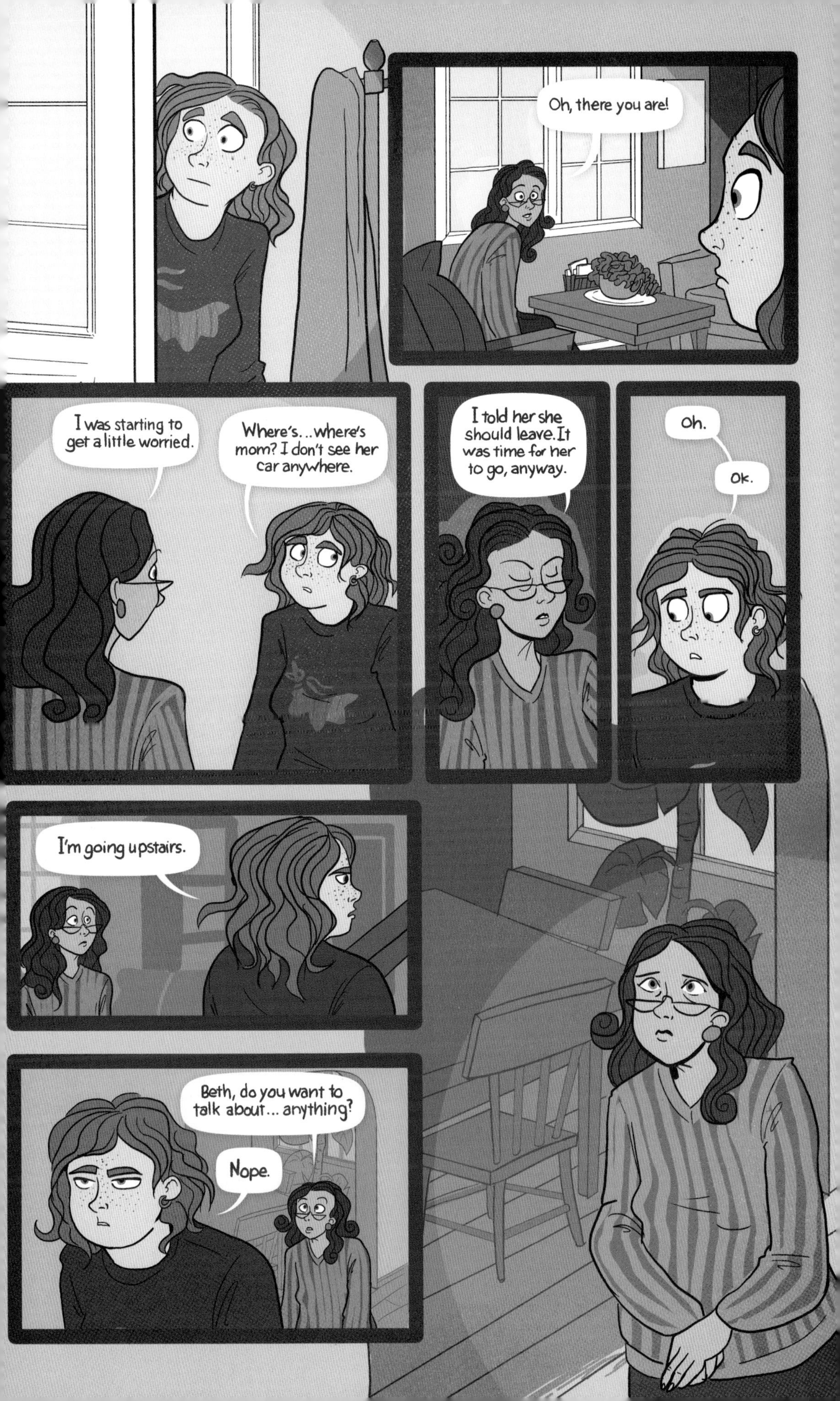
Oh, there you are!
I was starting to get a little worried.
Where's...where's mom? I don't see her car anywhere.
I told her she should leave. It was time for her to go, anyway.
Oh.
Ok.
I'm going upstairs.
Beth, do you want to talk about... anything?
Nope.

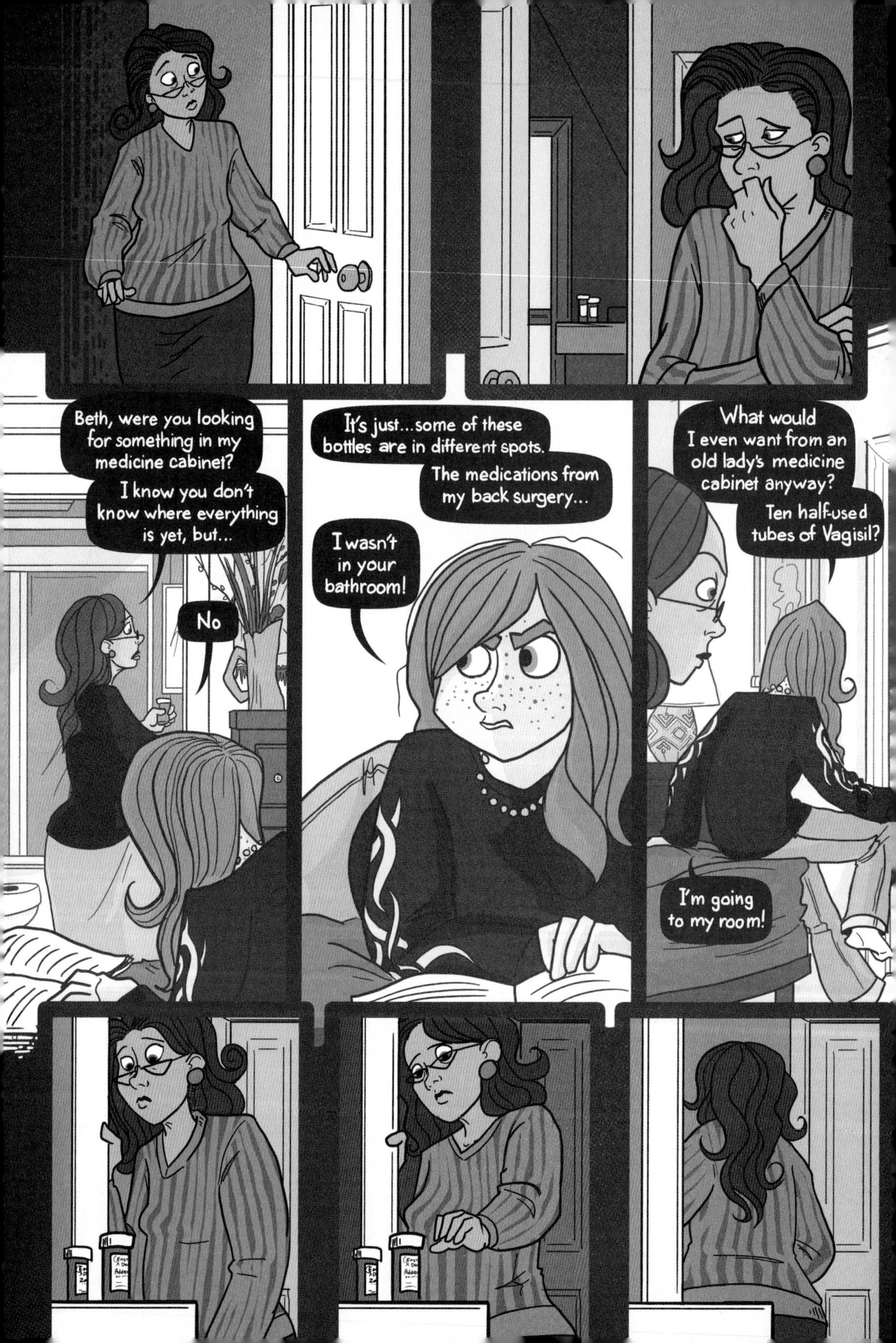
Beth, were you looking for something in my medicine cabinet?
I know you don't know where everything is yet, but...
No
It's just...some of these bottles are in different spots.
The medications from my back surgery...
I wasn't in your bathroom!
What would I even want from an old lady's medicine cabinet anyway?
Ten half-used tubes of Vagisil?
I'm going to my room!

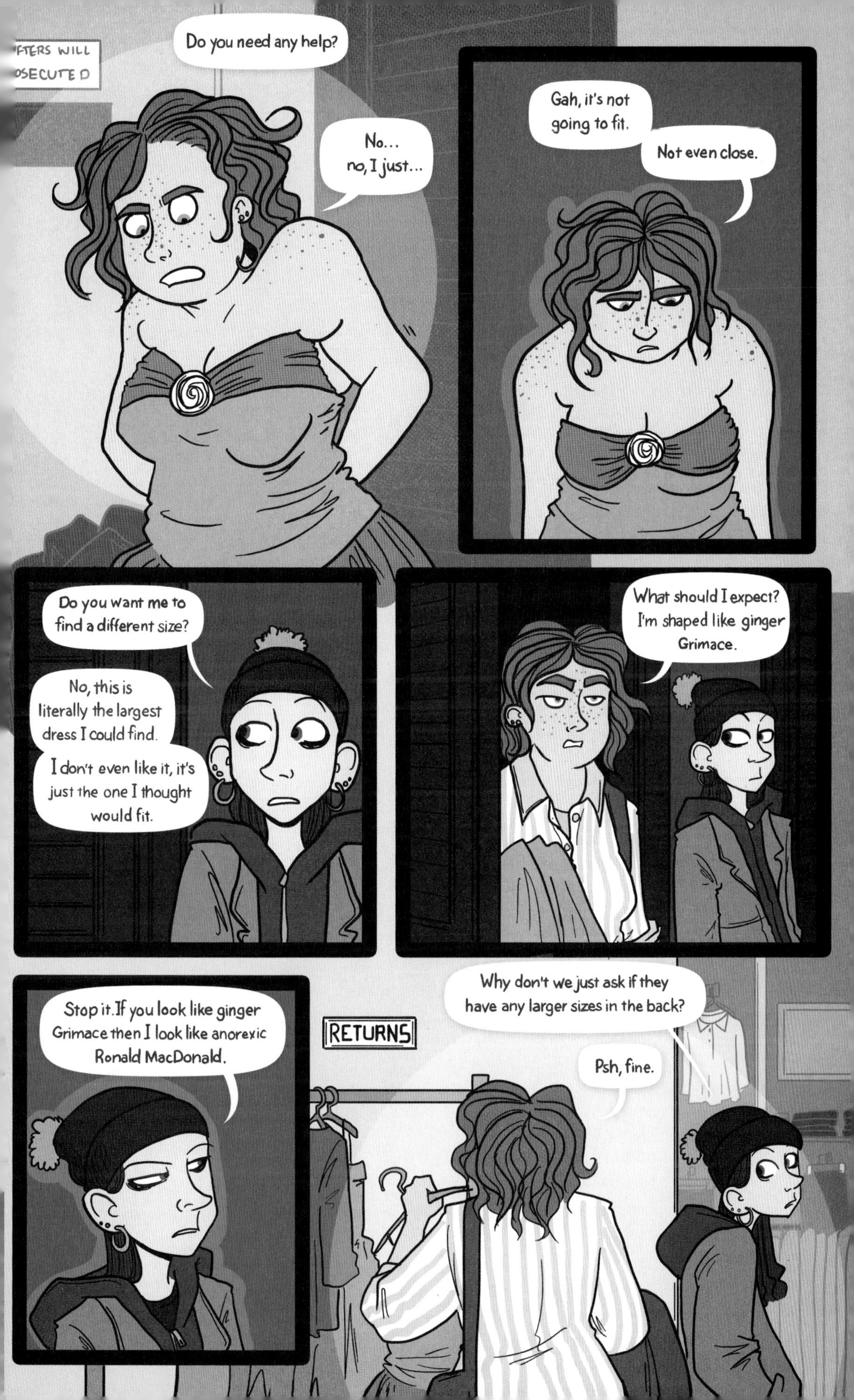
FTERS WILL
OSECUTED
Do you need any help?
No... no, I just...
Gah, it's not going to fit.
Not even close.
Do you want me to find a different size?
No, this is literally the largest dress I could find.
I don't even like it, it's just the one I thought would fit.
What should I expect? I'm shaped like ginger Grimace.
Stop it. If you look like ginger Grimace then I look like anorexic Ronald MacDonald.
RETURNS
Why don't we just ask if they have any larger sizes in the back?
Psh, fine.

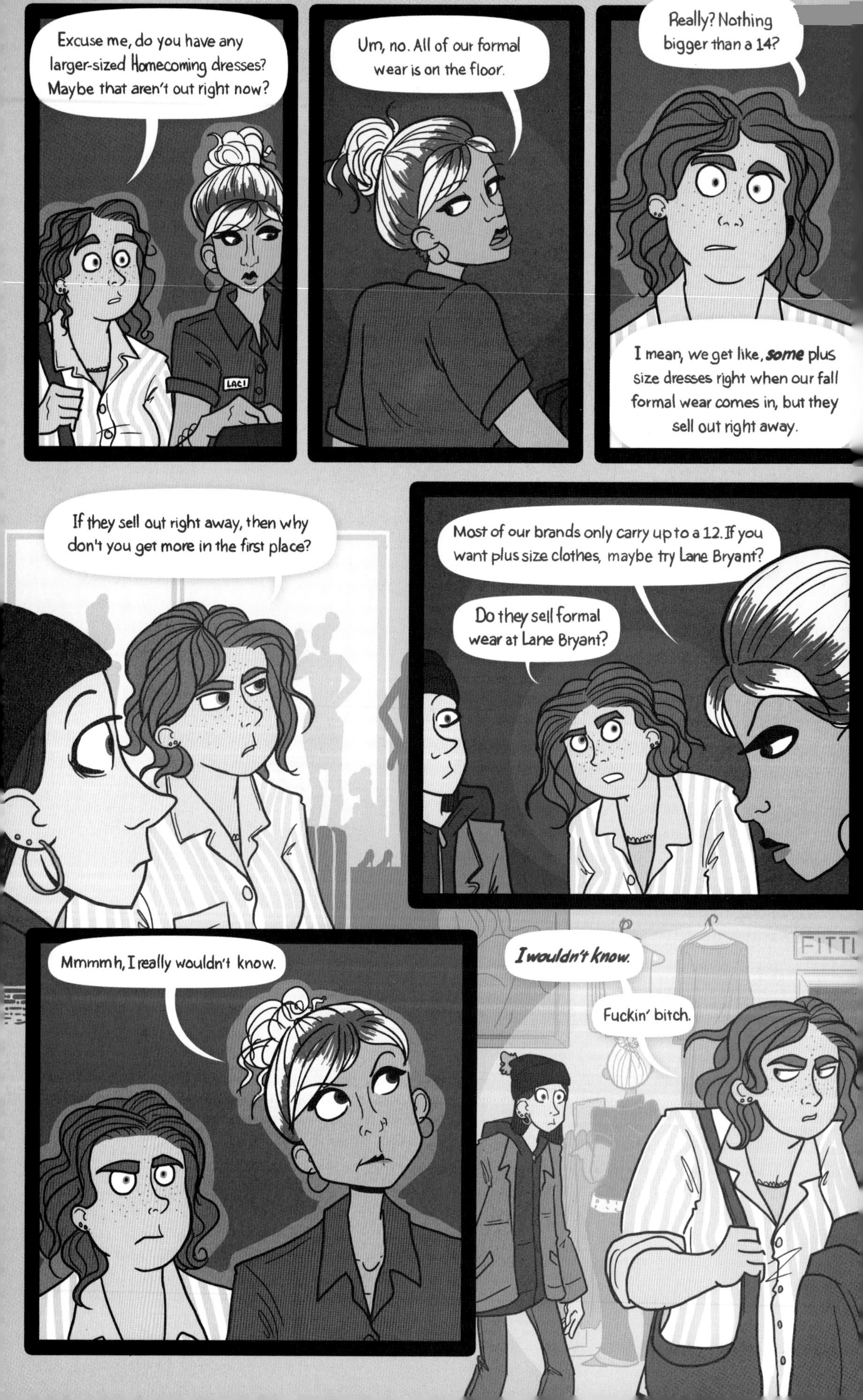
Excuse me, do you have any larger-sized Homecoming dresses? Maybe that aren't out right now?
LACI
Um, no. All of our formal wear is on the floor.
Really? Nothing bigger than a 14?
I mean, we get like, **some** plus size dresses right when our fall formal wear comes in, but they sell out right away.
If they sell out right away, then why don't you get more in the first place?
Most of our brands only carry up to a 12. If you want plus size clothes, maybe try Lane Bryant?
Do they sell formal wear at Lane Bryant?
Mmmmh, I really wouldn't know.
I wouldn't know.
Fuckin' bitch.

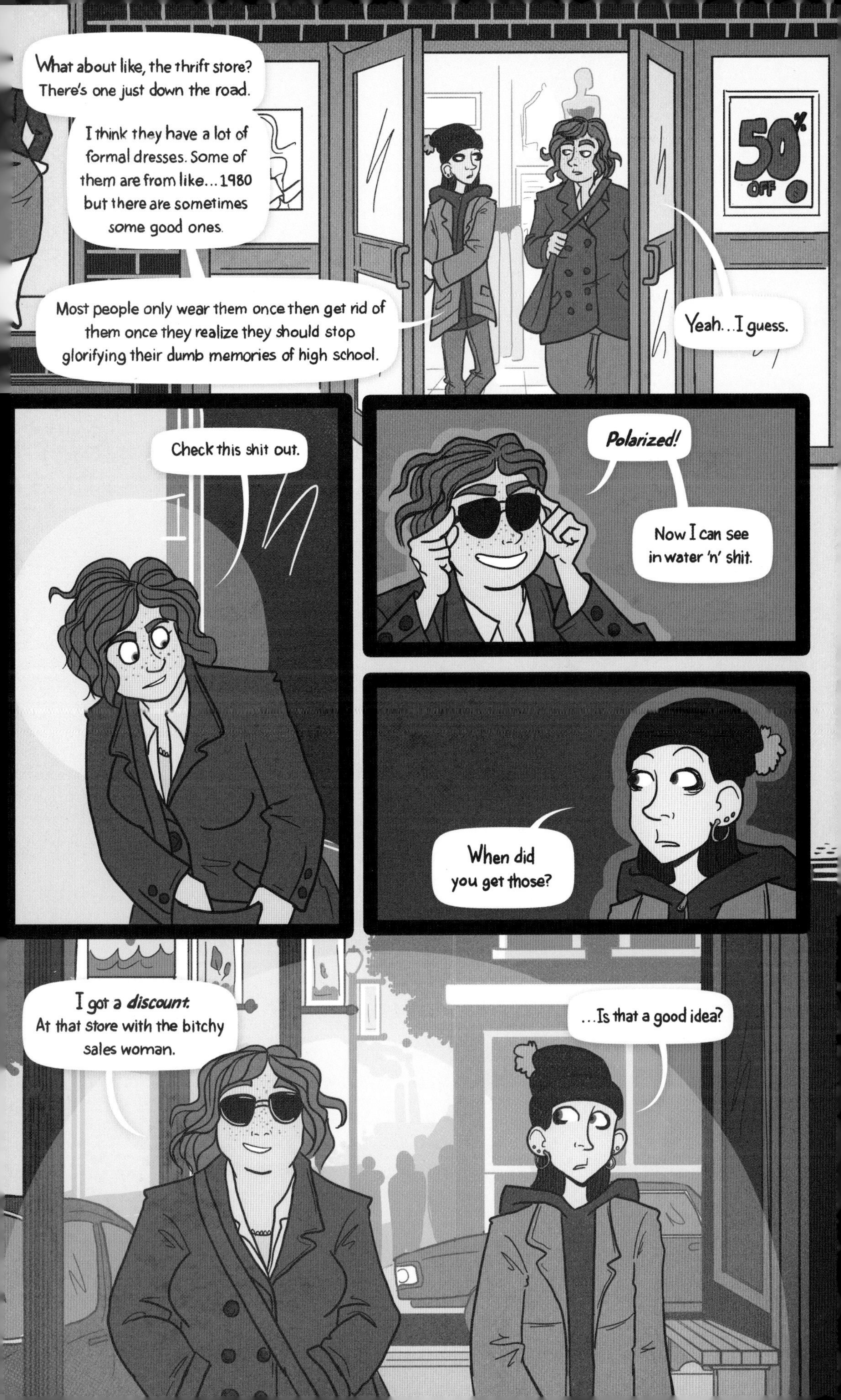
What about like, the thrift store? There's one just down the road.
I think they have a lot of formal dresses. Some of them are from like... 1980 but there are sometimes some good ones.
Most people only wear them once then get rid of them once they realize they should stop glorifying their dumb memories of high school.
50% OFF
Yeah...I guess.
Check this shit out.
Polarized!
Now I can see in water 'n' shit.
When did you get those?
I got a *discount.*
At that store with the bitchy sales woman.
...Is that a good idea?

Fuck that store!

Stupid bitchy sales people, ugly, tiny, overpriced dresses and sunglasses they think are worth $50.

Hey, do you think Jeordie and Jenna are good together?

I dunno, I guess. She seems kind of... rich and spoiled.

But maybe it works because he kind of is too.

Did he tell you he's going to have sex with her after Homecoming?

Oh my god.

You think it's a bad idea?

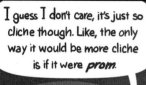

I guess I don't care, it's just so cliche though. Like, the only way it would be more cliche is if it were *prom*.

I'd be a little surprised if he actually went through with it, though.

Why?

I 'unno, he seems a little too self conscious to like...show his dick to anyone.

I mean, did you know he told me once he's never even pooped at school?

Haha!

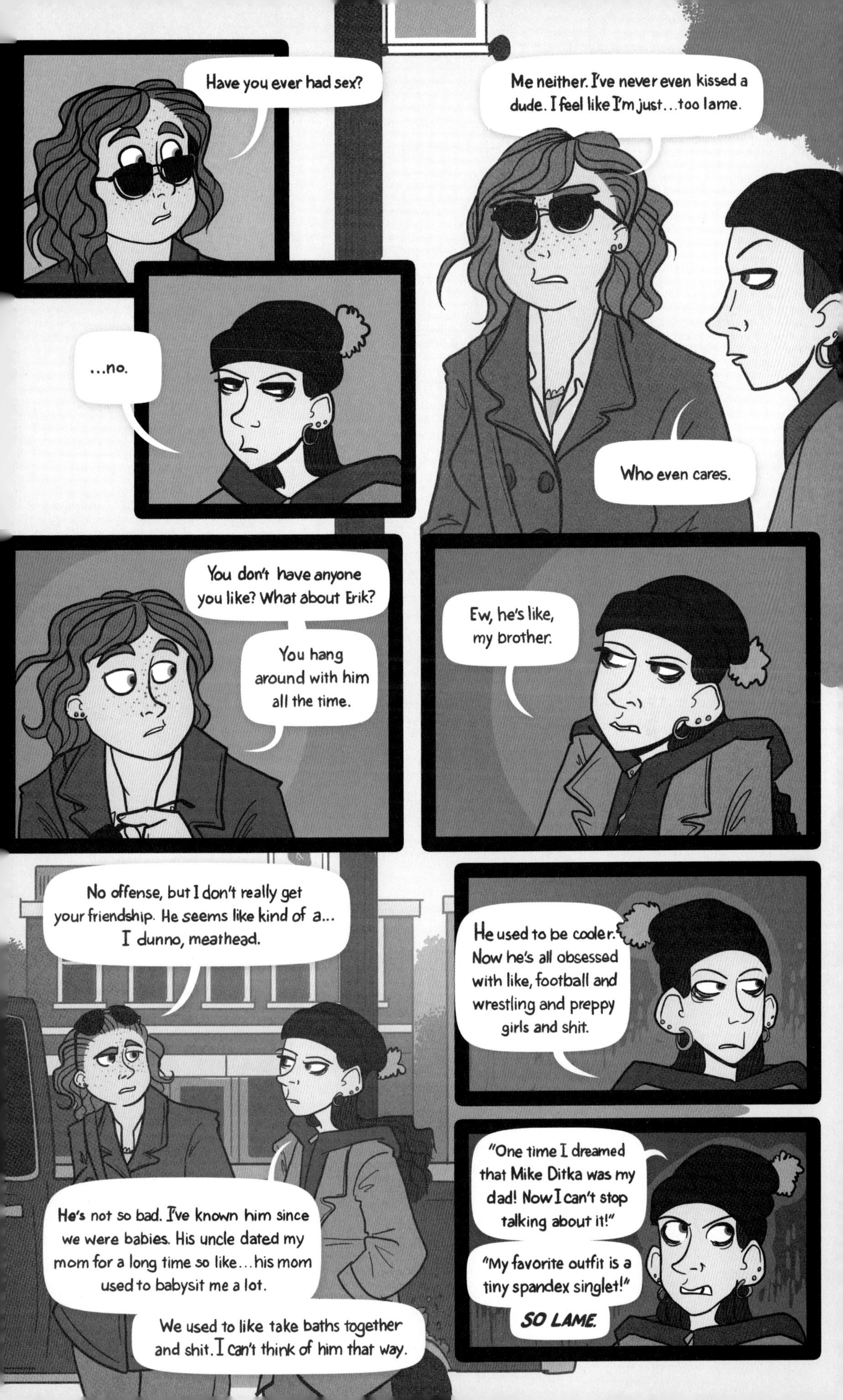
Have you ever had sex?
...no.
Me neither. I've never even kissed a dude. I feel like I'm just...too lame.
Who even cares.
You don't have anyone you like? What about Erik?
You hang around with him all the time.
Ew, he's like, my brother.
No offense, but I don't really get your friendship. He seems like kind of a... I dunno, meathead.
He's not so bad. I've known him since we were babies. His uncle dated my mom for a long time so like...his mom used to babysit me a lot.
We used to like take baths together and shit. I can't think of him that way.
He used to be cooler. Now he's all obsessed with like, football and wrestling and preppy girls and shit.
"One time I dreamed that Mike Ditka was my dad! Now I can't stop talking about it!"
"My favorite outfit is a tiny spandex singlet!"
SO LAME.

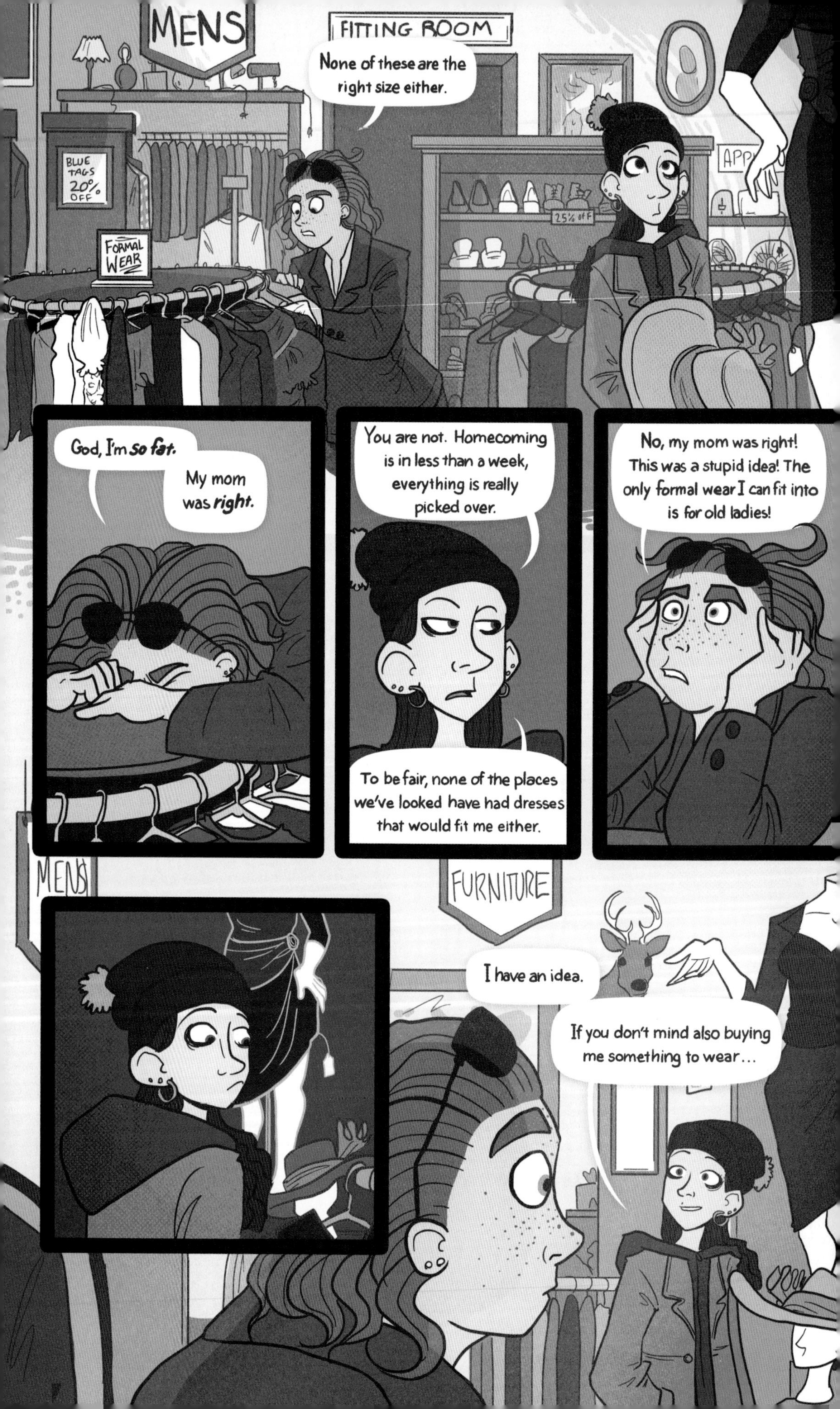
MENS
FITTING ROOM
BLUE TAGS 20% OFF
FORMAL WEAR
25% OFF
None of these are the right size either.
God, I'm *so fat.*
My mom was *right.*
You are not. Homecoming is in less than a week, everything is really picked over.
To be fair, none of the places we've looked have had dresses that would fit me either.
No, my mom was right! This was a stupid idea! The only formal wear I can fit into is for old ladies!
MENS
FURNITURE
I have an idea.
If you don't mind also buying me something to wear…

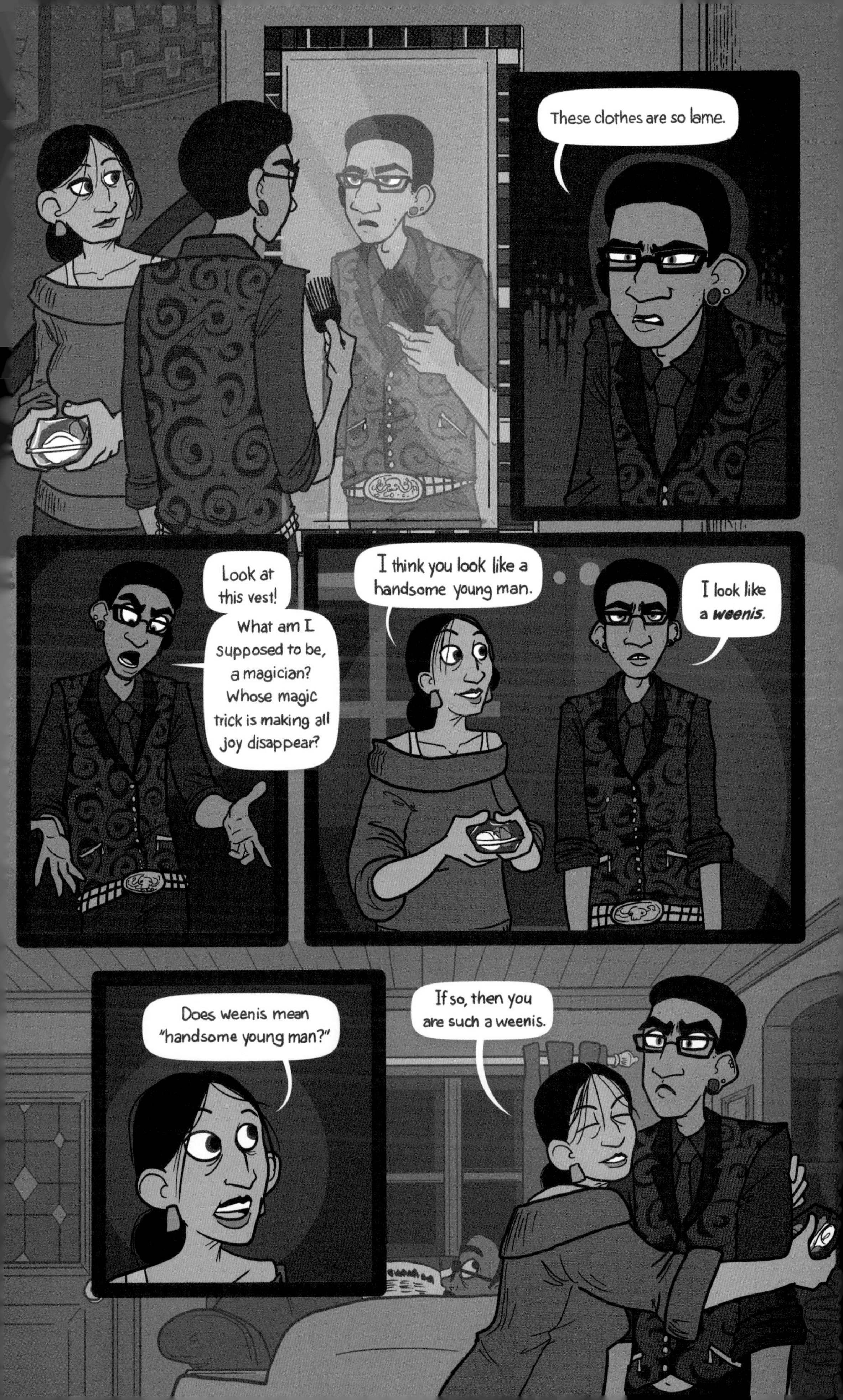
These clothes are so lame.
Look at this vest!
What am I supposed to be, a magician? Whose magic trick is making all joy disappear?
I think you look like a handsome young man.
I look like a ***weenis.***
Does weenis mean "handsome young man?"
If so, then you are such a weenis.

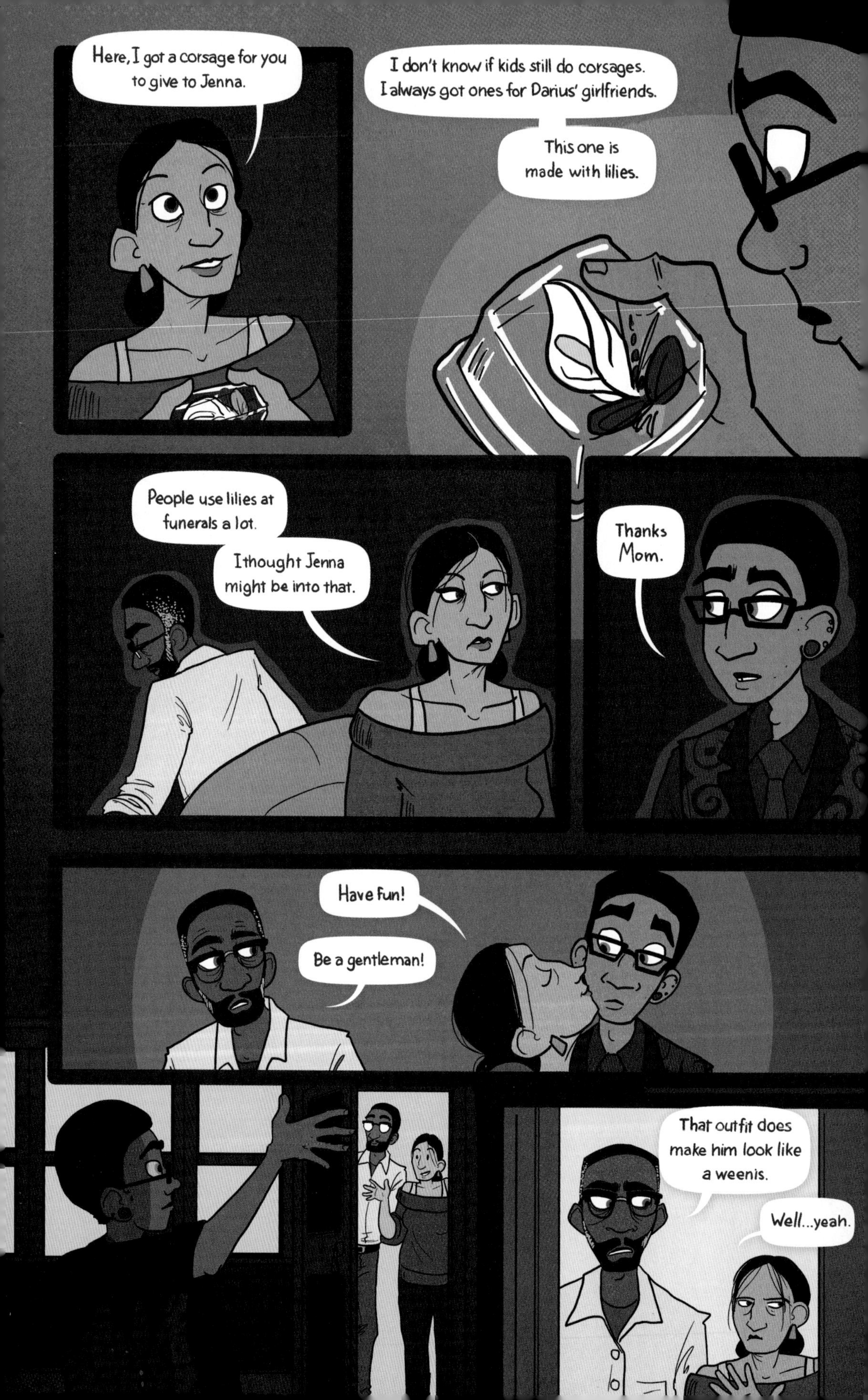
Here, I got a corsage for you to give to Jenna.
I don't know if kids still do corsages. I always got ones for Darius' girlfriends.
This one is made with lilies.
People use lilies at funerals a lot.
I thought Jenna might be into that.
Thanks Mom.
Have fun!
Be a gentleman!
That outfit does make him look like a weenis.
Well...yeah.

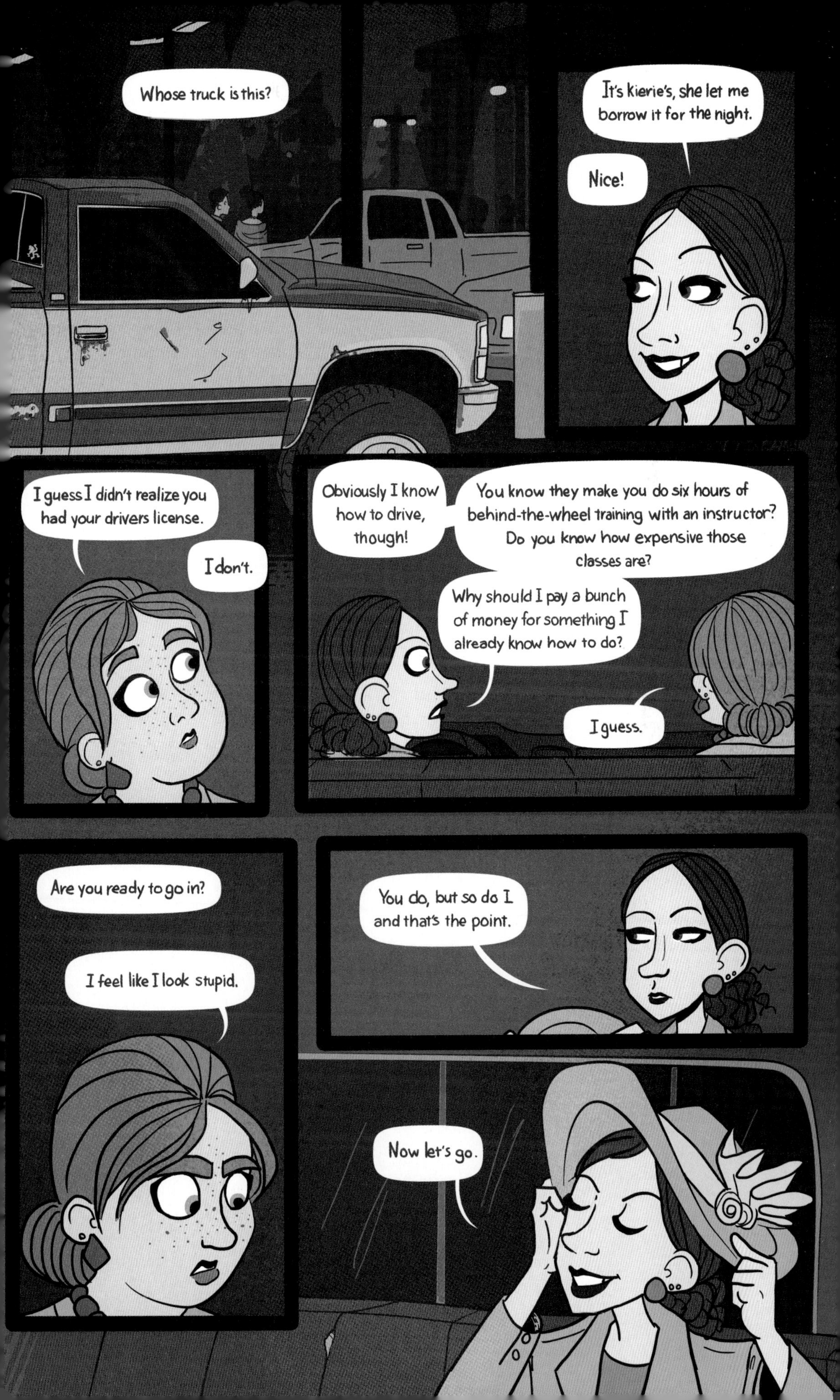

Whose truck is this?
It's Kierie's, she let me borrow it for the night.
Nice!
I guess I didn't realize you had your drivers license.
I don't.
Obviously I know how to drive, though!
You know they make you do six hours of behind-the-wheel training with an instructor? Do you know how expensive those classes are?
Why should I pay a bunch of money for something I already know how to do?
I guess.
Are you ready to go in?
I feel like I look stupid.
You do, but so do I and that's the point.
Now let's go.

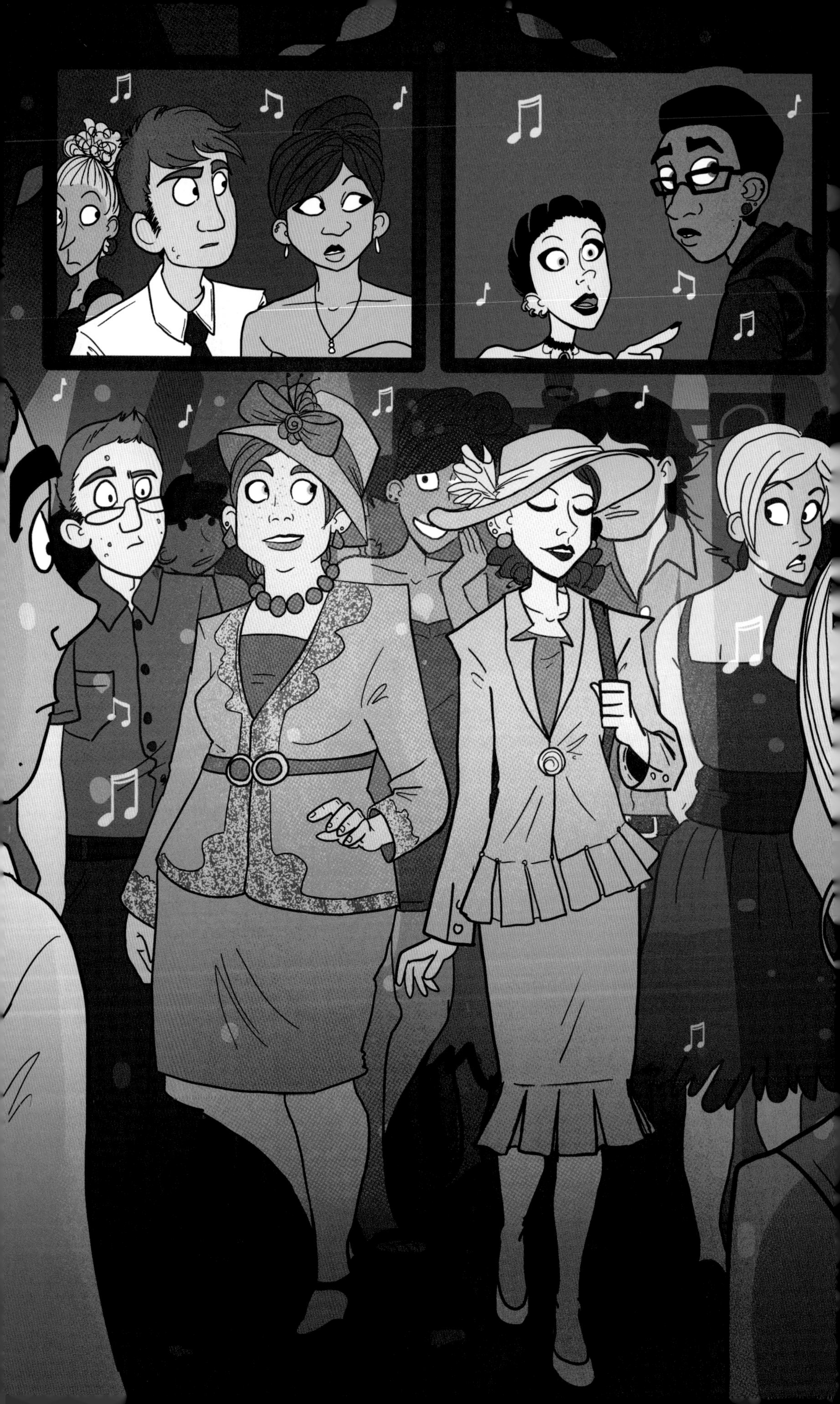

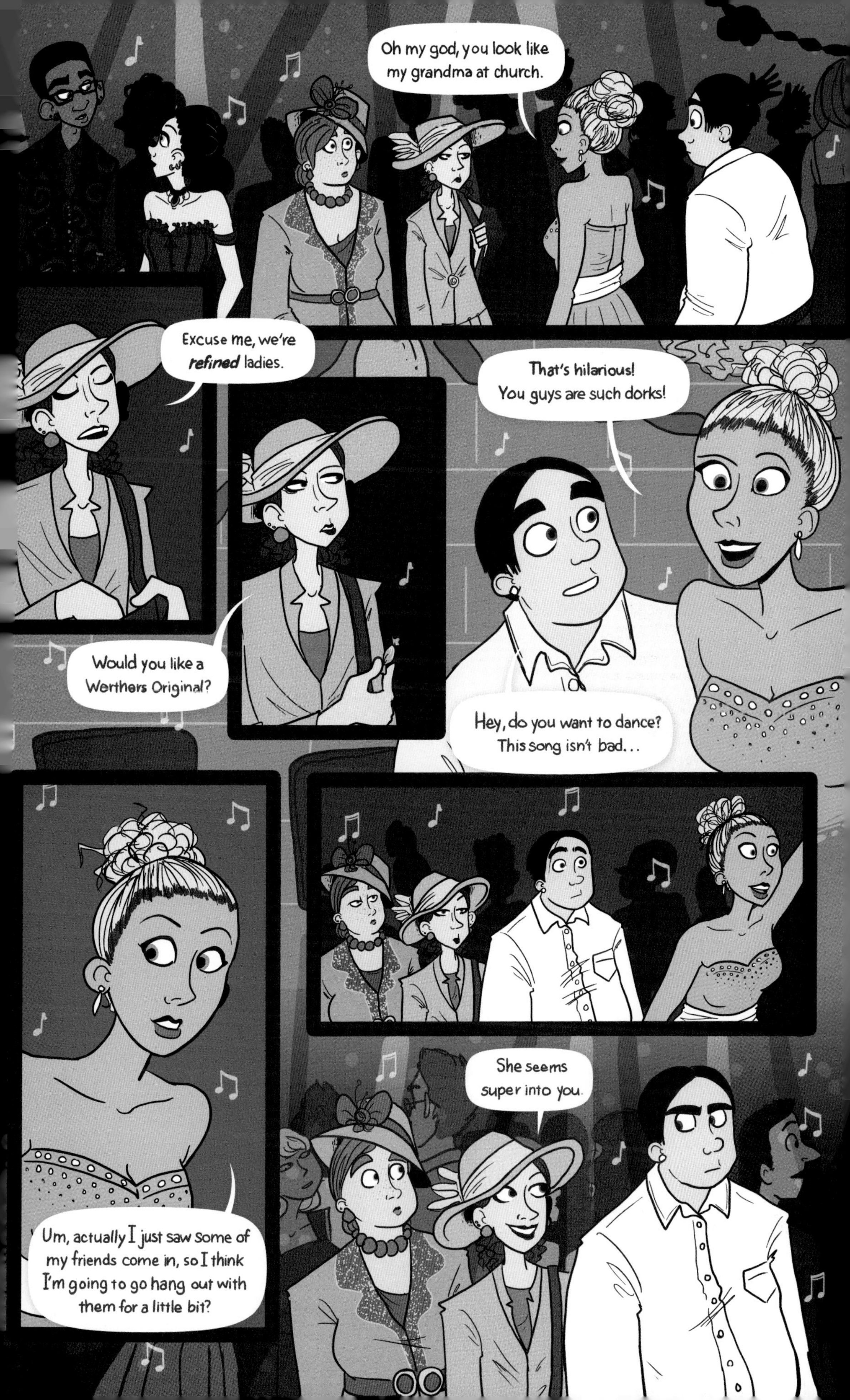

Oh my god, you look like my grandma at church.
Excuse me, we're ***refined*** ladies.
Would you like a Werthers Original?
That's hilarious! You guys are such dorks!
Hey, do you want to dance? This song isn't bad...
Um, actually I just saw some of my friends come in, so I think I'm going to go hang out with them for a little bit?
She seems super into you.

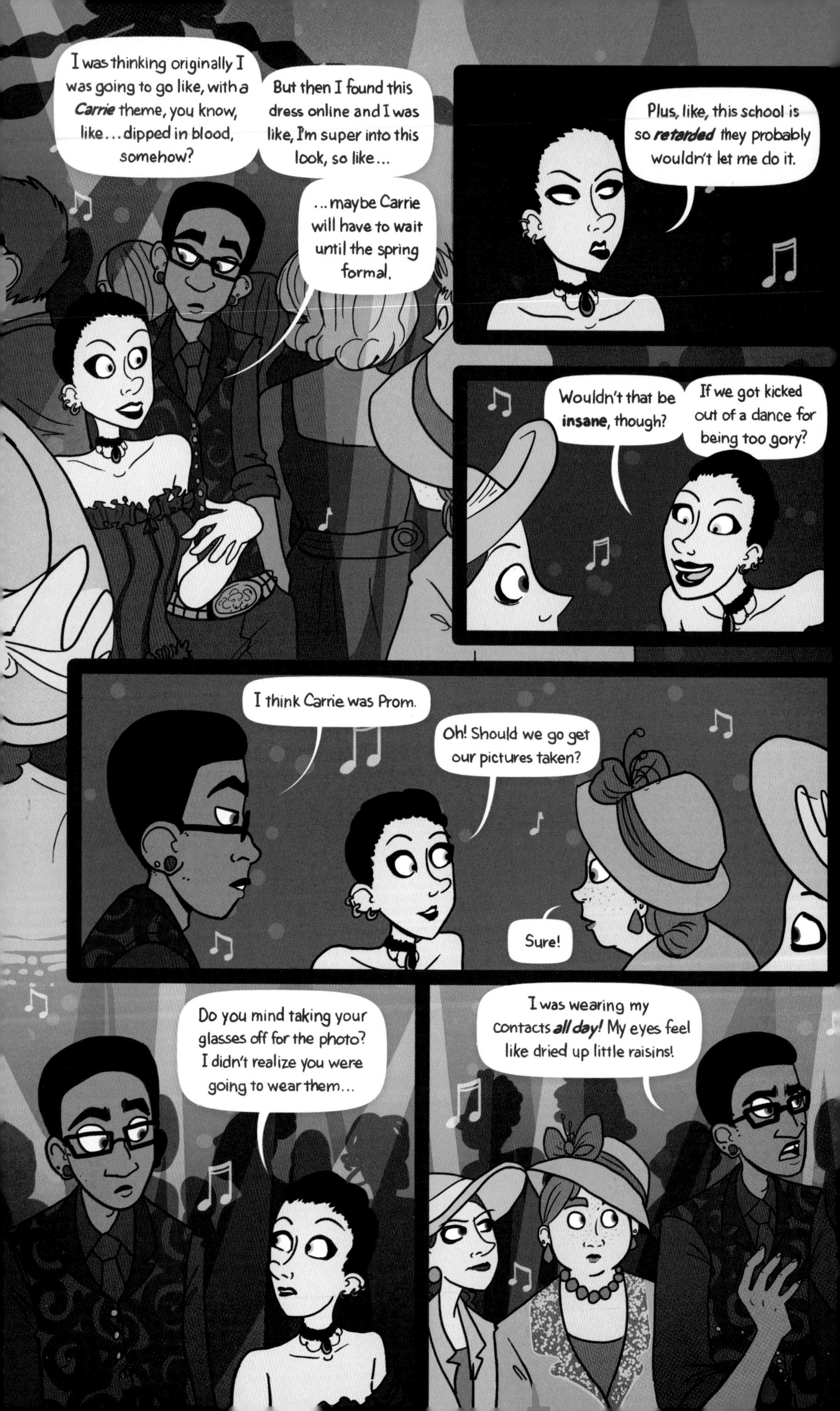
I was thinking originally I was going to go like, with a *Carrie* theme, you know, like... dipped in blood, somehow?
But then I found this dress online and I was like, I'm super into this look, so like...
...maybe Carrie will have to wait until the spring formal.
Plus, like, this school is so ***retarded*** they probably wouldn't let me do it.
Wouldn't that be **insane**, though?
If we got kicked out of a dance for being too gory?
I think Carrie was Prom.
Oh! Should we go get our pictures taken?
Sure!
Do you mind taking your glasses off for the photo? I didn't realize you were going to wear them...
I was wearing my contacts ***all day!*** My eyes feel like dried up little raisins!

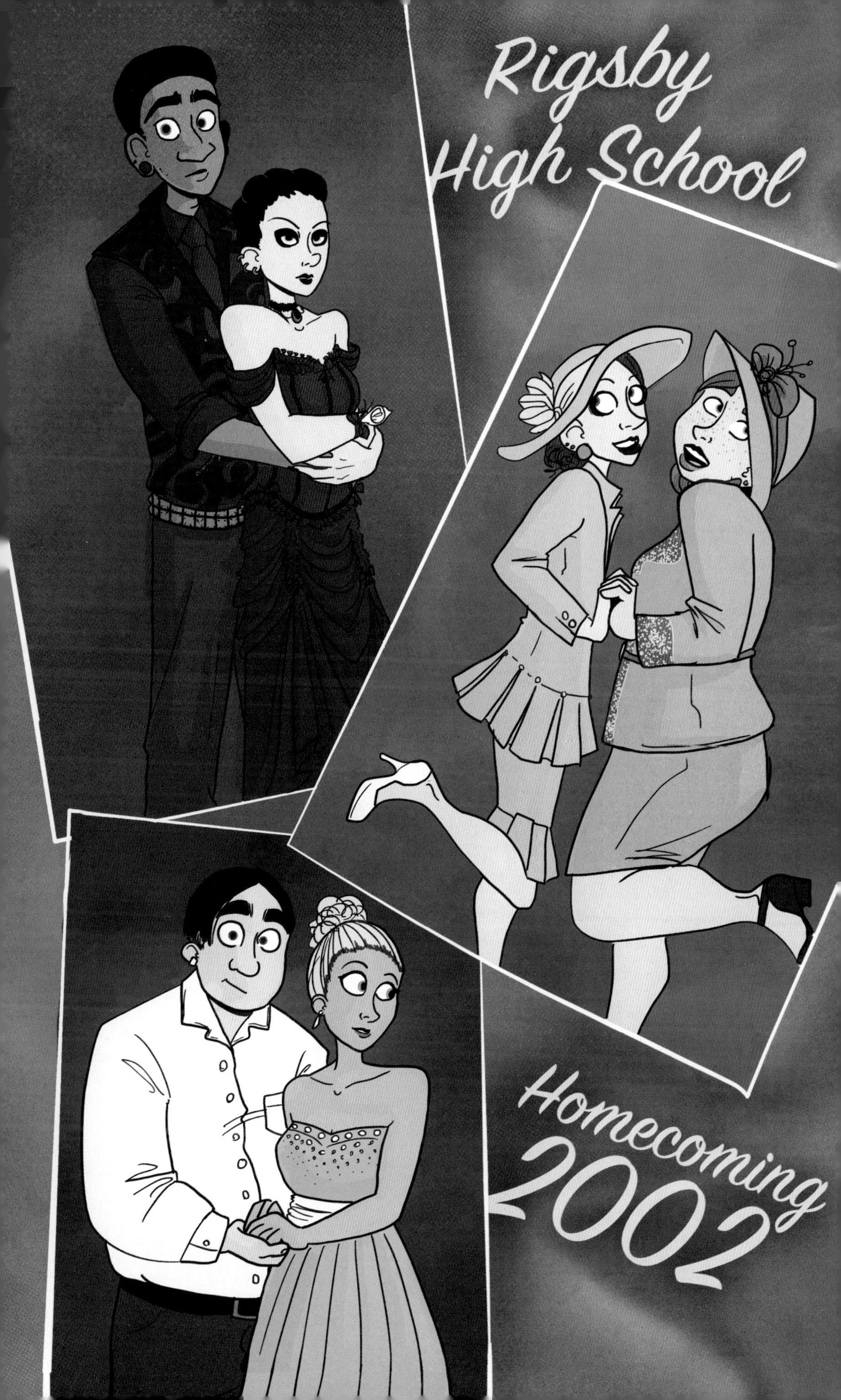
Rigsby High School
Homecoming 2002

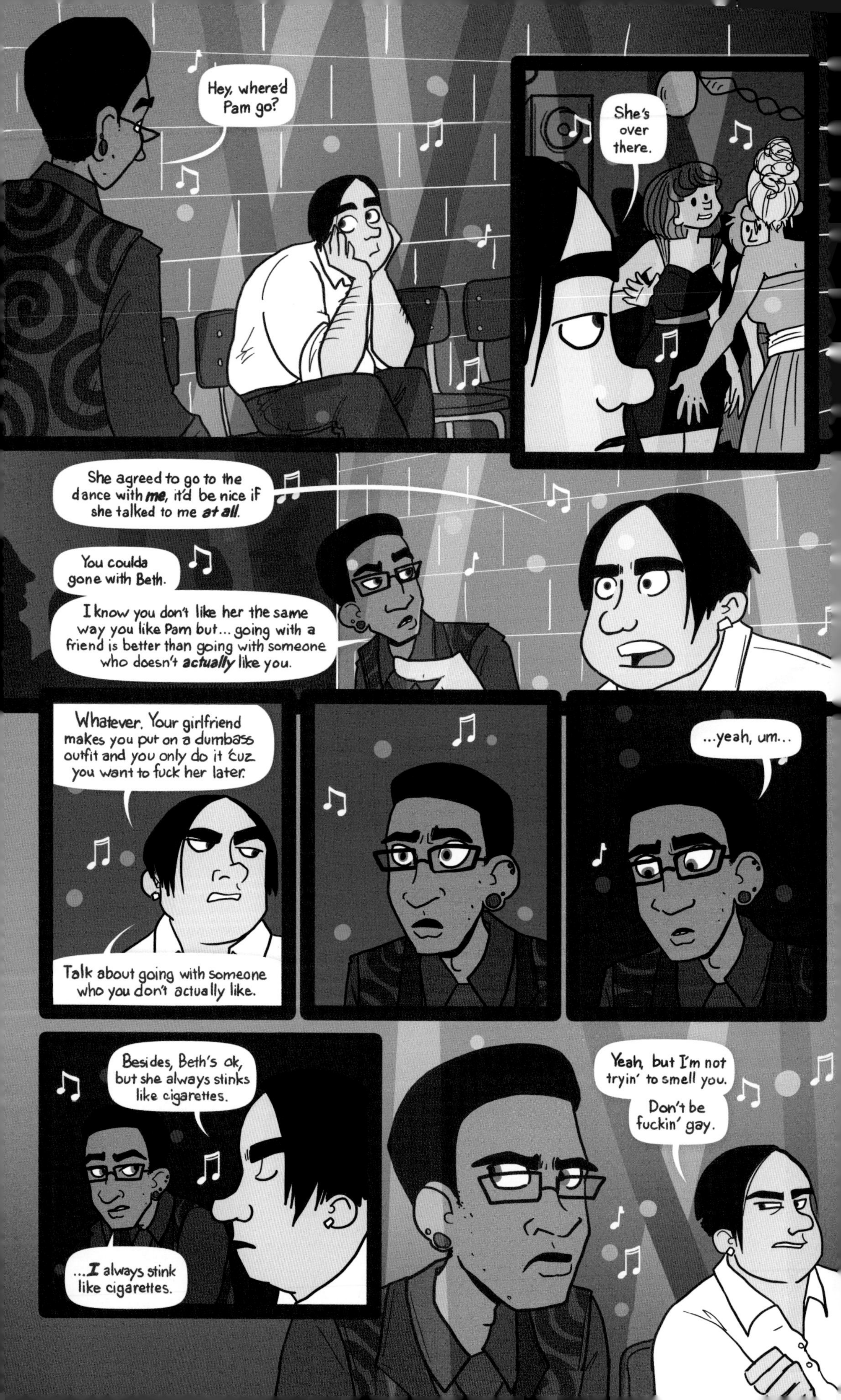
Hey, where'd Pam go?
She's over there.
She agreed to go to the dance with **me**, it'd be nice if she talked to me **at all**.
You coulda gone with Beth.
I know you don't like her the same way you like Pam but... going with a friend is better than going with someone who doesn't **actually** like you.
Whatever. Your girlfriend makes you put on a dumbass outfit and you only do it 'cuz you want to fuck her later.
Talk about going with someone who you don't actually like.
...yeah, um...
Besides, Beth's ok, but she always stinks like cigarettes.
...I always stink like cigarettes.
Yeah, but I'm not tryin' to smell you.
Don't be fuckin' gay.

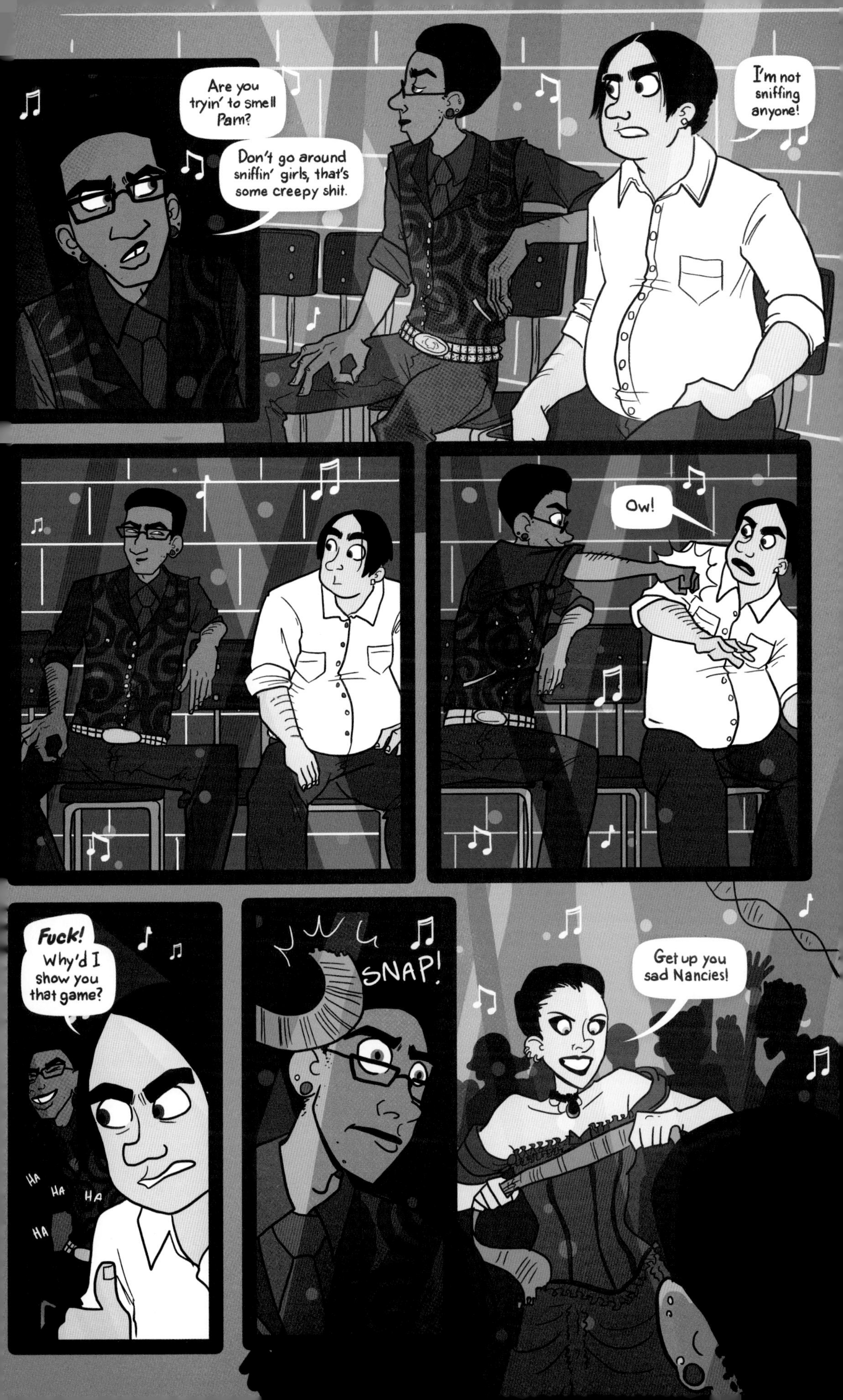

Are you tryin' to smell Pam?
Don't go around sniffin' girls, that's some creepy shit.
I'm not sniffing anyone!
Ow!
Fuck! Why'd I show you that game?
HA
HA
HA
HA
SNAP!
Get up you sad Nancies!

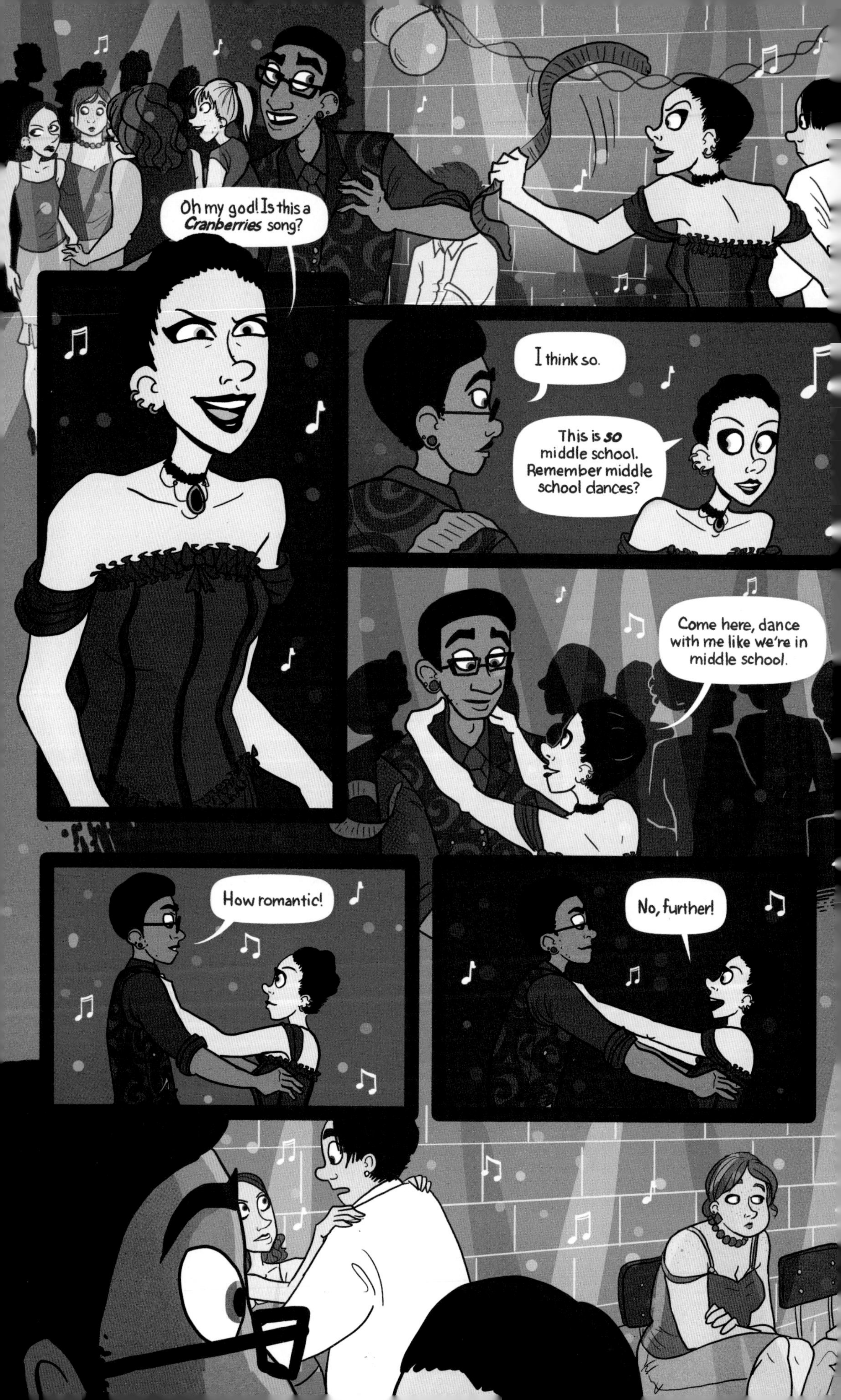
Oh my god! Is this a *Cranberries* song?
I think so.
This is *so* middle school. Remember middle school dances?
Come here, dance with me like we're in middle school.
How romantic!
No, further!

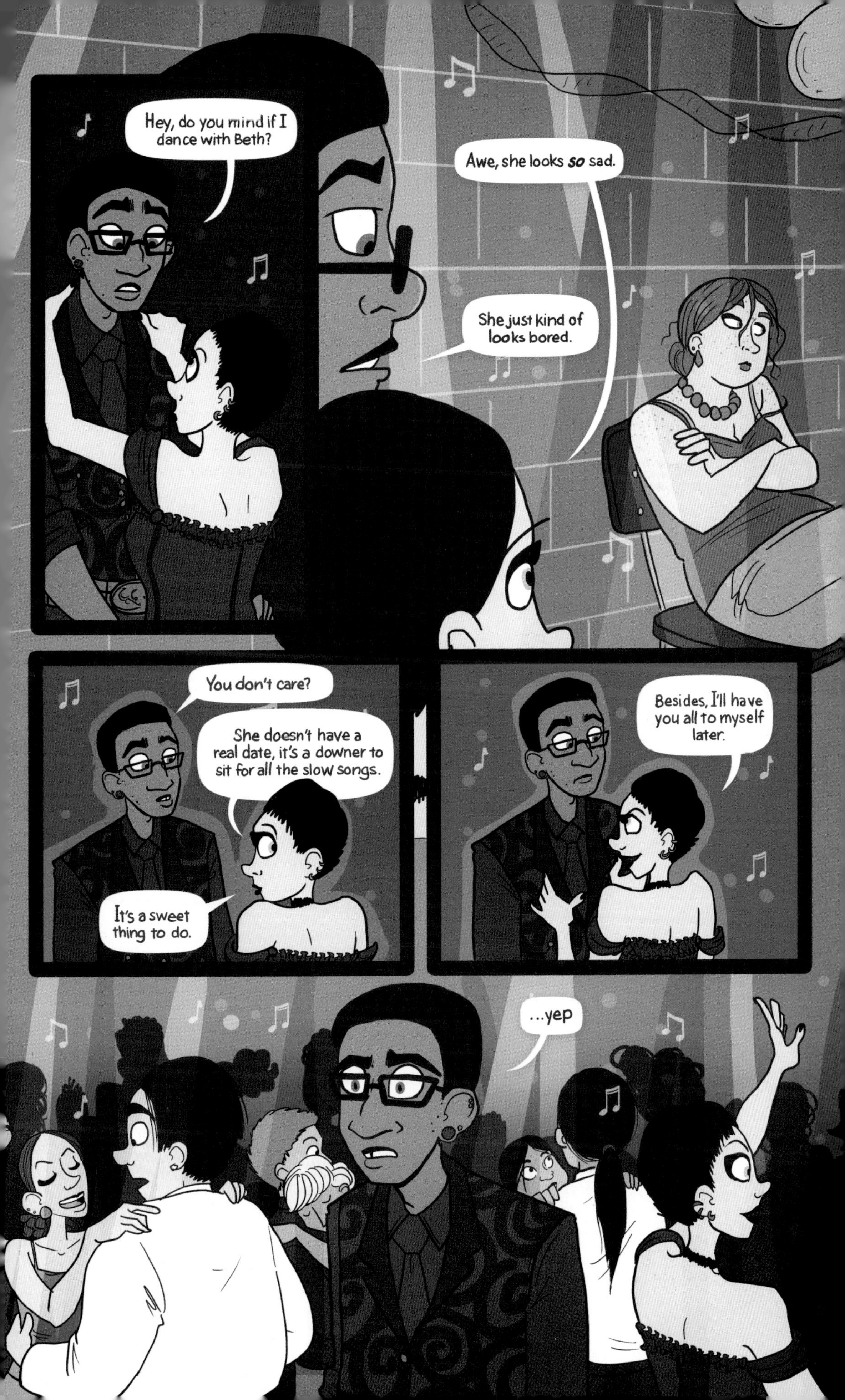
Hey, do you mind if I dance with Beth?
Awe, she looks *so* sad.
She just kind of looks bored.
You don't care?
She doesn't have a real date, it's a downer to sit for all the slow songs.
It's a sweet thing to do.
Besides, I'll have you all to myself later.
...yep

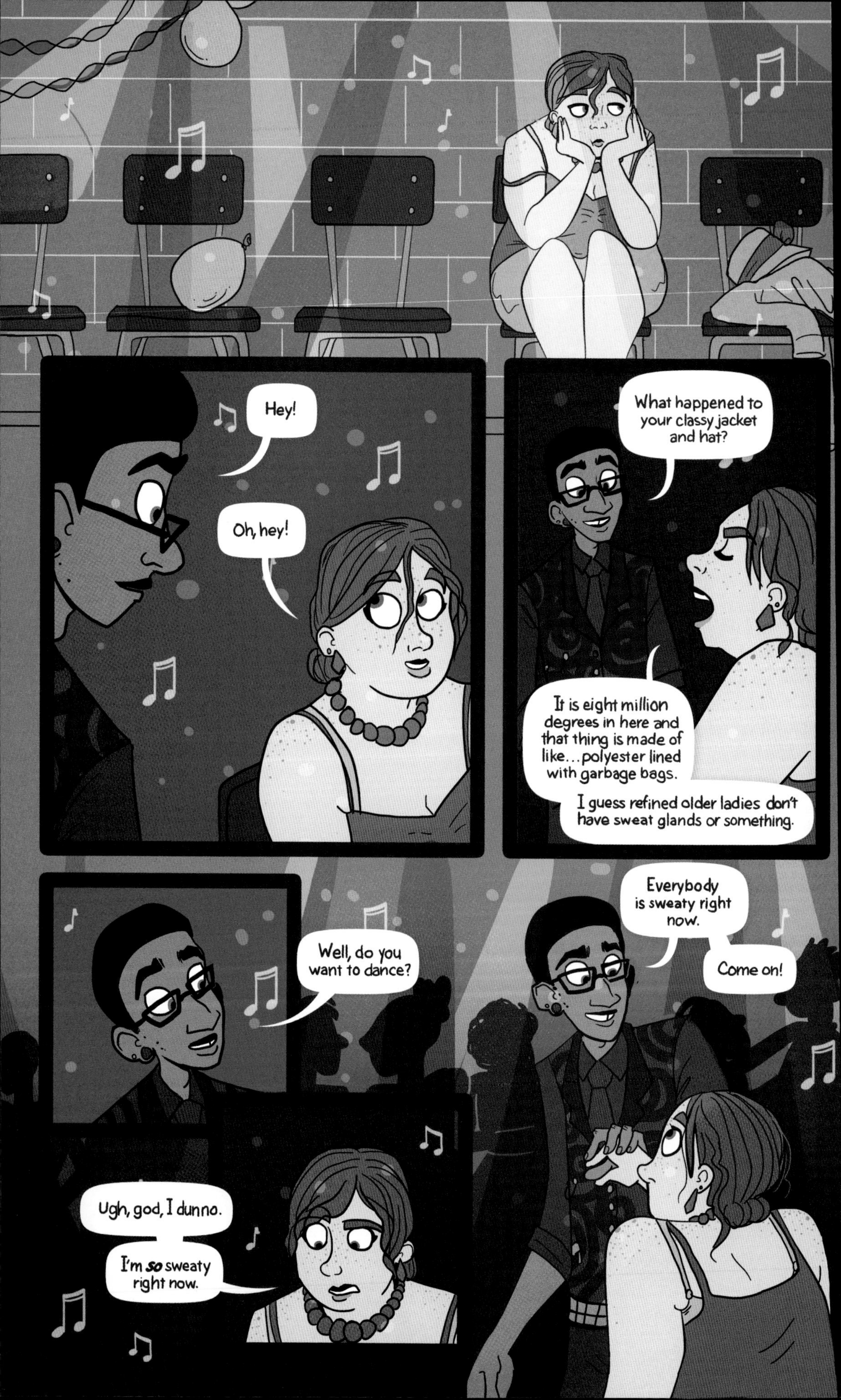
Hey!
Oh, hey!
What happened to your classy jacket and hat?
It is eight million degrees in here and that thing is made of like...polyester lined with garbage bags.
I guess refined older ladies don't have sweat glands or something.
Well, do you want to dance?
Ugh, god, I dunno.
I'm *so* sweaty right now.
Everybody is sweaty right now.
Come on!

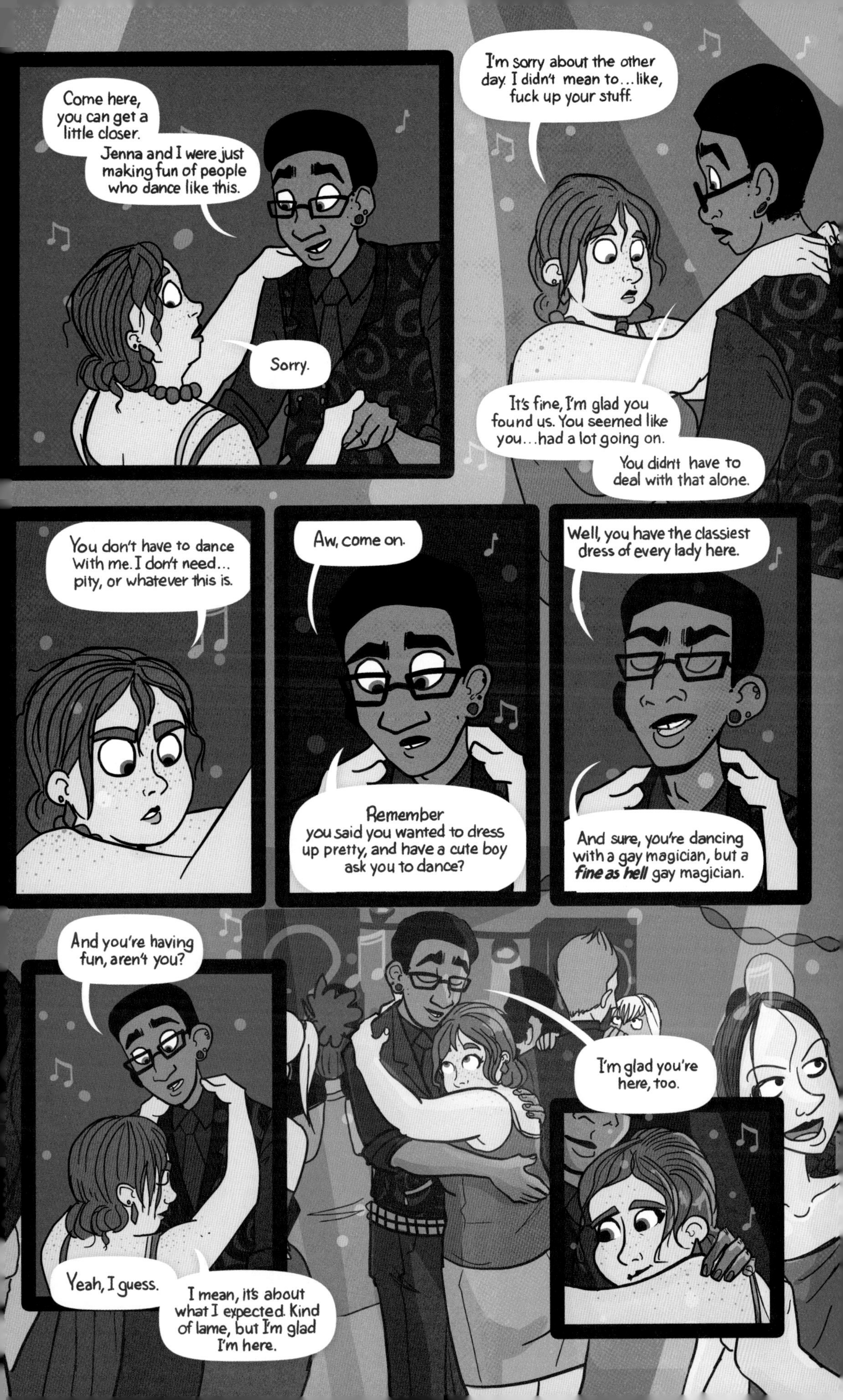

Come here, you can get a little closer.
Jenna and I were just making fun of people who dance like this.
Sorry.
I'm sorry about the other day. I didn't mean to... like, fuck up your stuff.
It's fine, I'm glad you found us. You seemed like you...had a lot going on.
You didn't have to deal with that alone.
You don't have to dance with me. I don't need... pity, or whatever this is.
Aw, come on.
Remember you said you wanted to dress up pretty, and have a cute boy ask you to dance?
Well, you have the classiest dress of every lady here.
And sure, you're dancing with a gay magician, but a *fine as hell* gay magician.
And you're having fun, aren't you?
Yeah, I guess.
I mean, it's about what I expected. Kind of lame, but I'm glad I'm here.
I'm glad you're here, too.

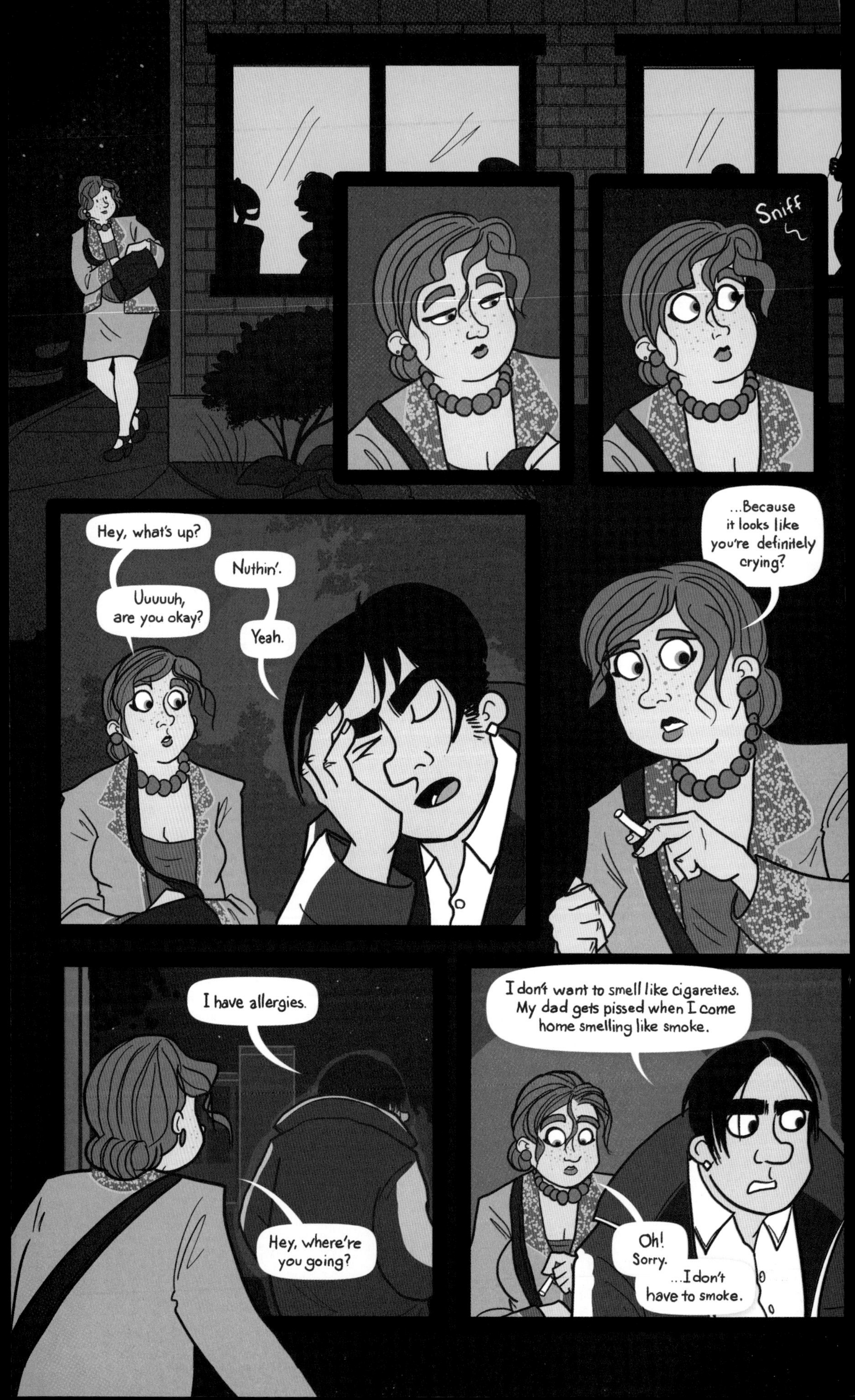
Sniff
Hey, what's up?
Nuthin'.
Uuuuuh, are you okay?
Yeah.
...Because it looks like you're definitely crying?
I have allergies.
Hey, where're you going?
I don't want to smell like cigarettes. My dad gets pissed when I come home smelling like smoke.
Oh! Sorry.
...I don't have to smoke.

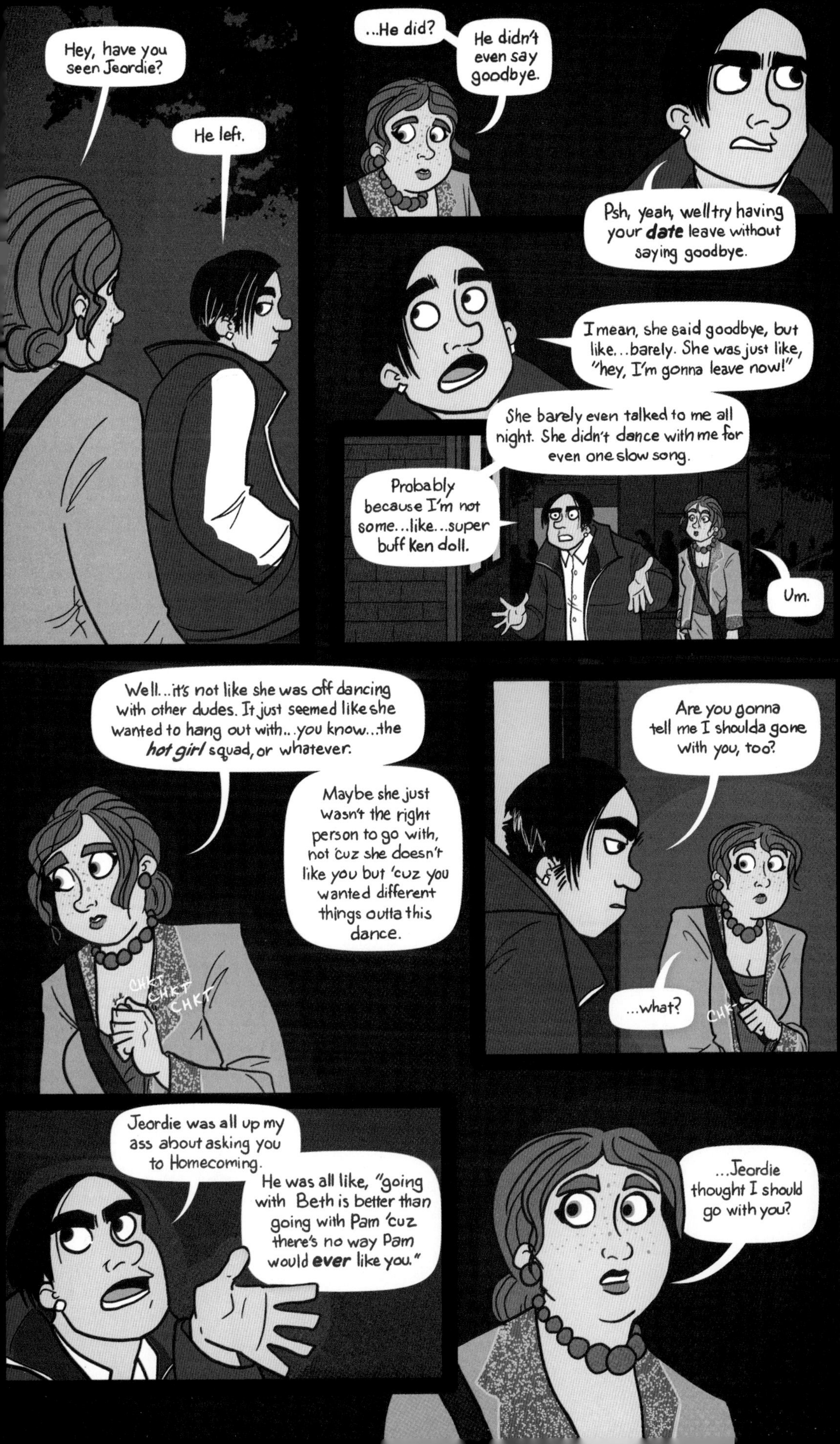
Hey, have you seen Jeordie?
He left.
...He did?
He didn't even say goodbye.
Psh, yeah, well try having your **date** leave without saying goodbye.
I mean, she said goodbye, but like...barely. She was just like, "hey, I'm gonna leave now!"
She barely even talked to me all night. She didn't dance with me for even one slow song.
Probably because I'm not some...like...super buff Ken doll.
Um.
Well...it's not like she was off dancing with other dudes. It just seemed like she wanted to hang out with...you know...the ***hot girl*** squad, or whatever.
Maybe she just wasn't the right person to go with, not 'cuz she doesn't like you but 'cuz you wanted different things outta this dance.
CHKT CHKT CHKT
Are you gonna tell me I shoulda gone with you, too?
...what?
Jeordie was all up my ass about asking you to Homecoming.
He was all like, "going with Beth is better than going with Pam 'cuz there's no way Pam would **ever** like you."
...Jeordie thought I should go with you?

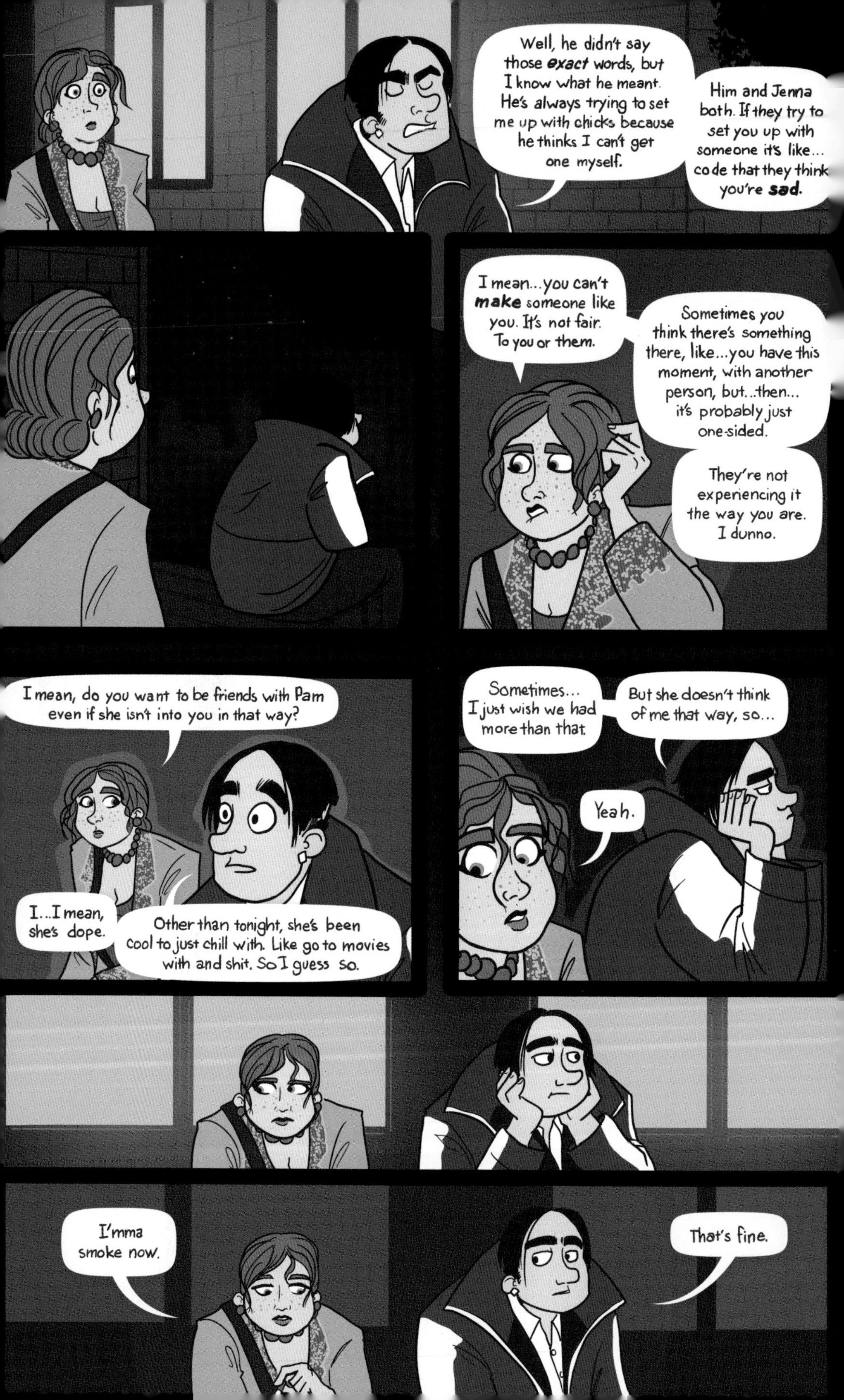
Well, he didn't say those *exact* words, but I know what he meant. He's always trying to set me up with chicks because he thinks I can't get one myself.
Him and Jenna both. If they try to set you up with someone it's like... code that they think you're **sad**.
I mean...you can't **make** someone like you. It's not fair. To you or them.
Sometimes you think there's something there, like...you have this moment, with another person, but...then... it's probably just one-sided.
They're not experiencing it the way you are. I dunno.
I mean, do you want to be friends with Pam even if she isn't into you in that way?
I...I mean, she's dope.
Other than tonight, she's been cool to just chill with. Like go to movies with and shit. So I guess so.
Sometimes... I just wish we had more than that.
But she doesn't think of me that way, so...
Yeah.
I'mma smoke now.
That's fine.

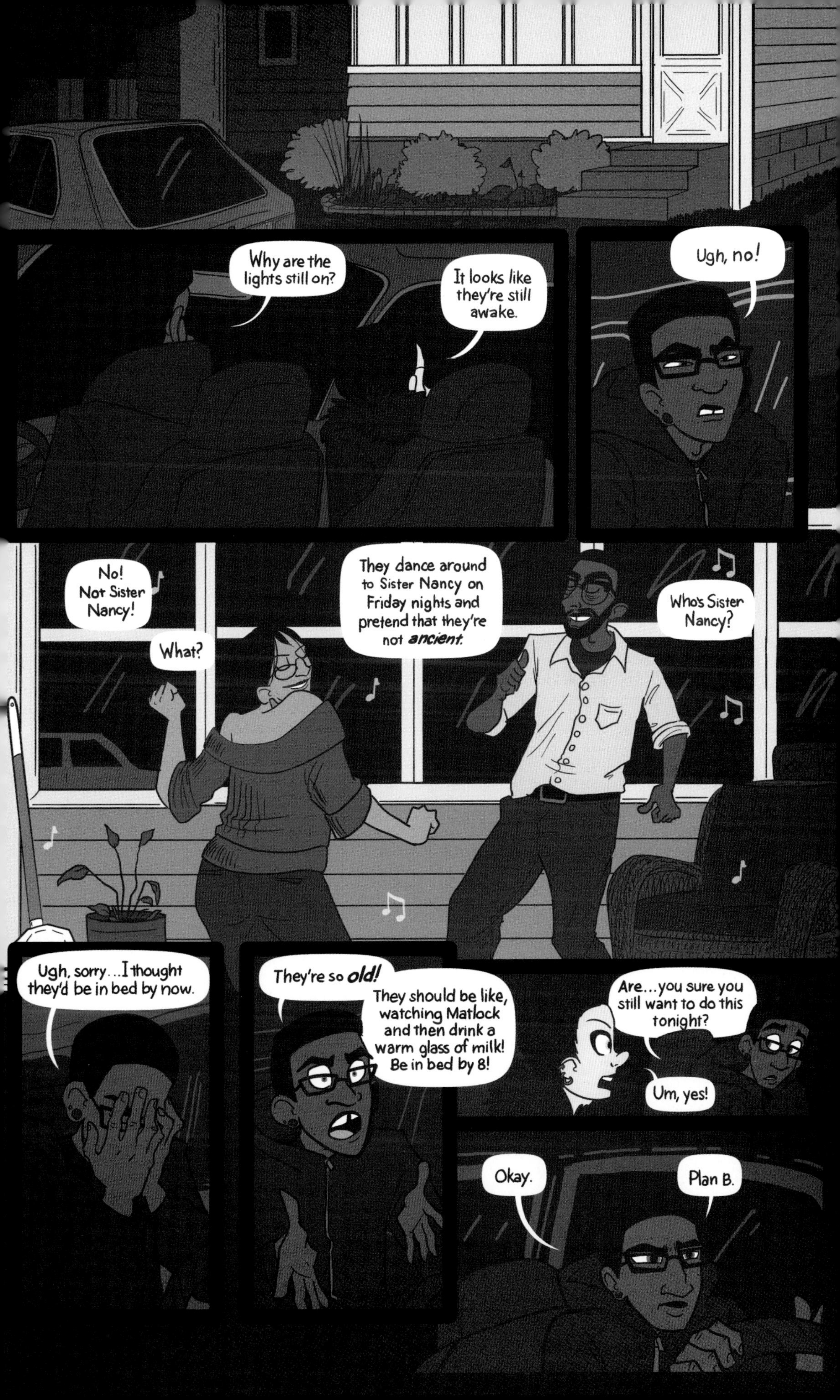

Why are the lights still on?
It looks like they're still awake.
Ugh, no!
No! Not Sister Nancy!
What?
They dance around to Sister Nancy on Friday nights and pretend that they're not *ancient*.
Who's Sister Nancy?
Ugh, sorry...I thought they'd be in bed by now.
They're so *old!*
They should be like, watching Matlock and then drink a warm glass of milk! Be in bed by 8!
Are...you sure you still want to do this tonight?
Um, yes!
Okay.
Plan B.

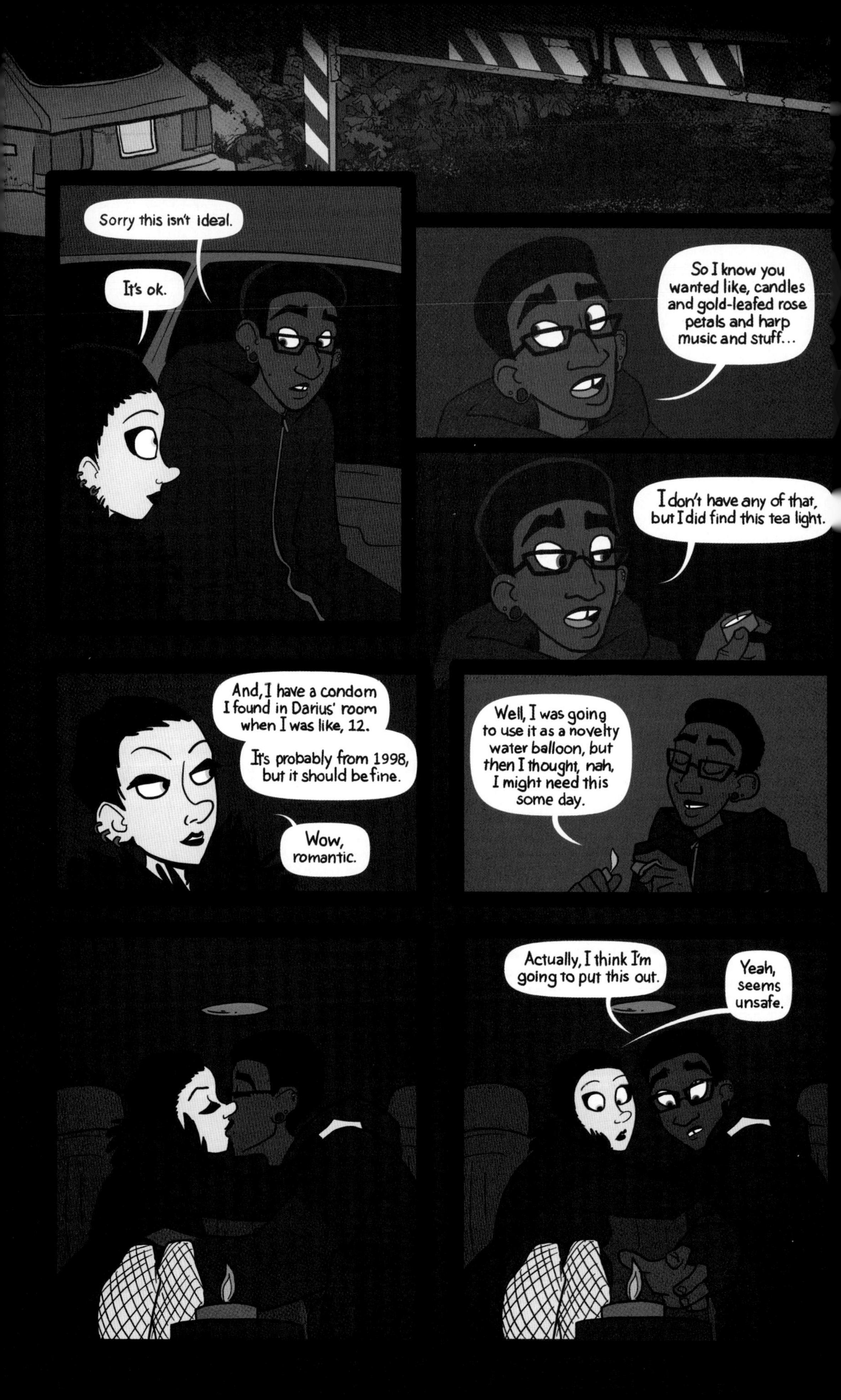
Sorry this isn't ideal.
It's ok.
So I know you wanted like, candles and gold-leafed rose petals and harp music and stuff...
I don't have any of that, but I did find this tea light.
And, I have a condom I found in Darius' room when I was like, 12.
It's probably from 1998, but it should be fine.
Wow, romantic.
Well, I was going to use it as a novelty water balloon, but then I thought, nah, I might need this some day.
Actually, I think I'm going to put this out.
Yeah, seems unsafe.

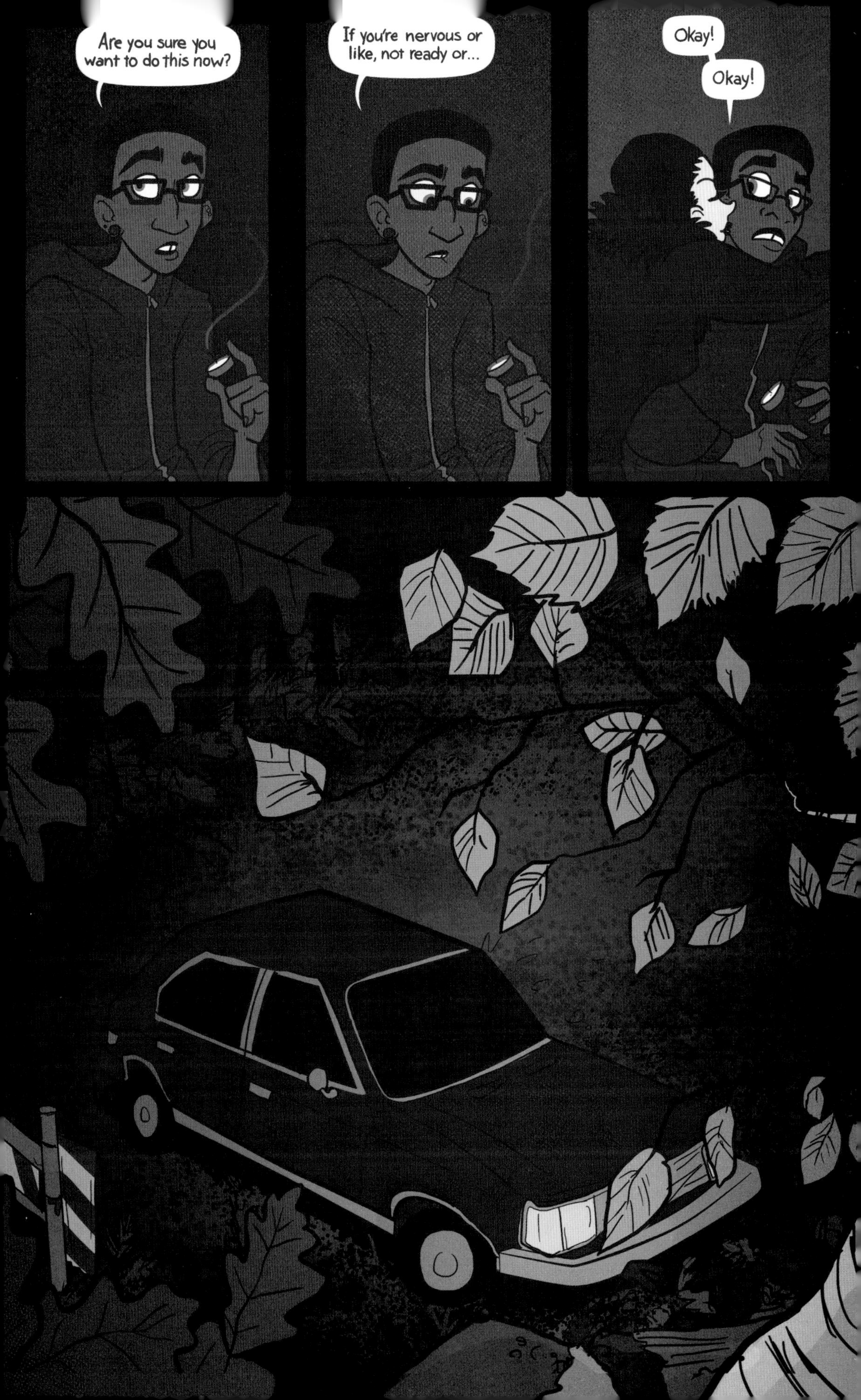
Are you sure you want to do this now?
If you're nervous or like, not ready or...
Okay!
Okay!

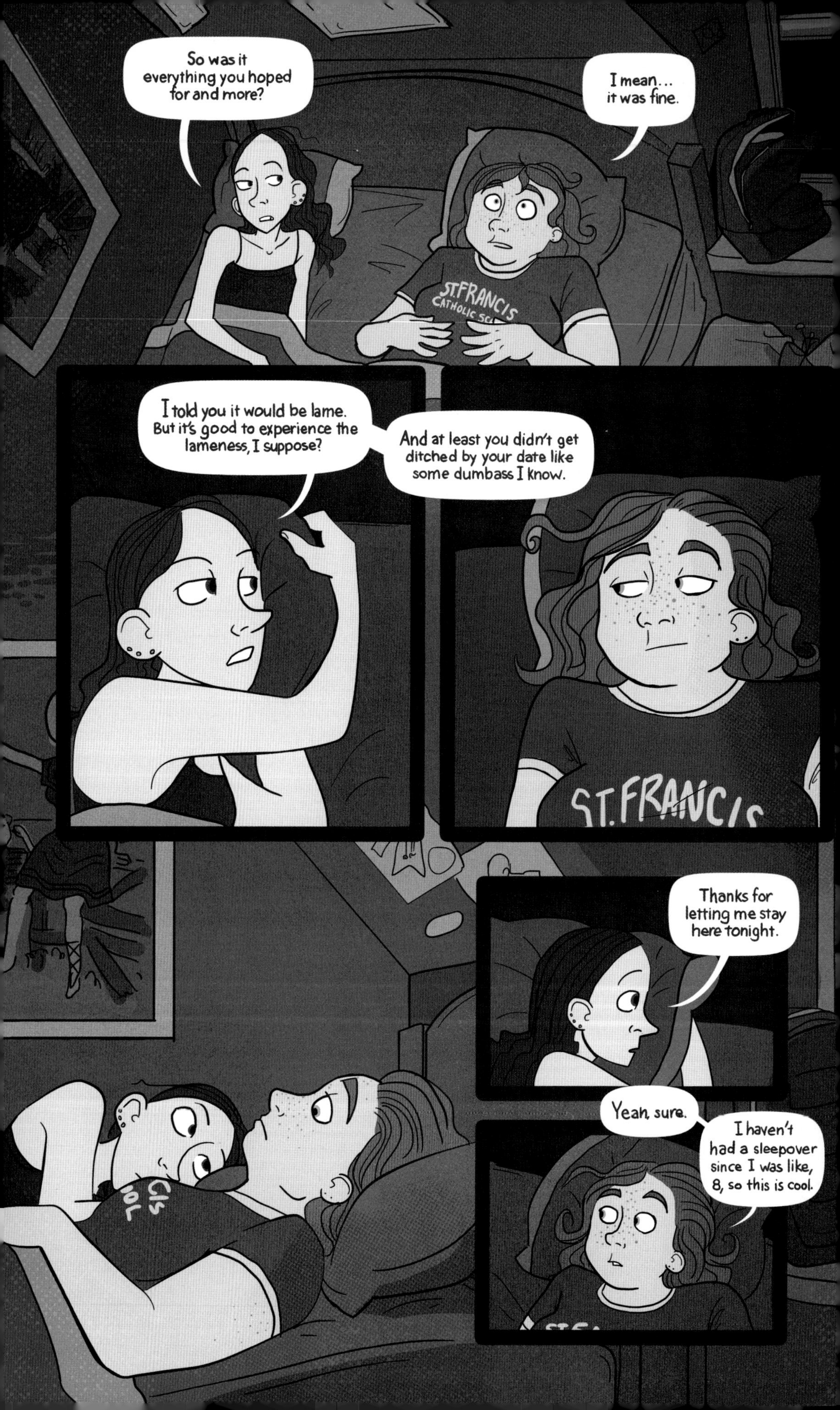
So was it everything you hoped for and more?
I mean... it was fine.
I told you it would be lame. But it's good to experience the lameness, I suppose?
And at least you didn't get ditched by your date like some dumbass I know.
ST. FRANCIS
Thanks for letting me stay here tonight.
Yeah, sure.
I haven't had a sleepover since I was like, 8, so this is cool.

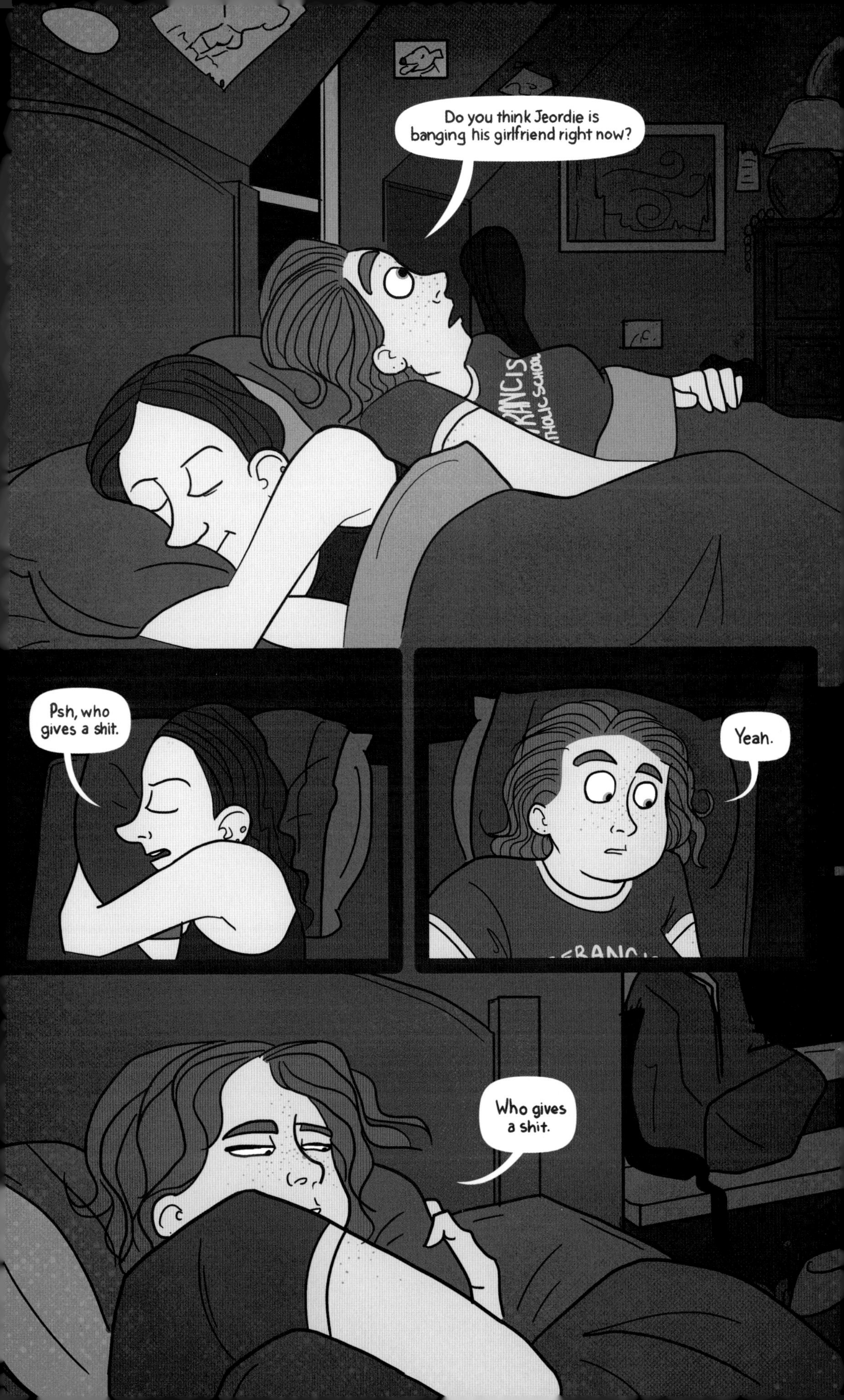
Do you think Jeordie is banging his girlfriend right now?
Psh, who gives a shit.
Yeah.
Who gives a shit.

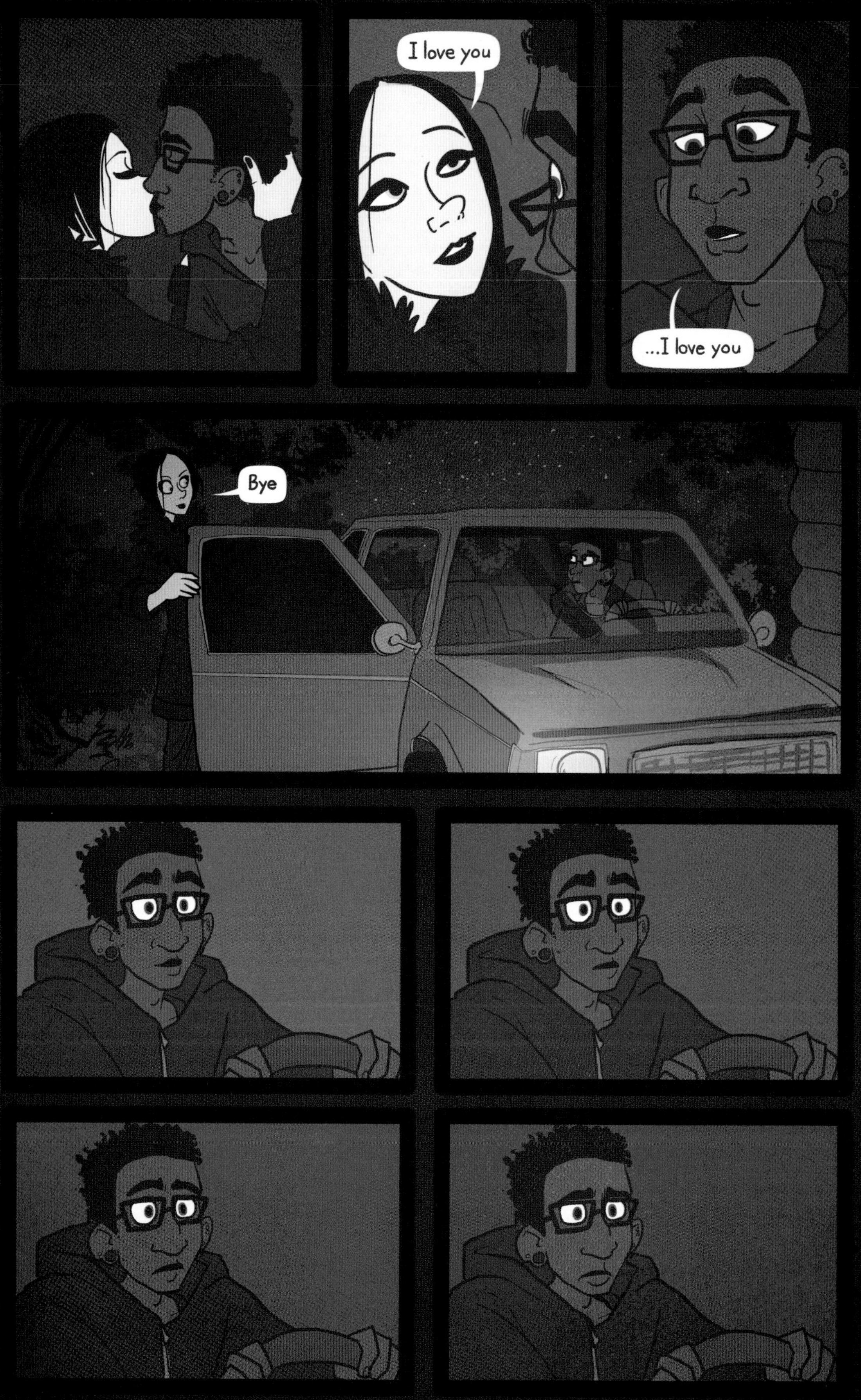
I love you
...I love you
Bye

BONUS COMICS

A SOLUTION

As the oldest girls in a very large, conservative family with emotionally detached parents, Beth and Jenny were the de facto caregivers for their younger siblings. Before she left to live with Alice, Beth bonded with her youngest siblings, twins Erin and Owen, in particular.

It is true that all babies look the same, with the exception of my baby, who has always been precious and unique. Also, I think it is possible to have identical twins that are born different sexes, but it's very rare.

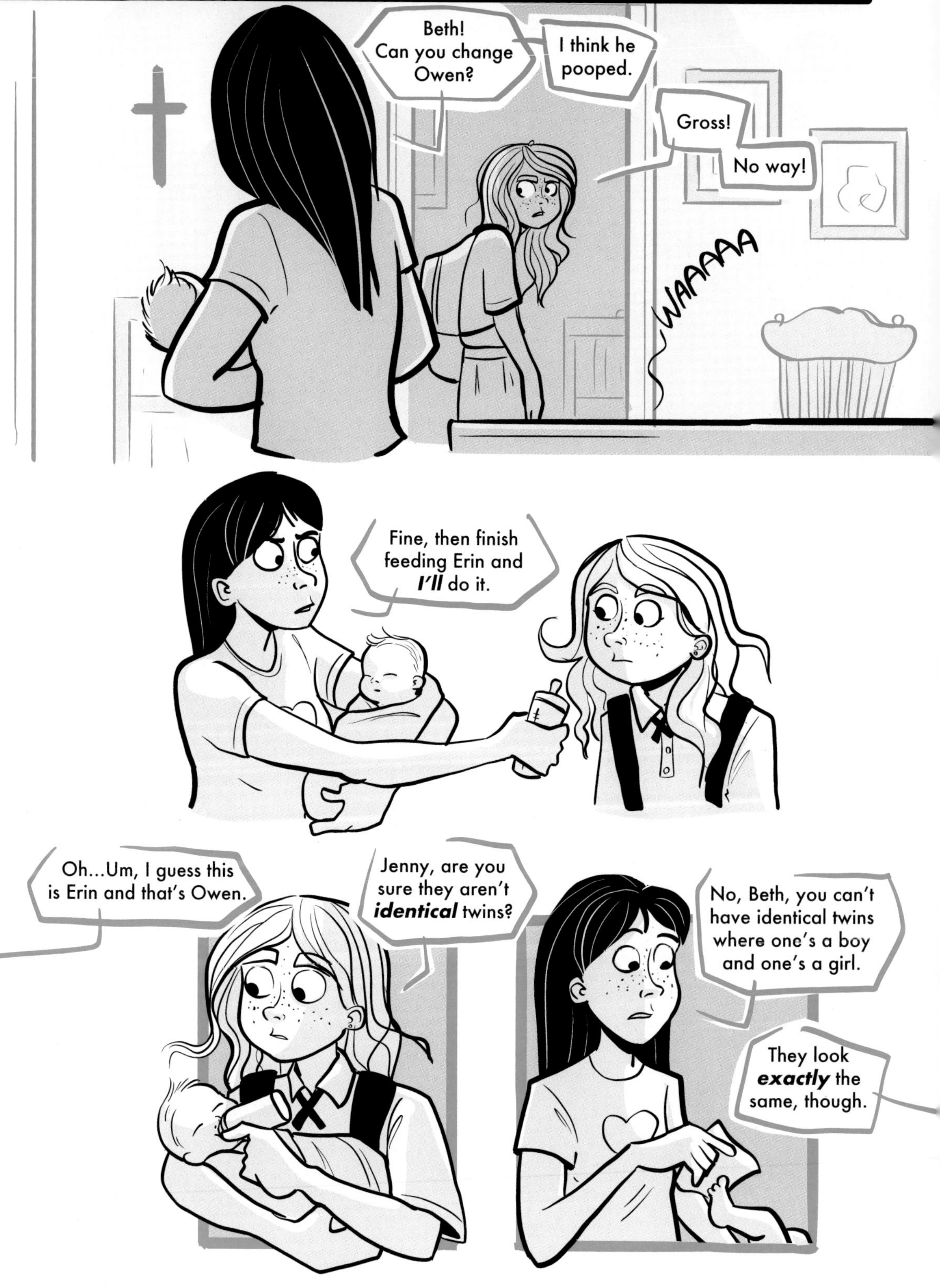
Beth! Can you change Owen?
I think he pooped.
Gross!
No way!
WAAAAA
Fine, then finish feeding Erin and ***I'll*** do it.
Oh...Um, I guess this is Erin and that's Owen.
Jenny, are you sure they aren't ***identical*** twins?
No, Beth, you can't have identical twins where one's a boy and one's a girl.
They look ***exactly*** the same, though.

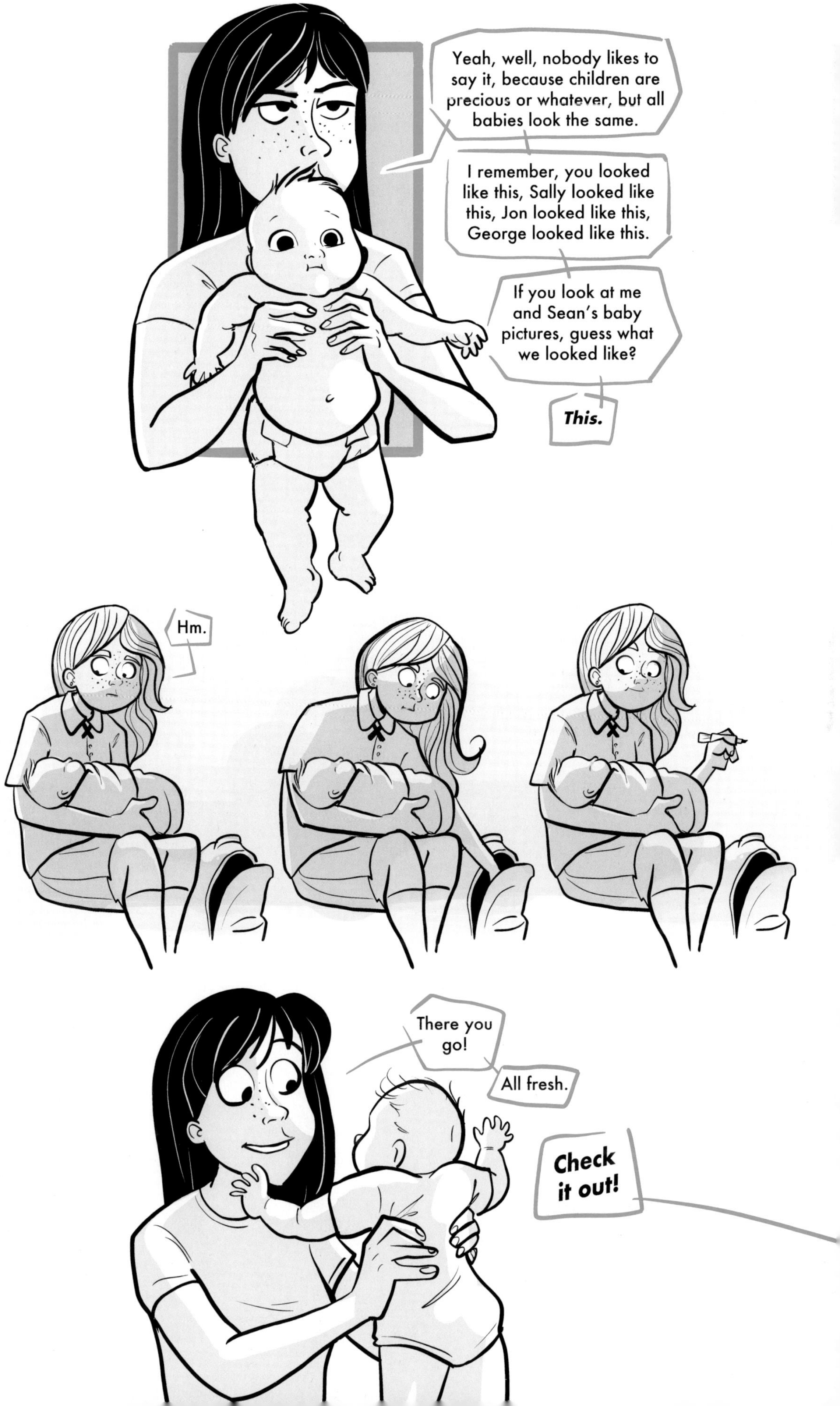
Yeah, well, nobody likes to say it, because children are precious or whatever, but all babies look the same.
I remember, you looked like this, Sally looked like this, Jon looked like this, George looked like this.
If you look at me and Sean's baby pictures, guess what we looked like?
This.
Hm.
There you go!
All fresh.
Check it out!

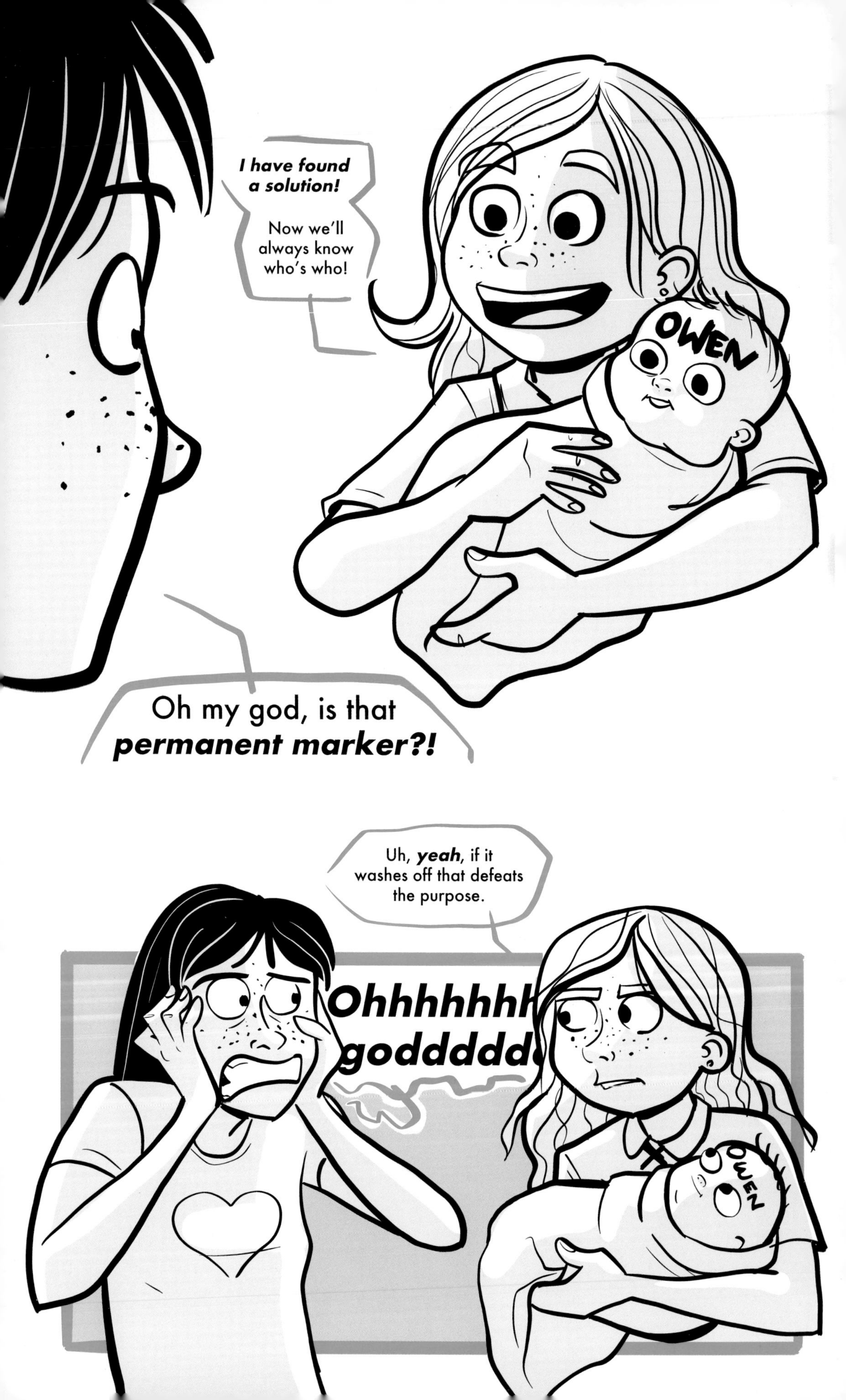
I have found a solution!
Now we'll always know who's who!
OWEN
Oh my god, is that ***permanent marker?!***
Uh, ***yeah***, if it washes off that defeats the purpose.
Ohhhhhhh goddddd
OWEN

HOBBIT TRAILS

Someone once asked how Jeordie originally asked Jenna out. I'm still foggy on how high schoolers actually "ask each other out," since I never really dated in high school, I just made out with my friends and felt varying amounts of bad about it later.

Hobbit Trails was a game a couple of my friends made up in high school, where they walked down a bike path and kicked sticks at each other.

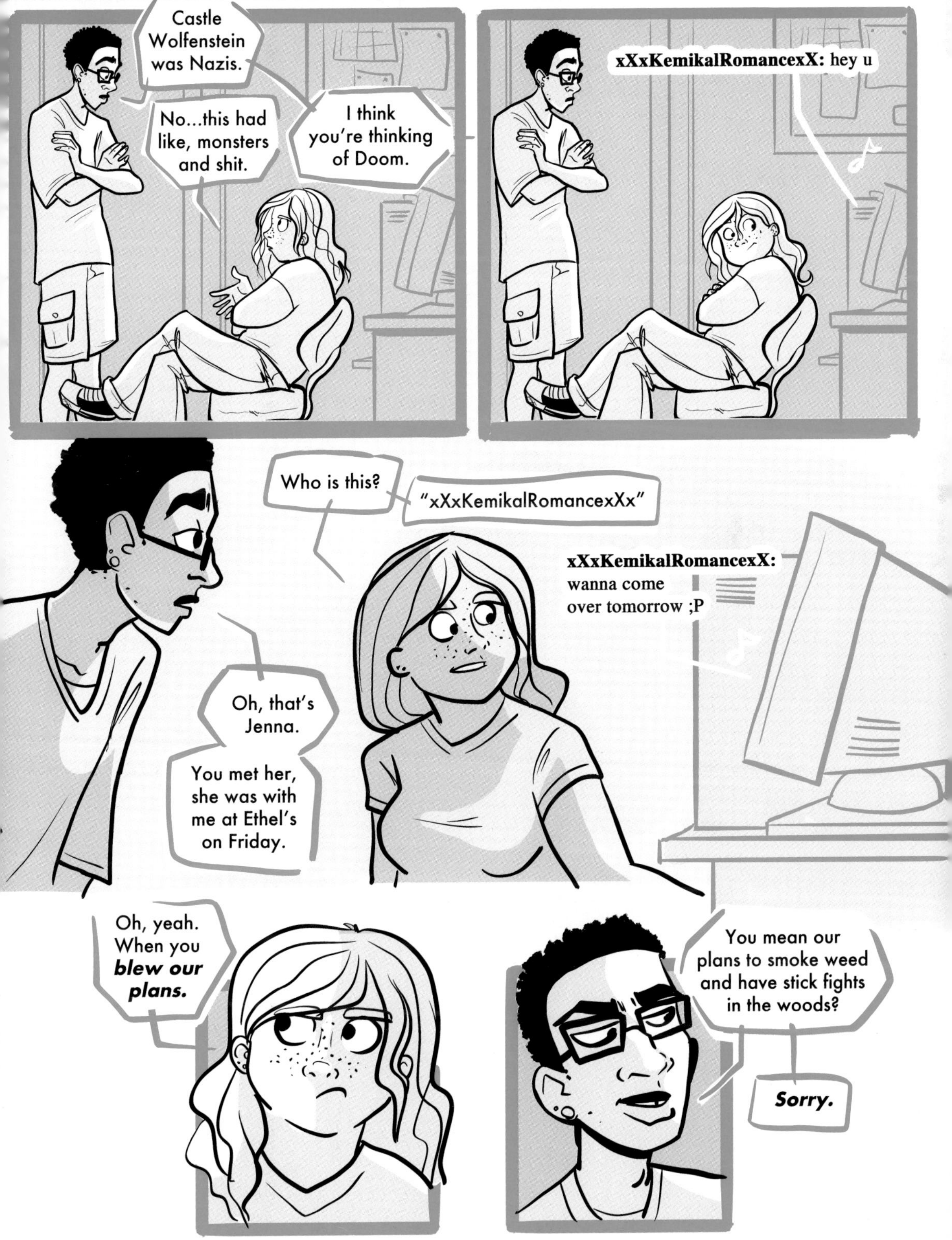

Castle Wolfenstein was Nazis.
No...this had like, monsters and shit.
I think you're thinking of Doom.
xXxKemikalRomancexX: hey u
Who is this?
"xXxKemikalRomancexXx"
xXxKemikalRomancexX: wanna come over tomorrow ;P
Oh, that's Jenna.
You met her, she was with me at Ethel's on Friday.
Oh, yeah. When you ***blew our plans.***
You mean our plans to smoke weed and have stick fights in the woods?
Sorry.

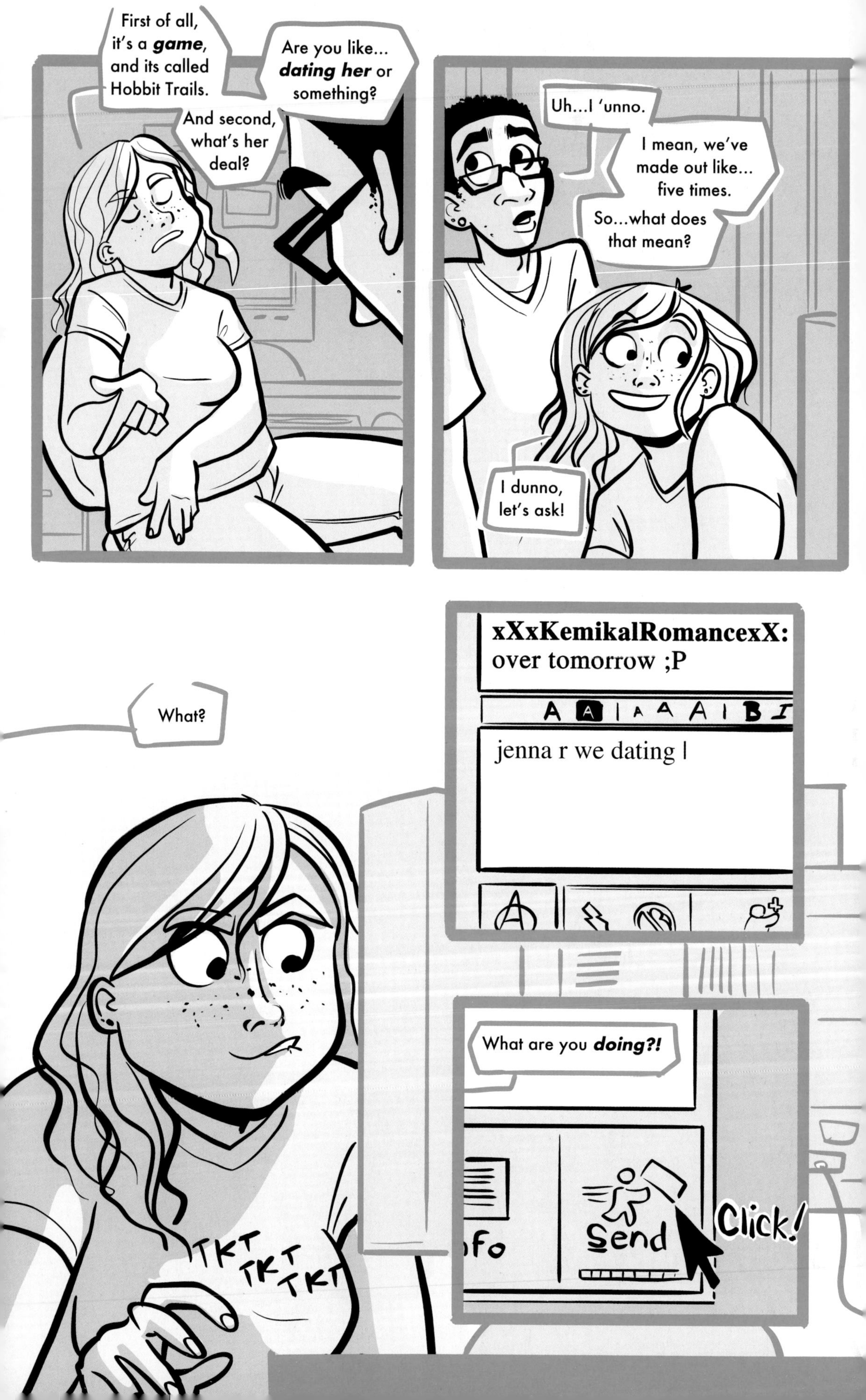
First of all, it's a ***game***, and its called Hobbit Trails.
And second, what's her deal?
Are you like... ***dating her*** or something?
Uh...I 'unno.
I mean, we've made out like... five times.
So...what does that mean?
I dunno, let's ask!
What?
xXxKemikalRomancexX: over tomorrow ;P
jenna r we dating
What are you ***doing?!***
TKT TKT TKT
Send
Click!

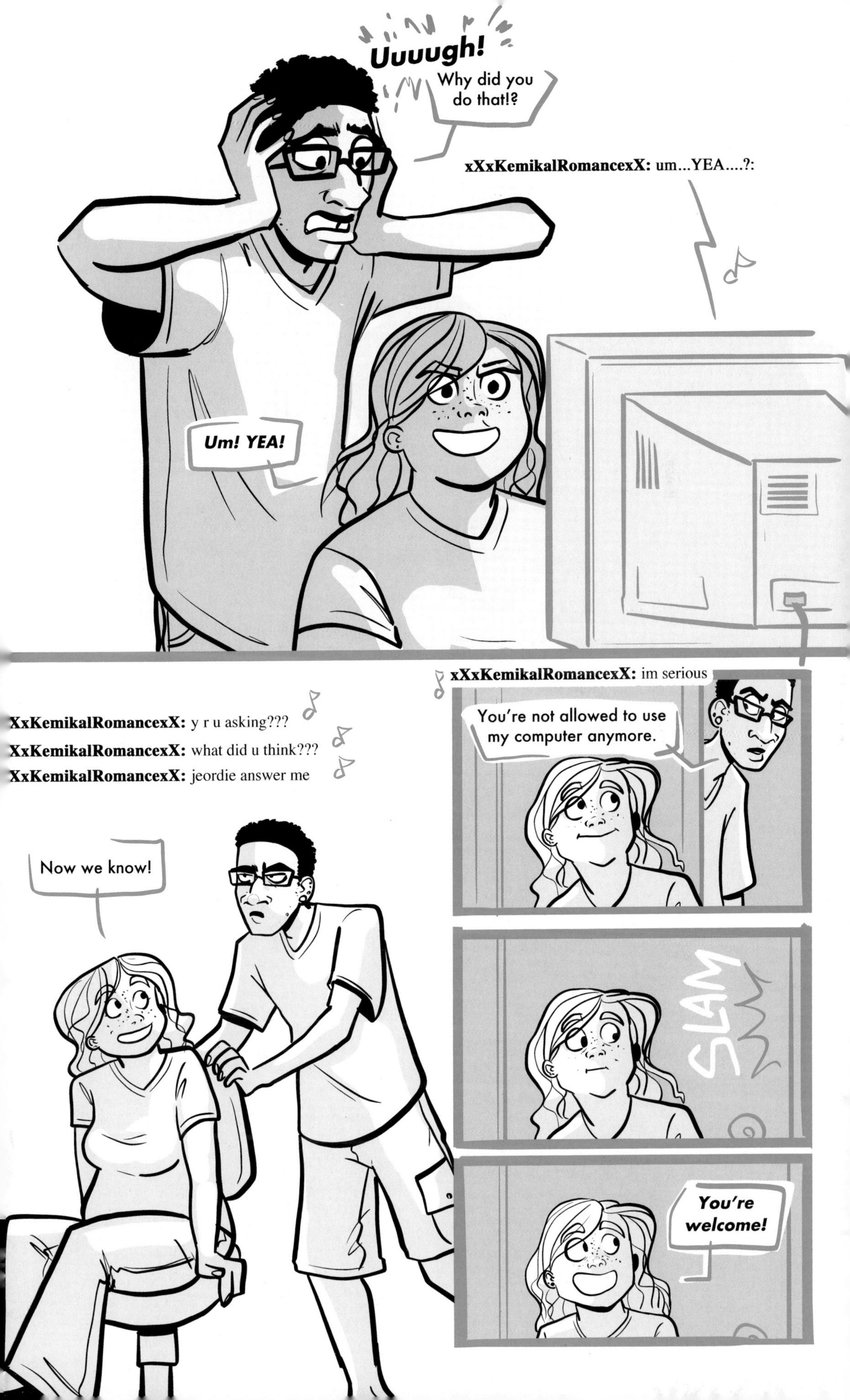
Uuuugh!
Why did you do that!?
xXxKemikalRomancexX: um...YEA....?:
Um! YEA!
XxKemikalRomancexX: y r u asking???
XxKemikalRomancexX: what did u think???
XxKemikalRomancexX: jeordie answer me
Now we know!
xXxKemikalRomancexX: im serious
You're not allowed to use my computer anymore.
SLAM
You're welcome!

GINGER FETISH

I was asked once if the reason Jenna thought Beth and Erik would be good together was because she thought their personalities clicked well, or if it was because they're both overweight. Honestly, it's a little bit of both. I think a lot of teens do this; I remember when I was in middle/high school/college, I was fat and any time one of my friends wanted to "set me up" with someone, it was almost always another fat person. Not that I had a problem with the idea of dating someone who was also fat; it just seemed like kind of a weird dynamic.

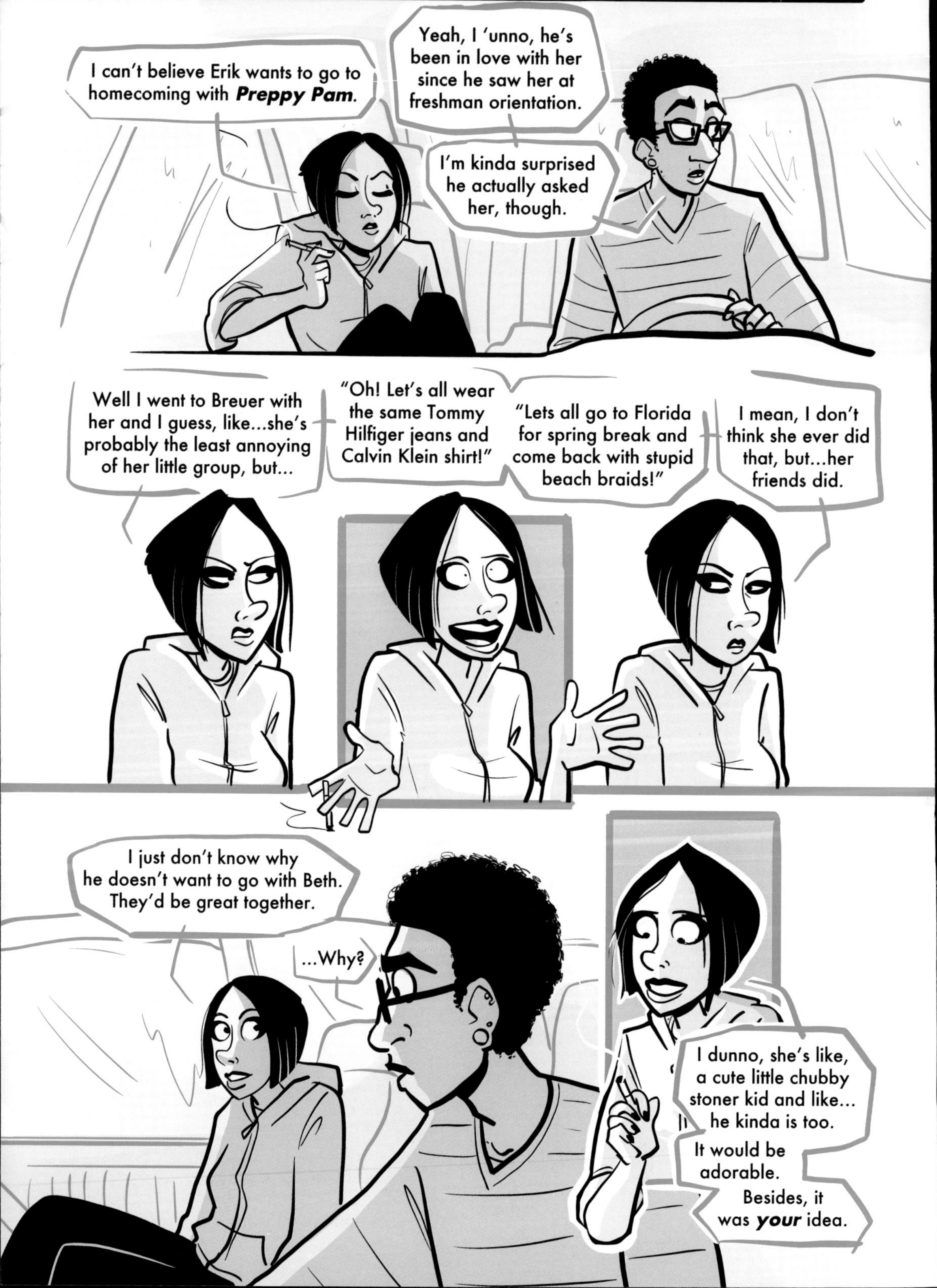
I can't believe Erik wants to go to homecoming with *Preppy Pam*.
Yeah, I 'unno, he's been in love with her since he saw her at freshman orientation.
I'm kinda surprised he actually asked her, though.
Well I went to Breuer with her and I guess, like...she's probably the least annoying of her little group, but...
"Oh! Let's all wear the same Tommy Hilfiger jeans and Calvin Klein shirt!"
"Lets all go to Florida for spring break and come back with stupid beach braids!"
I mean, I don't think she ever did that, but...her friends did.
I just don't know why he doesn't want to go with Beth. They'd be great together.
...Why?
I dunno, she's like, a cute little chubby stoner kid and like... he kinda is too.
It would be adorable.
Besides, it was *your* idea.

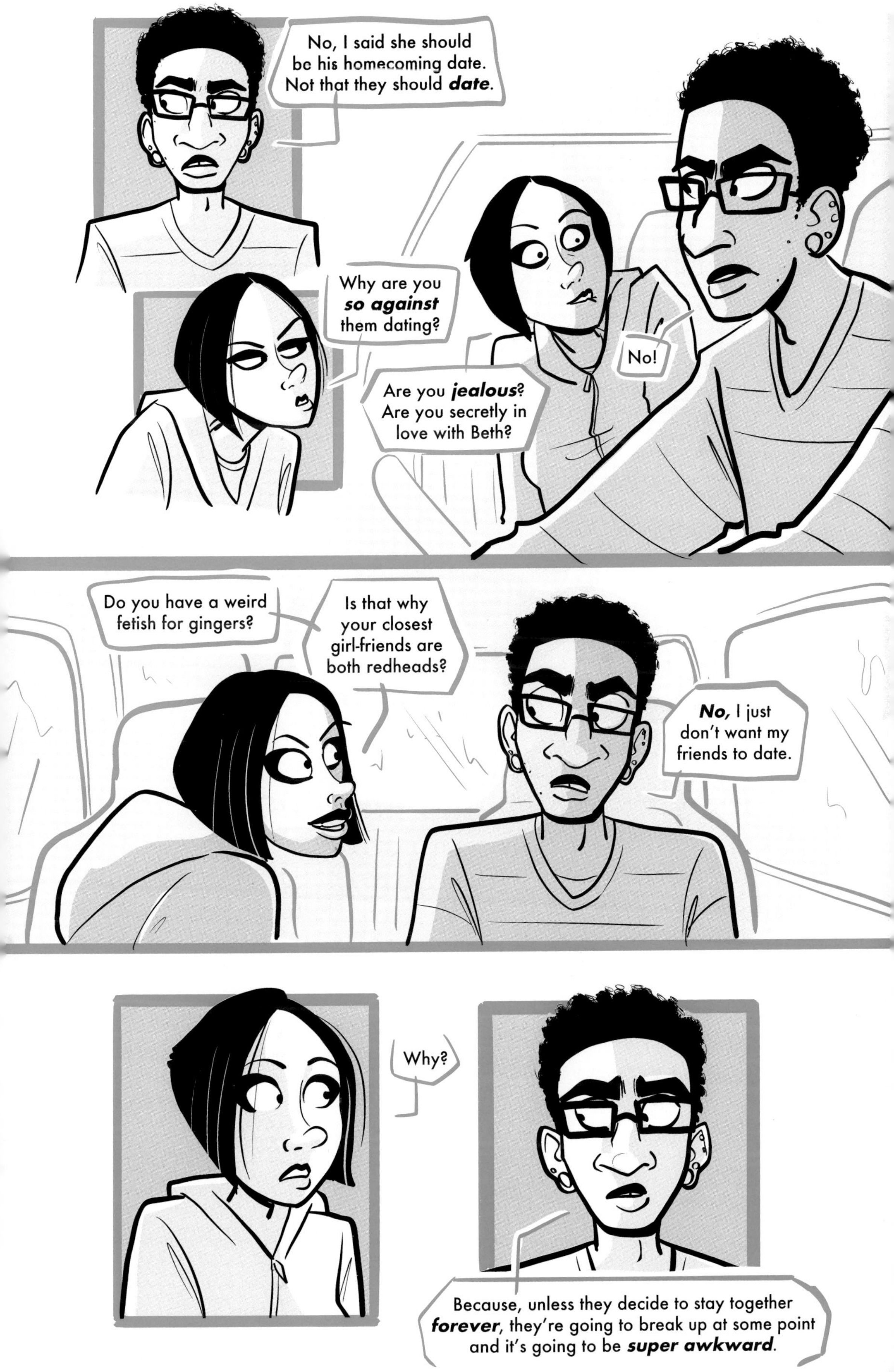

No, I said she should be his homecoming date. Not that they should ***date***.
Why are you ***so against*** them dating?
Are you ***jealous***? Are you secretly in love with Beth?
No!
Do you have a weird fetish for gingers?
Is that why your closest girl-friends are both redheads?
No, I just don't want my friends to date.
Why?
Because, unless they decide to stay together ***forever***, they're going to break up at some point and it's going to be ***super awkward***.

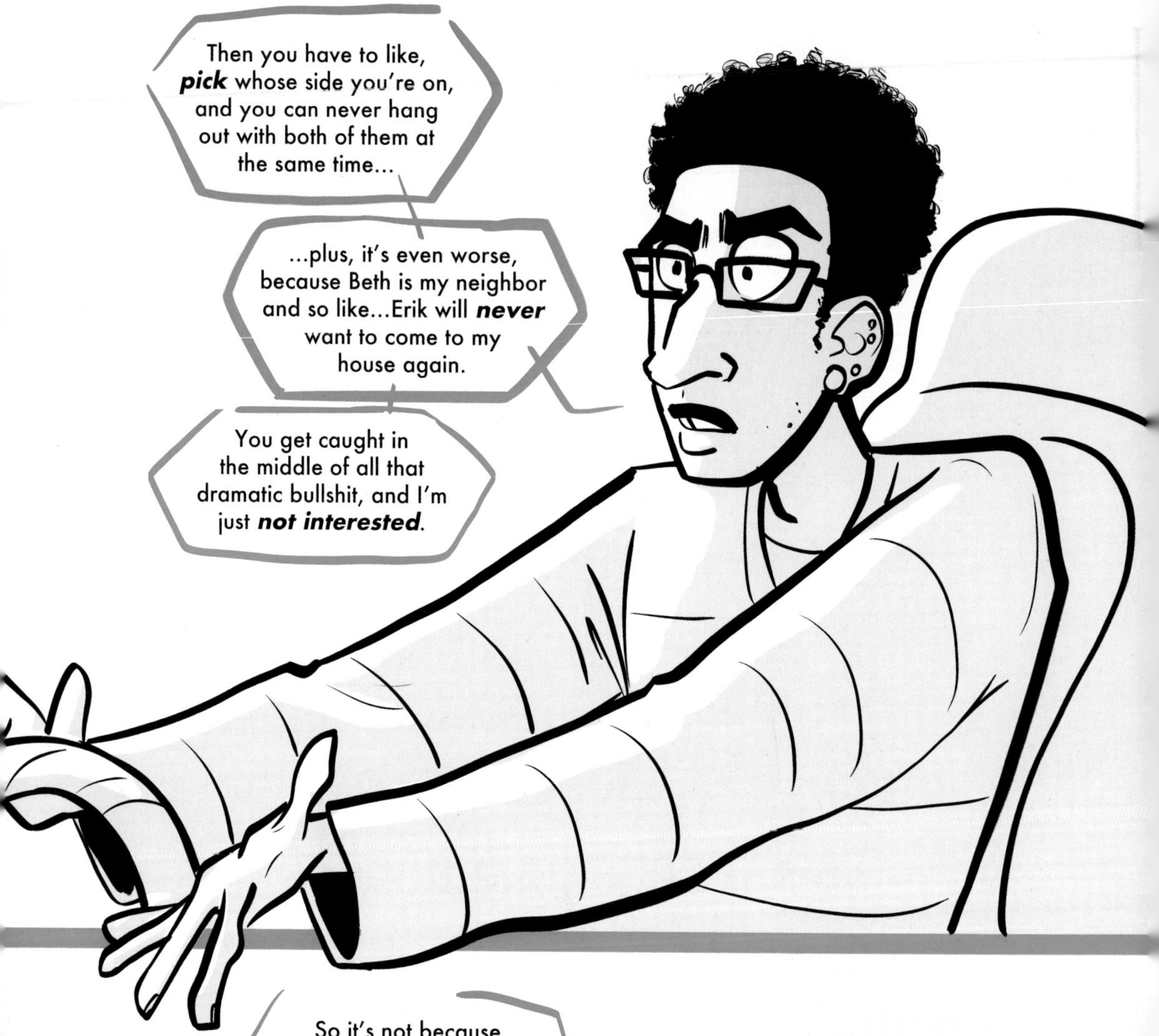
Then you have to like, pick whose side you're on, and you can never hang out with both of them at the same time...
...plus, it's even worse, because Beth is my neighbor and so like...Erik will never want to come to my house again.
You get caught in the middle of all that dramatic bullshit, and I'm just not interested.

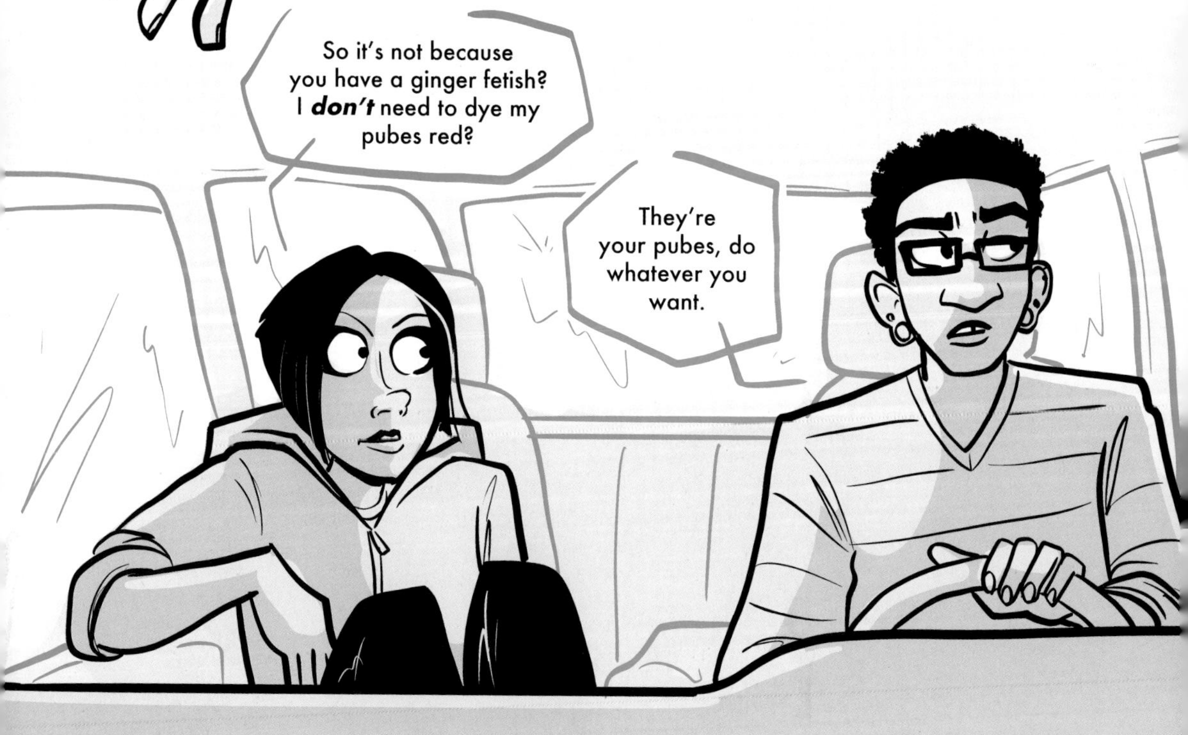
So it's not because you have a ginger fetish? I don't need to dye my pubes red?
They're your pubes, do whatever you want.

LADIES BE SHOPPING

I feel like I should have written more scenes where Jeordie and Jenna actually have fun together, they do actually like each other and have a decent rapport, at least at the beginning of their relationship. They butt heads sometimes because Jenna can be pretty selfish and tone-deaf, and Jeordie can be a little bit of a sourpuss.

I wrote two follow-ups to the scene with Jeordie and Jenna in the car after the 9-11 assembly, and both of them mention pubes. I am sorry.

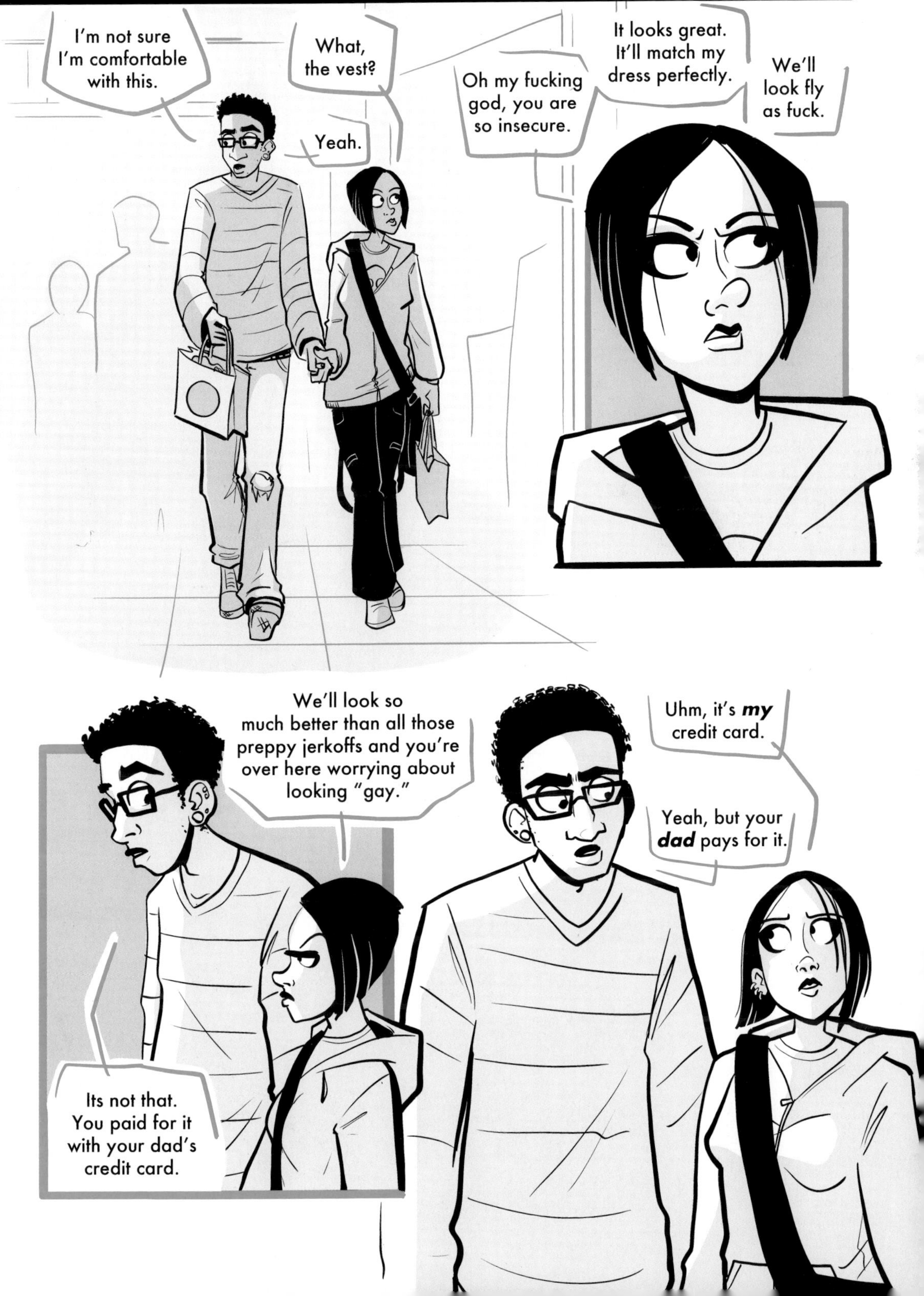

I'm not sure I'm comfortable with this.
What, the vest?
Yeah.
Oh my fucking god, you are so insecure.
It looks great. It'll match my dress perfectly.
We'll look fly as fuck.
We'll look so much better than all those preppy jerkoffs and you're over here worrying about looking "gay."
Its not that. You paid for it with your dad's credit card.
Uhm, it's *my* credit card.
Yeah, but your *dad* pays for it.

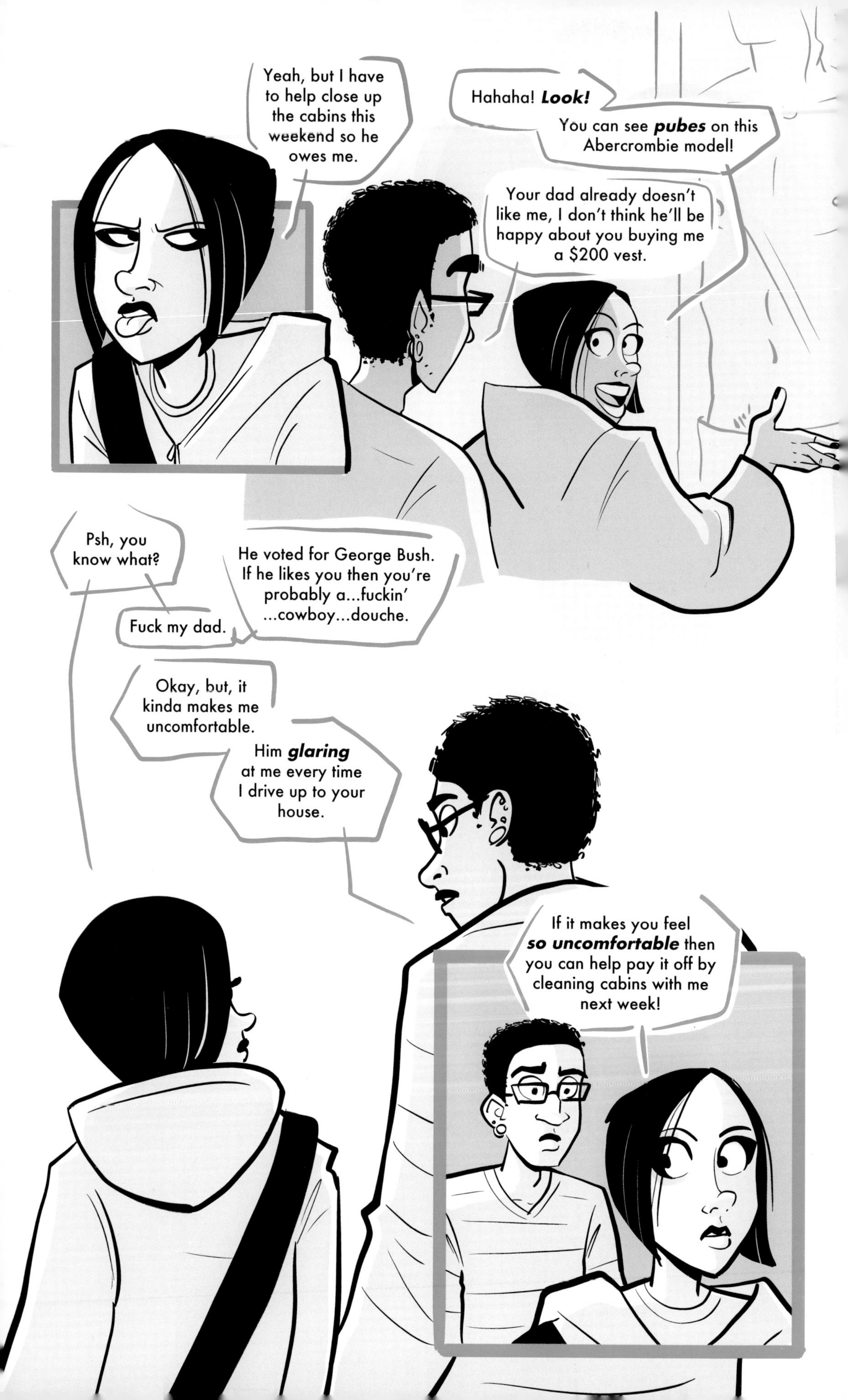
Yeah, but I have to help close up the cabins this weekend so he owes me.
Hahaha! **Look!**
You can see **pubes** on this Abercrombie model!
Your dad already doesn't like me, I don't think he'll be happy about you buying me a $200 vest.
Psh, you know what?
Fuck my dad.
He voted for George Bush. If he likes you then you're probably a...fuckin' ...cowboy...douche.
Okay, but, it kinda makes me uncomfortable.
Him **glaring** at me every time I drive up to your house.
If it makes you feel **so uncomfortable** then you can help pay it off by cleaning cabins with me next week!

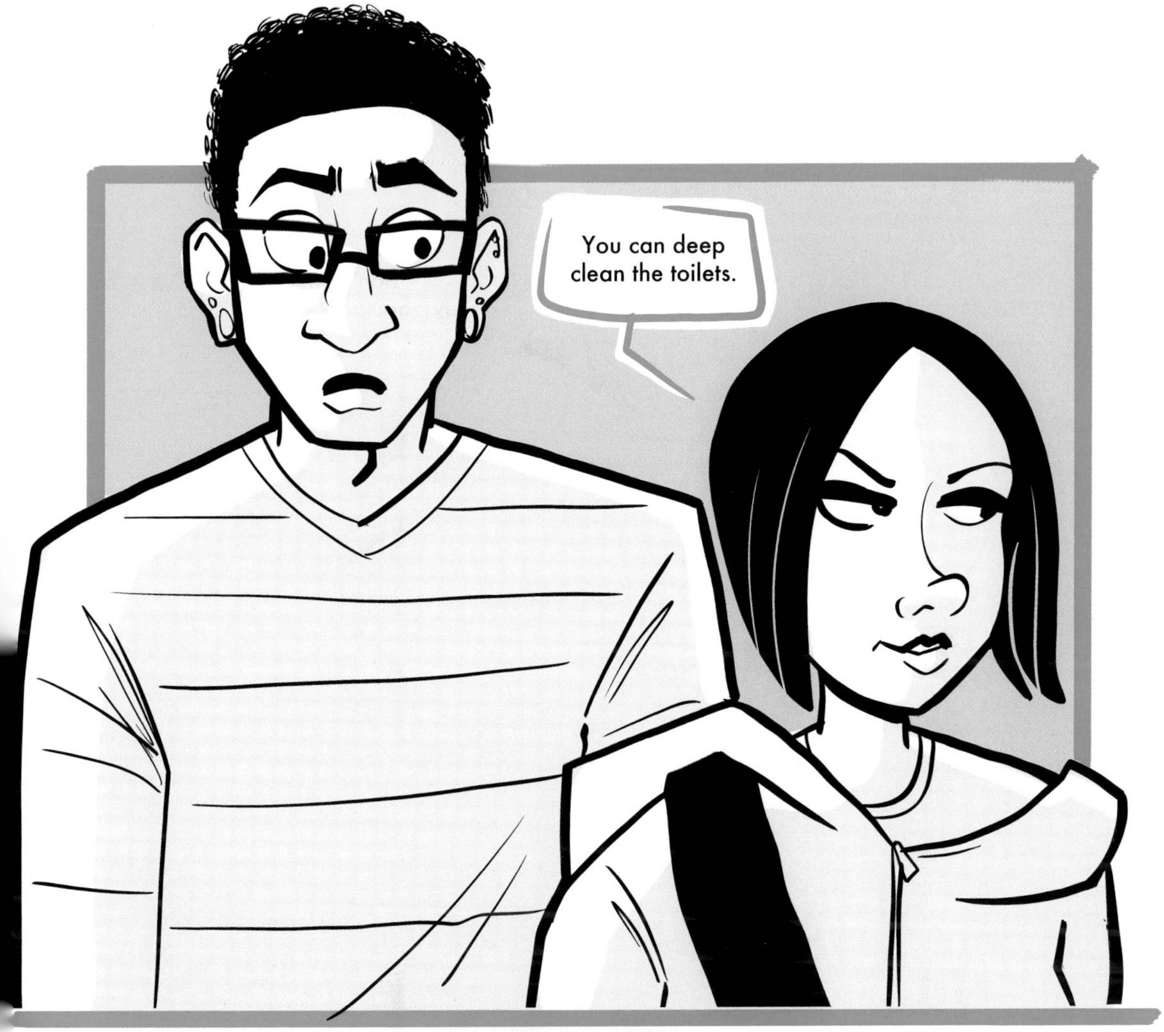
You can deep clean the toilets.
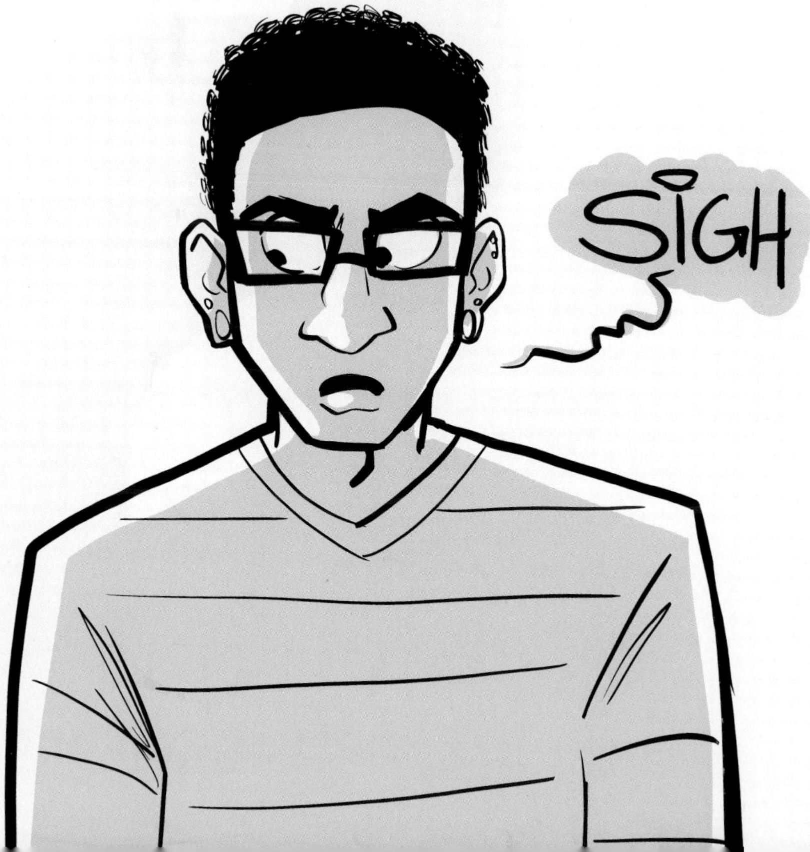
SIGH

THIS COMIC IS ABOUT POOPING

Between constantly weighing yourself and wearing the world's most unflattering uniform, wrestling must be a hotbed of eating disorders. It must be even harder for Erik when his two closest friends have hummingbird metabolisms but he gains a chin if he even looks at a piece of spaghetti.

This comic takes place a couple months after the end of volume one.

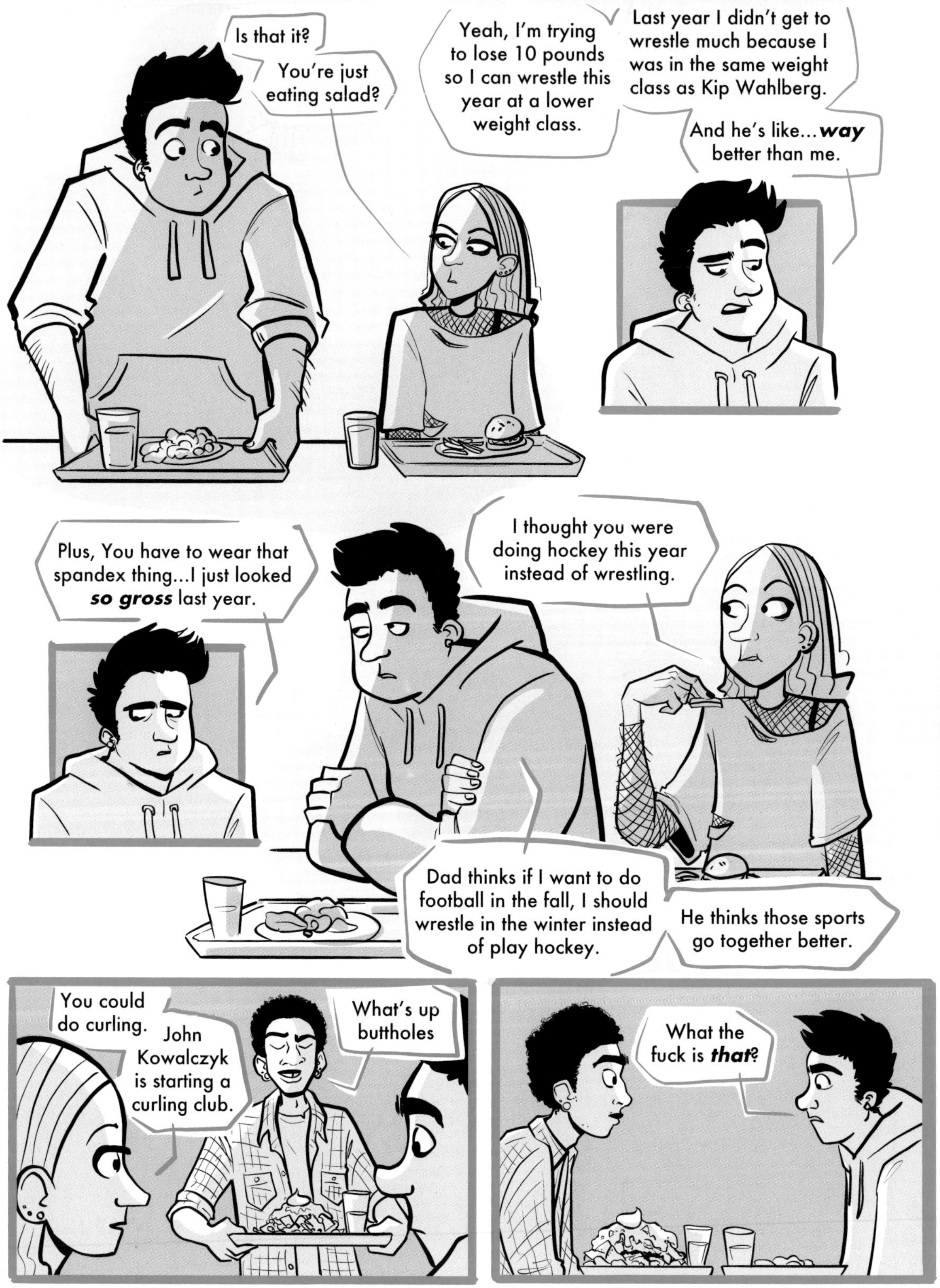

Is that it?
You're just eating salad?
Yeah, I'm trying to lose 10 pounds so I can wrestle this year at a lower weight class.
Last year I didn't get to wrestle much because I was in the same weight class as Kip Wahlberg.
And he's like...***way*** better than me.
Plus, You have to wear that spandex thing...I just looked ***so gross*** last year.
I thought you were doing hockey this year instead of wrestling.
Dad thinks if I want to do football in the fall, I should wrestle in the winter instead of play hockey.
He thinks those sports go together better.
You could do curling.
John Kowalczyk is starting a curling club.
What's up buttholes
What the fuck is ***that***?

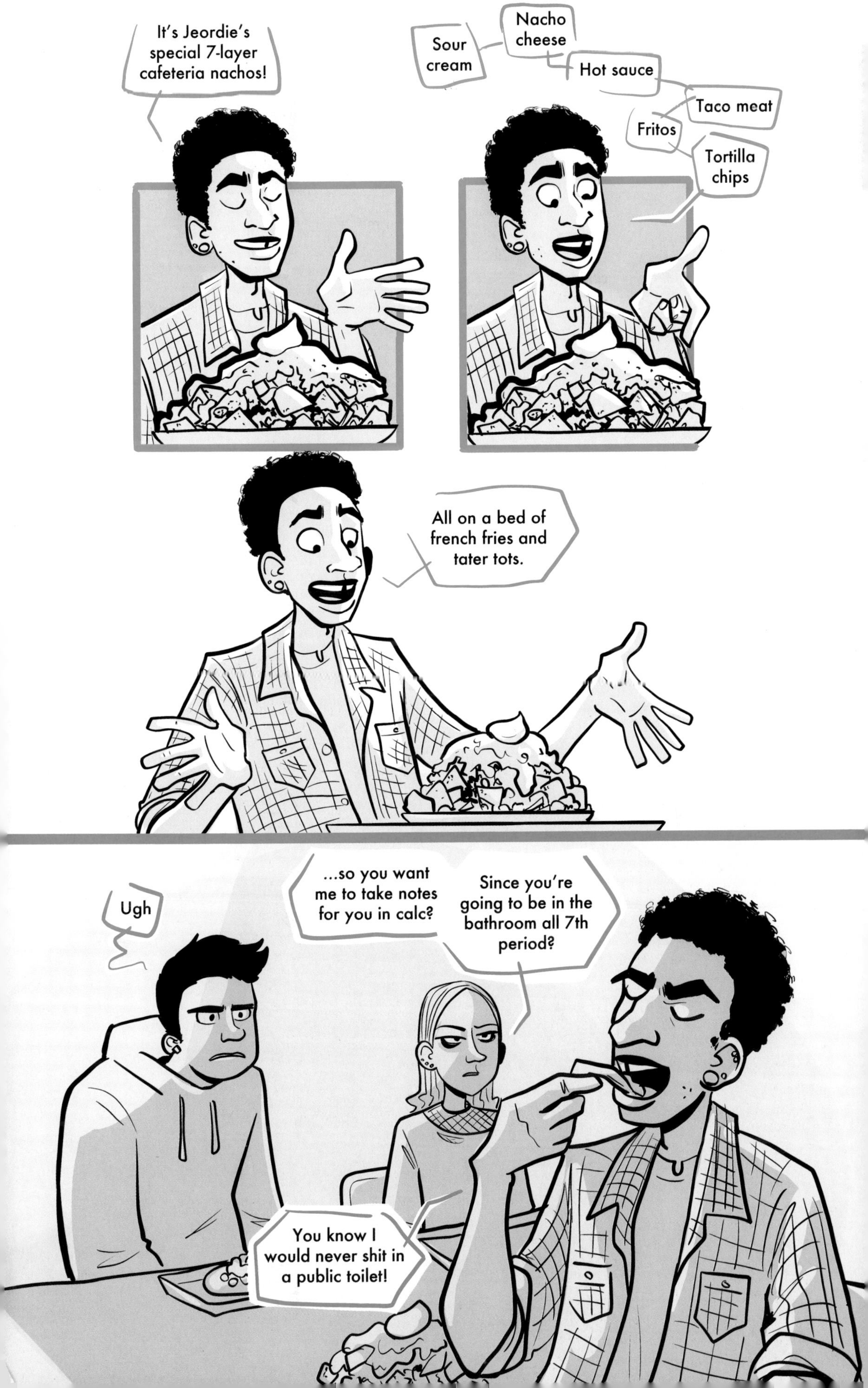

It's Jeordie's special 7-layer cafeteria nachos!
Sour cream
Nacho cheese
Hot sauce
Taco meat
Fritos
Tortilla chips
All on a bed of french fries and tater tots.
Ugh
...so you want me to take notes for you in calc?
Since you're going to be in the bathroom all 7th period?
You know I would never shit in a public toilet!

S.E. Case is an illustrator, writer, and designer living in Southeastern Minnesota with her husband, daughter, and dog. She is best known for her webcomics, *Cheap Thrills* and *Rigsby WI*. She enjoys creating comics about average people, with a particular focus on realistic characters, facial expression, body language, character interaction, and rich environmental design.

Rigsby WI is inspired in part by the people she has met and places she has lived in the upper midwest, including the Wisconsin Northwoods and Mississippi Driftless area.

S.E. Case may be contacted at rigsbywi@gmail.com.

RIGSBYWI.COM